DAVID MACE

NIGHTRIDER

ACE BOOKS, NEW YORK

NIGHTRIDER

An Ace Book/published by arrangement with
Granada Publishing Ltd.

PRINTING HISTORY
Panther Books edition published 1985
Ace edition/October 1987

ISBN: 0-441-57613-3

Ace Books are published by The Berkley Publishing Group,
200 Madison Avenue, New York, New York 10016.
The name "Ace" and the "A" logo are trademarks
belonging to Charter Communications, Inc.
PRINTED IN THE UNITED STATES OF AMERICA

10 9 8 7 6 5 4 3 2 1

MAN VS. MACHINE

"Nightrider, send them the signal saying we're okay, the Outsider is destroyed, and we're heading back. Give them a fix on our flight data so they'll know where we'll be if they want to signal back."

"Is it wise to signal, Shapir? It will inform anyone else there of our continued presence. If the lander team were tempted to reply, they would announce their position."

"They won't reply unless they think it's safe. Not if we don't specifically request a response."

"I still think it's unwise, Shapir. If we include flight data someone else might also obtain a fix on us."

"Look, Nightrider. We've wiped out everything that was there, and the lander team will want to know we still exist. We're their ride home." Sandra looked at Shapir. Shapir shrugged. "Nightrider, just send the signal. Okay?"

Nightrider apparently accepted.

"He's really getting talkative," Shapir said.

"No," Sandra said, "he's getting argumentative . . ."

NIGHTRIDER
David Mace

"Mace's writing has an exciting flair that's all too uncommon in the field . . . Take note: here is a major new talent!"

—*Locus*

Ace books by David Mace

DEMON-4
NIGHTRIDER

To Renate, with love

At the time of writing (Autumn 1983) NASA is confident that measurements over the succeeding years of the flight path deviations of Pioneer 10 and Pioneer 11, now leaving the Solar System, will reveal the location and mass of the unknown body responsible for the perturbations of the orbits of Uranus and Neptune. The nature of this object—planet, or dead stellar remnant with planets of its own—remains speculative.

The orbital and flight data appearing in this book are consistent, but derive from a mathematical model containing some simplifications and deliberate approximations. Further, by no means all assumptions as to distances, masses, propellant velocities etc. are stated in the text, and working backwards from the data given will produce at best a very loose fit.

A graviton propulsion system and a *high*-thrust ion drive are of course pure fantasy. A thinking computer is not.

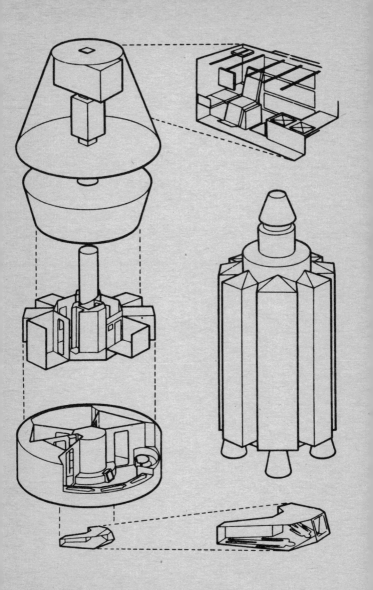

NIGHTRIDER

NIGHTRIDER fell from the Sun to Hades.

Nightrider fell through the empty dark, fell upwards and outwards from the Sun, retarded by the gravitational pull of the star and all its little planets so far behind. Nightrider slowed infinitesimally, approaching the null point where the pull of Hades would start to win. Gravitational drag is politically neutral. The Earth and the Moon slowed Nightrider's course just as much—proportional to their mass—as did the scattered Outsider colonies on their gas giant satellites, on Mars and on Mercury. Two political camps disputing the oh-so-important human future while united by natural law. So it has always been.

Nightrider fell past the null point, began to gain speed infinitesimally, fell gravitationally downwards, inwards towards Hades and its dark retinue, further from the dwindled light and further into the outer dark.

Hades was a corpse, the Hades System was dead. Its planets orbited a lightless cinder that curved in mutual circles with the Sun, out in the utter interstellar dark. A black dwarf, an extinguished, carbon-oxygen core, crushed to Earth size in the stupendous explosive catastrophe of death, cooled until cold and invisible. But still in death the absolute master of its own realm, the lord and commander of those condemned planets, holding them helpless in their endless circuits, locking them forever in a prison of perpetual night.

Black as the lost light, Nightrider fell for six and one half thousand hours, for two hundred and seventy-seven days, for nine months. There had been the sequence of long acceleration phases pulling out from the Sun, then the five one-day periods at low acceleration to compensate for the solar gravitational drag, to optimize the course, to maintain the crew's metabolic memories of weight gradients and cardiac loads. There had been the reversed series of low-gee pulls to kill the velocity slowly imparted by Hades' invisible mass, to trim the pinpoint aim, to keep the crew fit for planetfall. Now the sequence of long deceleration phases was due to begin, shedding flight speed, tailing in to a target rendezvous in the heart of Hades' black and scattered kingdom.

Nightrider had two propulsion systems. One of them radiated no light, no heat, no anything but a ghost of gravity, left no detectable trace other than an infinitely small shift in the net momentum of the rest of the cosmos—an invisible driving force, hence Nightrider's name. The other blazed with the violent furious fusion light of the stars—a torch flame streaking heaven.

Nightrider was all drive system and power reactor and support functions, feedstock, fusion booster ring, flight control mechanisms and a minimal payload. The payload consisted of a two-deck crew module capped with a planetary lander, and seven human beings. The lander and most of the passenger-crew had been opportunistically added to take advantage of the main mission target. Nightrider flew itself—in that respect the crew were redundant. For the fifty-one billion kilometre fall from the Sun they had nothing to do, three or four of them in rotation slept long sleep while the others—always including one of the two pilots—kept a normal day-night cycle. They were components waiting for use, mission functions like the lander and the fusion boosters and Nightrider's brain.

Nightrider's brain was constructed and programmed on the basis of the executive computers of the self-commanding ships used by Earth and the Outsiders alike. But it was intended for another role, equipped with supplementary deep programs and with the skills and data specific to its current mission book. The mission book was the mission, the parameters governing every decision made under unforeseeable circumstances in the pursuit of the defined targets. The goals were to be fulfilled and the constraint on the mission was one of maximum performance, because this was a first-use test of a purpose built machine. Nightrider was on trial.

Nightrider was a weapon, and the people were aboard to teach it to kill.

DAY 277

INTO your most private world, a voice intruding. Discreetly.

"Wake up. Sandra, wake up. Sandra, wake up."

Floating in a fetal curl, no up, no down, no touch, no pressure, nothing but scented darkness, sweetly warm. No orientation, no tension, no time.

"Time to wake up, Sandra."

Move, gently. Uncurl, unfurl arms and legs, reach, stretch out back-bowed into a taut tau, muscles toning, tightening, opening, lengthening, telling you that you physically are. The bliss of waking weightless.

Her fingertips touched a tufted, padded wall. Her heels brushed smoothness, softly resistant, the redundant floor of the redundant ceiling. Falling free in a little cosy nest of darkness inside a ship falling free between stars that were falling freely in immeasurable circles around the galaxy. Free of terrestrial restraint, part of the gravitational mechanism of expanding cosmological time, free to fall forever and never land.

"Time to wake up, Sandra."

She opened her eyes. Nothing but touching blackness. She moved her head. Down where her feet felt to be were the bright little chronometer numbers, hovering in nothingness. She hauled them gently from infinity to focus. 277 04:06. Nightrider was calling her minutes early, knew she always awakened slowly. Nightrider thought of everything. She sighed heavily, just an excuse to open her lips.

4

"A little light, Sandra?"

"Mm, a little."

The dim glow began, the cell became a space, tiny.

Her orientation was out. It always was. She had read the chronometer numbers upside down without even noticing. The diffuse little wash of the inset corner lights came from behind her, the smooth surface her heels had touched was nominal ceiling, not floor. Still a naked tau cross, she hung half askew, her feet to the ceiling at one end of the cubicle, her head almost to the floor at the other. Faun floor and ceiling, tawny brown walls, tufted comfortingly. Herself a browner body suspended across the middle of the space. A very little space—two hundred centimetres long, one hundred and fifty wide, one-hundred and thirty high. Not that long and wide and high and floor and ceiling and wall meant anything. Afloat you are as *you* are, you orientate the world according to your own direction, it tyrannizes you less directly. Let the ceiling-corner lights be behind her.

"Status okay?"

"Nominal," Nightrider said. "Drive activation is due at oh-nine-forty."

"I know, Nightrider." And between now and then the reactor had to be run up and the drive systems checked through, and for the first time for a long time, it wouldn't be just a routine running of check sequences, but work for a functional purpose, the first long deceleration phase, the beginning of the mission proper.

But a few moments more, a few luxurious little lazy moments. A moment is a second. In a second you fall ferociously, unnoticingly two thousand kilometres closer to Hades. Almost an eighth of a million kilometres in a minute. Two thirds of one percent of lightspeed, as fast as any human being ever moved. Yet so effortlessly, so utterly lazily. The inverted little figures glowing in the corner of the silvery screen read 277 04:09. Time to move.

Set in the side walls, softly padded, were the white fold-down doors to the personal lockers. She twisted around herself so that she could reach, grasped one of the recessed handles, and rotated herself in a wrist-twisting somersault, pushed herself with a last touch towards the corner screen, towards the little door beside it. A more elegant manoeuvre than bouncing off the walls—the cubicle was so small that by twisting around and stretching out you could span every dimension of your private space.

She touched the door pad. The upholstered panel slid aside behind the rest of the end wall, behind the flat little screen. The night-lit coolness of the ring corridor came in. She fingertip steered out of the door-hatch opening, drifted through the shadow towards the grab handle at the bend of the inner wall.

The ring corridor was octagonal, was a generous metre wide. In the centre was the transfer lock giving access to the lander wedded to the top of the crew module, was the ladder down to the main deck of the module, were the two flanking halves of the module's structure and service core, all very compact. Around the outside were the seven sleep cubicles and the hygiene room. The *private* world ended at the hatch door, was confined to the cocooning little nest box inside. The night-lit ring corridor was public space.

Naked and more awake in the coolness, she pushed off from the grab handle opposite Shapir's door, coasted through the full-scale doorway of the hygiene room opposite the ladder to the main deck. Nightrider put the lights on for her, flat, white, shielded light. She rotated in the bright space and touched the pad to close the door.

Another little box, but one you could stand up in when pulling gee. There was just enough room to rotate yourself between the screen door of the shower, the recessed hand douche with its mounted mirror, and the toilet sitting like the smooth rim of a high hollow saddle. She pulled herself round by the ubiquitous handles and settled into the coolly cupping toilet. Human beings are unclean machines, there was no way round that for the technologists—if you design in a human component you have to design in its collateral needs. At least there were foolproof ways of suspending ovulation and menstruation—you can't afford deep-space crews getting pregnant. And they could cure the men of their beards, poor things. But a human being likes its unclean machine: there she was, a nice naked negro-brown body in the white world of Nightrider.

She triggered the flush. A brief warm jet of disinfected water, a little thrill, then a soft warm drying breath, all sucked away scent free by a high technology abort. The flush was fun, little intimate caresses for them all from their guardian machine.

She slipped into the shower box, braced herself with the

recessed handle, and rolled the translucent door across. The shower box had to be loosely sealed from the free floating outside world. She pushed the soap button and shut her eyes. The sighing suction through the foot gratings began, then the brief spurt of atomized water hit her, pre-soaped and pre-scented. She opened her eyes and massaged the soap film to a lather, rubbed her hair, then pushed the water button. Again the extraction draught through the foot gratings, again water from the head end, but this time a needle spray from five directions, a washing rinse. Then the dry button. She bathed in a flow of warm air, luxurious.

Out of the shower again, she wedged herself lightly in front of the mirror mounted on the hand douche and finished off her hair with the detachable dryer. It was only very short hair, tightly curled, but it needed more air drying than her skin. Everyone's hair was cut conveniently short, and everyone used the hand dryer. All the haircuts were neat and orderly—how to handle the foolproof haircutter was one of the host of ancillary skills that space-experienced people had brought with them to the mission. The mission training had been more specific than that.

None of them were volunteers. Volunteers, like heroes, were a part of the past. In their various original jobs—ship crews, orbital station personnel, Earth-orbit or Luna-orbit shuttles, Luna ground station technicians—they found themselves provisionally short-listed for some undisclosed project. Then they were tested without explanations, and provisionally assigned. There were more tests and uninformative interviews, then they were each seconded and began training programs still too general to be an indication of the eventual task. There was a further shortlisting, another transfer, and there they were in a little group of fifty people, all training for who knew what. Finally they were all moved out into a sub-group of seven, isolated from everyone but their trainers and mission coaches, and at last told what they were going to do. They assumed that one or more parallel crews were also built up out of the fifty-strong sub-group and were trained as backup crews or as crews for other Nightriders that might already exist—if Nightrider was only the first to be used rather than the first ever to be constructed. But about that they had never heard even a whisper.

Sandra hooked the hand dryer back into its clip, grinned at

herself in routine sympathy for the limited morning toilet, so different from back home back in that childhood then. One of the last wealthy families in Montana, they had been, very probably among the last in the whole of Westamerica. Ah, then.

"Nightrider, is Shapir already awake?"

"Shapir is eating," said Nightrider's everywhere voice. "Akira and Yasmin are asleep. Ali, Kim and Samson are in long sleep. Samson is due to wake tomorrow."

A status report she didn't ask for, but he was only being helpful. "And it's my last long sleep I'm due for tonight?" She didn't like long sleep because you woke up so groggily after sixty hours or more.

"Yes. A low fibre breakfast, remember."

"I'll remember." She would be asleep for three nights and the days in between. A day is a count of the clock from zero to zero, 24 hours, 1,440 minutes, 86,400 seconds. Time units counting cumulatively from nothing to null. Two hundred and seventy-six times round since the mission began, now on the two hundred and seventy-seventh cycle. For the two hundred and seventy-seventh time she remembered to promise herself —when back home on Earth, in about a year, she would take showers for hours, baths lasting all morning, go for walks in the pouring rain and swim every day for a month. In about a year, about fifty billion kilometres from here.

Sandra floated back through the ring corridor to the lighted door hatch of her sleep cubicle, slid inside. She opened one of the fold-down drawers, unclipped briefs and pulled them on. Briefs were a regulation, they made the laundering of the day-long overalls that much lighter, a thoughtless automatic process. Briefs were necessary because human beings make dirt, they are animals, are products of evolutionary biology— they fit only problematically into the machine age. She manoeuvred into the day's white overall and zipped it more or less closed, pulled on the day's white slippers. A clean technological colour.

She glided into the corridor again and closed the door behind her, leaving the lights in there to Nightrider. She pushed off for the grab handle opposite Shapir's cubicle, pulled herself around it to the recessed ladder across from the hygiene room, changed grip and followed the ladder through its hatch rim into the main deck light. She arrived nominally upside down to it all, facing the ladder. To her left was the narrow doorway into the empty day room, to her right the doorway into the galley. Only doorways—on the main deck there were no doors, just partition walls separating the circular space around the central core. She jackknifed and pulled through into the galley.

"Morning." Shapir perched on the bench set round the table, his legs hooked under the seat. Most of the galley was filled by the little table alcove, the rest by the through-way to the adjacent exercise space. Shapir wore a short-sleeved white overall just like her own, just like everyone did. He had a data pad adhered to the table top, was looking through something like deceleration phase parameters. "Deceleration phase parameters," he said.

"Aha." At this stage they were still well within the predetermined frame of the mission book's flight schematic, there was no need even to consider departing from the pre-decisions until they were halfway through the deceleration sequence in towards Hades and Hel. But Shapir always liked to take another last look at the breadth of possible options defined by the space stretched out between the parameters. Which was probably why Nightrider was instructed to give Shapir's views a fifty-six to forty-four preferential weighting in the event of a protracted disagreement between Shapir and herself, to regard him in an extreme case as the senior pilot. "Nightrider said you were eating."

"I was. I just finished." His hand rested on the data screen's key pad, fingers pressuring the five keys in complex sequence, calling forth changes in the flat screen display. His fingers, his hands, his arms were a much paler brown, more like a rich suntan. Shapir came from the Moon, was born at Crisium Terminus, but his ethnic inheritance was one half pure Iranian.

Sandra pulled at the doorway rim to turn herself, hovered in front of the larder. She rolled up the door of the cool cupboard, eased out the weightlessly running yogurt drawer and coaxed a tub out of its clip. She left the tub tumbling vaguely more or less towards the table, fingertip swapped the yogurt drawer for the fruit squashes, selected sweetened pineapple and lime, let the drawer sail home, rolled down the door.

Shapir caught the yogurt, which was on its way towards a gentle bounce at the back of the table alcove. He stabilized it in space where she could reach.

"Thanks. Oh, you want anything?"

"No thanks." Then he looked hard at the larder roll doors and the microwave and thermal cookers filling the narrow wall behind her between the two doorways. "Oh yes." His face cleared. "We have to fill up the ices. I remember from yesterday."

The main stores were behind the table alcove, a solid packed volume between the galley and the outer wall of the crew module, inside the central service core, and inside most of the space between the workshop and the outer wall on the opposite side of the main deck. Replenishing the larder meant opening freezer hatches and extracting packets, variously rehydrating or thawing to reconstitute the contents, and then loading them into the keep drawers in the galley. A fully automated service waiter would have been possible, retrieving, reconstituting, and where required cooking everything, but then the crew benefited from something to do and above all from a feeling of involvement in their own sustenance. Planned psychology.

"Sleep well?" Sandra said, snapping up the drink tube to break the seal inside the bulb. "Make it with Yasmin? With Akira?"

Shapir shook his head. "Didn't feel like it. You didn't either?"

"No. I just watched a show in my box, then went to sleep. Do you think you're having an unadventurous phase? I think I am."

"Oh, sex is sort of up and down." And a slight smile from him. "We can't all do it with each other every day for nine months without *any* interruption. Couldn't even if it was a requirement and not a recommendation. We should pay attention if any of us shows a consistent reduction of participation, but not right now, not at the end of the transit phase." Not immediately prior to the deceleration phase, which in twenty-five days would bring them to their goal, to their target.

"A low psych-threshold, the mission book says. Does it give a predict on the copulation frequency for Day two-seven-seven?"

"Isn't the mission book's psych profiling independent of our particular group parameters? They told us our group parameters were self-defining around a compatibility norm. *That's* what the mission book is planned around."

"So they said. So they said. The mission book is crew-neutral, but the crew is selected around the norm parameters compatible with mission requirements. So they said.''

Any cohesive crew was to be selected from the repeatedly filtered pool of appropriately skilled and experienced candidates, so as to fill all the mission function slots in a coherent pattern of overlapping areas of responsibility—everyone on the lander team had to be able to program the vehicle for an automatic descent from or ascent to orbit, but not everyone had to be able to *fly* it. The primary criterion for selecting any particular crew—as far as they knew, the one and only actual crew—was that of psychological compatibility within a symmetrical peer group structured only secondarily according to the asymmetries of specialist functional responsibility. One was a pilot, another an information systems expert and medic and so on, but there was no leader role and there were no subordinate roles: the absolute reference authority was the mission book and its target requirements. One critical factor for psychological compatibility was specific sexual compatibility within a fully promiscuous self-norming and non-hierarchical group. There should be no selective attachments into couples or subgroups, preferences should be matched along dipolar variables such as heterosexuality and bisexuality, privacy against non-privacy, and so on, and those preferences should be defined by the group members' preference behavior. There could be no sexually dominant individual within the group or within any sex-subgroup, no more than there could be any consistently dominant partner in any other interactive constellation. The soft machine design aimed at complete harmony in a completely cohesive sexual economy, which then served to represent and thus reinforce the interactive psychological-functional status of the interdependent group. They all needed each other and liked it that way.

''Really,'' Sandra said, ''we should celebrate by having a good long seven-day orgy like we did at the end of the acceleration phase way back then. Sex is the best thing about space travel.''

The worst thing was the routine monotony. Nightrider's mission was mostly utterly uneventful transit phase, a long limbo fall from the Solar System into Hades, a gravitationally switchback descent towards Hel.

''We have to get something back for our dedication.'' Shapir wiped the data screen. ''But the time for another orgy is after the mission target. A long journey and then home to look forward to. And nothing else to do."

"Yes indeed, that's why I went spaceside. Well, a collateral attraction. Getting paid for getting laid. You know, sometime when I was a kid, just a little girl, one of the Westamerica Directorates drafted people's prostitution staff to fill a plan list of tastes and demand rates; and then the next Directorate executed most of the prostitutes. Back then the pleasure principle totalitarianists and the moral radicalists were still purging each other. Then the economy went the way of everyone else's, and pragmatic rationalism came in."

"On Luna we never had anything else. What was political instability like?"

"Oh—I'm too young to remember, really. But it didn't do my parents any good, did it?"

The entrance to the flight centre was in the day room at the base of the central core. Seventy centimetres square, and angled at forty-five degrees to floor and inner core wall, it was more a hatchway than a doorway. Not that the distinction mattered in free fall. A little crypt of highest technology, more than half recessed below the main deck level underneath the central core, the flight centre lay exactly on Nightrider's longitudinal axis, a location selected so as to minimize the disruptive effects upon the two pilots of sudden attitude changes during manoeuvring. Flush with the bottom deck were two acceleration couches like a pair of waiting sarcophagi, arranged almost as a "V," heads quite close together about half a metre in from the entrance hatchway, feet further apart. There was a strip of the padded deck between the two couches down to mid-thigh level, then they were seperated by an intrusive part of the solid structure that kept the crew module from collapsing at maximum gee. The flight centre was a split space, a tomb for twins, featureless except for the human shaped deep indentation in each couch, and a pair of flat and silvery screens in the slightly sloped ceiling an arm's reach above. There were no littering control interfaces, no running readouts.

There was a handle under the upper hatch rim. When pulling gee you went in feet first and then pushed yourself legs extended into the waiting couch. In free fall it was easier—you swung in feet first and steered yourself straight down the narrow slot that belonged to you. Sandra went in first, sliding to the right. The lighting came on, triggered by Nightrider.

She dug her heels into the couch recesses before letting go of the handle inside the hatch, then with ankles gripped by the couch, she had enough purchase to slide her hands into the arm troughs and wriggle neatly into place. Getting into the couch was one of the few things that was easier when pulling gee—getting out was easier in free fall. You fitted perfectly into the couch, flush with the padded floor. Its quilted material completely covered over your arms and legs, lapped round your sides, cupped your head so that you could only hear through the built-in earphones. Nothing pressed against you, it was like floating in a dry fluid, but the couch *held* you. It was essentially a water bed, an immersion tank. A layer of water a mere centimetre thick circulated around you, kept you hovering sweetly between cool and warm. The water layer could have been a millimetre thick if it wasn't for the risk of localized pinching of the immersion film because of a creased overall or a tensed elbow. Afloat was afloat. And afloat meant immunity to Nightrider's maximum ten gee.

At 10g acceleration the weight of nine additional breast-bones pressed upon your breastbones, an almost unnoticeable load. But ten times your Earth weight—your evolutionary *designed* weight—crushed your spine and pelvis into whatever you lay on, tugged your cheeks into your ears, clamped your tongue asphyxiatingly against the back of your throat, stressed your ribs almost until they snapped. If you were lightly muscled from your bone strength, and above all cardiac fit, then it probably wouldn't kill you unless sustained for too long, but you would pass out, which would make you useless. But immersed in a bed of incompressible fluid like water, be it only a suspending centimetre layer, the weight on your back was turned into evenly distributed pressure over your whole body. And because the human body, apart from a few air spaces, is essentially a water volume, then despite a weight gradient form breastbone and abdominal muscle to spine, the internal *pressure* was evenly distributed. The physical distress was largely cancelled out, you functioned the way you should.

Arms enclosed in the couch, Sandra slipped her fingers into the concealed gloves and touched the key pads, one for each hand. Each pad had five keys, you talked into it by pressing with fingers and thumb in varying patterns. All five at once meant "activate" and "space." You could talk with the left hand, with the right hand, or allegedly with both at once, holding two distinct conversations with the computers. She had yet to meet someone who had been proved to be able to do that. She swung her arms a little out to the side, the only movement accommodated by the couch, and found the joy-stick trigger grip on the left, the attitude ball control on the right. Those were the controls for manual manoeuvring, and they would never be used. Normally you just lay there and told Nightrider what to do. Otherwise you talked instructions into a key pad and then let the computation run the manoeuver. And both procedures were potentially redundant because Nightrider could do it all by himself anyway.

Shapir floated in, pushed his legs down into the left side couch, and then wriggled the rest of the way out of sight. "Hear me okay?" his voice asked in her ears.

"I hear you okay. Where do we start? Power systems?"

"As good as anywhere."

She keyed her screen to life. An arm's length in front of her part of the crystal surface darkened and featured reference codes she already knew by heart. She dug deeper into the retrieval routine. The key pad had a symbol pattern for everything, you entered a signal by pressing the appropriate pattern and separated the symbols by releasing pressure from all five keys at once. There were only thirty-one static key patterns, but every pattern above one-key pressure was internally variable. With a two finger pattern you could add two more values by releasing one finger or the other after the initial pressure, signaling the end of the symbol by releasing all keys. With a three finger pattern you could release any single or any pair of keys during the signalling of the symbol. With a four finger pattern you could release one, two, or three keys. With the single five finger pattern plus key releases, one symbol value was expanded into thirty-one. And the permutations went on. Instead of just fingering a full pattern and then releasing, you could release and then restore, release in sequence, or you could build up sequences by adding keys, or by adding and subtracting them. The possibilities went on and on. But the complexity was unnecessary. With static patterns and simple partial releases you arrived at two hundred and six separate signals—more than enough for alphabet, numerals, and a whole repertoire of shortened instruction codes.

Sandra and Shapir talked into their key pads almost as fast as talking with tongues, and never noticed the automatic skill. It was one of those things you learned over the professional years, from teenage initial career area selection to practising and practised ship pilot. It was just something that you could do, like all those other thoughtlessly miraculous accomplishments.

Sandra paused with her screen filled with coded retrieval gates leading to component and assembly status readouts. "How often do you ask yourself—why do we have to do system checks?"

"Every time we do one."

"Nightrider can do it himself. Part of him is nothing but a continuous systems check." Nightrider was behind them, below them, back beneath the couches and the base of the crew module, his central and peripheral brains located inaccessibly just inside the vehicle proper, down against the shielding plate that protected everything sensitive from the radiation surges.

"We back him up. And it keeps us in training. Okay, Nightrider—we'll run the check over the pilot interfaces."

"Okay, Shapir," Nightrider said. "Should I set up load simulations?"

"No need," Sandra said. "At oh-nine-forty we run a live load real-time. Do we have course refinements accommodated into the drive phase?"

"Not yet, Sandra."

"That can wait until after initiation," said Shapir. "The phase is long enough."

It would be fifty hours at 0.1g. Over the next twenty-three days there would be two such 0.1g phases, then four more at 0.2g. Then at Day 300 the final approach phase would commence, and they would already have shed most of their current 2,000 kilometres per second and would be almost in the heart of the Hades System. Before then they had to decide which of the approach options planned into the mission book they would take—tear straight in unheralded, or first take a long look at Hel from a faraway flyby or orbit, with the chance, just the wildest chance, of being seen.

Sandra gazed over the screen full of coded gates, wondering

whether they should start with output power monitoring and work back through the reactor plasma ring to feedstock injection, or the other way around. It was immaterial.

"Last night," Shapir said, "I was going to invite you to me, but Nightrider said you were watching a show."

"Oh, yes? So you're not as sexually down as you were saying over breakfast."

"Oh, maybe I am. Instead I took a look at the drive performance during the last course correction phase, anyway."

"What?" She tipped her head free of the couch, looked across at his visible nose and forehead. "Doing *work* in your little private box? That's perverse." She settled back in the couch. "How was it?"

"Optimal. Absolutely."

Which it had to be. Combined with a gravitational slingshot in the shape of a hairpin flyby course round Hades, the fusion boosters had just enough kick to slow them and send them off back to Earth again at such a low velocity that the fuel reserves in those boosters would be enough to slow them to a halt on arrival. But the fifty-one billion kilometre coast would kill them, would take twice a human lifetime. Only the drive could get them back alive. It might accelerate at an undramatic maximum of 0.25g, but it could sustain that for hours and days, could push them up to astonishing velocities, to the two thousand kilometres every second with which they still fell unchecked from the Sun towards its dead dark twin.

"Time we started," Shapir said. The chronometer between the screens read 277 05:07:39.

Sandra keyed up feedstock injection assists. Her screen rippled into numerical and graphic data. "Are Akira and Yasmin awake yet?"

"They are copulating," Nightrider said.

"Suppose we live-test the boosters? Give them a touch of two or three gee."

Shapir laughed. "Put some bounce into it."

"That would require a power-up of the main reactor to drive the pinch fields," Nightrider objected. "The fusion burn and the correction manoeuvre would waste propellant."

"It was a joke, Nightrider."

Nightrider didn't have a sense of humour program and sometimes made mistakes accordingly. Earlier in the short history of interplanetary space flight it had been discovered that isolating crews with witty computers was bad psychology.

Nightrider had a heart and guts and a brain.

Nightrider's guts were a continuous flow fusion reactor burning a deuterium and helium-3 feedstock. Deuterium and helium-3 produced no energetic neutrons during fusion, and thus none of the associated severe radiation problems. The reactor's continuous feed plasma did produce helium-4 nuclei and protons, produced in other words a charged plasma which served as a raw induction generator capable of inducing massive currents in the encompassing electric pick-up coils. The monstrous quantities of electrical energy went to feed the heart, the drive unit, where gravitons were kicked into infinitesimal existence, pushing the drive unit, pushing the vehicle built around it. Nightrider's heart was Nightrider's secret, operational for the first time ever. There was no exhaust trail, no light flare, no ion stream and associate synchrotron radiation, no magnetic field disturbance, no hard radiation beacon. There was no way to detect the black dragon in the lightless night of space.

Nightrider was a bulky flat-ended cylinder sixteen metres across and forty metres long housing feedstock, the reactor, the drive chamber, and the solid mass of associate and support systems. Inside its uppermost end, protected from the fusion sun fires by the shielding plate, was the brain and all the sensitive peripheral electronics and autonomous control functions. Attached to the top, equally protected by the radiation shield, was the two-deck crew module, eight metres wide, surrounded by a ring of all-frequency active and passive sensors, eyes that covered every part of the spectrum from X-ray through visual to radar wavelengths. Mounted on top of the crew module was the broad truncated cone of the planetary lander.

The lander was very temporary, the crew module also. The lander and its five strong team were only along to use the opportunities presented by this celestial hit-and-run commando mission. In future Nightrider was to operate with just two or three pilots accommodated in a much smaller module, with the rest of the payload capacity being taken up by a weapons platform that was still in the prototype stage. Eventually, if Nightrider learned well enough, it might operate without any crew, just its own brain and a maximized war load. The original conception had been self-operating, after all. Inceptionally and for part of its construction life Nightrider was intended as a high acceleration vehicle for a real-time returning —in other words coming back within a human lifetime— automatic probe to the nearest stars. To the real, burning, living stars, not to Hades. But priorities change purposes and applications.

Nightrider's brain needed teaching and testing. It had not been purpose designed for its function, but merely adapted from the most advanced available executive ship-computers, self-commanding within the operational frame of a flight assignment. Peripheral skills were added to cope with the specific capabilities of the vehicle, guidance and applications programming blocks that allowed the enactment of the new role, a supplementary knowledge base expressing everything relevant that was known or suspected about the capacities and activities of the Outsiders. And of course the mission book. The mission book was a knowledge complex containing the Hades System in every known detail, containing the approach flight plan and the return transit projection, containing the mission targets and the goal hierarchies, decision trees for the expected and decision rules and convoluted algorithms for the unexpected, containing all conceivable data on every isolatable component of the complete mission. The most subtle part of Nightrider's edition of the mission book concerned the crew. Like any executive computer coupled with a crew, Nightrider required structured data on what a human being was, how it was to be maintained within the available manipulable world of Nightrider's own interior, and what decision enactments were non-permissible because of what consequences for the functional status of that human being. And Nightrider required structured data on the functional role of each and every crew member and combination of crew members, together with a knowledge base defining the assignment of value indices to any communication from the crew concerning mission book elements, since the crew were to be Nightrider's guides in the fulfilment of the mission targets but the book remained the arbiter. Most crucially Nightrider needed an explanatory representation of the crew as socially functioning psychological entities and as a socio-psychological group, together with instructional advisements on how to steer communicative interactions with the crew.

The crew were Nightrider's helpers, were decision counsellors and tactic teachers, were mission book components second only in importance to Nightrider itself. Without Nightrider, of course, the mission book stalled.

Apart from the lander team's small arms, Nightrider currently had only one weapon. The main hull was completely enclosed in a girdle of huge expendable pods containing thousands of tonnes of deuterium-tritium propellant feed pellets. Four of the pods were nothing more than propellant tanks, four more were propellant tanks with through-flow fusion reactors mounted—four monstrously powerful rockets that could exert a continuous 10g thrust. Such high-gee manoeuvrability might prove to be as valuable tactically as the drive invisibility on target approach was strategically, but that was not the purpose of the fusion boosters. The combined plasma jet, a searing flood of charged ions and massive neutron flux and sheer sun heat, was a weapon trailing torching kilometres of absolute lethality.

Nightrider was the first of a new class, the first ever purpose built war machine of space.

DAY 300

THE exercise space was opposite the day room. Strapped to the bike saddle against free fall, Sandra faced the central core, had the galley doorway to her left. In the workshop Ali was buckled into one of the rotatable chairs, dividing his attention between a bench anchored tester module and the inverted, hovering, oversized shadow of a night-black suit. In the galley she could see Yasmin head on to her beyond the doorway, selecting breakfast from the larder. Yasmin had started the day very late. From now on the lander team had everything to do.

The exercise bike was usable in free fall because of the saddle strap; the treadmill beside it was only practicable when pulling gee. The work bars with their torsion pulleys mounted on the outer wall to the other side of the bike were equally good in free fall or gee. They were a torture devised to make you pull and push weight, to keep you healthily strong, to keep everyone fit for an eventual return home and to keep the lander team in training for their intermediary planetfall. None of it was relevant to coping with Nightrider's maximum 10g—for that you needed an acceleration couch. There were three of those for the lander team against the outer wall over in the day room; the other two were here in the exercise space, one against each partition wall, outwards from the doorway. By some untraceable agreement it had been decided that Ali and Kim, the lander pilots, would use the couches in the exercise space. If something indefinable suddenly happened when they got nearer to their goal, then everyone had to know where to go. And fast.

"You're not exercising," Kim said.

Sandra shrugged, pedalling hardly at all. "I had my workout an hour ago."

"Mine's still to come." Kim hated the programmed workouts, the more so because they had been a constant part of her life since earliest childhood. Growing up in lunar gravity, without the routine workouts she would never have acquired the physical condition to take a trip to Earth. And everyone living on the Moon had to be fit enough to do just that should the occasion arise: every other off-Earth colony had been estranged by divides of lifestyle and material conditions, by distance and political goals—Earth had no intention of letting its sky-commanding neighbour go the same way, separated by an unnecessary physiological barrier despite immediate communicative and cultural proximity.

Kim, stripped of her overall, hung upside down in front of the central core, tied to the med-tester by an umbilical bundle trailing from a blood pressure cuff and a pattern of cardiac electrodes, a slight human being on function test like the black suit under Ali's command in the workshop. Kim's cropped hair was auburn, her skin colour the palest of the crew. She was the lander's first pilot, besides being an expert for life support systems, astroscience, and for the determined degree of medicare skill. She and Akira, with the others assisting and the medical computer guiding and monitoring, could theoretically work their way through a medium complex operation.

Kim watched Ali rotating the black suit effortlessly in the air, a real human shape partnered by an imitative technological shell. She looked at Sandra again, strapped to the bike saddle. "You know, when I was a kid I had a real bike. Just a foldable, but good for racing down those long corridors when they were empty at off-peak. Serenity has the longest unbroken corridor on Luna, four-point-three kilometres from the North Industrial under the landing field to Admin Zone, and then a connection into Centre, up from Service Subsid and out to Management Sub. To have a bike was a real luxury. I was the only one in the Kombinat school who did."

"Different conditions, different economic priorities," Sandra said. "I had a new bike for my birthday every year. A racer. You could still get customized products then, I guess.

Creative market exploitation, or something."

"Creative market exploitation?"

"I think that's what they called it. You create a new product that nobody really needs so as to soak up a bit of the surplus disposable credit they don't know what to do with. I mean, I wasn't a professional racer. Just an amateur. A regular bike with adjustable saddle and handle bars would keep a kid happy for two or three years. And then your little brother. I had a little brother. But my parents spoiled us."

"That was positive capitalism, then? Surplus credit has to be circulated, not held. Weren't your parents purged?"

"The Directorate changed and my folks sort of found themselves on the wrong political side. Their credit was sequestered and they were taken off the data net, which meant they couldn't work. And there was no *manual* work to be had up there in the hills, and a freeze on residence exchange permits, and supra-local transport accessing had been impossible for years so they couldn't commute to city or industry laboring or anything like that. So they were unable to support themselves and were declared parasitic contra-capitalists, and me and my brother were taken into care. After the next Directorate switch down in Salt Lake I didn't have any family left to be given back to. Didn't get a new bike either."

"Your parents were sociometricians, weren't they?"

"My father was in sociometrics. My mother was into sociodynamics consultancy. Which I suppose in those days, with all the political switches and purgings, was like playing Russian roulette. There's a lot to be said for pragmatic rationalism."

Mutually upside down, Kim frowned at her. "You said that as though there was something to be said against it. Don't you like it? It's getting the world working at last."

"Well, let's say it's got most of the chaos back under control. It's a principle of pragmatic rationalism not to underestimate the problem by exaggerating your achievements. Of course I like it. It works and it's honest. Take us. It's a much more intelligent procedure to co-opt and assign the right individuals to fill your requirements than to condition people to volunteer on grounds of national or religious or political chauvinism. How can you target that kind of conditioning to be sure that exactly the right people happen to volunteer? If there's a job to be done that's evaluated as necessary for the

Earth, then whatever the job is, do it right.''

"You don't have qualificationist sympathies, then? Sometimes you almost talk as if you do.''

"Ah, that's just my flippant style. I wouldn't question the reasons for necessity evaluation. Think of the economic load Nightrider represents. We wouldn't be here if there weren't reasons enough. No, no—I'd just be *interested* in the reasons if they happened to be available. I just look at things that way. Maybe it's the political instability in Westamerica during my formative years. Not as serene as Serenity.''

Kim grinned. She started to unclip the cardiac electrodes. They left moist little fading love bites on her skin.

"We didn't have luxuries like bikes for children,'' Ali said from the workshop. He turned a tester probe idly in his fingers. Ali came from one of the lingering remnants left over from the dessicated catastrophe of the Allah's Garden resettlement of the Sahara, a disintegrated monument to fundamentalist Islamic coercion. "A bicycle was just a machine for travelling. That or foot. We ran a black market in stolen parts. You did for everything. Nothing ever got through to us—financial resources, high tech, wind generators, machine spares, water aid. Then one day the talent scout arrived with her psychometric tests for all the kids in the village. When she selected *me* I couldn't believe it. My grandfather refused to let her take me.''

"But you had a real education,'' Sandra said, stating the obvious. "You flew orbital shuttles. You're here.''

"I must have come out well enough on the tests for someone to make the effort. Or someone decided they had to show anachronistic family patriarchs who was running the place these days. Two militia came for me in a helicopter. That was the first real *machine* I ever saw that wasn't chalked on the school wall.''

Then Ali had grown up under the delegated care of the Earth's newer guardians, a system of informational oligarchy that permitted the magical application of *organization*, that was already consolidating and extending its power amid all the utter chaos. Now he used a magnificent little semi-automatic machine to test another machine, and both of them and himself elements inside an encompassing machine of unparalleled sophistication and power.

Nightrider spoke, a little deferentially, giving the standard time mark reminder. "Two hours to drive initiation.''

"Thanks, Nightrider," Kim said, turning to stow the blood pressure cuff behind its panel.

The chronometer said 300 08:02. Seconds were an unnecessary regime in the exercise space. At 10:20:00 the final approach deceleration phase would begin, fifty hours at 0.2g. They were presently falling 360 kilometres closer towards Hades with every second, were still almost thirty-five million kilometres from Hel. The decision had already been made to go straight into the target rather than into a high long-period observation orbit. They would arrive at midday on Day 302.

Yasmin tugged herself gently through the galley doorway, kept hold of the doorway rim to stop again. Arms and ankles and throat and face, she was pale milk chocolate brown against the contrasting white overall. Her close cut hair was silky black. In childhood and into her teens, her high caste nostril had carried a ruby stud. Not even the Bangalore version of Madrasi recommunism, not even the overlayering of established rationalism had quite eliminated that. "When do you want your turn on the bike?" she said to Kim.

"Might as well get it over with. As soon as Sandra finds something better to do."

Sandra shrugged, slipped the saddle belt, came adrift.

"Ali?" Yasmin said. "Isn't it recommended that we take the tester to the transfer lock and just bring the suits that far?"

In the workshop Ali took the hovering suit by its heavy black hand, an inverted friend. "If they'd designed an appropriate data channel into the dock connector we could test them in place in the lander."

Kim reached out and took hold of the hand bars of the bicycle, an almost naked soft machine temporarily stretched across the focus of its functional space. "But then there wouldn't be anything left for us to do."

Sandra coasted towards Yasmin's helping hand at the doorway. "Not before we arrive, anyway." She disappeared into the galley.

Even in the spatial freedom of free fall the black suit seemed to fill up most of the corners in the transfer lock. Its arms waved effortlessly as they pushed and pulled it. The suits were semi-rigid, with rigid structures and deformable sections at limb joints and mid torso—there was no way to fold one up to reduce its bulk. Nor were there any internal-external pressure gradient constraints to encourage the suit to assume a constant attitude when sealed, for example a maximum internal volume posture with the arms at rest. They were constant volume suits, the joint sections deformed to maintain constant volume and therefore constant pressure during flexion, so that the wearer wasn't working against pressure loads when moving and manipulating—a very wasteful way of getting tired. At least the suit was dead, devoid of its life support backpack and uncluttered by additional carry equipment. Otherwise Ali, suit and Samson might have been distinctly cramped in the space. This suit was Kim's. Her name was printed tiny and white on the black back padding inside the empty helmet. The little letters were the only part of the suit that gave back light, not even the curved helmet visor was reflective on its outer surface—these were not the brilliantly search and identification coloured suits of a science or maintenance party. This suit was Kim's, and Kim was the second smallest of the women while Samson was the biggest of the men, and the suit far out-bulked Samson's moderately substantial body.

Ali fingertip tugged himself along the ladder, past the break at the forward hatch seal—the upper hatch seal when pulling gee—and into the transfer tunnel. Handling the suit in free fall was inevitably tricky. If you pulled it feet first its arms always managed to catch behind the rungs of the ladder, if you tried to push it by its feet then the legs doubled up and the push came off centre and the whole suit tumbled and blocked the tunnel. They really needed a hauling harness, but it wasn't worth the trouble of rigging one.

The tunnel was narrow and the ladder reduced the free space still further. It was three metres long, but you couldn't quite comfortably turn round in it. Ali coasted on to the open docking hatch leading into the lander.

The lander was a truncated cone, eight metres across its base, four metres across its top, and five metres high. Docked, its circular roof represented Nightrider's nose, flat to frictionless space. The lander was mostly propellant and oxidant tanks, with a narrow crew space tucked up under its roof and a centre axial lock below connecting with the transfer tunnel. At the moment, in free fall and with all the hatches open, the ten metres from the lander's crew space ceiling to the deck of the transfer lock made by far the longest uninterrupted linear dimension aboard Nightrider.

Ali went through the deformable docking rim section, through the lock well and into the broader lock. He caught a rung of the ladder continuation, turned a somersault, and then headed back into the docking tunnel. Samson had managed to coax the suit's head and shoulders through the transfer lock hatch. Ali hooked his feet against a ladder rung, took hold of the suit helmet with both hands, and pulled slowly. The suit came towards him, its arms cleared the hatch seal.

"Okay, that's enough."

Inside the lock, Samson braked the suit with a pull at one of its ankles. In Earth surface gravity it weighed forty-five kilos, sixty with the backpack. It was more or less like tugging a human body about.

Ali stretched around the suit's helmet and shoulders and eased the elbow joint of one arm into flexing cooperatively, then took hold of the elbow and wrist and rotated the arm up around the shoulder joint, just like a real arm, until the massive glove was waving past the top of the helmet. He took the suit by the hand and started to work his way rung by rung backwards along the tunnel towards the lander. Samson followed, ready to brake the suit again.

Passing through the tunnel, they passed through the hollow centre of the lander's ring-booster, a support stage eight metres across and two metres deep. The ring-booster was just motors and propellant-and-oxidant tanks and pumps, good for a 180 second 3g burn, then only good for dumping. But three minutes at 3g would take them most of the way down from a low or grazing incidence orbit, and leave the lander proper with enough reaction mass to finish the descent, hover for minutes on end to check the terrain at the landing site, then launch up into orbit again and do as much orbital manoeuvring as could foreseeably prove necessary. It was good to know when you made your first touchdown fifty-one billion kilometres from home, with nowhere to go but back, and that only possible after redocking with Nightrider, that you had more than twice as much fuel aboard as you actually needed to get up into orbit again. It allowed for margins. And the lander had four rocket motors delivering 3g together. If one of them failed you just shut down the diametrically opposite motor for the sake of stability, and you still had more than enough thrust to get up again.

Ali hauled the suit through the docking rim section and

through the lock well into the lander's lock. There he had more room and pulled it in beside him. The lock was also the lander's wash down space and toilet—the toilet just a fold-away suction abort—and a hard stores space. Ten backpacks were racked in one side on recharge and replenishment, two suits were stowed opposite each other in support clamps because they would be "standing" when the lander fired manoeuvre burns or rested at touchdown. The fourth side accommodated the toilet and wash towels dispenser, and stowed ground equipment. The ground equipment could toler-ate vacuum. There was nothing else but vacuum starside of Titan.

Ali got the suit into the lock and then backed out feet first into the crew space while Samson eased in past the suit's ponderously aimless floating feet. This lock really was not big enough for all three of them.

The crew space was going to be cramped for five people. It was three and a half metres by two metres by one point seven metres, a rectangular place just under the lander's roof. The closeable hole in the centre of the deck opened from the airlock, the panel in the centre of the ceiling concealed the emergency hatch, the route by which they had entered Night-rider three hundred days ago before the voyage began. Through the transfer lock, and through the lander when docked, was the only way in or out of the crew module.

The crew space wasn't empty, even with Ali as the only human occupant. On each side of the airlock hatchway the deck rose as stores lockers that ran out to each end wall and bent L-shaped to fill up the deck in the rear outer corners. Every square centimetre of the locker sides and the four walls was equipment drawer or storage door. Besides all the expend-able and non-expendable equipment for use after touchdown, the lander had crew consumables enough to keep five people alive for twenty-two days.

Acceleration couches were mounted in two pairs on the lockers—just padded and lightly contoured couches, these were intended to help a human being through a mere 3g manoeuvre. The left-hand pair were for Ali and Kim, beside their seat sections were set main thrust regulators and attitude motor joy-stick triggers, just in case real flying was ever called for instead of pre-programmed computerized sequences. A fifth couch was stowed against the forward wall at the deck: it could be mounted in the gap between the lockers over the airlock hatch. The two outer fixed couches were deployed flat, reaching headrest to footboard right across the two metres from rear to forward wall. Their partnering data screens mounted on ceiling slides waited blankly level with the headrests. The two inner couches were tipped up as seats facing the forward wall, their data screens dropped perpendicular as wall panels at the forward ends of their ceiling slides. The screen for the stowed fifth couch was flat up against the ceiling.

Not up, not really ceiling or deck or wall. This was still a free fall space, and Ali was diagonally between the tall backs of the seat-deployed couches, feet to the forward wall and forehead to the deck. He anchored himself against a seat back and began to haul the black suit through. Its night skin started to swallow light in the crew space. The crew space was a terminus. Next came only the emergency hatch and heatless hard interstellar vacuum beyond. Lightless yawning nothing encompassed by infinite stars.

With Samson pushing at the knees and Ali half hugging the thing, they got the suit bent and turned into the free space behind the seat backs. Then Samson floated in, a cheery Trinidad brown in contrast to the black machine man. He pushed the suit to the ceiling and stopped it from bouncing back while Ali twisted into the space behind the lockers and rolled open the door to the lowest of the three suit racks in the rear wall.

"How's your bowel regulation?"

"What?" Ali said, opening up the restraint clips inside the rack.

"Maybe I've been staring up this thing's arse too long. This is the third one, and each time as brake man." Ali had tested three of the suits down in the workshop, leaving just the pair in the airlock. Drive initiation was due. Those last two would have to be lowered no further than the transfer lock, and Ali would have to make do with using the tester in the inconveniently restricting space. You couldn't expect the designers and mission planners to have got *every* detail right at the first attempt. "You said your bowel regulation wasn't so good yesterday."

"Back under command," Ali said. Such things were a matter of general concern—if any physical parameter deviated from the functional norm the whole mission timing would have to be restructured to allow for recovery. "I shit when I tell myself to. I assume that I won't when I don't." Ali twisted himself round to receive the suit when Samson started to ease it towards him.

"Better hope so," Samson said. "You don't want to let go inside one of these."

Ali laughed. His face lit up but his eyes stayed hard. Strange darkly gleaming desert Arab eyes, those. At the beginning Samson had been surprised to find how tender Ali could be. Over their endless sexual permutations he had taught them all a little of that. Ali reached for the drifting suit. "At least we'll be on a planet. It would run down to your boots. Imagine that in free fall."

"Getting into your helmet." Samson grimaced. "You'd think they'd be better off building robots than training people."

"They don't have a robot can do our job." They turned the suit around so that it would lie on its back in the rack restraints. It folded it's own arm behind its back, playfully. "Nightrider's pilots, yes. Sandra and Shapir are redundant, Nightrider can fly himself. But we don't know what we're going to find down there."

Samson steadied the suit while Ali sorted the arm. "Their job is to *make* themselves redundant. They're not redundant yet. Nightrider can fly, but he needs showing what he can do with it. They don't know how to program survival instincts yet. Have to let a machine learn to imitate them."

Ali braced himself against the lockers to push the suit into the rack, Samson curled up between the seat back and the suit rack wall and ensured that the legs followed the body in.

"Learn how to kill designated threats," Ali said. "Good instinct to imitate."

Samsom wedged himself lightly, feet on the ceiling between the slides of the forward deployed screen, head against the deck. He settled the suit's legs into their clips. "What use would a machine with a sex instinct be?"

"We're machines with a sex instinct. Are we useful?"

"We keep the other machines going."

Nightrider spoke to them softly, spoke to everyone. "Drive initiation due. Please secure loose equipment."

Shapir's voice followed almost immediately. "Do you two have that suit in the rack? There's no hurry. We can be flexible, you know. There's a time window."

"That's okay," Ali said. There was no need to move to a microphone, the intercom system cleaned out all space effects that thinned and echoed machine received voices. And the intercom was permanently on everywhere if you chose to listen in. Only the sleep cubicles were private, except for Nightrider's guardian attention.

"Okay, then. We're coming up to the mark."

Gently, so very gently, the deck kissed Ali's shoulder and side, his hip and his knee. Samson planted his hands beside his head and began an impossible body folding towards the deck, except that now it was *down,* and he was descending elegantly, sweetly slowly, from an effortless headstand. Ali was in the way. He could push up from the deck, use the increasing purchase to propel himself sideways, turning, to sit on the back section of the flat deployed couch against the end wall. Samson's feet touched the narrow piece of deck between the open suit rack and the airlock hatch. The world acquired an up-down orientation again, the deck became a floor, the hatch a hole leading to the lock below. They could sit, kneel, stand, pieces of language took on meaning again. Well not stand, not quite here. Samson had to stoop under the ridiculously low ceiling.

They fastened the restraints round the suit and then rolled the rack door down. Samson stepped across the hole in the floor and sat in the chair-deployed pilot couch.

"Are you going to stay and help me get the other two suits down to the transfer lock?"

Samson grinned. "Like to see you do it by yourself."

At 0.2g it would be possible, but not at all easy.

Samson tipped the couch right back to its flat mode, lying on it lazily. As he tipped the couch the attendant screen folded up along the ceiling and slid backwards until it was placed directly above his head. "Have to wait between lifts, don't I?"

Ali shrugged, stood up stooping and stepped to the hatch. The composite ladder led down a narrow eight metre drop.

Samson slipped out the key pad recessed in the side of the couch. Each couch had a key pad. He called up systems data on the screen. "I like to work lying down."

Ali grinned at him, then braced himself against the locker

sides and dropped slow-falling down the first stage of the descent.

In almost six and one half hours at 0.2g Nightrider had shed 46.6 kilometres per second velocity, fell tailwards towards the target at 313 kilometres per second, was still twenty-four and a half million kilometres away from Hel. So deep inside the heart of the Hades System, falling obliquely towards its centre, the gravitational pull of the primary was beginning to take a noticeable effect, stretching out the deceleration phase, imparting new energy and thus velocity to Nightrider. At twenty-four and one half million kilometres, Hel's tiny attractional pull was minuscule. Blackly invisible, a dark companion to the distant Sun, Hades ruled here.

Hades had once been a living star of light. Estimates put its one time mass at between one hundred and fifteen and one hundred and twenty-five percent of that of the Sun. It had outshone its still active partner in a binary dance of aeons duration. Both stars had condensed out of the same primal nebula of gas and dust, primordial material left over from the beginning of all things and detritus and molecular debris of the deaths of stars of earlier generations. Two primary iron cores had formed, it seemed, one for the Sun and one for Hades, had slipped inevitably into mutual orbit and thus determined the dynamics of the nebula's accretion disc and the slaved orbits of the circling lesser cores destined to become planets. Proto-Sun and proto-Hades had defined the plane of the ecliptic. But Hades was fatally flawed. The mechanism still had to be worked out, long research was needed into the marks of the catastrophic event left on its forlornly circling children. Hades had been an irregularly variable star with an undue proportion of hydrogen in its composition, had somehow shed too much of that hydrogen during its wild flarings, had become unstable and died.

Hades had suffered a carbon-oxygen core explosion of a type I supernova.

The death must have been appalling. There were some half-eradicated traces of the event left in the ice layers of some of the satellites of the Sun's outer giants—those with liquid-water mantles and subject to cold vulcanism under the conjunctional gravitational tides of their primary and satellite neighbours. On Earth and Mars and Venus there was no surface structure that old that had not been weathered, on Mercury or the Moon all traces on the surfaces of the unchanged rocks had been long degraded by solar wind and cosmic ray particles. Probably the only substantial leftovers were the rarer comets of untypical composition, not remnants of the original birth nebula but re-accreted material blasted out from Hades but still chained within the gravitational thrall of the binary pair. The age of the event was still undetermined beyond a wide window, the nature of it still not understood. Had it been a fullscale supernova, and if so then why was the Solar System apparently so little affected, or had it been a somehow dampened cataclysm, and by what mechanism?

The age window centred on six hundred and fifty million years ago. The first known mass extinction had occurred on Earth about then, a wiping out of most of the forms of algae. External causes for mass extinctions were popular again, weaker leftover events caused by collisions with recaptured fragments of the ejected shell from the vast explosion. Hades' death might have shaped the development of life on Earth. It ended anything in its own System.

Hades was its own grave marker. The explosion had left a rapidly extinguishing core remnant hardly more than half the mass of the original star. It had been a condemned white dwarf that had faded rapidly away to black, to nothing, to undetectable cold. It still had a magnetic field, thermal and perhaps thermo-nuclear mechanisms must still be lingering in its heart, but as a star it was clinically dead. The corpse was less than two-thirds of the mass of the Sun, was compressed into a lightless lump little bigger than the Earth. In death it still held its planets in its gravitational grip.

That last remaining self-assertion had given it away long ago, the Sun's invisible partner perturbing the planetary paths from afar. In looking for the cause they had found Pluto, but Pluto had turned out to be minute, not massive enough. Not until the first probes left the Solar System and suffered deviations from their predicted paths was it possible to pinpoint Hades and lift the Sun's atypical ban of apparent solitary isolation. Not until the first probe flew there and measured its own course deviations was it found that the night dark mass had planets of its own. There was no reflected light to see them by and no chance of a telltale star occultation visible from Earth. The detailed extent of the system that night-mirrored that of the Sun was still unknown.

Hades was an aborted sun, a dead star.

They sat on the curved couch in the outer corner of the day room at the workshop end. Most of the rest of the arcing outer wall was taken up by the three acceleration couches rowed head to tail, ten gee refuges for Akira and Samson and Yasmin. Halfway round the tight curve of the central core, inset into the split bench seat at its base, the door of the flight centre hatchway was rolled closed. Sandra was in there rehearsing manoeuvre games across a simulated Hades System. That they had done now in months of specific mission training and months of eventless flight. The day room swept a full third of the curve of the main deck. From the couch corner at the workshop end they could hardly read the chronometer over the ladder space doorway at the far end, and had to lean forward to read the one up on the partition wall over the workshop doorway. And the ceiling mounted screens partnering each of the high acceleration couches were dead. It was the only place aboard besides the shower where mission elapse time didn't stare at you.

Not that the mission cares went away. Not twenty-four and one half million kilometres from target.

Shapir had propped the data screen on a tape reader on the little circular table. Its surface showed a plan view of the known elements of the Hades System. Hades in the centre, a tight little ring around it almost too close to resolve representing Hel's orbit, the much wider ring with an occupying dot for the gas giant Tartarus, and a ring much further out still for the smaller giant Yama. Death-gods or death-realms all. Inside the orbit of Tartarus and between that of Tartarus and Yama were shaded bands representing two families of regularly circling planetesimals—dozens known and thousands presumed. Not represented were the few known wandering lumps of rock and comet nuclei. Data on planetesimals and comets was rarest of all—everything there was surmise. In the utter night they were detectable only after long on-site investigation and careful measurements of flight path perturbations and fortuitous star occultations. Not that many probes had ever been here, and only Outsider ships most recently, and those secretly. The Outsiders had presumably found out more since all scientific co-operation with Earth was ended, but they kept it to themselves. They wanted to keep the whole Hades System to themselves, and until now Earth had been far too preoccupied with its own internal troubles to consider stopping them. The Outsiders blamed the initial breach and the entraining spiral of disintegrating understanding to their abandonment back at their fearfully vulnerable birth by the resource rich mother world. All rebelling colonies need a political excuse—Earth could not forgive them for selfishly looking after themselves while the mother world's fragile and so falteringly restored consensus had been ripped apart again. It had taken more than a generation, and the restoration of consensus and control was anything but complete, but Earth was coming out beyond the orbit of the Moon again. Earth might only command two planetary bodies to their ten or twelve or more, but the population balance, the sheer proportion of the human race, went the other way. How dramatically no one knew. Earth had no knowledge of the true numbers of the Outsider population except that it was tiny, possibly not half a million in all, and neither side had the faintest idea of how many people still lived and starved and died on Earth better than to the nearest half billion.

Earth had lost the Solar System short of waging a war. Which Earth would lose despite its vast advantage in material and human resource, if only an informational oligarchy could finally be established that could *organize* it all. Earth was steeply gravitationally downhill of everywhere except Mercury, flight energy disadvantaged. Earth was one planet and its single moon, one double target. Earth was soaked in an atmosphere that conducted shock waves and heat and circulating fallout, an atmosphere that everyone breathed, that could be bombarded by a cascade of blindly descending nuclear warheads, mere bombs coming black from the blank sky. The Outsider cities had to be remotely hit with almost pinpoint accuracy by robot weapons that could be equally remotely destroyed. A direct war would be the final disaster, and although there was no way to tell if the Outsiders were ready for a war, they were after all human too.

But Earth wasn't going to let them steal the further future, not the first stepping stone out towards the stars. The stars, perhaps, held knowledge. And in the longest term, knowledge is the purest form of power.

Akira tapped the dot representing Tartarus. "That's where

to look for a second base if any. But after Hel.''

Tartarus, as far as Earth knew, had at least three moons, Tantalus, Sysiphus and Ixion. Like any gas giant satellite, they were the obvious place to make ship reactor fuel—hydrogen slush, water-ice or methane crusts, and only a minimal gravitational field to lift it out of. If the Outsiders really wanted to open up the Hades System, really intended to pour precious resources in, they would need a refuelling station to rationalize the payload to propellant ratio of their supplying ships. Up to a year ago they had done nothing at Tartarus. A year ago Earth's last robot probe had been here before climbing up clear of the ecliptic and the danger of random interception and laser firing its data harvest back home. The data had come in just in time to update Nightrider before departure. Since then silence—the risk of chance discovery was too great.

''We can still take Tartarus first,'' Shapir said, just testing that the option was out. ''Flyby at Hel to take a snap look from way out, long loop round Hades and out to Tartarus. Twenty to twenty-five days, maybe.''

''Shall I run a determination on that?'' Nightrider asked.

Shapir looked at Kim and Akira.

''No thanks, Nightrider,'' Kim said. ''Inside a year they couldn't have more than a work station set up at Tartarus. Which wouldn't be able to defend itself even if it was warned by us arriving at Hel first. But going the other way round a warning might go to Hel, and they might have expanded in the last year.'' And they were so close, and falling on a course that would take them in less than two days to a perfect planetfall. ''Besides, we're nearly there.''

''Prime target first,'' Akira agreed. In a sense Kim and Akira were the two lander team leaders, Kim when the lander was in flight and in all matters attending the vehicle and its flight planning. Akira on the ground in general because of matters of fighting in particular. Yasmin was no less of a weapons specialist than Akira, but Akira had real ground combat experience. He had found himself in a real war, having to cope with ambushes by, pitched battles with, and the massacring of the endless murderous waves of the Messiah's little boy and girl children, every now and then supported by regular units capable of higher-tech war. There had not been many suitable candidates for the lander team who were experienced in both long confinement spaceside operations and true terrestrial ground fighting.

"Good," Shapir said. Taking the mission the linear way meant juggling less convoluted futures in your head. He keyed a scale change so that the diagram expanded until everything disappeared from the screen except Hel and Hades. The to-Sun direction was straight down to the bottom of the field. Hel was out to the right, forty degrees advanced upon its orbit. Shapir keyed up their present position and course predict. A little arrowhead marked Nightrider and a string of punctuations skipped out to contact Hel. There was no predict beyond Hel. At present, if they maintained 0.2g deceleration with no lateral component whatsoever, they would eventually collide with the planet at a sedate eight kilometres per second.

There, on the rotation locked Hades side of Hel, secreted away in this domain of utter night, was the Outsider base.

Eight years ago it had not existed when one of Earth's rare probes had flown by long-range low-resolution radar sampling an equatorial stretch of the biggest known terrestrial planet besides Earth itself and Venus. Four years later it was already there, a minute little heat source in the very centre of the face locked blind towards black Hades. The base had presumably not seen the probe, since the probe had survived to report back. The base was a secret that Earth had supposedly never cracked—both sides watched each other via remote surveillance probes in the Solar System, but what was there to snoop for out here? Who would have supposed that the scattered Outsiders, stretched to the very limit to remain cohesive, to consolidate and simply to survive, would marshal the proportionally gargantuan effort required to establish and maintain a base fifty-one billion kilometres out into nowhere. Their resource economy was alledgedly not up to it. But they wanted to secure the future for themselves, and somewhere to develop in safety far beyond the reach of mistrusted Earth. Insofar as the detection of transitting vessels allowed the assumption, they seemed to run an irregular service of ships to the Hades System. There was no way to tell if one was there now.

"Next decision," Shapir said. "Do we go into orbit in the same sense as the planetary orbit, or reversed?" Should they loop round the back of Hel, the side of the planet permanently turned away from Hades by ancient tidal locking, or should they come straight across the front and over the base? Nightrider had the acceleration and the time to do either with ease.

"It doesn't matter which way. They'll never see us coming."

"And," Kim said. "Do we orbit and then take a look first? Fix the base location. Or do we try to take it out on the first pass? Lots of variables."

Akira nodded. "Like the accuracy of the base location predict."

"And who else is there," Shapir said. "If there's another ship and we notice it, then it's probably best to be able to unload the lander first before taking it on." The lander's maximum structural tolerance was 5g—if Nightrider pulled a full 10g burn the lander would collapse, along with the overloaded supporting structure of the crew module. "But. If there's a ship and we don't notice it but it somehow notices us, then it could be a mistake to separate the lander from Nightrider's protection."

Akira nodded. "We can't defend ourselves with small arms. Not against a ship."

"Not against a ship with weapons," Kim said. "But we have no reason to expect weapons."

"Not to expect them, no."

"But," Shapir said. The mission book had its unknown variables under control, locked into predicted limits. But they were there.

Kim leaned to look up at the chronometer over the workshop doorway. "Sixteen-thirty-three. We don't have to decide all that for hours yet."

"About twenty hours," Akira said. "Right, Nightrider?"

"The decision window is from now until Day three-oh-one fourteen-oh-oh," Nightrider confirmed. Then they would be just twenty-two hours away from Hel.

They stared at the little target dot. A planet much bigger than Mars, with 0.6g at the surface. A planet suddenly seared by its sun and then transfixed in a frozen ice-death that would linger until the end of the galaxy.

Samson's sleep cubicle was blue, all the padded fabric of the floor and ceiling and the tufted material of the walls a powdery Wedgwood blue, and the padded finishes to the locker doors in cream. Somehow it set off his skin colour well. Sandra slipped inside, sitting in through the door and pulling her legs in after, and touched the door pad. The cream upholstered door slid shut, closing off the night-lit corridor. The music glided up to its pre-set volume, enclosing.

"Not too loud?" Samson asked through the thick surround of tropical sound. He lounged naked against the rear wall, filling much of the space from floor to ceiling.

"No, nice."

He grinned, stretched a little. "Glad you were free. Didn't feel like a threesome tonight."

Sandra smiled. "Me neither tonight." She unzipped her white overall and shrugged it off her shoulders, slipped it under her hips, over her legs and free from her feet. Kicked it carefully into the adjacent corner. The lightweight material settled so softly, deflated so slowly in the gentle deceleration gee.

"Nightrider," Samson said, "dim the lights down to about half, please."

The little translucent ceiling-corner lights dimmed. The blue became a shady dusk hue, the music closer, caressing. Sandra slid free of her briefs and fingertip freed them to slow fall onto the overall, discarded second skins.

"See." Samson held his spread hand against her side. "Get the brightness right and we come out exactly the same colour."

Sandra nodded, smiled. She stretched her legs and rubbed at her thighs. A little distraction signal to start with. "A little cool, maybe?"

"Like it a little warmer? Nightrider, a couple of degrees more, please." The silently seeping night scent air came instantly shadily warmer. Summer dark beach breath under music surf from a simulating machine. He slid his fingers silkily along her thigh from hip to knee, from knee to hip, slipped his hand behind her.

In the fish-eye they slide together, elongated, shrinking, huddle half sitting against the rear wall, talk and touch. The fish-eye sees everything, the disused corner clothes, even the peripheral hint of the chronometer glow from the adjacent screen. This eye is better with its backup processing, even in the low light it can see the clear difference in their skin colours. When Sandra extinguishes the lights in her cubicle and calls it black, she is still visible to the eye in the faint glow from the chronometer. And her breathing is audible, her muscle movements. Her body heat is detectable from the extracted air, her metabolic level from the humidity and trace excretions signature. Designation: *crew monitor-function*. Crew communication lexicon: *safeguard, protect, watch over, look after*. Application: isolation avoidance. Purpose: crew viability maintainance, post mission performance analysis.

300 22:32:17. Velocity 270,000 ms -1. Drive 80%. Deceleration 2.0 ms -2. Range to-Hel 18.013 Mkm. 300 22:32:23.

Ali and Kim move from the corridor lock-side fish-eye into the lens in Kim's cubicle. Kim pushes Ali. Laughter. In another fish-eye Shapir and Yasmin are tangled limbs under the lens and Akira rests, watches. Four cubicles are empty. The main deck is black. The lander reports functions nominal, zero event. The drive function is nominal. Power systems nominal. The electro-magnetic surveillance shows star background plus zero.

Nightrider saw all, supervised all. Nightrider flew itself, falling through the void darkness.

DAY 301

KIM hated the weights and the exercise periods. Always had. Round and round the main deck, hopping the partition doorways, jogging the continuous curve. Round and round and round. Ten times round. Exercise space, galley, ladder space, day room, workshop, exercise space. Round and round. It made a break from the treadmill band. Ten times round, fifteen metres a circuit winding down to one hundred fifty. Stop and turn. A little idiot orbiting round and back and round and back. A dumb human being jogging to mission book rules round the central core primary of a living space dictatorship tacked as an afterthought to the top of a perfect machine. A little idiot orbiting.

Skip both the doorways in one shallow stride. Don't even touch the deck at the foot of the ladder. At least you got a breeze on your skin. You ran stripped to your briefs rather than sweat your overall through. You got a breeze on your skin. The only one outside the shower box. The only cool one at all. Through the doorway into the workshop. Breathing easily and cursing the weights. Strap-on strips filled with lead powder, they brought every part of your body up to its apparent Earth weight. You wore them round your ankles, thighs, wrists, upper arms. Black coronet round your skull, heavy girdle round your hips, yoke around your shoulders too heavy to bounce. Into the exercise space. Stripped, weight bejewelled, Shapir toiled away steadily on the exercise bike. The weights

40

make for muscle tone and muscle strength. Next day or the day after, they would be down in three-fifths gee, down on a planetary surface instead of in Nightrider's smooth cocoon. You couldn't switch from one-fifth to three-fifths just like that and still function unless you were fit. Into the galley. One, two strides. Skip both the doorways at once. Don't even touch the deck at the foot of the ladder. She was used to exercise weights, of course. Used to running round things too. Bigger things. The one gee outer rims of the huge centrifuges back home. She always hated the heavy workouts there and the compulsory runs round the big wheels. Some people did it for fun as well. Since she could remember doing it she could remember hating it. Must have hated it even back then before she was aware of doing it. But it made you fit. Running in ridiculous circles, breathing easy, sweating lightly except where the weights wrap. Over the sill, into the workshop. Stupid sills. Just six centimetres at every doorway. Stupid little six centimetres. But every time, *every* time. The first run after a long free fall phase she never picked up her feet high enough, tripped at every door sill, sometimes falling the long lateral stumble to cannon slantwise into the outer wall. Bruises. From space travel. Into the exercise space. No tripping now. This was the second day of this deceleration phase, the twelfth pulling gee in the past twenty-four days. Shapir pedalled steadily on the bike, going nowhere. Two ship pilots, jockeys of the fastest things the human race ever made, both going nowhere. One round and round and one even less. Shapir from Luna too. They weren't physically disadvantaged. All that lovely exercise. Had done all the on-Earth training with the rest of them. Into the galley. She had held up under the terrain-training in the nights on mountain and glacier and ice cap just as well as the rest. Shapir had come in for some of that too, making sure that Nightrider's pilots shared everything with the lander team. Flitting through the ladder space, never touching the deck. Making sure the whole crew stayed cohesive. Minimal splits resulting from mission duties. Two of the four pilots from Luna. Two million people on Luna, several billion on Earth. Not surprising. Space related professions were a front runner career off-Earth. She and Shapir got even less dizzy than Ali and Sandra. The others got dizzy, had to take a break from the baby orbiting jog and run on the treadmill band. Space familiarized, but they got dizzy after two times ten

circuits. They preferred the bike. Other advantages in coming
from Luna. Into the workshop. Bare toes grazing the door sill.
Careful. That hurts. You didn't mind the utter monotony, the
cramped little unchanging world. Serenity was all enclosed,
but had those long corridors, Dome Park, and the endlessly
different little rooms and spaces. In Crisium Terminus Shapir
had grown up to far less variety and far less space. The others
needed more psych preparation. Exercise space. Shapir hammered at the pedals, obediently hitting an energy delivery
peak. The men's weights were heavier than the women's,
bringing them up to their Earth load. Sweat ran on Shapir's
skin. The others needed psych preparation. Ali said he missed
having anything far away to focus on. Yasmin wanted sunlight
and shadow, harshness as well as Nightrider's light softness.
Into the galley. Two strides. Round and round, winding ten
times up and times ten down. Again and again and again. Sail
the ladder space to the day space. Running round and round
like Nightrider's days. A day was just mechanical time, a
digital divide, a sequence of slipping numbers. Nightrider
woke them and Nightrider sent them to sleep. And in between
another day wound up. Up and up. Not like the jogging circuits
up and down. Pointless, pointless. Enough, enough. Had quite
enough. Jogging and pedalling she'd had the weights for half
an hour. Hated them for half an hour. Enough. Into the
workshop. Slowing suddenly down. Who was counting circuits? Winding up or down or neither it was enough. Round
and round like an orbiting idiot. Only *step* through into the
exercise space. No more. *Walk* in front of Shapir pedalling
madly on the bike. Walk to the open rack beside the torsion
bars, the free fall torture. Snap the weights from wrists and let
them just fall into the rack. Slip the lead headband and throw it
in after. Ah, your head is lighter than a free fall load on your
neck. Rip the weight bands from upper arms. About time for
Nightrider to be polite.

"You should do forty minutes today, Kim. You still have six
minutes."

She hauled off the yoke, held it high, flung it down.

"You should really go for a few minutes more."

Off with the hip girdle. The skin over her pelvis was pressed
red. It always was but for once it mattered. Everyone has to
self-assert now and then. Off with the ankle weights.

"Don't you want to continue, Kim?"

"No, Nightrider. I *don't.*" And off with the weights wrapped around her legs above the knee. "I'm fit enough. I'm the first lander pilot. I'm life support systems specialist. I'm astroscience specialist. I'm a medic." Snap the rack door closed. "What I'm not is a weight lifter!"

Shapir had slackened off, was hardly pedalling at all. He shrugged.

She grabbed her overall from the foot of the acceleration couch and went out into the galley. She rolled up the cool cupboard door, wrenched out the fruit squashes drawer, snatched one, snapped the drawer back home and slammed the roll door shut. No messing with the drinking tube and low gee spills. She ripped off the top and drank it down. Sweetened cherry. She should watch what she was taking. She hammered lid and empty cup through the hatch of the disposal shute. She lost her overall but retrieved it on its retarded way to the deck, hitched it over her shoulder. Now that was better. Much better.

"Would you like to continue now, Kim?"

"No, Nightrider, I would not. Is the mission book going to block if I behave a little flexibly?"

Nightrider knew how to handle arguments with a low function correlation with the mission book targets. He didn't answer.

Self assertion did you good. It was even expected in the psych set-up. They all had to retain the ability to take the initiative when it really mattered. She glanced back at Shapir and grinned. Shapir shrugged, already pedalling steadily again.

She turned and stepped through to the foot of the ladder, hauled herself up arm over arm effortlessly.

She stepped from the recessed ladder into the ring corridor. Stopped. There was almost nowhere else to go to. Yasmin sat in the angle between the hygiene room and Shapir's sleep cubicle, perched legs crossed at the focus of a litter of loose components. Beyond her, the tightly angled metre wide corridor was blocked by a piled clutter of weapons and sights and scopes. Round the other side of the central core lay hand charges and grenades. Akira appeared, picking his way through the litter, the aiming block of the grenade launcher in his hands. Kim stepped to the open doorway of the hygiene room to get out of Akira's route to the ladder. But Akira stopped. He had obviously been intending to sit down next to

Yasmin on the only bit of clear deck left, right where she was standing.

Getting past Yasmin was impossible. Kim's cubicle was round the other side of the central core, opposite the transfer lock. She leaned to look past Akira. The whole of the little deck appeared littered, choked.

Akira looked behind him. "You want to get past?"

"Yes. No. Never mind. I'll shower first. Saves one trip. There's room down below for whoever's next for a workout. Shapir's on the bike." She turned through the hygiene space doorway. Nightrider put the lights on for her. She touched the pad and closed the door.

Akira looked at Yasmin, martial Japanese at fatalist Indian. "You want to go first?"

Yasmin shook her head. "I'm still right in the middle of a batch." Her hand arced index finger down over the fan of loose components. "You go."

Akira nodded. He put the grenade launcher down on the deck, stepped over the ladder well and slow-dropped from sight.

Yasmin started to reassemble the dismembered rifle. That was the variety in being one of the two weapons specialists—a small part of the things you were responsible for were good old fashioned mechanical, rather than electrical. A small part. Most of it was solid state sighting and guidance, timing triggers and surveillance. But she and Akira were the nearest of the whole crew to people doing things themselves, rather than through instructed machine intermediaries. A little further away from technology servitors and back towards handicraft skills, but still a mission function. Hopefully a reserve function. What a thing to class as a handicraft skill—killing other people with hand held tools. It might come to that, it should not. Akira had been in a real war, adventuring away from his Peruvian émigré homeland and some of the time soldiering in Latin America and Africa, which slipped him smoothly onto the side of the spreading pragmatic consensus. No Japanese would come out of Japan any more, of course. Japan had long gone the same way as the other northern powers, eastern North America, Europe, western and south eastern Russia, most of China, places like Korea caught in between. Places that didn't exist any more. Funny how the will to organize and mobilize still came from the northern hemisphere, spreading from India and Indochina through to northern Africa, reaching West america and Central America. There still wasn't much pragmatic rationalism south of the Equator, not yet. But then Africa and Latin America had always been more internally preoccupied, while the stable anchor of the pragmatic consensus—though never really its focus, not its power source—had inevitably been the Moon. The people up there were necessarily realists. Up there! *Back* there, ten months' transit time away. But that was an interesting question, one of those answers that Sandra would like to know for the sake of knowing. Where were the informationalists behind it all—was the rational half of Earth running the Moon, or was the Moon running the rational half of Earth? And did it make a difference?

Akira had killed people. All those endless waves of the Messiah's little children, shrieking with machetes and pistols and grenades, seeking a despatch to Heaven, sex and sin free, or as a consolation at least unbeliever prisoners to play with and send to Hell a piece at a time. They'd used adult hides, he said, stripped from the living and sewn up and inflated to symbolize the spiritual emptiness of the enemy. All those endless waves of the Messiah's little children, shrieking shredded by machine guns and shrapnel and scorching under napalm rain. And some people looking at the world, still wanted to know *why* absolute obedience to an absolute authority bound to rational response to the dictates of pragmatic contingency. Well just look at the world. Since it began.

Yasmin had never killed anyone, not even during her schooling secondment to the People's Militia, not even out on the streets during the Mysore riots, eyeshields and bayonet rings against stones and incendiaries and slingshots and even spears. It was always another squad that had been finally ordered to fire.

Perhaps it would come this time. It shouldn't.

The assembled rifle was blunt and ugly. All rifles are ugly. It fired a low calibre round at super-high velocity, it was all breech and recoil-reloading mechanism, snub barrel and long muzzle brake. The butt was nothing, just a flat buffer pad. You held it two-handed like a police marksman but with the butt jammed against the chest of your suit, high up over the heart.

The breech and the block magazine were behind the trigger grip so that it was back heavy when loaded, awkward to aim unless butted securely. To aim beyond point blank range you snapped the sights up and forward, open sights or else with an infrared or starscope aimer fitted—you couldn't crane your head to line up a shouldered weapon, not in a spacesuit. Aiming was easy unless you wanted to shoot for kilometres, when you had to use a laser ranger that imposed a trajectory lift on the sights. Closer to, the trajectory would be virtually flat in Hel's 0.6g, and with no atmosphere to retard it the bullet arrived as fast as it left the barrel. Which was very fast. And that achieved with a minimum recoil kick because of the muzzle brake. The design was just a futher improvement of what was standard. The brake deflected the propellant gases into an X-cross of four streams, two angled up and two angled down, an arrangement that neither blinded your aim while firing nor seared your leg while kneeling nor killed the friend beside you. Handling the rifles was far too easy.

And the rounds were fearful. Pointed little four millimetre things, part solid bullet and part glued on caseless charge, such low bulk and weight that you could carry hundreds. Those bullets would go through the shell of their own suits. They would hopefully go through whatever the Outsiders wore. The bullet sheared and fragmented on penetrating a rigid suit, it *shredded* any flesh on the other side. If it hit unprotected flesh it tumbled, dumping all its momentum in shock waves. Bones struck directly disintegrated, others connected to them shattered, soft tissue was just exploded kinetically.

Not that the weapons were to be used. When Nightrider had done passing over the Outsider base there wouldn't be anyone left down there to interfere with the intelligence snooping of the lander team. The weapons were for just in case, for self-protection and for mopping up. It had to be a clean raid with no one left to tell how it happened. The object was to eliminate the Outsider presence and prepare the way for a terrestrial one, thereby restoring future parity. Advertising that you *had* capabilities was inevitable, but you didn't have to tell the other side what they were.

Yasmin put the reassembled rifle aside and started to strip another. One more after that, and then came the IR and starscope sights and imagers. There was no light down there but starlight. Hades was just a corpse, black and cold and too far away even to make a visible hole in the sky backdrop.

Kim came out of the hygiene room, clothes in her hand. There was still no route past Yasmin, so she started round the other way.

"Are you dry? Don't drip water on those things."

"I'm dry. I just wanted to go back to my box and dress."

Kim picked her way over the jumble of killing things, half the time hauling herself clear of the deck with the free fall grab handles. She skipped over an array of recoilless grenades and landed between the transfer lock and her own cubicle door. She looked at the grenades. They were just flat ended cylinders sitting on the ends of one-shot disposable firing tubes. No streamlining or flight stabilization was needed. There was no atmosphere down there, only gas-ice and water-ice and rock and ice-rock powdery surface and a smear collected through the long circling aeons, a smear of cosmic dust. The grenades had electric capacitor heads which would need charging up before storing away again in the lander—the lander's system couldn't supply the necessary power. The grenades were the first ever weapons type designed exclusively for space use. The huge electrical potential discharged almost instantaneously into whatever was hit—building structure or vehicle or whatever —causing dispersal currents that vaporized the material and inducing secondary intense and disruptive electric fields. All the energy was dumped into the target. In contrast explosives were debilitated in a vacuum, with no pressure damping to confine the force of the detonation and no medium to transmit a shock wave. Even if an electric charge grenade only hit near its target it would cause such thermal disruption of the ground that debris would fly as from a fragmentation blast. What it would do to people Kim didn't know. They hadn't shown her. All that was for Akira and Yasmin.

Yasmin leaned round the sharp curve of the ring corridor, bending over her pile of ordnance. "Ali's in the lander with Samson. Program checks. They said would you like to go up and see."

Whether the Outsiders down there on Hel had things like that with them. They shouldn't, of course. There was no war yet and no one would ever expect it to happen out here. Not out here. "Yes. Sure. In a minute."

She opened the little door to her cubicle, ducked and tumbled inside.

So there were two sides to the Solar System. The Outsiders scattered from Mercury to even Pluto but only really concentrated on Mars and Ganymede and Triton. So few of them with such limited material and energy resources, and people scarcest of all, surviving somehow since their seeding and sudden abandoning by the collapsing mother world, perfecting a culture of purest high technology and even spreading from ice ball to ice ball in desperate pursuit of the raw resources of life support. And huge and teeming and still mineral rich Earth, but self-crippled and with only its Moon in tow.

But this was a *planet* at the target end of Nightrider's approach path, eight times further from the Sun even than Pluto. A medium sized terrestrial planet with a rock and iron core, with the chemical crustal composition of Earth, with uranium decaying deep in its heart making *heat*. A planet with the chemical resources and the thermal engine needed to produce *water*, be that water now mostly frozen in a funeral crust of ice. A planet with water and oxides to produce oxygen, with frozen nitrogen to complete synthetic air, with deep heat to generate limitless geothermal power, with light and heavy metal ores. Only life based hydrocarbons were missing to make chemical manufacture feedstocks. There was no life and there never had been. Hel was too close to hot and variable Hades for life to start, and even if it had, six hundred and fifty million years ago the vast explosion had wiped it all out, and since then there had been no light energy input and therefore no photosynthesis, but only the black geothermal warming at crushing pressures under a solid crust of ice and rock. But even without hydrocarbon feedstocks, with free energy, on site plastics were composable from their constituent elements.

In short, Hel was a *world*. A potential place to live. A world where a colony—based on the surface or buried in the ice—could grow and grow richly and limitlessly once ever established, until it outproduced Earth in power and purpose. Only the years and years of vastly expensive investment were needed to choose a suitable starting point for a growing colony, a seeding bed, and the Outsiders would have an empire and a home world safe in the outside dark. And despite the monstrous proportion of their total resources required for the task, they had already started the search for the seeding bed.

And the rulers of Earth—rulers absolute over some areas of the planet and barely at all over others—had finally noticed, and had finally decided that the prize belonged to them.

The Outsiders had already moved from a loose to a tight federation. They had not liked it a quarter of a century ago when Earth had sent more ships again to expand the never quite broken bridge from the Moon, not when those ships brought shifting political petitioners and a pervasive assumption of the right to call the suddenly cut off children back to heel. The Outsiders had grown through a generation of their own too, not physically destructive like the change on Earth, but just as divisive. And then when Earth began to regroup itself and pour its culture outwards, treating the little outer worlds as natural dependencies to manipulate so as to back up power dances on the stage back home—then the schism had begun, and with it the little incidents. The Outsiders needed no one else's convoluted rationalism. They had a pragmatic principle of their own, that of sheer physical survival.

So the Nightrider program had been diverted from its original purpose and developed for use as needed, and Nightrider was the first of a possible line. And now the Outsider's presence in the Hades System was to be eliminated, brushed out of the way and kept out of the way until Earth decided to do something with the planet. Earth had the right, after all. The historical imperative was there as surely as for the Outsiders, and so was the means to do it. And so was the will. Those are the key components of any justifying rational theory of action, politically phrased.

301 12:25. Both chronometers over the day room doorways said so, two telltales of the cycle of time, one hundred and twenty degrees apart. Time to be ending the midday communal meal, the reinforcement ritual of the little community communicating with itself, exactly as prescribed in the mission book.

The best thing about pulling gee was that you could eat open-dish food instead of the tube foods and the pastes that stayed in their tubs and cartons and had to be scooped out. You could eat curries and casseroles, or soya steaks with side dishes, mayonnaise stirred or sauce soaked salads, all ready made and reconstituted in sealed bowls or subdivided trays, to be eaten not just with spoons, but also with knives and forks. Or chopsticks. Everyone today used chopsticks. In unspoken solemn solidarity twenty-four hours before target, they had all selected from the same cuisine, from the Chinese derived menu list. Chinese derived dishes were easy to cope with, meats sweet and sour, prawns or crab meat or crustacea portions fried in batter balls, fowl in nut or citrus fruit sauces, always sitting on a bed of rice in shallow single portion tubs, all tastily traditional. You could eat with spoons, of course, but chopsticks were available and had been employed for the oriental menu lists without exception since the beginning of the mission. Akira had been the only one who had to learn the trick.

"Hel encounter," Sandra said. "We have to decide our tactical pattern." She sat shoulder to shoulder with Samson on the convex curve of the bench seat between the workshop partition and the flight centre hatch. She tweezered the last batter ball out of Samson's bowl. He stole a piece of sauce steeped fish in redress, along with a glue of rice all around it. You can pick up a lot at once with chopsticks.

"The target approach," Kim said. She sat with Shapir and Ali on the curved couch between the last acceleration couch and the workshop partition. Akira and Yasmin sat cross legged on the deck. "Which way do we go round, and where do we select for orbit injection?"

The decision would be an easy one, limited only by the parameters of their own intentions. The Outsider base was located almost exactly on the planet's equator, and the planet's rotation rate was tidally locked to its orbital period—from the base, Hades was directly overhead forever. Approach paths for voyagers sailing the plane of the ecliptic couldn't be easier, parking orbits for anyone intending to land couldn't be simpler in energy terms. Which was why the Outsiders had put their base there.

"Flyover from the east or west," Ali said.

Shapir put his bowl on the little table, the chopsticks neatly paired across the top. "It's just a choice as to which way we can most easily pick up the target. If we approach from behind we come in from the west, so we come in over the plain.

If we come in from the east we come in over the mountain upland."

"Continent," Samson said. "Probably. Geographically speaking."

"Mountains anyway," Yasmin said. "A real jumble. But that gives us a profusion of approach markers."

"Profusion is right," said Sandra. "Almost enough to mix up. And they're all pattern markers. A sharp peak next to a rounded peak next to a cleft valley next to a table top, and so on. It's all peaks and valleys and plateaus. The plain is broken and rifted, but it's all level, minimal topographic variation. There aren't so many markers but they're all distinct, something in nothing. Single feature fixes, mostly."

Ali shrugged. "There's nothing in it. I think so, anyway. At least from the terrain simulations we have. If the mapping is out in either measurement or interpretation, well then that's different."

Kim scooped rice together in the bottom of her bowl. "In what way?"

"Well—if the terrain diverges from the predict, then broken and irregular terrain will be more difficult to match than flat terrain with isolated features."

"I think so too."

"Anyone disagree?" Shapir asked.

"I don't disagree," Samson said, "but still. Level terrain with a low feature density and low marker density presents its own problem. Suppose we see a low plateau with broken scarp to the left of track. With no other potential markers to correlate with, we don't know whether it's an unmapped feature we should ignore, or something mapped as a high plateau with continuous scarp that should lie to the right of the track. Depending on which is the case, and depending on which we assume and whether we correct our course, we could stay wrong or go wrong and miss every other marker."

"We don't have to make such decisions on one marker," Sandra said. "At least not usually. Mostly they come in series."

Samson spread his hands, bowl and chopsticks diverging. "I said I wasn't disagreeing."

Akira put down his bowl. He uncrossed his legs and stretched them, leaning back on his hands. "The other factor is the target visibility. If we come in over the plain instead of the upland we get a longer view. Assuming we're approximately on track, we have a higher chance of making a fine correction in order to overfly the target on the first pass.''

''We don't need to hit it on the first pass,'' Shapir said. A little carefully, consciously steering an argument he seemed already to have resolved.

''But it has advantages,'' said Yasmin. ''If we think we're as likely to find the target approaching from east or west, we should select the option that maximizes a first pass strike.''

''Well that's the west approach,'' Kim confirmed. ''The mapped area could be mislocated in any direction by sixty kilometres. It was scanned by three different probes, all of them from more than eighty thousand kilometres out. That degree of possible error is irrelevant to an east or west approach. But the error on the base predict inside the mapped strip is five kilometres. The further downtrack we see it the better.''

''If we can take it clean out or damage it the first time we see it, so much the better. There's always a chance they'll see us when we see them. If they just happen to have radiation shelters, then no matter how many passes we make *after* we've located the base, there's always too good a chance that there'll be people down there waiting when we land.''

''Which we want to avoid.''

Yasmin nodded.

Ali stood up. ''Anyone want ice cream?''

''Yes,'' Sandra said. ''But get me a spoon?'' Ali liked to eat ice cream with chopsticks too. Nobody else could cope with that.

Ali smiled one of his smiles that didn't affect his eyes, left them darkly desert gleaming. ''Flavour?''

''Oh—anything. Not chocolate.''

Ali nodded and crossed to the ladder space doorway.

''A first pass strike?'' Shapir asked.

Sandra nodded. ''Whether we do two or three or four strike passes, the sooner we start the series the better for all of us. For the lander team, for the survivors reason, and for us for manoeuvrability. Which is also good for the lander team.''

Samson nodded too. ''Because if Nightrider can't manoeuvre freely, Nightrider might have problems. We don't know if there's a ship on station there or some orbital defence system."

"Unlikely," Akira said.

"But possible. And we might be seen. We'll certainly be visible while taking out the base."

"If a ship or something *is* there . . ." Sandra said.

"If so," Kim said, "we want to get the lander down on the ground where it's partially protected, so Nightrider's free to pull full gee manoeuvres and take care of the problem. Personally I'd feel safest of all right here. But the lander has to separate because the structure tolerances limit Nightrider to five gee, and I have to go with the lander, so I'd like us to be able to land at a safely levelled target rather than hang around helplessly in orbit. So the sooner the base is taken out the better."

"I think we're all agreed," Akira said. "Ali?"

Ali came back into the day room carrying two tubs of ice cream. "I heard. I agree. We should aim for a first-look first-strike on the first pass." He handed one tub to Sandra and went back to his seat. "Kim mentioned orbit injection. Let's select the *path* injection for right over the base predict."

"But stay supraorbital?" Kim asked.

Ali nodded. He picked up his chopsticks and started stabbing at the scoopfuls of ice cream in his tub.

Sandra spooned her ice cream in tiny tongue tip tastes. "We have eight kps as encounter velocity, if we don't course modify." Hel's orbital velocity at the near grazing incidence altitude they were going to adopt was 6.2 kilometres per second. "Nightrider, how much drive do we need to maintain an orbital path at eight thousand metres a second?"

"Seventy-two percent, Sandra."

"So we can do it. Transit time right round the path?"

"Three-seven-four-four seconds at twenty kilometres altitude."

"Thanks. And orbital period would be four-eight-four-oh. So an hour and a couple of minutes and something instead of an hour and twenty minutes and something. We'd come round for the second and each subsequent pass faster than they'd be expecting us. Even if they see us on the first pass without us managing to line up to take them out, we still keep an element of surprise."

"If they mark our velocity?" Yasmin said.

"Highly unlikely. We're black and invisible so they won't see us except occulting a star overhead. If we occult two stars and they time it, or if they react fast enough to turn a radar on us and get a reading—which is unlikely in the extreme—they'll see we're at supraorbital, and they won't see our drive operating so they won't know we're doing anything about it."

"So they'll think we're at perigee of a highly elliptical orbit and won't be back again for hours," Kim said.

"Exactly. Anyone seeing us anywhere along the orbital path—for whatever unbelievable reason they see us—will think the same. Which will fool anyone trying to predict our path for an intercept, and will leave the base thinking we're taking ourselves back out where we came from."

"You're thinking," Samson said. "I like it."

Sandra shrugged. "Ali's idea."

Ali just balanced a half impaled, half tweezered lump of ice cream into his mouth. His secret was that he liked to eat ice cream in large chilly gobbets instead of neat snippets. He swallowed the ice. "But I'd only thought as far as the reduced path transit time, not the course camouflage."

"Well," Shapir said slowly, "that seems to be decided. We go in west to east. We decelerate to eight kps over the base location predict and maintain that in a supraorbital path for as long as it takes to destroy the base. Then if there's no trace of any other presence to complicate things, we drop down to orbital velocity and go over a few more times to take a good look, then the lander goes down while we run orbital guard. All as in the mission book. Modifications?"

No one seemed to have any.

"Okay. Nightrider, course modification from now to bring us round for a west to east flyover at encounter. We'll look at the fine parameters in a while."

"Check," Nightrider said, and a second later, "Initial modification enacted." A fractional shift in their orientation and thus in the axis of deceleration, far too small for them to register.

"What," Akira said, "if there's a ship, and we see it fire a burn to take it out of orbit?"

"Go on taking out the base," Samson said. "Then the lander team goes down and Nightrider chases the ship. Mission priorities."

"We let the lander go as soon as we know we've hit the base," Shapir added. "A ship can signal home as easily as the base. More easily. At the present orientation the base has most of the planet between it and the Solar System."

"They'll have some sort of comsat," Yasmin said.

"So the base still has to go first. The Outsiders back home will know there's a war on out here as soon as the reports cease, or as soon as someone sends an alarm signal. But we have to eliminate them before they can figure out and report *how* it's all happening."

Kim looked slightly confused. "I didn't know we were thinking in terms of a *war* out here."

"Oh there's a war," Samson said. "We're it."

Sandra nodded. "The first ever interplanetary war is also the first ever interstellar war. Two firsts with one kill."

Ali and Kim spent most of the rest of the day in the lander, running through the various options for a landing sequence from a west to east orbit. The lander's computers held a mathematical map of the relevant part of the physical universe —Hel and the coarsely mapped section of its equator that contained the base—all reproduced in variously appropriate degrees of detail, but for its proper functioning it had to know its exact starting point within that map matrix. The touchdown target was a designated site six kilometres southwest of the base predict, on the protected blind side of a low east-west running escarpment. If they descended from a low enough orbit, the approach angle would be so shallow that the base would be hidden from them all the way down—which meant that they would be hidden from any survivors inclined to shoot holes in the vulnerable vehicle. To be able to reach the touchdown target, the lander had to be supplied with repeated position and motion data updates and short-term predicts right up to the moment of separation, an updating responsibility that the mission book assigned direct to Nightrider. With adequate start data, knowing where it was and where it was going, the lander was then able to go from orbit to target touchdown all by its automatic self.

The rest of the lander team went through the remaining battery of equipment and systems tests, then switched to runs of the simulated approach path, examining the intimate terrain again, revisiting all the memorized markers. It was impossible to know the topography too well, you had to be able to cope with a consistent change to it *all*, to elevation or gradient angles, if the remote mapping turned out to be seriously in error. The mapping had been done from a long way away by laser point-sampling of the ground elevation and by starlight photography after all—high resolution radar scans would have given the probe away, along with the knowledge that Earth knew about the place.

Sandra and Shapir ran course predicts and manoeuvre simulations, and ran the target approach over and over. They had covered every conceivable angle at every imaginable altitude a hundred times before. But they did it all again.

Sandra sat alone in a day room darkened to dim light, to machine world night. With a data screen on her knee, she ran yet again through the simulated from-west approach to the base predict. The screen showed a fine rectilinear grid beautifully distorted into the ground topography as seen from a simulated fifty kilometre altitude. Via the key pad she made the graphic move as if sliding forward over it, as if sliding back, dropping down, sliding again, moving left, dropping again. Stop. She switched to the horizon profile, just a green line on black, slightly irregular, slightly curved. She switched to the horizon silhouette and the green line disappeared. Instead she had the star field on black, a dense dust of little light points, cut off irregularly by a sudden nothingness. She ran the simulation forward again. Nothing seemed to happen, except that the cut-off changed shape slowly and only minimally, and the star field slipped barely perceptibly as the simulated viewing point cruised a simulated orbit beneath a simulated sky. The features this far downtrack were just plateau blocks and fissure patterns. She waited for the horizon rise of the fourth marker, the first key marker, a little centrally peaked upland mass like an island in a petrified sea.

In the fish-eye she sits with the screen on her knee, the screen readout clearly visible. She sits lower right. Opposite the eye, lower centre, is the flight centre hatch in the central core, open on black. She sits in dimmed light. The screen readout is directly experienceable, is accessible in real time as she accesses the mission book database. The day room is dim, the other spaces of the main deck dark and empty in chronometer light. Akira comes down the ladder, falling and handgrip braking. He enters the day room, crossing curved from mid left. Sandra looks at Akira.

Akira: *you should stop now Sandra—you should relax—we all gave up hours ago—even Shapir.*

Sandra: sighs: *I'm tired.*

Sandra puts the data screen flat on the table.

Sandra: *you just want sex.*

Akira: *don't you too?—it's good for you.*

Sandra: *sure I do—recommended psychologically and socially isn't it—helps us function better—keeps interactive tensions down—and come tomorrow we'll be far too busy for a few days.*

Akira and Sandra leave the day room. They climb the ladder, Akira following Sandra, his eyes fixed on her close buttocks. The data screen glows in the dimness, a star silhouetted frozen horizon line. Ali is in Yasmin's cubicle. Naked, he massages her naked back and buttocks while she purrs and curls and uncurls her fingers. Samson is wedged wall to wall across the fish-eye distortion of Shapir's cubicle. Kim and Shapir try to remove his clothes and Samson laughs.

Already naked, Shapir clambered over Samson to attack from the other side, distracting him. Kim dug her fingers suddenly into Samson's waist and he collapsed and curled with a shriek. He gave up and let them strip him. Only Kim was left clothed, eyed at bay against the back wall. She smiled one of those smiles, she unzipped her overall and shrugged it from her shoulders, slipped her arms out of the half sleeves. She stuck out her legs at them and lifted her hips so that they could pull the overall down to her ankles, then over her feet. She slid out of her briefs, still smiling. We shed our overalls, we slip out of our briefs, we slide out of one skin and into another. We set one role aside and perform a different function.

Yasmin spreads her thighs, lifts her buttocks. Ali slides over her, reaches under and enters her from behind. Akira and Sandra squeeze opaquely into the shower. They run the water in bursts. Dim day room light to zero. Data screen off. The lander reports functions nominal, zero event. Drive function is nominal. Power systems nominal. Electromagnetic surveillance shows star background plus zero.

Nightrider sensed every one of its own myriad functions, watched the motionless stars, listened to every empty frequency in the rushing void.

DAY 302

SANDRA came back into the flight centre, swinging in through the hatch under the bar just inside the ceiling, twisting to slide herself into the right side couch. Her legs went into the enveloping folds, she pushed against the bar and let her hips slip over the padded edge. She wriggled down until her feet touched the tailored ends of the leg recesses, pushed her arms into the closed side slots, and lay back into the couch's caress. Its hydrostatic sides lapped her, almost overlapped her, sweetly cool warm. It enclosed her head, half circled her throat. She checked the arm swing freedom to the manual flight controls, then settled her fingers back on the key pads. She pressured up the couch. It gripped her gently, entirely.

An arm's reach above her, between the screens set flush into the slightly sloping ceiling, the chronometer read 302 11:44:09.

She activated her screen. Its silvery surface dissolved into a display pattern identical to its slanted twin over Shapir's couch. Readouts. Drive 100%. Acceleration—0.25g, —2.5 ms^{-2}. Velocity 10,700 ms^{-1}. Drive output parameters; power output monitor; fusion boosters one to four pinch fields activated and run up to half, feeds open. And a view of the world beside them.

A view without image intensification. A view synthesized from the planetside nose and tail sensors, a hemispherical field.

A thin ring star field of differing density, speckled pinpoints and dusty clusters on night velvet. And filling the centre almost to the rim, a lightless hole, a nothingness, a starlight trap, a gaping black negation giving nothing to the eyes.

A closeup look at Hel.

"They're welcome to it," Shapir's voice said into her ears. "At first sight, they're welcome to it."

"The lander team?"

"The Outsiders. In resource terms it might be a hundred times—a thousand times more valuable than everything else they have apart from Mars. But they're welcome to it."

"It's just the lack of rosy sunglow. No beauteous lightswept world swimming in a celestial sea, and all that. But it's the best piece of dirt available besides Earth. Hel's a little piece of heaven to them." Sandra cancelled the stars in her own view, brought up the image intensification, reinforcing the back-washed starlight reflected from the low albedo surface. In a black ring, Hel became a dark grey, indistinctly varying. Nothing down there was mapped. It would be a frozen wasteland, a mess, a meaningless jumble of rocks and ice, a dead world killed by a suicide sun.

"Who's in the couches?"

"Everyone but Kim and Ali. They're up in the lander locking the couches flat."

"Kim is in the lander," Nightrider corrected. "Ali is in the hygiene room."

"Last of the last trips to the toilet," Sandra said.

"Okay. We're seventeen minutes from target. Give me lander and hygiene room, Nightrider. Hey, you two. Get down here and into the couches. We're at target minus sixteen and a half."

Kim stood up stooping under the low ceiling, pausing between the footrests of the flattened couches. The four fixed couches made a second, contoured deck bridging both halves of the crew space from front wall to back. Only the space between the floor lockers showed a strip of the real deck, and that divided in two by the open airlock hatch. In a few hours, a few orbits, this shoulder to shoulder space would be their second home. They would ride down to Hel in it, and then she would be counting every sliding second until they lifted off again for Nightrider, for their chaperone voyager and the long transit home.

The chronometer showed 302 11:45:51. Kim turned, stepped back over the open hatchway, and let herself fall.

She touched briefly, straddle legged, on the airlock deck, then she let herself fall again through the lock well, the docking collar, down the transfer tunnel, braking and guiding with her hands sliding down the ladder sides. Through the top hatch of the transfer lock onto solid deck. "Close the lock, Nightrider."

The top door slid closed, sealed.

She went out of the lock, swinging round the door rim, three steps running round the half octagon of corridor. Ali came out of the hygiene room in front of her, stepping straight from the doorway to the ladder well. She slow fall followed him down.

She bounce landed and strode long steps across the galley, over the sill into the exercise space, turned to the couch against the partition wall beside the doorway. Ali was already lying back like a retiring vampire in shortsleeved white into his couch. Kim sat on the rim of her own, swung her legs over and dug her heels into the covered recesses, then lowered herself into the waiting cocoon. She wriggled into enveloped place, found the key pads and pressured up. The couch gripped her, safe within Nightrider's power. She activated the screen in the ceiling above and looked at the same blank blackness of Hel.

Altitude 25,700 metres. The altitude was measured from the deduced surface mean, and that in turn calculated back from the gravitational centre of the planet. Every second the range laser pulsed almost at minimum to measure the terrain elevation with respect to the surface mean. Elevation—309 metres, depressed plain. The laser pulsed almost at minimum so that no one else but themselves, no one elsewhere orbiting, would see any light scattered from the surface dust.

They flew tail first at over eight kilometres a second, decelerating at full drive, at one quarter gee. Orbital path entry, still at supraorbital velocity, was set for directly over the base predict. There they would burn the base in a technological Passover, then flip head down towards Hel and use the drive thrust to counter the centripetal force of the too-fast orbital flight and keep them in a tightly curving path around the planet and back to the base again. They would burn the base when they found it.

They flew tail first, tearing past the planet, cocooned in their couches, searching their screens. They used every permutation between them, watching an unmodified view of the horizon ahead or left or right, looking image intensified at the moving terrain, split screen or overlay matching with the approach simulations, searching for the markers. At their altitude, a flat plain horizon was just over five hundred kilometres away, they saw a circle of Hel a thousand kilometres across. Any feature appearing on the horizon ahead was beneath them a minute later and had vanished over the horizon behind a minute after that. In bright shadow scoring sunlight over broken terrain it would have been breath-taking, in the shadowless image intensified view a ripping rolling world would still have been dramatic enough.

Except that there weren't any features.

They were a third of the way into the approach run, three minutes already gone. They were looking for the fourth marker, the first key marker. Markers one to three had not appeared.

"The burn," Shapir said. "What value should we set?"

"Give it full lander tolerance," Sandra replied. "Five gee."

"Yes." He watched the blank forward horizon silhouette in his arm's reach ceiling screen. The marker should appear there, breasting the horizon just right of centre, just to the south of track, a raised little upland mass with a central peak. It should already be halfway down to them. Instead there was just the plain. "But do we give half thrust on all boosters or full thrust on two? That would give a more concentrated tail jet, more intense but less spread."

"Let's wait until we see the base. Structure dispositions."

"If we see it." He switched to an intensified image with cancelled stars. Blank grey sped beneath, a broken lateral line slid rapidly down from the distance. Ali had sampled it with a laser sensor as soon as it had appeared. It was a shallow step, a rising fault line of almost a hundred metres meandering across the plain. It shouldn't be there. He watched it whip accelerated out of the bottom of his view.

"I see something," Samson's voice said suddenly. "Right horizon, seventy degrees from track."

"Good," Sandra said. "Give us your view."

Shapir split his screen, his own view in the upper half, with the flight readouts blended in over black sky, and space below for Samson's picture. "Ali, Kim—concentrate on the track."

Someone had to help Nightrider look ahead.

Samson had a silhouetted horizon line cutting off frozen stars, and dislocated below it the grey ghost brightened image of the blank world. Left of centre, growing slightly, moving right, was a tiny pyramid bump. "Is that it?" said Samson's voice. "From the north."

"It's over the horizon." Akira. "Six, seven hundred kilometres off track?"

"I have a predict on its profile from this angle." Yasmin. "Put it on the net, Nightrider."

A little green horizon simulation interposed between the two half pictures, real profile above, ghost terrain below. A long falling ridge, an elongated saw-tooth irregularity in the line, tracking right. The lengthened simulation and the twin real world little pyramids moved out to the right, shrinking.

Samson: "That isn't it. Where is it?"

Kim: "That wasn't it? Where are the markers? There's just nothing ahead."

Shapir wiped the failure from his screen. Altitude 25,300 metres. Terrain elevation—110. Time to target 282 seconds. "Nightrider, what's our track error?"

"Altitude minimal. Left-right one-three kilometres."

A thirteen kilometre error couldn't account for the missing markers. The target predict would come over their horizon at minus sixty seconds, in three and one half minutes. They had to find the markers and adjust their flight path so that they came right over the real base right on track, aiming their fusion lances directly at it. Time to target 260 seconds. The second key marker should come peeling down from the horizon line, breaking the grey ghost desert.

"Where are the laterals?" Sandra's voice. "The ones on our north and south horizons. The mapping error can't be so big that one side or the other isn't in sight."

"An error of sixty kilometres." Ali, cynically.

Akira: "Here it comes. Late, but there."

A darker thread across their track, creeping down.

Shapir: "Nightrider, what's our track plus-minus error?"

"Four-nine kilometres."

A dark line meant sunken, less starlit ground, a mighty fissure across fractured smoothness. Someone blended a range counter on it dead centre, little figures racing down the kilometres in tens. Two hundred. The foreshortened zigzag ninety kilometres left of track should be starting to show, an abrupt sidestep running parallel to their track.

Kim: "Is anyone still watching the left and right horizons?"

Yasmin: "I'm looking left. North."

Samson: "I'm still looking right."

Ali: "There's no break. No break."

Kim: "It's not right."

Sandra: "Samson, Yasmin, watch it as we overfly. The break can't be displaced over our horizon."

Ali: "Everything else is."

The fissure slithered out of the field, stubbornly straight. No second key marker.

Samson: "I don't see any break. Yasmin, you see it?"

"No."

Time to target 187 seconds. Altitude 25,200 metres. And no markers, nothing but anonymous cracks in the ice ground.

Akira: "That had to be the right fissure. We're just displaced way out to the north or south. Therefore the uptrack error."

Samson: "Does that help?"

"Sure. The fissure can't run forever exactly north-south. It must be offset. The uptrack error should tell us whether we're left or right of track."

Shapir: "We're at minus one-seventy. We can't recover a lateral error of five hundred kilometres in three minutes. We figure it later."

Sandra: "The burn. Five gee? Make it full thrust on two boosters? That gives us a longer effect range. If it turns up way off track we might still manage a hit."

"Okay. Burn on one and three. Feed from pods A and C." The booster pods one to four each had their own hundreds of tonnes of reaction mass propellant, but the four pure tank pods alternating with them in Nightrider's girdle had to be drained first for jettisoning. The fusion thrust steadily reduced automatically as propellant mass was expended and pods dumped, keeping constant the gee forces on the tolerance limited structures—five gee with the lander docked, ten without it.

"Right. Come on, Nightrider. Something for you and me to do."

Kim: "Shapir, did you mean this is a miss?"

Shapir: "It looks like it. Minus one-thirty-three and no marker yet."

Yasmin: "It would be nice if we got a track indicator, so that we knew which way to displace on the next pass.''

Samson: "Keep looking. Just keep looking."

Ali: "Hey, what's this? Look at that."

In star field profile or ghost ground grey, the horizon ahead was disintegrating, segmenting into little breaks and jags, turning into a profiled mountain range rising against the night. The disruption spread along the horizon, faster to the north than to the south.

Kim: "That's our broken upland behind the base."

Akira: "Not the right upland. It's too soon. Unless those peaks are elevated twenty-five kilometres."

Ali: "Put a laser on one. Range it."

Shapir: "No. Match the profile. Find the base."

They needed a raised line with a central cleft, that notched skyline bedded between higher serrated peaks. The base would be down in front of it, visible as they came closer, on a long flat tongue retreating into a valley between a ridge on the left and a shallower rise on the right. Behind the left-hand ridge there should be an isolated towering pinnacle pointing vertically at invisible Hades. Their final base marker, its death warrant.

Akira: "The mountains are already down from the horizon. Two hundred kilometres? It's minus seventy-five. They're three hundred kilometres too far down track."

Ali: "I see no match."

Sandra: "Our track plus-minus error is forty-nine. Huh."

Kim: "I can't see a match."

Akira: "There isn't one."

Sandra: "We can forget the burn."

The mountains were marching down the screens, more jagged peaks rising behind them, more behind those.

Shapir: "Nightrider, how are the star occultations by Hades? Are we on track?"

Nightrider: "The occultations follow the predicts exactly. Our left-right error is one-one kilometres."

Sandra: "Minus forty-five. Stand by for orbit path injection. Do we forget the burn?"

Shapir: "Yes."

Akira: "Here come the mountains."

The screens filled with downward rolling peaks and ridges, the surging storm surf of a giant, petrified sea. The terrain elevation raced up thousands of metres, pitched down again, tossed high.

Shapir: "Minus thirty. Injection manoeuvre at minus five. Reduce drive to seventy-two percent at minus ten. Manoeuvre duration five seconds."

Sandra: "There you go, Nightrider. Easy if you don't have a burn to execute at the same time."

Kim: "We all keep looking. Uptrack markers east of the base predict. We have to pick up *something*. Samson and Yasmin keep scanning the side horizons. Ali, look back the way we've come."

Nightrider: "Drive adjustment, mark."

A stepped decrease of weight from one quarter gee to just under a fifth, like the soft beginning of those falls as you drift into sleep, without the sudden start of waking.

Nightrider: "Manoeuvre, mark."

A sweeping feeling, sliding sharply feet forward. The counter thrust of the attitude jets, sharply sliding head first.

They flew on, pitched perfectly nose down to Hel, pointing the lander at its monstrous planetary goal. They flew on faster than orbital velocity, the skyward kicking thrust of the drive holding them in the orbital path. They lay there in their close couches, an entire planet balanced just above them.

Altitude 25,000 metres. Velocity 8,000 ms^{-1}. 302 12:02:12.

Sandra: "Perfect, Nightrider. At least your part of the mission is working."

Akira: "Nobody saw the base?"

No responses.

Nightrider had switched from tail to nose sensors automatically. A chaos of pitched and broken slabs and pinnacles swept by, dark grey in the boosted starlight.

Shapir: "First decision. Abort, or consider coming round for a second pass?"

Nightrider: "Excuse me, Shapir. Mission abort or this attack abort?"

Shapir: "This attack abort."

Sandra: "Don't panic, Nightrider. The mission's safe."

Kim: "If we try a second pass displaced north or south, we have the simplest manoeuvre if we just adjust the path inclination at ninety degrees round from the base predict meridian. Right?"

Shapir: "Right."

Kim: "Which is in fifteen minutes. So we have time to think."

Akira: "No abort yet."

A lightless chaos of ice and rock, shattered and smashed and jumbled, rolled by above them.

302 12:09. Drive 72%. Acceleration 1.8 ms^{-2} (vector angle 90° to flight). Velocity 8,000 ms^{-1}. Altitude 25,000 metres. Elevation +7,100 metres.

"It's rising plateau," Sandra said. "We should think about adding another five thousand altitude."

"Are you watching the ground?" Shapir asked. He was key pad talking with Nightrider, setting up parameters for the range of possible orbit adjustments that would bring them round again to search for the target northwards or southwards from the first pass. All they needed was something to base a decision on.

"Yes, I'm watching. It isn't interesting." She had a screen full of irregularly undulating blankness, no mountains coming up ahead, but the terrain steadily rising. The black horizon line and its star field backdrop would have been more interesting, but she would have lost herself studying the rising star patterns, and risked missing the warning bump on the horizon that would mean a towering mountain rushing towards them.

Yasmin's voice. "I think I've got something. I've been re-checking the north horizon. Please put it on the net, Nightrider."

Sandra cleared half her screen to accept the networked recording. There was more of the grey chaos of shattered mountain belt, receding away forever into the north, to the left of their track. The picture was frozen with a time marker blended on the black sky: 302 12:05:41.

Yasmin again. "The orientation is due north, ninety degrees left of track, three minutes twenty-nine up track of the base predict. Now look at this from the simulation." A bright line appeared in the sky above the horizon, roughly matching the real recorded horizon profile.

Akira: "That's an approximate fit."

Kim: "I don't recognize that at all. Haven't I studied the horizon profiles well enough?"

Yasmin: "Oh, Samson should recognize it."

Samson: "I should? I don't."

Yasmin: "Look at the centre, due north. A flat table with a sharp peak at the right end going down to a deep cleft, then a jagged rise, and at the left end a shallower cleft and a concave rise to the adjacent peak. I call that a good match."

Ali: "It is. It is. But the left horizon shouldn't look like that. What is it?"

Yasmin, with a hint of the successful conjurer. "It's the right horizon reversed. The back view."

A thoughtful silence, suspended beneath a mighty turning world.

Sandra: "Clever."

Kim: "Is it valid? I mean, can we trust a match like that?"

Samson: "It's the only match we've got."

Yasmin: "All the other matches you'd expect along the north horizon could be missing simply because of mapping error. So this is the only marker that shows up. Or—it could be a coincidence."

Samson: "It's a persuasive one, if it is. So we conclude that the mapped strip, the base predict, the whole thing is displaced massively north of the predicted track. Do we?"

Ali: "Why not? We have to conclude something."

Akira: "So we go north for the second pass. How far north?"

Yasmin: "That's the reverse of the predicted horizon profile as seen from on track at ten kilometres altitude. It's three hundred twenty kilometres south of track. And that real feature is at just over five hundred kilometres from our path."

Kim: "Eight hundred and twenty. That's about ten degrees of latitude. What's ten degrees, Nightrider?"

Nightrider: "Eight-two-five kilometres."

Sandra: "Well then. We tip our orbit to bring us over ten degrees further north. Simple."

Shapir: "Okay, it's twelve-eleven-forty. We have to make the manoeuvre at twelve-seventeen-fifty. We still have time to discuss it if anyone has reservations. We'll have to start the final setting up at minus two minutes. So?"

There was the persuasive little match of the horizon on the screen, with its nimbus self, its mission book snippet of idealization hovering just above it. The only feature match and the only marker that they had.

"I'm just wondering," Ali said. "Not a reservation—what

else do we do? Just wondering. What kind of mapping error displaces a whole strip of a planet's surface by ten degrees?"

302 12:29. Velocity 8,000 ms^{-1}. Altitude 50,000 metres. No rising mountains could reach out *that* high from a three-fifths gee planet to snare them. They were indifferent to the topography turning above their heads, had cancelled their screen views or else watched an endlessly rising miracle of pin-prick stars suspended over a well of black nothing. Only Nightrider recorded the terrain as the mission book instructed, amassing data for delivery to Earth. They were Earthside of Hel now, tail towards home. Not that there was any point in looking that way—from Hades the Sun looked like any other star.

"Incident radar," Nightrider said calmly. One corner of each flight centre screen rippled into data readouts.

"What?"

"Incident radar for two milliseconds."

You could *hear* the instant attention from all the other couches, from all the other little humans who thought they were flying in an invisible host. Detected?

"Thirty megaherz," Sandra said. "Ten metre radar. Coarse mapping radar?"

Ali: "What direction?"

"It's approximately straight out," Shapir said. "From a higher orbit. Maybe. Nightrider, what's the direction accuracy?"

"A seven degree cone."

"Search it visually, infrared. Anything you see. From the contact position outwards."

"Two milliseconds." Sandra stared at the data, trying to compel it to explain itself. "Was it a two millisecond pulse aimed at us, or a longer pulse we just flew through?"

"I have more data," Nightrider offered. "There was a coincident backwash from the terrain exactly below our position. The backwash source appeared one-one-three kilometres south of our position and tracked through to six-nine kilometres north."

"How fast?"

"Seven-six-oh milliseconds."

Samson: "A rapid scan mapping radar? Building up a map from a series of profile sections? How often would they scan?"

"There's been nothing else?" Shapir asked.

"No."

Yasmin: "Would we register against the ground echo?"

Kim: "If the equipment's good enough we would."

Ali: "Why don't they fire again?"

Hel turned, a vast frozen globe of inscrutable ink, as they traced their path around it. And somewhere further out something else moved too.

"Let's suppose they're mapping," Sandra said. "Or *it* is. So—is it a satellite or a ship?"

Samson: "A satellite would be mapping automatically. What's happened to the next pulse?"

Kim: "So it's a ship with a crew. Someone noticed our anomaly and is trying to figure out what it means."

Ali: "Why should someone want to monitor the trace in real-time?"

Kim: "Equipment test. Boredom. Who knows?"

Akira: "It could be a satellite with a performance monitor. It picks up an anomalous echo—a fifty kilometre error—so it runs a systems check."

Samson: "It should run a calibration check. Repeat the scan."

Ali: "Maybe."

"We'll know if it signals," said Shapir. "If it signals, it saw us. Doesn't matter what it is. Except that if it's a sat, nothing can possibly happen until it tells someone it saw something, but if it's a ship it can respond immediately."

Akira: "Respond how?"

If it was a ship, did it have a weapon? Could it track them and destroy them from range, or did it have a fusion torch like Nightrider's? Did it have a *drive* of its own, would it slide in unseen and sear them?

"They can't predict our position from the radar contact," Sandra said. "With our flight direction perpendicular to their viewing direction they'd get no doppler, no velocity reading. Not even our flight direction. They can't deduce our path and never that we're traveling an orbital path at supraorbital. To get a predict on us they'd have to *track* us first."

Yasmin: "Could they track us visually? The surface must be bright enough in an intensified image for us to show as a silhouette. If they have the imaging system for it."

Ali: "Maybe they saw us first and fired a radar pulse as a range check."

Akira: "Then why a sweep across one hundred eighty kilometres? To fool us?"

"Speculation," Shapir said. "Just speculation. So let's speculate some more. If it's an automatic satellite that ignores anomalous signals, then nobody knows we're here. If it's a ship or a satellite that only registered us but isn't tracking, then they can't predict where we are, and they can't tell anyone else unless they signal, and no matter how tight a beam they use we'll pick up side leakage and we'll know the warning's been given. So then the priority would be to take out the base before they can act on the warning. Okay so far?"

Akira: "And if it's a ship and is tracking us?"

"Then there's no advantage in manoeuvring, because it will see exactly what we do. If we abort the attack it will see our departure path and could track us in infrared maybe to I don't know how far out. But. If it's in a higher orbit it's circling slower, so before much longer it's going to be unsighted as we disappear behind the limb of Hel. If it's orbiting in the opposite direction it will just lose us sooner. So we go on and take out the base and then immediately insert into a new flight path that it can't predict. We could go up to a higher orbit and take a look at what happens, then maybe leave the lander in a parking orbit somewhere way out and come in to take out the ship."

Akira: "And if it's manoeuvring right now to intercept us?"

"Unless it had a drive like ours we'd see the burn. Nightrider would. And if it manoeuvres after we're round the limb it still loses us. The priority is to take out the base while we can. That's the only place they can *predict* that we'll turn up. The only place they could pick us up again once they've lost us."

Hel turned, a vast black nothingness over their heads. And somewhere further out was another something, perhaps another someone who had seen them and was caught in a quandary of their own. Anyone tracking them would know where they were going and what they might do. And couldn't interfere.

"Okay."

302 12:59:30. Four minutes into the approach, and something quite obviously wrong again. Velocity 8,000 ms^{-1}. Drive 72%. Acceleration 1.8 ms^{-2} (to-flight vector 90°). Altitude 20,000 metres. Terrain elevation −4,600 metres. They sped nose down just twenty kilometres from Hel, they had a horizon

at four hundred and fifty kilometres out. Intricately factured plain rolled through their nine hundred kilometre circle of sight, grey sight in magnified starlight. Cracks and fissures and dislodged blocks squeezed up out of their fault perimeters, little crevasses like cobweb lines, gaping chasms like cruel wounds in a bloodless and frozen corpse, hacked by some frenzied murderer. 13:00:04. Terrain elevation −4,300.

No markers, no features. Just this shattered plain depressed more than four kilometres below the surface mean, but rising.

"We can use the same burn as before," Samson said. "If there's anything to burn."

"There won't be," Sandra said. "There won't be."

"Full thrust on one and three, feed from A and C."

"Sure. Just somebody show us a target."

Akira: "No one sees anything?"

No answers. Elevation −3,800. Time to target predict 261 seconds.

Akira: "That big fissure we thought was the second key marker should be over the horizon now. It runs up here. Can anyone see it?"

Samson: "In that mess?"

Kim: "That's a giant hillside down there. Look at the elevation climb. Minus three thousand two."

Ali: "The fracturing is getting worse. What does it?"

Elevation −2,400.

Yasmin: "You can *see* the rise on the side horizon. You can *see* it."

Shapir: "No sensor contacts, Nightrider?"

Nightrider: "No sensor contacts, Shapir."

Nothing signalling, nothing radar scanning, nothing doing anything except perhaps looking, perhaps seeing them as a light-drinking silhouette speeding against the deep dark of the starlit ground. And only then if that something knew they were there and knew exactly where to look.

13:01:00. Elevation −1,200.

Samson: "Overriding. Plate boundary. That's it. Plate tectonics. Plate tectonics. The planet's still geologically active. It's a plate collision zone ahead, ocean plate and continental plate running into each other."

Yasmin: "Is this the *continental* plate? Doesn't the ocean plate go under the continental plate?"

Samson: "Yes. Yes. The continental plate overrides, the

ocean plate is subducted into the mantle. The continental plate's leading edge crumples. Mountain building.''

Kim: ''Shouldn't we see mountains coming over the horizon soon? That's still a clean line ahead.''

Ali: ''We should see the northwards extension of the mountains we flew over last time. They're due.''

Samson: ''Of course. That's the continental plate. This is ocean we're flying over. But it's frozen ocean. The ocean plate is dipping down there ahead, is being subducted. But the ocean is ice. It doesn't flow. It's getting piled up there ahead. It overrides the continental plate like a giant glacier.''

Sandra: ''They wouldn't put a base there, would they?''

Samson: ''Oh, but it happens slowly. Very slowly.''

13:01:50. Elevation +1,500.

Shapir: ''The ground's really coming up. How high is it going to get?''

Ali: ''No higher than that ahead. The horizon line's breaking.''

Showing notches against the infinite black, as if all the cracks and crevasses and chasms ran to an edge where the world dropped away. A topsy turvy concept, because this world hovered twenty thousand metres above them.

Elevation +3,100.

Kim: ''Peaks coming up behind it. A lot.''

The night horizon sprouted a forest of pyramidal trees.

Samson: ''The ice crust overrides the rock crust and the whole thing grinds together. That's how the planet gets an ice-rock layer over its entire surface. The process repeats and repeats, infinitely slowly—but it repeats. You get a frozen mix from the surface down to the real lithosphere. Must be kilometres deep in places.''

Sandra: ''At least one of us is happy.''

Akira: ''Here comes the edge. The elevation's going to reach plus six thousand.''

A jagged edge of severed terrain sped down to the bottom of the screens. Behind it came another petrified sea of monstrous chaos, huge slabs and pinnacles shattered upwards, yawning clefts filled with tumbled debris cascaded down from the advancing ice sheet. A sand box visited by hellish Titan children in a rage.

Samson: ''Further south the boundary is stable. Locked. Here it's active. *Look* at it. The most incredible glaciation phenomenon in the known universe. I'll call it after me.''

Yasmin: ''Oh, some Outsider already has his name on it.''

Nightrider: ''Incident radio frequency.''

Rippling data readouts in each flight centre screen, erasing mere natural splendours.

''UHF,'' Sandra said. ''What's that, an area broadcast?''

''The orientation,'' said Shapir. ''Tailwards. That's straight out to Hades.''

''Nightrider, is that coming from Hades?''

Akira: ''It's still coming in?''

''It's coming from the direction of Hades. Yes, it's still coming in. I'm recording.''

''Can you make sense of it?'' Shapir asked. ''Decipher it?''

''The signal is narrow bandwidth, digitized, probably data, picture, or voice. The bit rate is four-six kilobytes per second.''

Ali: ''Some picture. Some voice as well! Forty-six kbytes.''

Akira: ''I think that's the warning going through to the base.''

Kim: ''So all we need is the base.''

Yasmin: ''Minus twenty to target. If anyone's interested.''

''Can you decipher it, Nightrider?''

''I'm sorry, Shapir. Not at the moment. Their encryption is divergent from ours.''

''Huh,'' from Sandra. ''Now that's a surprise. By the way, that was a target *predict*, Yasmin. There's no target here.''

''Is the source moving?'' Shapir asked. ''Is the orientation changing?''

''Six arc-minutes every second with respect to our orientation,'' said Nightrider. ''But that is our flight orientation change. The absolute direction is constant.''

''From towards Hades. Absolutely constant?''

''Absolutely.''

Kim: ''It's a comsat.''

Akira: ''It isn't orbiting.''

Kim: ''You wouldn't want it to. Hel is rotation locked to its orbit round Hades. The planet turns every couple of hundred days. Orbiting comsats would always be tracking across the sky, and who needs a ring of satellites anyway? There's only the one base, with no one else to talk to but back home. Half of the planet's orbit the base can transmit direct to the Solar System, but for the other half it's on the blind side of the planet. So they put a comsat out at the Lagrange point, where the orbit time round Hades and the gravitational pulls of Hades and Hel all balance out. It keeps perfect pace with Hel's orbit, it stays stationary in the sky, lined up directly with Hades. The base is only cut off from the home for the day or two when Hel cuts across the comsat's signal path to the Solar System.''

"We have the same arrangement on Luna," Shapir said.

Kim: "Sure we do. The Lagrange points are the only way to fix a comsat in the sky. And from the comsat you can talk to orbiting mapping sats for half of every circuit."

Yasmin: "Or orbiting ships."

Samson: "Whatever it was that registered us."

"That they did, all right," Sandra said. "That we know."

Akira: "That would explain the delay in sending the warning. There's only one comsat, fixed at the Lagrange point, and whatever vehicle picked us up had to wait until it had orbited clear of the planet's limb before it could signal to the base."

Ali: "Which is what it's doing."

Nightrider: "The signal has ceased. I'm only receiving carrier frequency. That has ceased."

Shapir looked at the readouts and the frequency spectrum suspended in the ceiling screen just above him. If only the signal was decodable it might tell them something about the source, the thing that had sent it. Whether it was a ship, and whether it could threaten them. And where it was. And what they might be able to do about it. "The question is—the same as last time. Do we abort or do we continue?"

302 13:10:49. Altitude 20,000 metres. Velocity 8,000 ms^{-1}.

The base wasn't north of the equator. In two passes they had seen all the terrain out to fourteen degrees north on the Hades side of Hel. No conceivable mapping error or programming error during the long progress of the data from raw visual input through endless processing phases to the mission book database could possibly translate the target further northwards still. So it had to be south, wherever it was. They could change from their current orbital path again a quarter of the way round Hel from the Hades meridian, inserting into a new path that would bring them round again for a third pass south. The peak Samson had seen over the south horizon on the first pass might just have been the first key marker, despite the discrepancy in its profile. The gross errors were huge, after all, so such a small divergence from the simulated predictions hardly seemed improbable. They could insert into a path that would bring them round eight degrees and six hundred and sixty kilometres south of the equator, a last attempt to find the base.

The path change had other advantages. It would minimize the chance of any searching surveillance eye picking them up on the almost hour long circuit. That, coupled with the non-predictability of their position along their flight path because of their supraorbital velocity, should make them safe from any other presence that could intercept and harm them.

Should.

And hitting the base as soon as possible so as to free them from its attention focus was as desirable now as before. Setting down the lander team so that Nightrider could hunt the ship—if ship it was—unencumbered remained the most logical course of action. And the mission book priority rated the base as primary target, more important than any unknown that might be found. So important that they should take out the base almost irrespective of any collateral risk.

So the decision was due.

"Any votes to abort?" Sandra asked.

302 13:50:00. Drive 72%. Velocity 8,000 ms^{-1}. Altitude 50,000 metres. Seventeen minutes from the new base predict, the time point when they would once more cross the Hades meridian, this time eight degrees south of the equator. Had Hades still been a sun, it would rise blinding brilliant from the limb of the black night planet directly ahead of them in just two minutes' time. But Hades was a gravity compressed cinder, lightless. From now until the end of things there would be no more *day* here.

"I'm picking up radiation," Nightrider said.

Shapir had been rubbing his eyes, his bent arm raised up out of the couch. He pulled his arm in again in a reflex retreat to safety, ramming his elbow down into the enclosing arm-slit of the pressurized couch and forcing his forearm to follow. A tortoise starting back into its shell.

Sandra had already keyed up a display representation for both their screens—a curved cut-off of the limb of Hel, and above it radiation intensity colour contours, a laminated circle sunrise spreading from a dull red central crescent out to indigo regions fading into black. Beneath were the numerical and graphic data readouts and keys.

"Synchrotron radiation," she said. "From a particle cascade. Is Hel's magnetosphere powerful enough to trap particles?"

"It is," Shapir said. "Comparable to Earth's." Hel could keep a vacuum density swarm of captured cosmic ray particles. Any high energy particle flux streaming through the captured swarm would trigger off an avalanching cascade of interactions of reducing energy, a spreading cone of fundamental fragments that would spiral along the direction of the magnetic field, shedding further energy as electromagnetic radiation as they went. A high energy particle flux from where?

It was rising ahead of them, its energy focus at the limb just a few degrees off to the left of their flight path, to the north. That energy focus was a new laminate colour of reddish orange.

"What do you think that is?" Sandra asked. "No kind of natural phenomenon?"

"No." Nothing natural inside the Hades System fired focused streams of charged particles across space. "Stand by to manoeuvre, Nightrider."

The energy focus had a new heart of brighter orange.

"Think it might be aimed at us?" Sandra asked, and then ignored her own question. "Nightrider, can you work back through the particle cascade to orient the whole thing in three dimensions? Essentially I mean so as to compute a range on the source?"

"I'll work on it, Sandra."

"There's the source. Direction, at least."

A bright yellow dot had appeared and detached itself from the representational limb of the planet. The circle of brightest orange around it was beginning to close.

Kim: "That's a ship, that's what it is. Tail on to us."

"Any visual contact, Nightrider?"

"No, Shapir."

Kim: "There'll be nothing to see. It's an ion drive."

An ion drive ripped atoms apart into positively charged nuclei and negative electrons. It wound the nuclei and the electrons up to higher and higher velocities in accelerator rings and then spewed them out in alternating packets as relativistic particles streaming from a ship's tail. It was just another kind of rocket motor, which maximized its efficiency by maximizing the propellant velocity, the reaction mass comprising not electrically neutral chemical combustion products but electrically charged fragments of atoms. Fragments which themselves spiralled and radiated in a magnetic field, and which collided with the particles of any medium through which they passed. Such as the vacuum thin captive haze in a planet's magnetosphere.

The yellow centred orange circle had separated entirely from the limb. The red laminate ring was preparing to part company.

"You mean we're looking right up its arse? Nightrider, is the effect consistent with an ion drive?"

"It's a particle accelerator, Sandra. I estimate the range at seventeen-point-four thousand kilometres, error plus-minus two thousand."

Kim: "For particle accelerator read ion drive. We use them, the Outsiders use them. They're standard for deep space propulsion systems. We're the oddity. There's only Nightrider has our kind of drive."

Ali: "She's right. It's an ion drive. If there's anything unusual about it, it's just the power. It's powerful. Maybe that's a big ship, or it's accelerating fast. But it's an ion drive."

Obviously. The coloured onion display sun was lifting clear of the planet's limb. It wasn't a weapon waiting for you, aiming death at you. It was a ship about seventeen thousand kilometres ahead and accelerating, running away. Anyone could work that out. If they had the leisure, they could estimate the energy output while tracking the position to measure its acceleration, and thus arrive at the mass of the ship. But small, large, or very large, it was running away. An Outsider ship trying to escape from an unknown quantity, from the black intruder it had briefly seen speeding past the back of Hel.

"That's what saw us," Shapir said. "An Outsider ship that was presumably in orbit, surface mapping or something, when it picked us up. It sent a warning to the base over the comsat as soon as it came round the limb, and is now shifting out to a higher orbit. At least an elliptical one with the apogee way out towards Hades."

Samson: "You mean running clear instead of protecting the base? That would mean it isn't armed."

Akira: "They don't know that we know they have a base

here. They could be hoping to distract us.''

"They must know their drive lights them up like a beacon,"
said Sandra. "Maybe they want to lead us away. Or maybe
they want us to see where they're heading. For the comsat.
They'll know we picked up the signal and know where it is.
We have to take out the comsat, too, if we want to stop all
signalling back to the Solar System. Maybe they want us to
know they're protecting it. My guess is they're armed somehow.''

Yasmin: "Reasons?"

"Because they're being visible. They don't know if we're in
orbit, or on flyby, or whatever. They don't know when we
might or might not be unsighted by the planet. They could have
just kicked out of orbit and then coasted, and we'd never be
any the wiser. As it is they're letting us see them. They want us
to follow like Akira says and ignore the base. But that's a big
risk unless they can defend themselves.''

Samson: "The ship could have a priority instruction to draw
intruders away from the base and sacrifice itself if necessary.''

"Maybe. But let's not rely on them being a soft target.''

"We'll find out," Shapir said.

Akira: "First priority is the base. Then the lander team goes
and Nightrider can deal with the ship and the comsat. Do we
assume the departure of the ship removes any immediate
danger to us in taking out the base?''

"I think we can," Sandra answered. "Shapir?''

"I think so." A glance at the chronometer. 13:56:42. Just
over ten minutes to the base predict, the third one. "Target
approach due in seventy-five seconds. As before, Samson
monitors the right horizon, Yasmin the left. The rest of us look
up track.''

Kim: "Let's hope we see something this time.''

302 14:00:00. Drive 72%. Velocity 8,000 ms^{-1}. Altitude
25,000 metres. Terrain elevation −250 metres. And still no
markers, nothing clearly recognizable as some feature to which
the simulation marker was some remote mapping approxima-
tion. But it couldn't be another dry run, not another. That
isolated peak which might be the first key marker should be
appearing over their up track horizon in a matter of seconds.
Next came that huge transverse fissure that was supposed to
have a sharp sidestep making the second key marker. This time

they should be able to line up and locate the base, even overfly it and burn it on the first pass.

"I have a result tracking the Outsider," Nightrider said. "I have the acceleration."

Ali: "Something on the horizon immediately right of the track."

Kim: "I see it. That's Samson's peak."

A grey ghost pyramid, tiny, surfacing against the black, star wiped sky. A grey ghost pyramid with an extending base, blending into the horizon line.

"The acceleration, Nightrider?"

"Two point four metres per second squared."

"Two point four?" Sandra sounded their joint surprise. "Two point four metres? An ion drive? That's a factor of ten above standard."

Nightrider: "The figure is correct."

"Two point four. We're going to have to chase him. Really chase him. That's going to be something."

Kim: "The match is poor. The sides have no scarps. We know the peak isn't elongated east to west. Do we take it as the marker?"

Grey on synthetic starlight grey, a little island on the blank plain, coming down. But an island without the sought for cliffs.

Akira: "The right displacement is too small. Accept it as the marker. Nightrider, how far off track are we?"

Nightrider: "From the marker, forty-five kilometres right displacement. Correction manoeuvre?"

Shapir: "We can cancel again. At drive one hundred percent, and keeping the supraorbital compensation thrust, what's the to-track lateral thrust vector at what orientation?"

Nightrider: "One-point-seven-three-metres. Attitude change yaw four-four degrees."

Shapir: "Okay, Sandra, work it out to let us overfly the base predict. Nightrider, manoeuvre as follows. At minus two-nine-five, attitude change yaw forty-four left. Three second manoeuvre. At minus two-nine-two, drive to one hundred and maintain."

14:02:01. Time to target 299 seconds. 298. The assumed island marker slipped out of the bottom of every screen.

Nudged sideways to the left by the couch, like a lurch in the perfect ride. Then the compensating push to the right, stopping them angled still nose down to the planet, but hanging skew at forty-four degrees. No, your body wants to orientate the universe according to the weight it feels. The planet had slopped sideways above them, went on spinning madly as they lay immobile in their couches.

Sandra: "Ninety seconds from minus two-nine-two. Then cancel and reverse manoeuvre. We'll have a lateral component of one-five-six metres per second to bring us over the predict exactly."

Shapir: "Okay. Nightrider, give us a decision call at minus two-on-two."

Kim: "Here comes the fissure."

The screens still showed level views. A blank grey desert of smooth ice and pulverized rock, but with a darker lateral thread peeling down from the horizon.

Kim: "Is that the step to the left? Is that the step?"

Akira: "I think so. Nightrider, how far off track does that put us?"

Nightrider: "Three-seven kilometres right displacement."

Sandra: "That's perfect. That's where the correction should put us. This looks like it."

A vast chasm came sliding down the screen, a chasm with an abrupt zigzag breaking its otherwise straight run out towards the northward horizon.

Samson: "It seems to reduce a couple of hundred kilometres south. The simulation says it shouldn't."

Kim: "Let that go."

Ali: "The simulation isn't exactly perfect."

Yasmin: "Samson, what is that? It looks pulled apart. Some sort of tension fracture?"

Samson: "It could be rifting. But two thousand kilometres north of here we've got compression."

Nightrider: "Reverse manoeuvre at minus two-oh-two?"

Shapir: "Yes. You take it, Nightrider."

14:03:34. Altitude 23,000 metres. Elevation −110. Drive 100%. Nothing but blank starlit plain again, image intensified. Drive 72%.

A nudge to the right, then a nudge to the left. They were aligned again perfectly nose down to Hel, still tearing east at eight kilometres every second, but with enough lateral velocity northwards to bring them exactly over the track again just where the predict said that the base should be.

Sandra: "Burn as before? Full thrust on one and three, feed from pods A and C."

Shapir: "Okay."

"Okay. Nightrider, run one and three to full pinch field at minus sixty. We'll pick the twenty second burn commencing at minus ten option if we see the base soon enough. We don't worry in advance about post-burn flight corrections."

Akira: "Third key marker in sight. The ridge looks right."

A raised rib in the blank plain was coming down towards them from the horizon, lying diagonally across their flight direction, slightly curved. The curve was convex, coming in from the left and pointing the way towards the base. If the base was really there.

Akira: "That looks higher than it's supposed to be. Are we going to overfly the eastward extension? We're too far to the right."

Kim: "Sandra, does our displacement match with our to-track correction?"

Sandra: "Can you check that? I'm kind of busy."

"Okay."

Yasmin: "I estimate the ridge as one hundred thirty kilometres long, which matches. But the simulation has a two thousand elevation, and that one must be at least four thousand."

Ali: "The simulation's already nearly seven hundred kilometres out. We can accept that."

Kim: "Yes, we're still right for track convergence at the base predict."

Drive 72%. Altitude 21,000 metres. The eastward reach of the curved ridge rushed away beneath them, out to their left.

Yasmin: "Minus one hundred and ten-mark. The end of—the ridge marks at five seconds after predict."

Akira: "Then we're fine."

Sandra: "Okay, I have the burn set up. Twenty seconds at five gee, ten seconds down track of target to ten seconds up track. If it's displaced laterally we just aim skew but keep the timing and thrust. Resultant to-track velocity vectors depend on the aim displacement, but we'll emerge with eight thousand still along track."

Shapir: "Fine. Okay, Nightrider—burn initiation will be at minus ten to flyover. Take the parameters from Sandra. We'll fix the flyover mark when we see the base."

Ali: "Mountains ahead."

Synthetic grey skyline against synthetic starless black, a skyline wrinkling, peaking, breaking into a mountain wall wave front. Here came the plate boundary chaos again, limb rising and spilling down towards them.

Kim: "There's the marker. Dead ahead."

Exactly where their track would take them was a lowered level break between serrated peaks. In the middle of the break was a deep notch. The notch filled with looming mountains behind. The base would be down in front of it, not yet resolvable in the level distance. Falling broken ground ran out from the mountains and blended into the plain. Two last little ridges amongst all the others ran paired directly westward, each a scarp to the south and a long shallow dip to the north, the northern one of the pair much higher than the southern. On the flat strip between them should be the base. The pair were marked by an isolated needle of rock rising a kilometre further north than the summit of the northern ridge.

Akira: "I see the base marker. Nightrider, net my view."

A closer view into the long distance. Rising mountain wall with jumbled foot falling to flat plain. End on levelled ridges. A little rock pinnacle sticking up from the one in the centre of the view.

Shapir: "IR, Nightrider. Overlay hotspots."

Bright pinpoints in the flat gap between one scarp and the next rise. Two points.

Shapir: "That's it. Laser range it. Fix to-target time."

Nightrider: "Two-three-two kilometres. Two-nine seconds."

Sandra: "Burn at minus ten. Aim at target and orientate to maintain target aim during burn. We're going to pass four point five kilometres north, altitude twenty."

Shapir: "Close tail sensor shields. Manoeuvre at minus seventeen—drive to zero and attitude change to aim burn."

Akira: "Wait. The base is spread out. Hottest point left, flat structure centre, hot point right. Thousand metre spread?"

Sudden cessation of weight. The enclosing couch pushes and pulls as Nightrider flips tail to target.

Shapir: "Centre aim between left and central structure."

Nightrider: "Burn initiation, mark."

Weight. Something. Even in the couch bed. A ripping at cheeks and eyes. Feel the weight of thin overall on chest and stomach. Tongue wants to curl back. Swallow to prove you still can. Prove you won't choke.

Sandra, slightly laboured: "Buildings spread across a thousand metres. Will the burn focus take everything out?"

Shapir: "Should do."

Nightrider pitches over, stands tail down to the planet belching solar fire, a black night dragon burning light into Hel. Not a sound. The furious plasma streaks out of its fusion focus through a magnetic lens, *touches* nothing. Nothing but the iron ice and vaporizing buildings and any people there.

Nightrider pitches further, nose to flight.

Nothing. No pressure. No strangling tongue. No tearing at your face. Free fall freedom in the grip of the couch.

The massive petrified chaos of mountains coming down from the forward horizon and passing beneath. A world visited, unchanged.

Shapir: "Open tail sensor shields. Let's see."

Mountains, and then plain out to nothing night. The base already hidden behind them and the pinnacle marker sinking. Vanished.

Shapir: "Nightrider, how was the burn alignment?"

Nightrider: "Constant alignment at focus between north and central structure from initiation until termination."

Sandra: "It was. The burn spread will have got them both. It probably didn't reach the southernmost structure."

Akira: "That was the smallest one. I'm looking at the last view we had. The south structure looks like some kind of square twenty or thirty metres across. The central structure is around one fifty metres across. The north structure is taller and twenty or thirty metres across. It was making the real heat. Must be the power reactor."

Yasmin: "Look at that behind us."

In the downtrack view, choking up with foreground mountains, a little cloud of half-opacity was rising against the further plain. Rising from where the base had been.

Yasmin: "What's that? It can't *burn*."

Samson: "Get it's temperature, Nightrider. Put a laser on it to measure back-scattering."

Kim: "We did something to it. We did something."

The mountains pushed the cloud, shrinking with distance, towards the horizon. For a moment it was a ghost dome against the black backdrop. Then it sank from view.

Ali: "Did you see how bright it was? I just looked at it in natural light. It *glowed*. I'm running it again without the light intensification. It looks as though it's lit from below, like a fire."

Yasmin: "It can't *burn*."

Nightrider: "I have the data. Would you like to look, Samson? I can't interpret it."

Altitude 30,000 metres.

Shapir: "Sandra, we're rising faster than the supraorbital should account for. Work out the components the burn gave us. Nightrider, attitude manoeuvre to put us nose down to the planet, then drive initiation at seventy-two percent to maintain path. Manoeuvre duration five seconds. Initiate—now."

The sideways nudge of the couch again, and then its countering compensation to stop the attitude pitching. Then weight, a sweet little weight leaving you lounging on your back in the deep and cocooning bed. Nightrider flies nose down to Hel again. The planet hovers massive above you, kilometres away.

Altitude 33,000 metres.

Sandra: "We've picked up thirty-one metres a second laterally northwards. That adds to the correction component we gave ourselves to make one-eight-seven north. We have an away from Hel component of one hundred and three metres a second. Suppose we cancel them one at a time?"

Shapir: "It's easier. Away from Hel first. Just increase the drive."

Sandra: "Okay. At one hundred percent we pull back oh-point-seven metres every second, so we need—one hundred forty-three seconds to cancel. Okay, Nightrider. Drive to one hundred percent and maintain for one-four-three seconds. Initiate—now."

A little more sweet weight. Just a little.

Samson: "I've sorted it out. The cloud was water vapour with a particulate mix. I assume that must be re-freezing as the vapour radiates thermal energy. Whatever kind of mixture the ground is down there at the target, we vaporized the water-ice."

Ali: "The glow? What would that be?"

Samson: "Incandescent melting, I suppose. Either the base structures, or rock particles. Maybe a rock bed just under the ice. I wouldn't expect the plasma would cut very deep."

Akira: "But you think the ground was disrupted?"

Samson: "Oh yes. That's for sure."

Akira: "So—what structures weren't destroyed outright have probably collapsed or even sunk."

Samson: "Possibly. Can't be sure unless we take a look. But we must have made a mess of the *site*. So it won't have done the base any good either."

Akira: "Sure. Don't worry, I'm not trying to unload the responsibility onto you. I'm just trying to establish a decision basis for whether or not we go down in the lander without taking another look first."

Yasmin: "We hit the base. No mistake there."

Kim: "How hard?"

Shapir: "There's another factor to consider. Stress—to *consider*. Ground decisions aren't my domain. It's just that the Outsider ship is accelerating at two point four metres every second. Our sustained maximum is two point five. If we start out after him and he keeps on going, then it's going to be a long chase. If we start out from orbit at the counter base position this circuit, he'll already have something like a two hour start on us. Three, if we go round again. If we leave this circuit we won't catch him until he's about as far as Hades. If we wait another hour that's going to go up to well over a hundred million kilometres."

Yasmin: "So far? Really so far?"

Kim: "Ah, it's his start velocity. Nightrider starts with zero towards Hades, but he's already making speed. So he builds up an enormous spatial lead before Nightrider catches him up in just velocity terms. And then you have to close the gap again."

Nightrider: "Correction manoeuvre termination, mark."

A little less weight. Just a little.

Akira: "So you think the lander team should go right away?"

Shapir: "Not necessarily. We can leave the lander parked in orbit here while we all stay to chase the ship. We'd probably be back in six to eight days. Then we could take another look at the base before you go down. I'm just saying that Nightrider has to get after the Outsider this time round, in about—twenty-five minutes from now."

Kim: "If we go, we go with just twenty-two days' life support endurance. You'll be sure to be back before then?"

Sandra: "We'll catch him in three days at the most. We can't lose him while he runs his drive, and if he cuts it we'll be able to predict on him from his start position and known coasting velocity. We'll be back in time.''

Shapir: "If we lose him we'll be back in time. Let's put a seven day safety margin on the lander endurance. Whatever happens we'll be back to pick you up within fifteen days. We won't overrun without consultation, even though that would mean breaking communications silence.''

Ali: "We don't have to go down without taking a look first. We can orbit in the lander and overfly the base, and go down the next time round if we think it looked damaged enough.''

Shapir: "Maybe that's the answer.''

Akira: "Yes, I think so. Kim?''

Kim: "That sounds okay. After all, the Outsider is out of the way, so we're safe from him.''

Sandra: "Oh, he's out of the way, okay. He'll have seen what we did to the base. He's running for his life.''

302 14:35. Drive zero. Velocity 6,200 ms^{-1}. Altitude 60,000 metres. Free fall in a real orbit. No sensation of weight and so no absolute orientation but your own. Hel is neither up nor down, not above nor below. The planet is merely *out there*, sixty kilometres away. And then comes nine and a half thousand kilometres of rock solid and rock molten, and then the base, or at least the place where the base used to be. And then nothing but nothing for another seventy-five million kilometres. And then Hades.

Kim eased herself hand over hand along the ladder in the transfer tunnel, following Ali's feet. No hurry and no urgency. Everything in the lander was ready to go, had been checked through and flight status cleared before they ever arrived at Hel. The four fixed couches were already locked flat in flight configuration, the systems computers already updated by Nightrider with the hard data they had acquired on the planet and on the base location, data that replaced all the mapping simulations stored in the lander's copy of the mission book. Nightrider was continuously updating the flight computer on their orbital parameters and position. There was nothing to do except get aboard, switch to onboard power, and then go.

Alone with a planet of iron ice, five little people in a lander vehicle whose only protection was its outer coat of absolute black. She sometimes wondered, when it got this real in her thoughts, why Earth had to come here at all, and why the lander component of the mission was thought necessary, and why they'd had to pick her.

She followed through the docking rim section and through the lock well into the airlock. She grasped a rung and braked herself—Yasmin was only just starting along the tunnel behind. She looked round. The two suits staring empty at each other were secure in their clamps, all ten backpacks were locked in the stacked replenishment rack, the ground equipment lockers were fastened, the toilet and wash towels dispenser closed up. The check was just Kim being a pilot on automatic—everything had been finally secured three hours ago. But she knew what it was like when equipment came loose during free fall manoeuvring, which was the one time you noticed and the one time that mattered.

She pushed herself on through the ceiling hatch and into the crew space. Nothing in front of this but the lander's roof, and then vacuum. She caught hold of the two levelled couch backs and pulled her feet in through the hatch. Four couches in two pairs filling the space from front wall to back, from headrest to footrest, decking the space from left wall to right, leaving room for just one more centre couch to be rigged for Samson. A five person space tailored round five little people.

Ali was already stretched along the couch by the left wall, the single belt buckled across his stomach. She levered herself sideways over the neighbouring couch and pulled the hip belt out of its reels. Pulling out the belt pulled her back against the couch. She snapped it closed, and was no longer floating free.

Yasmin came in through the hatch hole and on between the couches, turned herself and pulled over to the right-hand end couch, belted herself secure. Akira came up beside Kim, pitched himself forwards, footwards, to tackle the centre couch stowed along the front wall behind the footrests. Samson's head and shoulders appeared. He waited, keeping out of the way.

Kim slid out the key pads attached to her couch and looked at the screen deployed against the ceiling in front of her. There were five screens mounted side by side across the ceiling, one for each couch. Ali already had systems readouts called up and running. Everything was optimal, living on power channelled through from Nightrider. The screen-corner chronometer said

302 14:37:20. Just less than four minutes to separation. Then Nightrider would be free of them and could accelerate out of orbit to chase the Outsider. And they would be on their own.

"Hatches?" Ali asked.

She nodded. She keyed up power cell data and display.

"Okay," Ali said. "Outer hatch closed. Samson?"

Samson looked down between his dangling feet. "Is closed."

"Airlock outer—closed."

"Is closed. Don't close the next one. You'll take my legs off."

"Such lovely legs, too," Yasmin commented.

"Okay, Nightrider," Ali said. "We're sealed for undocking."

"Thank you, Ali. Docking hatch and transfer lock outer closing now."

Akira had freed the fifth couch and was turning it to line up with the others. It had to go over to Yasmin's end so as not to interfere with the pilots. Anchored to her own couch, Yasmin took hold and steadied it while Akira got clear of the space, curling up at the foot of his own couch. Samson curled up at the head. Yasmin held him fast with one hand.

"Airlock inner closed, Samson?"

"Is closed, Ali."

"Floor hatch closing?"

"Is closing."

Four shields between them and the devouring vacuum night. But only two of those seals.

Akira and Samson started to manoeuvre the couch into the gap. Once locked in place it could deploy as a seat like all the others, but it went in flat.

The internal power output was perfect, the cells ready for load. "I'm switching to onboard power, Nightrider."

"Thank you, Kim. I'll reduce umbilical when the load is off."

Akira and Samson were bracing themselves between couch and close ceiling to snap the thing into its seat support clips.

She switched the power. The output graph traced the time-fractional load uptake drop and recovery—shallow enough, fast enough. No problem at all.

"No system alarms," Ali said. "You?"

"No." He didn't need to ask—he could read her screen, too.

Samson had turned and was buckling himself to the couch beside her. Akira was already anchored between him and Yasmin. Kim transferred her right hand from the key pad to the attitude jet trigger grip control.

"That's phallic," Samson said beside her.

She looked at her hand encompassing the trigger grip, finger wrapped round the thrust control trigger, thumb teasing the locking switch. A joy-stick to turn the lander whichever way you wanted it. Was that why it was called *joy*-stick? From the handgrip steering you could do to a man? "Samson, we're busy." This was Kim coming into her function at last, something to *do* instead of lying locked in a deep couch. Sandra and Shapir were still there in the flight centre, still encased in communion with Nightrider. 14:39:53. "Okay, you two back there. We're ready to go."

"Nicely on time," said Sandra's voice. "You want to wait the full two minutes? Last messages? Wish us luck?"

"I'll wish you a quick return to pick us up.

"You two are the ones with Nightrider to look after you," Ali said. "And don't forget you're our only ride home."

"Oh—try to look on the positive side. You circuit once to check the base is out okay, then down you go to take a look round. A nice chance to stretch your legs."

"In a suit," Samson said. "A nice cosy suit."

Nightrider: "Propulsion burn. Five-two-one kilometres."

Sudden silence from everyone.

Shapir: "I see no object. You?"

Sandra: "No. Look at the predict. It's going to intercept. It sees us. Heat signature?"

Shapir: "Radar locate and track. Main reactor one hundred percent. Pinch fields run up one and three, feed A and C. Are you people flat on your couches up there? We can pull four gee with you on the couches."

"We're strapped in."

Sandra: "Two-two-oh and closing. It's too close. It's small. A missile?"

Shapir: "Laser illuminate it."

Nightrider: "Incident radar from object, continuing. Do we make an avoidance manoeuvre?"

Sandra: "Where to?"

Shapir: "Stand by to burn on one and three. Four seconds at four gee. Object is the target. Align."

A sweeping feeling as Nightrider pitches and yaws in an abrupt tumble.

Sandra: "Eight-two kilometres. Don't see it. Must be black. Seven seconds to intercept. Six. Five."

Shapir: "Burn."

A blanket of weight and your breath rushes out. The couch rams you in a one-sided press. A crash.

The crushing load gone again.

Sandra: "Fireball, twelve kilometres. Keep us tail on to it, Nightrider. See that? The fireball went straight through the intercept predict. Would have got us even after we got it. That was *close*."

Shapir: "It did get us. We've gone through it but it was already too tenuous. Damage, Nightrider?"

Nightrider: "Tail visual six disfunction. Nothing else."

"Samson," Akira said. "Hey, Samson?"

Samson wasn't there.

The couch had gone, Samson too. No—the couch was still there beside him, the edge of it. The rest was missing. Samson came drifting out of the gap, back to him, hugging himself. The crash?

"We've got damage," he said. "Injury. Samson's couch collapsed during the burn." Akira had taken hold of Samson. He twisted to look over at the couch. It was angled back from her own couch to the deck. She couldn't see for Samson, but the anchoring clips on the other side must have torn away. "What did you pull?"

Shapir: "Four gee."

Sandra: "Not four. Look at the burn record. Five at peak. You pulled five gee, Nightrider."

Nightrider: "Yes, I'm sorry, Sandra. I thought it best. The missile was close."

Akira was moving Samson round in front of himself and Yasmin. Samson hugged himself. Or his arm, his right arm—the fingers of his right hand stuck out straight, tense. His eyes were clamped closed and his mouth locked open. He *hurt*. Oh, he hurt.

Sandra: "He's right. I'm afraid he's right. The thing still got to twelve out before it blew. With a less intense burn it could have got close enough to kill us.''

Shapir: ''Looks like it. I initiated so late to make sure the burn was still concentrated. Same reasoning.''

Samson's couch had collapsed, tipping him onto his right arm. The couch had collapsed fifty centimetres at five gee, the same as a two and a half metre fall at Earth normal. Landing half on your back and half on your side from *that*.

Shapir: ''How's Samson?''

''His couch collapsed at five gee. How do you think he is?''

Samson shook his head from side to side, trying to dispel pain knives. ''My arm,'' he got out. ''My—*arm*.''

''Whereabouts?'' Akira asked gently, holding him by his wrapped over left forearm. ''The shoulder? The elbow?''

''The forearm. Right here.'' Samson still had his eyes screwed shut. He unfolded his arms slightly, rubbed his left hand up and down from right elbow to wrist. Gingerly, as if afraid of his own touch.

''Broken?'' Yasmin asked. She took over the job of holding Samson by his overall shoulder and side so as to free Akira to look at the arm. Akira was the trained medic. And Kim, of course—but Kim had to fly the lander if they still undocked.

Shapir: ''How's Samson?''

Sandra: ''Is he okay? Can he still go? I don't like to push, but we need a decision. We're already past our planned departure point.''

''Tell that,'' Kim said, ''tell that to whoever it was on that Outsider ship who thought of leaving a missile behind when *they* left. Give us a chance to find out how he is, will you.''

''This will hurt,'' Akira said. ''This is practical field medicine. I just want to see if your forearm's rigid. Your grip's all right so it's safe to try. This is a trick we learned under fire.''

Samson's face contorted again, paled under brown pigment. When he opened his eyes again it was to look at Akira in sheer astonishment.

''Sorry,'' Akira said. ''I know. I've had that done to me when I'd just got my arm smashed. I know. But it isn't broken.''

Samson went on looking at him. ''It wasn't.''

''That's not in the rules,'' Kim said.

"But it works."

"It's already showing swelling," Yasmin said.

"We'll get it bandaged. Maybe a surface vein's gone."

Shapir: "Do we gather Samson's okay?"

"Depends what you mean," Samson muttered.

Kim looked at Akira. "Can we look after him if it turns out to be a serious contusion? And can the team still function if his arm is out?"

"We can look after him."

"It's me and Akira who have to be fully functional," Yasmin added. "In case there's anyone left down there. The rest of you just have to look at the wreckage."

"So—do we still go?"

Akira looked at Samson. Samson just clutched at his arm. "Don't ask me. You're the medic. I just hurt."

"We go," Kim said. "Yes?"

"Yes." Akira started pulling Samson. "Relax. Relax. We just have to turn you and put you here between us for the undocking. The couch we can look at later."

"Okay." Kim straightened out on her couch again and took hold of the attitude jet trigger. "You got that?"

Shapir: "We got it. All the best, Samson. Okay—communication silence because you don't know what you might call down on your heads."

Sandra: "But listen for our call. We call you as soon as that ship is out of the way, one way or the other. Not until then. We don't want him to know where we are."

"Watch out for more missiles," Ali said.

Sandra: "We'll look after ourselves. You do the same. Be seeing you."

Shapir: "Undock, Nightrider. Good luck."

The display lights marked the release of the docking clamps. Nightrider did it so gently, backing off and leaving them hanging in independent orbit, that there was no residual tumble for her to correct. They orbited free beside Nightrider, but banned from communication, from voice or data contact. They orbited in isolation, all that empty way from home.

They cleared the limb of Hel at 14:59 and sighted the tail radiation of the Outsider. There was no more significant accompanying cascade of energized collisions and created particles—the Outsider was already beyond the veil of trapped cosmic ray components that the planet had wrapped around itself—but the primary beam of expelled ions still streamed at relativistic velocities almost directly towards them and there was still a magnetic field for them to follow, a field influenced primarily by Hel's immediate presence, but partly dictated by Hades' residual magnetism and by the Galaxy itself. The synchrotron radiation was weak, but it was there.

The Outsider had a head start of perhaps eight thousand seconds—almost two and one quarter hours. He had already accelerated up to a velocity of nineteen point two kilometres every second when they saw him and was almost seventy-seven thousand kilometres out in front. If he kept on applying the same acceleration at the same orientation, he would arrive at Hades in sixty-seven hours, whipping past the stellar corpse at six hundred kilometres every second. At that point Night-rider would be three thousand seconds and one million eight hundred thousand kilometres behind. But Nightrider could accelerate that little bit faster, would already be travelling at six hundred and five kilometres every second, would have attained an even higher velocity advantage at its own flyby encounter with Hades. Nightrider would be closing the gap ever more quickly. Wherever the Outsider headed after Hades, they would catch him. There was no escape for the Outsider even by shutting down his drive and coasting invisible in the black emptiness. Nightrider could comfortably see the ion drive out to more than the maximum separation they would achieve on the unequal headlong fall to Hades. If the drive cut out, they would know the other ship's exact flight direction and velocity and could predict its precise position from one second to the next. Nightrider would continue accelerating and merely close the distance sooner.

The hunting of the Outsider ship would be an inevitable and mechanical process governed by the predetermining technology of drive capabilities and by the immutability of physical laws. The absolute truth that the universe has, and the relative truth that the human being builds—both uncompromising and cold.

The sheer power of the Outsider's ion drive was a surprise—the things openly shunting around the Solar System generally attained only a tenth of the acceleration, although it was assumed that the Outsiders had managed to at least treble that. 2.4 ms^{-2} was almost enough to escape Nightrider. Almost. The research and development that had gone into it, the sheer resource commitment, must have been hugely disproportionate for the so desperately limited means of the allied colonies—an extraordinary achievement for a material economy already stretched beyond its theoretical capability by the establishment and upkeep of a base way out here. At least the *nature* of the technical breakthrough had stayed within the realms predicted by Earth's information bankers. It involved the improvement of an established technology until it was pushed to unheard of limits. But it wasn't wholly innovative like Nightrider's drive.

From the energy output of the ion drive coupled with the acceleration it imparted to its source, they could estimate the mass of the Outsider—twice their own. That was all they knew about their target. Except that it could leave a nuclear armed missile behind it, a missile capable of transferring down into a lower orbit and searching for an intruder—presumably by its radiant heat—and then homing in on it. The Outsider wasn't harmless, wasn't helpless.

Sandra appeared in his view, looming over him as she pulled herself backwards onto the tongue of deck between the heads of the two couches. She sat there hunched up, the hair on the back of her head brushing the ceiling between the screens, obscuring the chronometer figures. She looked down at him, sighted him between breast and hip. "You know, this is a little hole."

"A hole?"

"There's just you and me and Nightrider. Here we are with the whole place to ourselves—and here we are, stuck in here in our nice little couches. Believe me, I'm going to be glad to get back to my box for a real stretch. Four hours I've been in that couch. That's four hours too many."

"I wouldn't go too far away. What do you do if we find another missile sitting waiting for us?"

Sandra shrugged, almost touching the ceiling with her shoulders. "You think there'll be another missile?"

He looked at the smooth power parameters on the screen above him. "Actually, no."

"Me neither. Why don't you think so?"

"Because—he has no way of knowing that we're following

him. He doesn't want to leave a missile coasting uselessly to nowhere when he knows he might just need it later.''

''Assuming he has any more at all.''

''Oh, he has some more. They're not going to build in the capability to launch one, and then only *carry* one. Nightrider's proved he can cope with anything that he sees coming in, even without a full burn—but let's just hope we catch up with him unawares. That will be easier.''

''My thoughts exactly. Of course, it might have made sense to him to leave *two* missiles in orbit at Hel. Protect the base and all that. He left before he saw us hit it.''

''He did. We should have thought of that before we let the lander go. They can't defend themselves.''

''Maybe. But then they only have one and a half orbits to go before they land. The chances of a line up allowing an immediate intercept must be minimal. That sort of thing doesn't happen *twice*. And if a missile sights them and predicts where they're going to be next time round—well, they won't show up because they'll have landed. Besides, they'll think of it.''

''You think so?''

''Oh, I'm sure. That's a neat little vehicle, the best lander shuttle that science can design. But it's helpless against nasty little missiles. I wouldn't want to be hanging around in orbit in that. I'd think of that about one second after we disappeared if I was left behind in that thing. I'd go down on the first pass, never mind a look-see first. If there's trouble on the ground they can always hop somewhere else and wait until we come to pick them up. They have the fuel reserve.''

''Let's hope they have the motivation.''

''Ah, they'll have that all right. Left on their own way out here.'' She shook her head. ''Sooner them than me. Nightrider makes it all easy.''

The base had been easy, ridiculously easy, once they had found it. The missile had been easy. It had come within seconds of killing them, but it had been seen and so Nightrider's torch had seared it. The time had been lost in realizing what was coming in.

''Could you clarify something for me?'' Nightrider asked.

''Sure,'' Shapir said. ''If we can.'' Nightrider didn't ask many questions, but it had happened often enough for it to be no surprise. After all, he was impelled to meet his learning program targets.

"If the Outsider doesn't know we're following him, why is he still using the ion drive? Why does he make himself visible?"

"Aha," Sandra said. "Now that's a perceptive question. Why indeed? Why isn't he coasting somewhere where we can't see him, trying to get away safely or maybe even come back after us?"

"Well—he knows that if we *can* see him right now, then we can't lose him. We see him if he uses his drive, we predict his position if he switches it off and coasts. Okay?"

"Obvious," Sandra said.

"Good. Also, he's seen us once on ground mapping radar or whatever it was. He must have observed us well enough to put a missile down after us, so he must have observed us well enough to see that we were travelling an orbital path at supraorbital velocity, and that we have to have some kind of propulsion system to do that. And—that you can't detect that propulsion system in use."

Sandra nodded. "So he knows that we can follow him without him knowing it, so he *doesn't* know we're *not* after him."

"And he saw the fusion flare as we took out the base, so he knows we're dangerous. He doesn't know where we are and he won't necessarily get any warning when we arrive. His only chance is to keep on accelerating and just hope he can outrun us. It's the only chance he's got."

"Some uncertain chance. I wouldn't like to be the Outsider instead of us. That's for sure." She twisted over onto her hands and knees and crawled up out of the flight centre.

20:30 and they were still nowhere. Literally.

The descent had gone perfectly. Automatically. That was the problem. They had decided to go down after only half an orbit and dispense with a preliminary look at the base and then the eighty minute danger of another circuit round to the base position. If the Outsider ship could leave one missile behind it could also leave two, and now Nightrider wasn't there to deal with it for them. It would kill them. So they instructed the lander to take them down on the first pass. After all, they were not going to land right on top of whatever was left down there. The touchdown site was six kilometers southwest of the base, on the safe side of the southward ridge, and the descent angle would be ten degrees, so shallow that any hypothetical survivor left at the base would never see them coming down. Which also meant, of course, that they wouldn't see the base during the descent, which was why no one had thought to look for it. After all, the lander knew exactly where the base was, exactly where it had started out, and exactly what was involved in getting from the start point to a reduced thrust hover thirty metres over the landing site—where it would stay until either the fuel reserve was exhausted or its human pilots took over and selected a smooth piece of ground to settle on.

And they had better things to do.

Samson's couch had to be prised out of its useless sideways sloped position so that they could lay it flat on the deck for him during the descent burn. The lander pulled only three gee, but that was enough to need a couch of his own. They had no tools for brute *mechanical* repairs—such a requirement hadn't been planned in. They had nothing more than their muscles with which to tear the deformed anchor plates out of the catches on the locker side under Kim's couch. And when they had managed that they still had to secure the couch against the deck over the airlock hatch. Placed head to toe from front to back wall, lying between the lockers that supported the other four couches, the couch couldn't slide out of place under gee. But during the moment of free fall while the ring-booster was jettisoned it could still float up, maybe twist, maybe come down on top of Samson at the next kick of thrust and kill him. They had to secure it, which they managed to do by pirating equipment straps and passing them taut across it with the ends jammed in locker doors.

At the same time they had to do something for Samson. The fall with his forearm rammed against the deck and locker side must have burst a minor vein under the skin or only shallowly protected by muscle. He had no ordinary bruising to look forward to, but instead a ballooning contusion of softly gorged tissue. The escaping blood had to make room for itself somewhere: it came out in a smooth swelling above and below the bandage. What he needed was not a restricting but a supporting bandage to get him through the extreme discomfort he was in for during the three gee descent burn. So that had to be changed.

Anyone who had time to look at things spent it watching the lander's sensor alarms, hoping no missile came suddenly swooping in to kill.

Both Kim and Ali monitored the descent against the guidance computer's predetermined course, checking from the function readings that the lander was doing what the computer told it to do. But they never looked out at the ground, because the naked eye couldn't measure altitudes in thousands of metres, nor course precision to a thousandth of a degree. And all the others were looking for missiles.

It was a constant three gee burn, the systems computer automatically reducing thrust as they lost mass through propellant expenditure. The lander tipped to ten degrees down from tail forwards, and fired the ring-booster motors at minus 210 from site hover. At 15:20:25. After exactly three minutes the thrust cut, the ring-booster kicked free, and then thrust resumed on the lander's four main engines. The landing legs deployed, hydraulic insect limbs. The radar altimeter aimed obliquely at the target site ground and adjusted the burn accordingly. After 210 seconds all lateral velocity had been shed and the lander tipped to vertical with respect to Hel to kill the residual fall. Six and a half seconds later they were hovering thirty metres off the surface at one fifth of full thrust. Ali and Kim unlocked their couches and brought them up to sitting position, the attendant screens relocating themselves against the wall right in front of them, and took over the flight control. They examined the ground in an image intensified view because the hydrogen-oxygen flame gave too little light to illuminate it, and selected a level area. Kim nudged the lander across to it and then reduced thrust and let it settle on firm surface. Touchdown Day 302 15:25:21.

Ali and Kim began a first-step systems check, Akira made sure that Samson was still with them. It was Yasmin who took a first look round to make sure they were secure. She expected to see a level raised horizon to the north, the scarp behind which the base was hidden from view. She expected to see flat plain to the west, broken raised ground to the south, and a clefted high horizon to the east. They knew that was right because the data from Nightrider's single pass over the base had confirmed the local accuracy of the simulation.

She saw broken raised ground from north to east, falling from east to southeast, and all the rest smooth and almost featureless plain.

They were down in the wrong place.

They interrogated the guidance computer. The guidance computer said they were in the right place. The outside landscape of absolute midnight said that they were not. They ran a step by step check through all the timing decisions and manoeuvre enactments conducted by the guidance computer, they mapped those back onto the mission book's updated representation of Hel as oriented to their start position anchor. The flight path put them down at exactly the right position, an exemplary example of automatic navigation and piloting.

So there was something seriously wrong inside the guidance computer.

And without knowing where they were, and without a reliable computer to fly with, they would never be going anywhere again.

Ali was the guidance system specialist, Samson the computer specialist, Kim was the first pilot and lander commander. They began the long complex list of functions, programming and database checks. Whatever was wrong had to be located, erased, and replaced. Whatever effect it had produced had to be reconstructed in order to determine their actual position. Even with the computer fully de-bugged, if that could be achieved, and with all three inertial response units functioning to give a reliable consensus of movement sensing, they still needed to know exactly where they were starting from in order to go anywhere else.

Akira and Yasmin started searching through the Hel map database in the hope that they might just have landed somewhere on the small area of the planet that had been previously surveyed or that they themselves had seen. Given a position fix, it might be easier to unravel whatever was wrong with the guidance computer. And at least they would know where they were. They jumped in simulation from point to point across a four kilometre grid, setting the viewing altitude at seven metres to match that of the lander's roof level cameras. They tried to match horizon panoramas, hoping the simulations were accurate enough.

It was almost an hour before Yasmin realized what was wrong.

She was pausing from the screen, looking past Akira at Samson squatting on his couch down on the deck, having to look up at his screen, having to key talk with it left-handed when he was by strong preference right-handed. He held his right arm folded across his chest, hand holding onto his left shoulder in an attempt to reduce the blood pressure at the injury site as much as was practical. The outside of his forearm was a soft bandaged balloon. All because the missile had come in from so close, and Nightrider had exceeded the instructed burn and taken it up to the general structure limit of the lander and the lander-loaded crew module.

"The burn," she said. "When the missile attacked. Did the burn throw our start position data?"

They just looked at her in the dark light, realization filling up their cramped little life space.

The main computer log held no record of a velocity and position update after the burn. The lander had started out in independent life thinking that the movement predictions it made on the basis of conditions pertaining one hundred and eleven seconds before Nightrider's burn still applied. But Nightrider had given them a five gee kick in some unknown and unknowable direction. There was absolutely no way to reconstruct the manoeuvre. The lander's own inertial response units were designed to serve its own flight requirements, and the lander pulled a maximum of three gee. The accelerometers simply didn't read any further: the exact thrust-against-time profile of the burn was lost forever. Even its orientation was irretrievable. Despite an enormously greater mass, Nightrider could pitch and roll and yaw at a higher rate than the lander—a rate determined by the need to aim a fusion burn at a possibly rapidly tracking target. The lander's sensors picked up the direction and duration of any movement, but not the angular rate and therefore not the result of any attitude change.

There was nothing at all wrong with the guidance computer. It had performed perfectly on the basis of false information. Information that was gone forever. It had not been heading where it thought it was, and it had put them down at the exact point where it thought the touchdown site should be. Unless they had landed somewhere on the narrow strip of mapped surface, and unless the mapping was accurate enough to allow them to establish the fact, there was no means whatsoever of finding out where they were.

A computer malfunction might almost have been preferable.

Now it was 20:45. It was fifteen minutes since they had completed their search of the mission book's Hel representation. They had found no match.

And no one had said a word.

Ali was peeling bite-sized cubes from a ration block. *Spiced Apple & Bran Cake,* the opened wrapping said, *fine texture.* No one had stirred from their seats for five and a half hours except to fetch food and to make Samson move so that they could get down to the toilet in the airlock. Samson's useless couch had been stowed away—he sat back from and below the others on the deck, his legs dangling into the open hatchway.

"One option," Ali said, and swallowed. "We try calling Nightrider. Maybe they can fix our position."

Akira shook his head. "We'd have to send a blanket call. We don't know where Nightrider is. Anyone and anything would get an immediate fix on us. If Nightrider answered he'd give himself away. And by the time we'd got a fix and programmed it in and set up a hop to somewhere else, we might already be dead or locked into someone's tracking system. That's a last resort. I'd rather sit here for the full twenty-two days."

"Exactly." Ali put another cube in his mouth.

Yasmin had pulled up her feet, was sitting sideways on her seat, ankles crossed and leaning against the end wall lockers. "Assuming Nightrider can get us out when he comes back. Assuming he can. If we just sit here, what happens to the mission?"

"What mission?" Samson was out of sight in the shadow pool behind the high-backed seats. His tone was perfectly dry.

Their life was consumables limited. Without a point to start from there was no going home.

"It's a pity," Yasmin said, "that no one thought to check that the computer had been updated. I mean, the data is indispensable for navigation and piloting."

Kim balanced the flat-based drink bulb neatly on her knee.

She looked at the blank screen in front of her. "Who's that aimed at?"

"Pardon?"

Kim looked at Yasmin. She was tired. She was tired from the partly completed exacting examination of the guidance computer's software. She was tired from the unbroken hours of staring at real images and endless simulated mismatches. She was tired from sitting all this time in the unaccustomed weight after the touchdown after the missile kill after the long frustrating imprisonment in Nightrider's couch. She was tired of keeping watch on the door behind which sheer fear was locked.

"Hey, I just said—"

"There was Samson to take care of. *If* you remember. There was a go or no-go decision. *If* you remember. There was one hell of a hurry to take it. If you remember. It isn't my job to check up on someone else's updates. *If* you remember."

"Look, I wasn't—"

"You want to know whose job it is? Call up the mission book. Select lander separation procedure. Presep. Flight-nav data transference. Guidance computer mapping base instruct. Position lock function code block-seven. Look at the top enactment of the cycle entry." And Yasmin was beginning to look angry, as if she really had been caught out trying to insinuate unspecified blame. "Flight data updating, host to lander, execution automatic—"

"Executor Nightrider," Akira said, quietly.

"Executor Nightrider. And what's the responsibility apportionment?"

"Nightrider, one point zero," Akira said.

"Nightrider, one hundred percent."

Yasmin uncrossed her ankles. She set her right foot back down on the footrest, she sat up straight, tenser. "So?"

"So if you want to tell someone he fouled up, tell Nightrider. When he picks us up. Tell our great big friend that he and all his slave functions and dedicated peripheries have got us lost and maybe got us killed. Tell him he's blown his mission book. Tell him. Clear?"

"Hey, hey," Samson said out of the shadows. "Now don't let's all get excited. We have to keep a sense of fair play here. I can't fight for my rights left-handed. Don't let's all get so pushy, now. Don't forget I'm first in the queue. I get first turn having a little fun jiggling around with his power input. You all line up behind me.''

"Another option," Ali said. "If they send a signal over the comsat we'll get a perfect fix. After all, we're somewhere on the Hades side of the planet."

"They won't signal." Yasmin shook her head, agreeing with herself. "Any Outsiders left alive are going to keep quiet. Any noise out of them would be as much as their lives are worth."

Kim had tipped back her couch and lay looking upwards, left knee raised. The screen was against the ceiling above her. It held an unmodified view of the sky. Looking upwards. If Hades was in view it was invisible. Earth size and so far away, there wasn't a chance of it occulting a major star. It would be in front of *something* amid all that telescope magnifiable clutter of shrunken ancient light. But to find that would require a star field survey, an astronomical computer, and years of time. Except that an adequately programmed computer would match a star pattern and then know exactly where to look, could give Hades' position precisely whether coincidentally visible or not.

Samson was sitting at the head end of Akira's levelled couch, Akira at the foot. Samson poked his finger into the backrest padding. "Magnetic field. We could get an approximate position. For a determination we just need the angle of dip and the north-south orientation of the field. Easy. All we don't have is the instruments, enough detail on Hel's magnetic field, and data on the local anomalies. Stupid."

Akira shrugged. "They didn't send us here to do a geophysical survey."

"But they included me. It's one of my specialties. They could have given me the means to do it instead of just hoping I might find an Outsider computer lying around to pull data out of. I begin to think the mission planning was over specific."

"The problem is," Kim said, "that the computer is set up to navigate by math and inertial backup from a fixed point in its local map-matrix. There's no requirement for astro-navigation, so there's no star data available. Only Nightrider has that. I don't know if I know enough stars."

Ali turned, glanced up at the screen behind his shoulder. "Do you, a spacer, not recognize stars?"

"Oh, I recognize them. But do you know their absolute co-ordinates?"

"How could I? Why should I? That's for astronomers. Ships navigate by computer and by radio beacon matching."

"I know a few. I don't know if I know enough."

"Enough for what?" Akira said.

"If I know a star's position in the Earth sky. The lunar sky, but what's the difference? If I know its position, then I know its orientation with respect to the vernal equinox. Then I know Hades' present orientation to the vernal equinox. I know Hel's orientation from Hades with respect to the Sun-Hades axis. We have an exact location for the base and for the touchdown target with respect to the Hel-Hades axis. So. With the computer and Ali to check me, I can figure out where the star should be as seen from where we should be. Then I just have to find the star and get its apparent direction from here to work out our latitude and longitude by way of the angular displacement. Then I have our position relative to where we're supposed to be."

"Just like that?" Yasmin asked. "As simple as that?"

"No." Kim sat up in the middle of her couch, hugged her knee and stared at nothing. "I haven't used star fixes since I was a kid. My memory is poor. Maybe too poor. We'll have to run a whole list of stars to check the estimates. It's easy with a computer if you have the right data. Maybe I don't."

"What were you doing with star fixes?" Ali asked her.

"Didn't you know every second kid on Luna plays astronomy? It's the seeing—hundred percent every night and every day."

Shapir sat naked on the convex seat beside the flight centre door-hatch. He was still damp from a hurried shower, his clothes lay rolled up beside him. Sandra sat on the other side of the hatchway gap. They ate from trays balanced on their laps, a late substitute for the missed midday meal. Spun steak in butter sauce speckled with pepper grounds, potato and chive salad, apple and peach and hazel nut salad, chicory and asparagus and celery in mayonnaise. It was one of the standard compensations for the general tedium of space travel that you might eat rather synthetically, but you ate considerably better than an awful lot of people back home.

Sandra put down her knife and fork and pulled at the

underarms of her overall. "I've had this on too long. Should have put a clean one on after my shower. Don't make the same mistake."

Shapir shrugged. "Go and change before we set up the burn."

"I believe I will."

"About the burn manoeuvre," Nightrider said. "Are you really sure that taking out the comsat is a good idea?"

Nightrider's eye in the day room was up against the ceiling on the outer wall, directly opposite the flight centre hatch. Funny, but Shapir looked up at Nightrider's eye, even though they had all got used to the total monitoring and to talking to the air months and months ago.

"We just discussed that, Nightrider. The comsat is off to the left of our track at three point seven five million from Hel. We can reach it by flipping over sideways for a few seconds and firing a four gee burn, then flipping back. It will have no effect on our to-Hades velocity. We take out the comsat in a close pass using a burn sequence tailored not to affect our to-Hades velocity but adjusted so as to kill the imparted lateral component and bring us back for Hades encounter as if we hadn't gone for the sat."

"Of course. But is it necessary to take out the comsat at this stage? We could deal with the Outsider and then take out the comsat on the return."

Sandra shook her head. "We have to cut the communication link back home. At least, that's how we read the mission priorities. Chasing the Outsider could take us a long way out from a return past the comsat position. Depends on his final Hades flyby. So let's take it out as we go past now. Sure, we've picked up no radio frequency signalling, but we can't say that they aren't channelling data continuously over a laser link from the sat back to Ganymede or somewhere."

"If the Outsider anticipates that we might pursue him he will be monitoring our potential track. From a manoeuvre burn followed by a burn at the comsat he will deduce our exact position and drive acceleration and course predict."

"So he'll know we're behind and theoretically able to catch him, so he'd better keep running and hope we give up."

"He might launch a missile against our predict."

She looked at Shapir. Nightrider was out-thinking them, at

least when it came to following through the consequences of an initial deduction. If at some future time he learned the trick of making the initial deductions as well, then one day he really would be flying under his own command. But the inspired guesswork that set up the constraints on subsequent reasoning was the real trick. A machine *should* out-perform an inattentive human when it came to the follow-on thinking within a defined paradigm of possibilities. Whether the planners had given him a good enough knowledge manipulation capacity to emancipate himself on the first level was still open to test.

"We'll take turns," Shapir said. "Always one of us in the flight centre in a couch. That will cut the response delay down to the time it takes Nightrider to tell us something is coming in. The other one stays on the main deck in reach of the other couches. If we sleep off watch we sleep in a couch. Okay?"

Sandra nodded. "That's going to be a hell of a lot of fun. We have the entire place to ourselves, and we end up living in an acceleration couch."

In the fish-eye they are far away, below centre-field on each side of the flight centre entrance. Shapir is naked. He eats. Sandra eats. Shapir's skin temperature pattern is stable at his unclothed resting norm. His skin has dried. There is no longer any evaporation cooling. The decision base is somehow not satisfactory. The mission book is not sufficiently specific on this eventuality. The mission constraint to follow pilot advice is clear, however. Additionally, self-motivation analysis is aware of a non-statable reason for preferring the return delay entailed in taking out the comsat after engaging the Outsider. The motivating condition requires further analysis. It is possibly influencing the assessment of the decision base adversely, therefore the pilot decision will not be further challenged.

Shapir: *Nightrider could you set up the manoeuvre burn for twenty-one-fifty—we'll take a look at the parameters when we're through eating.*

Instruct: guidance function, manoeuvre pre-set, 302 21:50:00.

Sandra: *first one to finish gets not to take the first turn in there after the burn.*

Shapir: *I'm eating not racing—strange.*

Sandra: *what?*

Shapir: *after all this time—to have the whole place all to ourselves.*

She'd got the fix! She'd got the fix. They were six degrees of circumference away from the target site, 508.4 kilometres, located 172 degrees east of north from the base. If she was right, they were. Together with Ali she had run two stars to get and confirm the fix, two more to check for certain, and two more again just to be sure. A beautifully close correlation. That was one up for the human component against the machine. It meant they could go where they were supposed to be and get on with mopping up any survivors they might find—or being mopped up themselves. It was 23:10 and the transfer hop was all worked out, a sub-orbital lasting 532 seconds in all, commencing with a forty-five degree launch burn of fifty-eight seconds and ending with a mirror descent burn. One hundred-sixteen seconds of fuel, half as much as they would need to reach orbit.

The decision was the same as it had always been at every hold up since the first pass over the false base predict. Go or abort. Transfer to the target site or sit there in a safe and known position until Nightrider came back for them. It was a predetermined decision this time—the planners back home wouldn't be too pleased.

"The advantage of going up high," Yasmin said, "is that we get a look at the base on the way down."

Ali shrugged. "We were just thinking of fuel conservation. The shallower the path the nearer it is to an orbit, so the faster, so the more fuel used."

"What are the risks of being seen?" Samson asked.

"Can't say." Kim tipped her seat back to a halfway lounger. The last hours had been too long. "We'll be over the base's horizon for more than half the trajectory, so if they just happen to be doing a radar sky search they'll pick us up. But why should they?"

"And the descent burn?"

"Oh—if they're looking directly at us with a close-up view they might see the glow from the heated motor venturi. Maybe even see the exhaust flame. It's just about possible. Of course, anyone looking at the sky in our direction with an IR imager will see the exhaust heat like a beacon. No way round that."

Akira studied the display figures still glowing against the

darkness on Kim's screen. "In a worst case, how quickly can you set up an abort manoeuvre? Say an orbit injection?"

"That would be the easiest." Kim stretched, fingertips reaching the ceiling. "We can set one up in advance so that we can cut in at any point in the trajectory right down to touch down. And beyond, of course, so we'd have an escape function ready the whole time. Launch at a touch. Firing it during the transfer would be expensive in fuel if we went for a low inclination orbit. We'd have to cancel the northward velocity component. But we could do it."

"And the fuel consumption?"

"Fuel status is no problem. After the transfer we'll still have enough propellant to do two more of the same, for an ascent to orbit and for an in-orbit manoeuvring reserve. Not so much of a reserve, but some."

Akira nodded.

"Well," Yasmin said. "I suppose we go."

No one disagreed.

Akira nodded again. "We go tomorrow. Right now we need some sleep. Would you prefer to set up the abort manoeuvre now or before we make the transfer?"

Ali grinned, his eyes staying mirthless. "I'm tired. Kim's more tired. Tomorrow."

"Okay."

"Nine hours." Yasmin reached forward to touch her toes, stretched out against the forward wall. "Nine hours just sitting in these seats."

"You'll miss it," Kim said. "It's going to be more cramped inside the suit."

"But at least you get to walk about. Here we just have the drop down to the toilet and back."

"If we're sleeping," Samson said, "I'd like a pain suppressant. It's not so bad, but it's uncomfortable." His forearm was still swelling, a shallow and soft ballooning extending from wrist to elbow like a massively deforming muscle that had gone to fat, but taut skinned.

"Do we need to run a watch this far from the base?" Ali asked.

Akira shrugged. "We have to. Someone has to send the others to sleep."

For three-hundred and one days they had been going to sleep by choice by asking Nightrider to trigger the implanted command supplied to them during mission training. They were thoroughly conditioned. Without post mission deconditioning it might be months before they could adapt to sleeping unaided again, might be days before they could even sleep properly at all through sheer exhaustion.

Yasmin smiled at Akira. "You're óur alphabetical leader. You can take the first watch."

Akira shrugged.

DAY 303

THEY knew whereabouts the comsat would be, but not its exact location within a lens of space that qualified as the Lagrange point. It was safe to use a search radar on the final approach, because whether or not the fleeing Outsider picked up side leakage from their radar beam and located them, Nightrider's burn a few minutes later would blaze their position across the inner Hades System for everyone to see. The search radar picked up and locked on the comsat at 05:47:55, at a range of 83,000 kilometres. They were tearing towards the satellite at 137 kilometres every second. They had nine and a half minutes to adjust the burn to a finely tuned manoeuvre that would take out the comsat at its determined location, and still bring them back onto track for Hades encounter in the wake of the Outsider. Nightrider presented the manoeuvre data and they checked over the readouts. Two eight second burns at five gee each, one approaching the one leaving the satellite. Two scorching caresses from an anonymous intruder slicing through the night.

"Okay, Nightrider," Shapir said. "We'll run the burn at full thrust on two and four this time. Feed still from A and C pods. Run the attitude manoeuvre between burns so as to keep us oriented tail towards the sat. Minimize debris damage if it explodes."

They would streak *past*, not *to* the satellite. It was nominally stationary as defined in respect to Hades and Hel, but they were not stationary with respect to the satellite, and the aiming problem was that of hitting a moving target. But with complications. To start with, each plasma shot would last eight seconds, so they had to swing the aim to keep an extended jet trained exactly on the target. The next complication was that expelling the low mass plasma at enormous velocity from the fusion rockets imparted a much lower but momentum conserving velocity to Nightrider's bulk, a five gee acceleration kick in exactly the opposite direction—a direction that swung through an arc as they approached on a near miss course towards the target. The aim had to be adjusted accordingly and the adjustment changed the direction and so the effect on the aim of the reaction velocity, and so on continuously. The third complication arose from the same imparting of velocity changes to Nightrider. Each infinitesimal slice of the plasma jet had to be aimed so that its direction of launch and Nightrider's existing velocity and direction-to-flight relative to the target coupled together to ensure that the slice of plasma flux hit that moving target. But although the plasma was expelled from the fusion rockets at a constant velocity, the velocity of those fusion rockets through space changed. With a five gee burn lasting for eight seconds, the tail end of the plasma jet fired at the target would be travelling four-hundred metres per second slower than the leading end. The jet grew in length on its brief trip to its goal. The problem was one of hitting a moving target with a long and flexible and elastic shot, all of which had to hit to ensure destruction. Nightrider's autonomous computation could handle the working out fast enough to make the weaponry viable—human agencies could do no more than dictate target, burn intensity and application time.

05:56:00.

"I still have no visual contact," Sandra said. "Laser illuminate target, Nightrider."

"Encounter minus eighty," Shapir said. "Burn minus fifty."

There it was, a speck in the centre of the field, spotlit in Hades' absolute night. The viewing magnification snapped a magnitude higher. Another.

An off-balanced thing. A parabolic dish pointing straight at them, past them to Hel. A matching phased array antenna. A bulking fuel pack and position correction motor. A little snub barrel on a turntable mount underneath, trained off left—a laser link to the Solar System. A long imbalancing boom with the block of a radionuclear power pack at the end. No light in this space to power it, no sunlight to see it by.

"Burn minus ten. Drive to zero. Aiming adjustment."

Weightless again in the grip of the couch. The first free fall since leaving the lander at Hel. The visual image blanked as the sensors ceased to bear. An almost sickening six second whirl as Nightrider flipped right over tail to target.

Nightrider: "Burn initiation, mark."

Weight even in the couch bed, tearing at cheeks and eyes and chin. Even the overall presses your stomach. Nightrider belches silent solar fire. You belch breathing air expelled by your leaden ribs.

Nothing, no pressure, no tearing, no weight.

"Tail sensors. Illuminate and track."

Briefest drama in stopped down brightness. A flexible searing plasma snake still stretches away and devours in a dragon kiss. Recedes. Disperses.

"It's still intact."

"They built that to last."

Nightrider swings slightly, increasingly. The reflector dish turns from circle to ellipse. The long boom foreshortens in the sweeping view, momentarily pointing at them. An impotent finger trying to ward off passing death. Nightrider swings more gradually.

"Tail shields close."

Nightrider: "Burn initiation, mark."

Weight again. Your lips press your teeth, you live breathless seconds.

Nothing.

Not even an attitude change whirl. Nightrider was already lined up in flight orientation, tail towards Hel and heading for Hades. 05:58:50.

"Tail sensors. Illuminate target."

Nightrider: "Drive initiation one hundred percent, mark."

Soft weight again, sweet weight. A gentle up and down.

No fire serpent to see, the searing plasma flare already attenuated and faded. No satellite to see, just a cloud of twinkling, turning pieces.

Nightrider: "Radar contact faint and dispersed."

"Kill the laser illuminations. Shut down two and four containment fields."

"It's still visible. Look. The debris. It glows."

A spreading cluster of light specks, remnants of a toy torn apart by a plasma touch. Bright little nuclei in a luminous veil.

"We vaporized it. Two little eight second shots at around three and a half thousand kilometres range each, and we just *vaporized* it. I'm glad I wasn't at that base. I'm glad I wasn't. Believe me."

"I believe you."

They watched the incandescent cloud, for the first time slightly appalled by what they commanded, secure within the directives of the mission book.

Nightrider: "Do you think we might analyse the flyby option range open to the Outsider at Hades encounter? The range is open, of course, depending on his velocity and range at encounter, but perhaps you could identify more probable options with respect to his future course."

"It's always worth a look."

"We'll think about that later, Nightrider," Shapir said. "Right now it's my turn to sleep."

"Leave Nightrider and poor little me to do all the work, all the post-check on systems performance. I should have been with the lander team after all. There's going to be nothing left to find of that base. All they have to do is sit around or go for midnight strolls until we get back."

Free fall in mid flight, leaping high above Hel's crust of iron ice. They were strapped in a divided row to the levelled couches, Samson and his couch buckled against the deck behind them. The base was in full intensified view. What was left of it.

They looked north along the cascading mountain rim, in close-up they peered down past one escarpment edge into a broad flat valley bounded by a second scarp, higher. On the valley floor was a tiny rectangular building block. North of it—about five hundred metres they knew from Nightrider's pass—was a much larger flat platform laid out on the ground. They had thought it was the main structure, the accommodation and work block of a base much bigger than the mission planners had anticipated. Now they could see that it was a foundation raft or a landing pad or something else not built upon. Whatever it was, it was ruined. It broke apart irregularly at its northern side, had part disintegrated, was less than half its original size. And there had been another block structure further still to the north, radiating so much heat that it must have been the power unit for the complex. It had vanished.

They were travelling towards the base with a lateral velocity of over twelve hundred metres every second. And they were falling as Hel's reach reclaimed them. Yasmin was keeping the base view trained—they had no computer guide to do that for them. The viewing angle was sinking, the valley floor fore-shortening, the nearer escarpment rising.

There were tiny little things like stacked pallets or store dumps scattered across the space between the first structure and the broken platform. They stopped in a neat east-west line level with the platform. North of that line the ground was lighter, reflecting more of the dim starlight for the camera's imaging system to multiply.

"Right across as far as you can see," Yasmin said. "A huge strip of it. Is that from the burn?"

"Must be," Samson said. "If the ice surface was melted all the rock dust would sink. When it re-froze you'd get a clean ice surface with a higher albedo."

"What happened to the power unit?"

"Sunk." Akira was staring intently at the surviving structure that the burn had missed, misdirected to the apparently bigger targets. There should have been no missiles and no ships so that Nightrider could have made a second pass. "I suppose."

"Burn minus twenty," Ali announced. "Stand by for the attitude manoeuvre."

Kim rested comfortably with her hands tucked into the couch's stomach belt. This part of the proceedings the lander could handle all by itself, like free wheeling on your childhood bicycle down the gentle corridor grade from Serenity's Admin Zone to Service Subsid, hands on hips and feet trailing.

Short hisses from the attitude thrusters. The base pitched out of sight and was replaced by stars. Yasmin killed the screen.

"Stand by for the burn. Mark."

Weight and a roar and the couch ramming your back. Up and down returning with a vengeance. Not a real up and down— they were plummeting at forty-five degrees to Hel's vertical.

Thrust was nominal, 30 ms^{-2}. Ali cut in the landing radar so that the guidance computer could take them down to a precise thirty metre hover. Kim took hold of the attitude jet trigger grip control with her right hand, moved her left hand to the couch lever, next to the key pad and the main thrust throttle slot.

"It's broken ground. Look at the radar scatter." Ali keyed up a tail camera to look down through their transparent exhaust flame. "It's nothing but fissures and junk."

Ten seconds to hover. The angled ground was a jumble of blocks and fragments interweaved by cracks and crevasses. Some place to try to land. One second to hover.

They pitched up to vertical and their overloaded weight sank to a fifth.

Kim brought her couch up to a sitting position, matching Ali's rise. The data screen slid across the ceiling for her and deployed itself against the forward wall. She keyed a lateral external view. Too dim. She raised the image intensification. The scene outside was like a monstrous gravel bed, jagged blocks tumbled about, blocks as big as the lander.

She thumbed off the locking switch. The trigger grip functions were aligned to match its mount orientation. Pull it up and you could fire thrust tailwards to nudge the lander noseward, ceilingward. Push it down and you went tailward, push it bodily forward or back, left or right, and you could give the lander a lateral nudge in the corresponding direction. To pitch, yaw or roll you had to tip the grip forward or sideways, or else twist it. The amount of thrust you gave was determined by the trigger movement.

Fine, but where to go? They hovered at twenty percent thrust.

"Hopeless," Ali said.

Kim had a forward lateral view, and now she was flying by touch. The direction indicator in the field top centre gave her the azimuth orientation inertially deduced from the lander's math map of Hel. East of north. She twisted the grip left and fired a brief pulse. The chaos ground started to drift right, the azimuth counter gave her north zero, and then counted degrees slowly down from 359. Rotating anticlockwise.

The lander pirouetted sedately, hovering on four pale pencil flames in a frozen vacuum night, tantalizing the waiting touch of the star-black shattered ground. Inside they looked at its ghosted grey confusion swinging by.

"Looks better over there." Samson was sitting on the deck between the other couches, sharing Akira's screen.

"That's due south," Akira said. "We don't go that way. Would take us hours on foot to cross this terrain."

The view swung east, and then north again. Nothing but smashed and shattered ground. This was the site selected by the mission planners from fifty-one billion kilometres away.

North again. Kim twisted right and fired a counter thrust to stop the turn. The escarpment lay square across the screen two kilometres away, its crest smooth against the infinite sky. The ground appeared to lift below the foot of the scarp, seemed less ruinous. Kim pushed the grip forward and fired a longer thrust. They glided at hover over the boulder wreckage and ice knives.

After a thousand metres the blocks began to reduce in size, the clefts hidden beneath them closing. Another hundred metres coaxing the lander at hover up a slight rise, and it was merely a severely broken pavement beneath them.

"There." Ali pointed at a clear patch higher in the screen field. "It's smooth enough if the level's right, and there's no more mess from there to the scarp. Could reach it okay on foot."

She took them over rising ground, another two hundred metres, then braked the lander with the forward thrust. They hovered and examined the ground. Smooth but sloping.

"I think it's okay. You think it's okay?"

Ali nodded. "Within our limits."

"Yes." She eased the main thrust back fractionally. They began to sink, gaining speed so very slowly. The forward leg indicator showed ground contact, hydraulic compression. Then the right leg indicator, then the left. Less thrust because the hydraulics push you back from the ground. The forward leg was nearing its telescoping limit. In a moment it would lock and they would begin to tip. Not dangerous but not nice.

The rear leg touched. She killed the thrust.

303 07:14:07. After 315 seconds of hovering they had touched down at the planned site. Only a little late.

The suit was a shell of midnight black, a made to measure monster bulk. With flexible joints and rigid trunk and limb sections, with deformable material in the joint sheaths that kept a constant volume during flexion and extension so that the one-atmosphere suits stayed at constant pressure during movement, with a mass tailored to bring occupant and technological shell up to no more than the Earth equivalent body weight, the suits hardly impeded mobility. But they made you feel so big.

They were one-piece shells, the helmet and shoulder yoke folding down over the chest to allow the wearer to squeeze inside. The easiest way was to lay the suit on its back and wriggle into it, legs and body and arms, and only then stand up, duck your head with your chin pressed to your chest, and close the yoke and helmet. But Akira's and Yasmin's suits were stored upright in the airlock, and the deck down there was little more than a metre square. So Yasmin steadied Akira's suit, free standing in the close space, while Akira climbed down the ladder from above and lowered himself into it. That involved leaving one arm out until last, and then coaxing it in with an almost impossible contortion, but it was quicker than hauling the suit up to the crowded crew space. She helped him fold the helmet closed over his retreated head, and snapped the clips at the backs of the shoulders closed. He looked out at her through a panoramic visor that reflected no incident light, almost as if it wasn't there. He helped her extract a backpack from the storage rack and she secured it to his suit, mating the sealed service connection and then turning the locking clips. He was self-contained. With brute black fingers he pulled a plug cable from the lock control panel and fitted it into the waist socket of his suit, communicatively reunited with the rest of them.

The same procedure got Yasmin into her suit, except that Akira in suit and backpack took up far more space than Yasmin had done, and made the task even more precise and dexterous. When the helmet went over and she could straighten her neck again, she looked out through the visor, looked out from a dead acoustic, just herself and her breath. Akira fitted her backpack while she plugged herself into the comm net. They asked Kim above to seal off the lock and begin pumping it out.

Power came on and activated the suit's systems. The heater-cooler circulation mesh built into the inner lining started to transport heat away, to surround her with coolness. Left hand playing the broad-spaced keys on the right forearm, she adjusted the ambient temperature slightly, the value the suit would hold her at whatever she did. Switching to the keys on her left sleeve just to check that they were functioning, she cut in the status displays. Little lights glowed inside the visor's chin rim. She activated the suit's orientation readout, switched it to the planetary program. The visor might have been nonreflecting on the outside, but it was totally reflecting for appropriately angled light on the inside. Projected from the helmet dome, figures floating at infinity in front of her forehead told her that she was facing 239°.

You had an excellent view through the visor: sixty degrees up, ninety degrees left or right, fifty degrees down. By leaning your head until your hair touched the visor you could see your own feet, by then looking left or right you could almost see your own shoulders. Not quite—but then if you were using the shoulder lights to illuminate your way through the darkness, you hardly wanted to be blinded by them. She leaned her head forward. She tested that the glucose nipple and water nipple were working.

They clamped equipment onto the belt girdles—a rifle each, an ammunition pack, infrared and light intensifying imagers, a hand grenade charge.

The light dimmed down to virtual blackness, leaving just the luminous outline of the airlock's floor hatch. The lock was fully evacuated, the outer hatch below already open and the ladder deployed. Nothing to do but go. They stepped aside, half hanging from the airlock ladder. Black panels opened on black nothing at their feet.

It wasn't really black, not utterly sightless night. With properly dark adjusted eyes it is possible to see by unattenuated starlight—just that it isn't possible to see such a lot.

They walked out from beneath the lander and across the slight slope. Carefully. Adjusting to the dark and the dusty smear and the grainy ice-rock soil beneath. Time to stop and look around.

The lander squatted evil, a depthless shape, not a circular section truncated cone, but just a trapezoid hole in the world, blacker than sight. On the broken ground they could make out the baldest of details close at hand. The distance was opaque, the horizon a terminating tear at the bottom of a cold star field dome. To have a real *horizon,* to have *distance* again after ten months aboard Nightrider should have been such a delight. But they could only see distance details through the starscopes, and those formed a fixed image focused at infinity. A synthetic landscape, not the real thing.

Akira pointed towards the scarp, blacker arm against merely black background. After reaching the top or after making a first attempt to ascend, they would pause and plug themselves together with a comm cable to talk. Radio communication would be private, of course, the signal encrypted indecipherably—but even completely incomprehensible communication would alert any radio receiver that just happened to be lying on their own side of the horizon. They had the advantage of virtual invisibility. There was no need to shout.

A last look at the lander, black in the naked eye night, black still in the starscope view, hot white through the infrared imager. The lander had been their reduced home after Nightrider. Now they were down to a skin moulded round their own body shells, and outside of that nothing, literally nothing at all.

They started to climb.

They returned after nine hours, the backpacks seventy-five percent exhausted.

They clambered up into the lock and closed the floor, came in from a cold near to absolute zero. They eased up the light and locked into power and service umbilicals. With the external power supply they could heat up the entire outer surfaces of the suits, whereas the backpack unaided could only heat the visor. That was vital, or else when the air flooded back into the lock its water content and even its constituent gases would freeze onto the outer surface and blind you for long minutes. With the visor heated up you could see, but the rest of the suit stayed iced up and lethally cold. Without heating the entire suit surface you would have to wait a long time before you could risk clambering out of it and accidentally touching its vacuum cold material.

They talked to the others over the comm net while the lock repressurized. The top of the escarpment ran flat and smooth for a while, and then dipped down towards the nearest of the base structures. That was at four and a half kilometres from the rectangular building. The last two kilometres looked from a distance as though they would be easy—level valley floor as smooth as a salt flat. But the shallow slope in between was impassable. It was as badly broken as the ground downslope of the lander, but fractured apart instead of crushed together. Splits and cracks and crevasses made a fissured maze between flattopped blocks and sliced off pillars, holes opened up in the fracture floors, side collapses choked them. That was what had taken the time—proving that there was no way down from the ridge to the base.

They rubbed each other clean with wash towels and then pulled on their stale clothes again. They climbed up into the crew space to eat.

"This strip with the higher albedo shows hot through the IR imager," Akira explained. "It's hottest directly across the valley where the power unit used to be. Now that can't still be from Nightrider's pass, can it?"

"Must be the reactor pile," Samson agreed. "They must have been powering the base so far from a fission reactor, wherever they got the uranium from. A fusion reactor would require too much supply payload from the support ships, and just isn't efficient enough on a small scale. A fission reactor would produce thousands of times the output a little building like that could need. But then they'll have been planning to expand."

"They need power to develop materials manufacture," Ali said. "They can't ship the stuff here that they need to open up geothermal power. Have to make it on site."

"We assumed the ground is hot because there's melted water under an ice crust," Yasmin said. "Does that make sense?"

"Suppose so." Samson nodded. "Suppose so. If Nightrider's pass disrupted the ground enough for the reactor to collapse and start to sink, then the core would go on melting its way down until it hit bottom. Maybe the ice is shallow here. This is the ocean-continental boundary, if I read it right. These parallel ridges we're down between must be upthrust override features. If the reactor core is sitting a few hundred metres down, then maybe it can keep a column of water heated almost to the surface. Maybe."

"This thing over here," Akira pointed, "really is some sort of flat platform. Nothing else. Maybe it was the foundation for your expansion program. All these things are crated loads on some sort of pallet. They're scattered so wide apart they really could be soft-lander pallets brought down from supply ships. This here and this look like perfectly regular materials dumps. The interesting thing is the building. Here's a close up."

"Oh."

"Is that a tractor parked?"

"A small one. A walker. What else in this terrain?"
What else.

"And the building?" Kim said. "Is it occupied?"

"It's heated. That's for sure. It looks to be a hollow rectangle, I'd say about thirty-five metres east to west and about twenty-five north to south. It's on raised foundations, presumably to stop it melting the ground underneath. You can see from the tractor it's one storey high except at the southeast corner here, from the antennas and those little things—cameras maybe—we assume it's the communications room. That little slit *might* be a window."

"What would they want windows for? What is there to look at?"

"The tractor," Ali offered. "People working outside. Guiding the touchdown of one of those soft-lander pallets. Cameras can break down."

"This southwest corner is where the heat seems to be coming from. There's machinery running in there. Presumably life support operating on auxiliary power."

"So people are alive in there?"

"Looks like it."

"So the base hasn't been taken out at all."

"Oh it has. Their reactor is gone. If we don't interfere they're just going to take a long time to die."

A little rectangular building with some lives inside. Lives condemned to the night by a sudden lick of fire.

"Are we going to interfere?" Kim asked.

Akira was silent for a moment. Then shrugged. "We can't walk down to the base. The ground's impassable. We can't walk round the ridge because it runs another twenty kilometres or more out to the west. We have the choice of sitting up on the ridge and shooting the building apart with grenades, or flying in and storming it. Can you fly us there?"

"Sure. No problem. But if we want to?"

"The deciding factor," Yasmin said, "is the intelligence trade-off. We're only down here at all to learn what we can. Here's a chance to do something better than just picking over a mess of wreckage."

"Let's shoot first and then go in," Samson suggested. "It should still be higher value wreckage than Nightrider would have left, and it will be safer. Much safer."

"They won't know we're coming," Akira went on. "The place is no kind of fortress, there are no visible weapons. It can't house very many people—not for long stay occupation, anyway. We should be able to take prisoners. And that could prove useful just in case there are any more of them wandering around somewhere who might otherwise turn up and surprise us.''

"And we have psychotropic drugs for interrogation. The mission book foresees the possibility.''

"Interrogating their computers would be more valuable,'' said Samson.

"I'm suddenly not so happy with the mission book,'' Ali said. "It's made a mess of two things in a row—the base predict and the landing site target. Three, if you count Nightrider missing our start position update. But then—on the other hand.''

"On the other hand?''

"What else do we do while we're waiting. How do we get in?''

"Through the locks.'' Akira pointed. "The tractor's docked at one at the southwest corner. This one in the centre is free. This right at the southeast end under the communications block has steps up to it. We go in there. If we can't open the doors we just blow them.''

Samson shrugged. "That would take care of the prisoners.''

"On the other other hand, I'm really not so happy with the mission book.'' Ali shook his head. "It's more guess than plan.''

"No, it's plan. We're planned in. A human component to allow flexibility. Otherwise they wouldn't have sent us out here.''

DAY 304

THIS was flying. This was real flying.

They sat in their bulky black suits like evil starship troopers in a dark world, the lights out and the screens dimmed to minimum to aid dark adaptation. The lander and its airlock were evacuated, pumped down to hard vacuum. Only the bottom hatch was closed to keep out the flame heat. Kim flew and Ali monitored, the others watched the approaching target. Akira knelt over the floor hatch, sitting on his heels, his knees either side of the opening, a waiting Japanese warrior in massive armour lacquered matt. Yasmin sat in his seat, Samson sat in Yasmin's seat against the right wall. Samson was going to stay. That would have been Kim's job, but now Samson had his swollen and half immobilized arm that had made getting into the suit so awkward and painful. He could still handle the easy-use weapons, but less dexterously, so he would stay aboard to watch and to defend the lander against sudden intruders. Kim would go out with Ali, pulling on their backpacks and grabbing their weapons and waiting beneath the lander to cover the other two until they went into the base, and then to follow them. Yasmin and Akira already had their backpacks in place, but like the others they took comm and power and life support from the umbilicals. For another few seconds yet.

This was flying. Balanced on its four throttled down invisible flames, the lander swept over the ground downslope.

Not perfectly balanced, but perfectly *imbalanced,* leaning slightly into its flight and letting gravity pull it over the gentle slope. She had brought them over the ridge with a lateral velocity drift, and then tipped the lander perfectly. Down they raced over fissures and blocks and crevasses, gaining speed all the way. It was a manoeuvre far finer than flying out over the base at hover and then coming down. She was proud of that.

The slope was levelling out. Tip the grip back and give the trigger the slightest squeeze to ease off the tilt. Forward to correct, or the lander would gradually flip over onto its back. The great clumsy gloves were not so bad. You couldn't pick up pins, but you had feeling enough to handle an egg.

No sign of movement from the base.

"As intended," said Akira's voice in her ears. "Put us down two fifty metres southwest."

"Okay. Almost there."

"Yasmin." Akira again. "Down into the lock."

A glance sideways past the visor edge. Black in shadow, Yasmin's suit substitute slipped its umbilical and swung out of the seat. Bejewelled about the waist with a black rifle and black charges, it dropped down the centre hatch.

Level ground now. Tip the lander to horizontal hover or it will crash. It sweeps on momentum-driven in an airless world. Air would freeze here. Using fuel all the time at twenty percent to maintain the hover. The only emergency escape straight up to the stars. A little sideways kick to aim for the touchdown point, a rotation reorientation to face exactly in the new direction. Akira's suit leans forward and drops out of view. Target point approaching. Give a first lateral kick backwards to retard. Still no movement from the base. Too fast an approach leaving them no time at all to react. The base is a little level block corner on, raised up on a lattice frame, a six legged tractor docked at the near corner. A second retarding kick.

Akira's voice in her ears again. "Ready to go."

Ali's voice. "Stand by."

Ground as flat as ice. It is ice, mostly. More retarding thrust. More still. Altitude twenty-seven metres and steady. Cut back main thrust by a fraction. Fly by feel. Target coming up. Long retard. Reduce main. Restore to stop an *accelerating* fall. Altitude ten. Nine. More retard. Five metres. Four. Final retard to zero lateral. Touch down. Main out.

"Okay, go!"

They opened the outer hatch and then the sealed floor under their feet, and dropped out without a ladder. Two and a half metres in a heavy suit at six tenths gee—a soft bounce on granular ground. Run folded forward and black blind to get clear of the hot exhaust flanges. Straighten up and see.

See the base lurching nearer in the visor view, a black block on black ground under a black night with stars. A myriad stars.

Akira runs beside you, a monster shadow with a gun in its hand. Detach your own stub rifle on its retainer cord. Lope over the easy ground. No star-shadow unevennesses ahead, nothing to fall over or plunge into. The six leg tractor stands backed against its docking lock, not moving, not stretching its limbs to turn to you. This corner has the heat exhaust, must have the auxiliary power and life support plant inside. How many people? No light from the little raised corner block where Akira is going to go. Those *are* windows up there, one little eye in each face. Check the ground ahead again. Smooth right up to the corner and the tractor. The tractor's limbs still stationary and its windows blank black.

Akira goes right around the front of the tractor. Go left, go close along the shorter wall, running beside the waist high frame supports holding up the one-floor structure. Smooth wall. No lock. Probably some variation on plastic-ceramic foam. Standard structure used everywhere off-Earth. Load-bearing, insulating, light weight. Stop at the corner. Look round, blunt gun butted two-handed to your chest. No one. Nothing along the north wall but a lock at the far end.

Back a pace. Detach a charge and slap it onto the flat wall, slide it hard so that the molecular hooks tear and then grip. Set it to remote, this the diversion. Run back the way you came, along the wall, out past the tractor. Stop in front of the sweep of its front legs.

Akira was a black shadow on the star dark ground, leaving the halfway lock without steps, running to the one right at the far corner under the raised block. The world was a sweep of opacity under a level sky tear. The lander a black decapitated triangle on splayed legs, Ali and Kim covering cut-out shapes just clear of it. Her own breath gasping in and out inside her minimal space, and nothing else but radio silence. She held the gun in her right glove, keyed the right sleeve with her left fingers, ready to fire the charge.

Akira's shadow stepped back from the lock, signalled sweeping once with its arm. She fired the charge.

A snap flash of light across the world. Ground, slope, distance etched. And gone again. Only Ali and Kim and the lander were untransformed, black as nothingness, light eating.

She ran along the building side to Akira.

Skid to a halt at the airlock steps. Look back. The other two coming. Look up. Akira already has the outer door open. He claps a hand over his empty visor at her, turns and goes inside. Visor heater on. Up three steps and squeeze in, hard body shells in a jammed space. The luminous panel says HAND-BUP. Akira throws one control from OPEN to KLOZ, another from VAK to AIR. *Sound* as it comes in. Stare at the luminous letters because you'll meet the light on the other side. HAND-BUP must be manual backup. No visor icing. No problem. Akira's hand throws another control from KLOZ to OPEN. The lock is cycled. The door cracks. Light.

Briefly blinded blinking.

A narrow end space, ladder in front going up. The space opens left. Jump out. Go left.

Standing in the corner of a room.

A room that goes further west than north. Maybe six metres by ten. A lock doorway in the north corner, open. A slide doorway in this east end, closed. Another lock doorway in the far end, also closed. Frame furniture, light and basic. Couches, chairs, two tables. Things on the walls. Displays, pictures, decoration colours. And other colours.

Four people standing stock still. People with suntanned scalps and skins, bald and smooth and young, in sleeveless tops and shorts and sandals. Simple clothes all colours. Four astonished people.

Staring silently at two monstrous black-suited apparitions that had come in from absolutely nowhere at all.

Yasmin stepped back, turned bodily to see the lock control, threw the finger lever from OPEN to KLOZ. Now the other two could cycle the lock and come through. As she watched, her sheen slicked arm and hand grew a white rime, matted with grainy ice. Her rifle was coated too. The bulky back of Akira's helmet, his shoulders, his backpack.

They started shouting, voices dull but loud from outside the suit. Suddenly all in motion, arms waving, faces yelling. The nearest man stepped at Akira—

Crack and the man exploded and flew onto his shredded back.

Screams and side-leaps from the others. Akira stepped out along the wall. Yasmin moved after him, gun trained too. The dead man was still dying, quivering in a blood pool.

A sound behind. Spin round. A man still straightening from landing at the foot of the ladder. Straightening to a muzzle brake pointing into his face.

She backed, carefully so as not to throw Akira. She beckoned the man with a blunt glove. He came wide-eyed and terrified, slid round the corner and backed away to join the others. Four fearful people and a dead man, and two fearsome figures dripping fragments of ice. Akira had switched to transmit. That was his sharp breathing too in her ears. She switched to transmit. Nothing to say. Just them and the four people facing them, facing the impossible invaders from the utterly empty outside.

The lock door opened at the right edge of her visor view. A black suit with Ali's face in it came through. The black took on an ice sheen. Kim followed. They looked at the space, looked at the people, looked at the twitching blood-pooled death mess.

Her gun was turning wet slicked and faintly dripping. The sights were frozen folded down, but the range was too small to need them. Through the open northward lock she could see a retreating corridor, empty, another lock at the far end. Closed.

"Ali." Akira's voice in each of their closed worlds. "Check in there right."

Ali moved to the sliding door of the closed off end compartment, opened it. He couldn't peer inside in his suit of ice—he had just to step through. Half hidden inside the space he faced left and right, then turned and came out again.

"Kitchen. No one."

"Good. Kim, come over here. I'll look up above. Yasmin, watch me."

Akira went behind her to the ladder in the closed corner, leaned back to look up, then started to climb. His suit sloughed ice, glistened wetly like black oil. He disappeared to the waist. A long pause, then he started down again, reaching the floor with his gun trained upwards. Sandalled feet followed him, smooth synthetically sun-brown legs, orange shorts with indigo side panels, a loose blue-green tee shirt, smooth shoulders and arms. A smooth scalped, smooth faced woman moving with anxious slowness, who slid away to join the others, who looked wide-eyed at the dead man on the floor.

Yasmin looked from the woman's face to the others, from one to the next. There were only two faces among them. Two men and three women, but only two faces, each one moment male and the next female. The confusion was perfected by the lack of hair. The man on the floor amid his death mess had the same face.

Akira again. "Kim, go out through the lock. Tell Samson we're okay. Five prisoners so far. We're going to search the base."

Kim went back to the lock, still iced.

Five prisoners with two faces and brightly coloured flimsy clothes. Five shocked people without the faintest idea of what had happened to them.

Akira and Ali went through the west end airlock, opening both doors. They found another long space. The near end was a narrow corridor with a walled off lab or workshop on each side, then came a broader walk with loaded racks and shelves arrayed left and right. Between two stacks of shelves on the left was an airlock, the inside of the unoccupied tractor dock.

The next interior airlock stood open, a receding corridor beyond. That section was dimly lit, but they had no way to turn up the lights. Shadows threaten you when your vision is limited and you can hardly hear. But then the suit was tough enough to afford protection, too.

Walled off workshops left and right, then a compartment on the left filled with plant machinery, with open shelving running off the opposite side of the corridor. And then a cross corridor at the end. An airlock closed each end of the cross corridor, the one leading to the docked tractor, the other into the next section leading north along the west side of the base. The closed off space filling the end of the section was filled with tight-packed machines and service connections—the running life support plant. Ali went through the double lock into the tractor interior and found it tiny, empty. Akira led the way north into the next section.

A central corridor again, with nothing from one end to the other but rows of loaded shelving. And when they went carefully along, hiding between rows of shelves, a woman.

The suit she had been breaking out was white, with broad arm-band colour markings. White was a sensible colour in the absolute night outside, it threw back the maximum starlight, made you as visible as possible if you lay injured somewhere, your backpack power out. It was a flexible suit, not semi-rigid like their own. It lay in an insulation thick heap at her feet, the end of her escape to who knew where. In the tractor maybe. Perhaps she had been on her way to investigate whatever had happened to cause the explosion at the northwest corner. And perhaps she had been warned of the invasion by the woman who had stayed a minute or two longer at the instruments up in the communications room. But she was caught.

The next lock would lead through to the northwest corner where Yasmin had sprung a charge against the wall. The lock was closed. Over it a light flashed. ALARM—VAKUUM.

They took her back to the others. Six prisoners now. They must all have been gathered together to plan a reaction to the sudden explosion, two of them going up to read the status from the control instruments. It had been real easy so far.

Akira took Kim with him through the other half of the base.

The east end section was taken up by four screened spaces, two on each side of the central corridor, and at the end they had come in by, two toilets and two showers. The screen walled spaces looked like sleeping accommodation—the floors were softly padded, there were little personal lockers with mattresses rolled up beside them. Little pictures were mounted on the walls. It would be an austere home.

Through into the next section they entered a cross corridor, another airlock opposite them leading to the black outside. The walled off end space on the right was filled by a duplicate life support plant, this time not running. The main corridor ran left, four spaces opening off it. One had an examination couch and must have been a sick bay. Another held anonymous machinery, another something that might have been for some sort of processing, the last held hydroponics support machinery—pumps, nutrient feeds, a water reservoir. They went through the end lock.

A central walkway with side branches ran between green walls and green curtains. The whole low-ceilinged and harsh lit place was festooned and choked with growing green. Water pipes ran everywhere, lazy fans in the obscured corners circulated the air. The section was the garden, the hydroponics farm that must have provided most of what the base lived from. Akira went ahead covered by Kim. He went very slowly, checking left and right, brushing stems and leaf cascades aside with his hard arm, patiently ensuring that no one was hiding against the back wall of the pumped water jungle, hoping that no one with a weapon that could go through his suit was waiting for him. Deaf to the surrounding space, half blinded by the visor limits, closed in by the solid curtains of living green.

The lock at the far end would lead into the northwest corner section. It was closed. A light flashed ALARM—VAKUUM. They went back.

Akira paused at the northeast corner. The exterior lock there was closed. The *inner* door was closed. When he went to open it to check that no one was hiding, he found that the door control didn't respond, that the lock was at vacuum and the outer door open. As if someone had gone out.

They hurried back. Ali and Yasmin had moved chairs and table aside, had got the Outsiders down on their faces on the floor.

"Someone might have got outside," Akira said to them all so intimately inside their suits. "Looks like a lock there has been cycled. Kim, check Samson's okay."

Kim went out through their entry lock. Akira went up the corner ladder and Yasmin followed.

The space above was tiny, their suits filled it all. It was dark but for instrument glows, control desks with inset monitors ran round three walls. There were two chairs, one pushed in under the instrument board, the other, back to it, pulled out. Akira pushed the chair, stood with his back to her but spoke almost inside her head.

"She was sitting here. Look."

The instrument board showed a glowing plan of the base, sloping like the panel. The plan was a lighted outline, but the west end section where they had found the woman, the northeast section where the lock had been cycled, were fully background lit. His hand knocked aside a stalk mounted microphone.

"She was warning people to get out. I should have noticed."

"There was enough to do at one go."

There was a blank little window in each wall. She tried to

peer out, visor against transparent pane, but saw nothing but perfect black. Her eyes were no longer night adapted.

Kim's voice. "Samson's okay but he's mad as hell. Says he's been trying to reach us for nearly ten minutes. He's seen three figures run out from behind the base and head south. Says they just disappeared behind some ground cover at the foot of the slope. He wants to know if we're going to do anything about it or just wait to see if they start shooting up the lander."

Out in the iron night again, the perpetual vacuum blackness.

Yasmin ran easily, a loping jog across hard ground covered with granular dust. Right in front of her she could even make out their tracks, scuffed boot-prints in the dark dirt. Ten metres ahead she could tell whether or not the ground was smooth, perhaps as far as fifty metres away she could have seen a boulder or a crevasse coming. Beyond that it was just formlessness fading to a black opacity that rose indeterminately far away to the brightdust wall of stars. Watching the ground was her job, seeing that they didn't run headlong into something. Akira was loping along behind, alternately catching her up and then pausing and falling back while he scanned with a starscope. He glanced regularly back at the base and the key-code locked lander. He swept the ground further ahead on the flat valley floor, and up into the fissured slope rising towards the southern skyline. He was watching to make sure that they didn't run headlong into an ambush.

They had dashed across to the lander to see what Samson had to show. The recorded camera view held three figures fleeing, three white suits with recognition armbands. The sensibly bright suits showed like beacons in a starscope image, just as their heat would flare in a lower definition infrared imager. Tracking and catching them in open terrain would have been easier than any training exercise. But they had disappeared into the shattered ground at the foot of the long slope two kilometres away, and they had carried things in their hands. Indeterminate things, perhaps weapons. They might have defensive weapons just for the eventuality, even though they certainly didn't have night camouflage suits. And where were they going? There was nothing over the far ridge but the next empty valley with its crush-chaos floor, impassable. Were they just trying to escape to the nearest cover, or did they have something to use from there, something that they could turn on the intruders?

If anything happened to the lander that was the end of everything. Nightrider couldn't come down and collect them. The next arrivals would be the next Outsider ship to come, in months if one was already under way, or else in years. The base probably had enough power to last a few weeks. There would be no need to worry about what arriving Outsiders might do to them.

They ran with radios set to receive—either could yell to the other instantly. They ran with the suit comm systems listening for any radio frequency transmission that the Outsiders might be foolish enough to make. They ran across the blank nothingness to where the skidding footprints disappeared into the first cleft, darker still under the star roof.

They consulted by communication cord, glancing at each other's barely lit visored faces, searching the climbing ground, the ex-soldier killer and his ex-militia assistant. They went into the deepening cleft, still not risking their shoulder lights. They had trained in the dark of lunar Farside at night. Carefully, they could cope with this.

The interconnecting cracks and clefts were the same tangled nightmare they had met on the previous day, trying to find a way down. Sometimes squeezing width, sometimes walk-wide, sometimes open alleyways. Walls sometimes smooth, or like jagged shear serrations. Floors that ran level, or that pitched wildly up and down, that ran like smooth winding path threads or phantom rivulet beds, that were choke blocks piled together with nightmare holes in between. But at least the tracks were easier to follow, even down in an almost total dark shielded from all but a slit roof of stars. Debris and detritus, chips and chunks, had collected down on the fissure floors since the initial sliding uplift had opened them, a fine talus deeper than the granular dust out on the ice plain. The tracks were broken but clearer.

But they had to use light. They had to let the forward angled shoulder lights glow at absolute minimum. The ice-matrix walls, where they were both contaminant free and overhung or deep enough to be shielded from the slow cosmic particle rain, glittered and gleamed in time fragments. Little eye jewels undiscovered, or a crystal place flashing quantized anger at animate intrusion.

After a toiling torturous hour they must have made up most

of the distance. Time and again the blurred tracks came back the way they had gone, returning from a blind route to take another turn. And the azimuth heading swung wildly but always swept back south, irregularly climbing. The Outsiders were just trying to get away—or else to reach the high ground.

Lights extinguished, eyes readjusted, they clawed and scrambled up a ragged wall and clambered up onto a flat block in a sloping night jigsaw of flat blocks all askew. They talked by comm cord and searched with starscopes. A whole tipped up landscape of indecipherable desolation.

A little white figure clambering in a cleft.

A bright little shape in synthetic grey shadow, in a cleft that climbed away from them and ended in a rising wall, up which the shape was slowly toiling. About four hundred metres away.

No sign of any others. They must have split up in an attempt to maximize the chance of one of them escaping. Where to and in order to do what?

Yasmin was the better long range shot. She mounted the starscope sight onto the snapped up rifle sights, knelt sitting on her heels, and butted the short and brutal thing against the chest of her suit. She flicked the magnification up to four, to eight. At four hundred metres there was no need to worry about ranging factors—the muzzle velocity was so high, the gravity field so weak, and air retardation non-existent.

A silent kick, and the X-flash spitting up left and right of the starsight. The framed figure went on climbing. The round must have struck so close, but there was no sound transmission to announce its arrival. The second shot missed.

The third hit. The suit jumped, and then slithered down on its face to the floor of the cleft. Yasmin detached the starsight. They took an azimuth bearing and scrambled down the side of the block again.

They came round a corner and there it was in the lights, a white suit face down, with red-yellow armbands. The suit fabric was bulky but crumpled—deflated. You had to search to find the tiny bullet hole in the backpack. It would have gone through to the body inside.

They turned the suit over. A blood-iced face was frozen onto the inside of the visor. It peeled off as the head fell back inside the helmet. It stared straight up into the galactic sky, stared straight up at Hades. The face was another copy of one of the only two shared by all those people in the base. And there were no weapons. What Yasmin picked up from the sloping fissure floor were power packs and air scrubber recharges, life extending replenishments for when the backpack reserves were depleted.

Highlights flashing flitting fading on the walls. Someone else coming, someone who had given up and turned back to follow an apparently more successful companion. They killed their own dim lights and waited.

The highlights came sliding round the corner, pushed by a walking white suit with a helmet light. The suit held something with a thin nozzle in its hands, something that looked like a cutting or welding torch. The suit seemed to register that it was suddenly following too many footprints. It raised its light to see two black shadows waiting above. It struck a searing pencil flame from the torch.

The X-flash from Akira's gun. The light went out and the flame flew away and guttered.

In their own lights the figure was dead, of course, again the same face twisted sideways behind the visor. A tiny hole in the centre of the suit was rimmed with air ice. The figure lay head and helmet downslope. Crystallizing blood collected inside the helmet.

They backtracked, trying to find the third trail, taking it in turns to lead, the leader using lights and the follower coming invisible behind the fissure filling silhouette. They found a one-way trail of single footprints. Yasmin was leading where the cleft opened into a little defile.

Up came the ground and she was flat on her face with a weight on her back, gasping. Something was pickaxe hammering at her hard suit. She braced empty hands in the ground dirt and tried to heave upwards. Too much weight. Pickaxe hammering. "*Akira!*"

The weight went away and she came up onto her knees. Black and light streaming, Akira backed away from a white suit slumped against the base of the ice-rock wall. Akira's gun came up.

"Hold it! Hold it. Let's take another prisoner."

If the prisoner lived. The suit was struggling to reconnect the backpack services umbilical wrenched out of the socket in its side. A detachable connection had to have automatic seals of course—without the backpack the occupant would just suffocate or freeze.

"Where'd he come from?"

"Up there," in her ears. Akira's black arm pointed skywards. Akira's gun still pointed at the Outsider. "Couldn't risk a shot."

"No." She cast about, turning her shoulder-light wash. She found the fallen gun and went to pick it up, stooping clumsily in the restraining shell. Something else gleamed on the churned up ground. She fumbled when trying to get hold of it, it was short and slender and so small in her black hand. A pair of pointed surgical shears. The pickaxe?

"He was stabbing at you with that." Akira looked at it when she held it up in his field of view. "Lucky he didn't hit a joint section. Might even have gone through."

An air escape slow or fast, depressurizing death.

The suit reconnected its side umbilical. There was a gas puff as the seals interlocked. Caught in their lights, a smooth face looked out at them, maybe even hearing their radio talk, but over a system that couldn't decipher it. The face was another of the same.

"How many is that now?" she said. "Seven back there. Eight, nine, ten. Two faces whether male or female. Two sets of twins. They're clone groups."

"Every time you kill one there's another left to haunt you," Akira's voice whispered in her ears. And then louder. "I wasn't going to kill this one anyway. We need prisoners."

"Need?"

"Have you thought how useful hostages could be if it's the Outsider ship that comes back instead of Nightrider?"

"I hadn't. Not until now."

"No. Neither have the others. Don't mention it to them yet."

"No." That was an impossible thought. Hostages or no hostages, without Nightrider they would never get out. There was no help coming, no rescue to hold out for. "Let's get back."

There was fruit to eat, real fruit! Their own rations, plus plunder from the base kitchen. There was a shower to take after the long labour in the suits—only cold water spurts for energy conservation on backup power, but a shower just the same.

The northwest corner section that Yasmin had blown open was a second hydroponics farm. Or had been. Now there was a hole in its end wall, and instead of air it was filled with—nothing. At the explosive depressurization all the water feeds had burst and vacuum boiled, and then the water vapour had immediately frozen onto every surface. *Everything* was rimed and coated, the floor walkways, the walls and ceiling, plant stems and leaves and once water borne roots. It was an ice house, a festooned garden of brittle glass. Everything they brushed against exploded in shimmering shards.

Samson and Kim had been sorting out the sense of the base's rectangular ring layout. It meant that there were two ways into every section, even the ones without external locks—always a second way out when a neighbouring section suffered an integrity loss, a minimized chance of being trapped. The duplicated life support plant at diagonally opposite corners doubled the safety factor again, allowed the service overhauls that permitted running times measured in years. Only the backup power unit was not duplicated because it was already an emergency reserve. The base had lived from the sunken power reactor. The backup power came from rechargeable fuel cells, but eventually the supply of oxygen and hydrogen gas would run out, the catalysing membranes would lose their activity. Without any external interference the Outsiders would have died along with their base in two or three months.

They had backed the Outsiders into the still functioning hydroponics section on the north side. Then they had scoured that and the northeast corner section for anything that might serve as a weapon—tools, surgical instruments, sick bay chemicals. The Outsiders could have the hydroponics and the northeast section to themselves. There was fresh food to eat, water to drink. Besides the sick bay and the hydroponics support space, the two remaining compartments were a food processing room and a water hydrolysis plant—they must have been cracking harvested ice and then storing the liquefied products at one of the outlying dumps, a little raw reserve for the industrial future. There was some hydrogen and oxygen stored in cylinders there, but the only thing they could do with that was blow themselves up.

They had no suits. They couldn't get out through the wrecked northwest section, nor through the northeast corner lock. Their only route was back through the sleeping accommodation section. And to stage a breakout they would have to go through a lock that had been sealed closed and then pumped out, and repressurizing it would take time and would cause the VAK light to change in automatic warning to AIR. There were no *lockable* doors in the base because there had been no such design need, but the telltale barrier and an armed guard watching it from the far end of the sleep section would do.

They settled in to camp in the main day room. A single space six metres wide and ten metres long and two and a half high was too good to miss. It was the biggest single space since the mission began. Ali had rigged a frequency matched relay to the lander, going over one of their own encrypt-decrypt units that Samson had managed to patch into the base circuit. When the call came through from Nightrider, they would know.

The labs and workshops and stores in the three sections on the south, southwest and west were full of everything a prospecting and mapping base could need. Instruments, equipment, seismology explosives, suits, and endless consumables stocks, an electronics and a maintenance workshop, and a geological and materials lab. There were chemicals, cutters, sonic drills, power tools, more heavy duty field equipment—a whole arsenal of hand to hand weapons. Even in a high-tech age, a screwdriver between the ribs can still kill. There was a little electronics toolkit packed beside every lock—including back in the sections where the Outsiders were detained. But then there was nothing they could do with those tiny tools.

The sleep section had to be searched, the four narrow little screen walled rooms flanking the centre corridor. In each room were three bedrolls and three lockers. More or less communal sleeping for twelve. They went through the lockers to confirm that the personal belongings sorted out into twelve piles for twelve people. They had captured seven and killed three, so two were left unaccounted for. And there was a second tractor docking lock, unoccupied.

The sleeping space was so sparse, so unprivate. A simplicity derived from Japanese tradition to serve the needs of isolated little Outsider communities crammed into a minimal living space. Akira wouldn't know: his great grandparents had emigrated to Peru. There had been nothing left of Japan, traditional or otherwise, since before he went to school.

Samson carefully put all the personal possessions back in the appropriate lockers. Why he wasn't sure—the Outsiders would never be living in the base as normal again, wouldn't be living at all once Nightrider returned.

Samson had already made some progress at getting through the computer into the base's accumulated data store. His next job was to get the external cameras under his control. He had already set up monitoring camera views of what the Outsiders were doing in their two sections, as well as identifying the telltale that would indicate to anyone up in the tiny control room that the intervening lock was being cycled. He could see the Outsiders and listen to them. They seemed passive, shocked or withdrawn. When they talked, they talked in whispers, knowing that they would be observed. The assembled survivors of two clone groups, each of mixed sex, all young and bald scalped and scantily, brightly clothed—they sat or lay almost motionless, meditating, holding themselves in check. Wondering what had and what would happen to them.

The vanished power plant had been a fission reactor in the megawatt range, small, self-contained, with two closed loops to generate power. Most of it must have gone to waste, waiting until there was a bigger base with a materials synthesis facility. Then they could have gone for geothermal power and for real expansion. The pile was still under there, somewhere, and the ice across the valley floor seemed to be getting warmer, heated by circulating convection currents. Whole areas of onetime base site and soft-landed supplies might vanish if the surface cracked. He had found out what was stored in all those pallets that were scattered around. They were all dated as having arrived within the past fifty days, so must have come from the Outsider ship Nightrider was chasing. Samson was happy with life, with nothing but pages and pages more of data indexing to fight his way through. All he needed was an arm that was no longer swollen but instead bruised with the splendid colours that would take weeks to fade, and of course that call from Nightrider. At least the swelling seemed to be going down slightly, leaving pallid skin more stiffly gorged.

On the padded floor of one of the sleep spaces, two and a half metres by four, the screens of the long wall separating it off from the corridor all slid aside, slumped against the hard outer wall, wearing red shorts and a blue tee shirt with green chevron stripes, sat the Outsider. He already looked dazed, sleep-stunned conscious, pale under an indoor suntan. The woman Akira had first found in the communications room, blue-green tee shirt and orange shorts with indigo side panels, watched him anxiously. Akira's witness to show that at least they didn't torture, just in case they ever found themselves negotiating for their lives.

The man was pallid pale, washed out colour in his face, on neck and scalp, on bare arms and legs.

"That's a genetic adjustment, isn't it?" Kim said. "No hair."

Ali shrugged. "Who needs hair, unless you're used to it. Most of the newest generation of Outsider kids have no body hair. A totally artificial environment, no open outdoors—makes it a useless adaptation."

"Cloning is a planned adaptation," said Samson. "Makes living together for years in such a tight space easier. But they're two clone groups instead of one, not a *single* family unit. That way you avoid feelings of resentment or gross intrusion when others arrive to expand the place." He looked at the woman. "Right?"

She only returned his glance. She wore the same face as two of the new dead. The drugged man shared the same face of the man or woman Yasmin had killed.

"He looks about ready." Yasmin bent down, hands on knees, to peer more closely. "You know what we've done to you?"

"Inject me with something." His voice was reluctant, somehow.

"It's what's commonly called a truth drug. It makes you predisposed to give precise straight answers to direct questions, to tell us what you think is directly relevant." She looked round at Akira, remembering their brief training experiences. "The only difficulty with the trick is targeting the questions."

Akira knelt on one knee on the other side of the man.

"How long has the base been here? In terrestrial years, please."

"Five years." He caught himself by surprise. He didn't like answering automatically.

"How long have the present personnel been here?"

"Five years."

"All of you?"

"Yes."

"No rotation?" He looked round at the others. Five years stuck in this tiny place, out beyond everywhere.

"No," said the man.

Akira shook his head, started again. "We want to know about the ship that was in orbit here. How many missiles does it have?"

"Four."

"Not tell them!" the woman said, then bit her lip when they looked at her.

"How many crew?" Akira asked.

"Four."

"How often do ships call?"

No answer.

"Must be an irregular timetable," Yasmin said. "When's the next one due?"

"Seven four days."

"Not tell! They wait for it!"

"You don't have to stay." Akira turned back to the man. "Why do your ships carry missiles?"

"Self-defence in Solar System, base defence here."

"Why do you want to defend the base?"

"Stop you attacking."

"You knew we would?"

"We've see a probot. Mapper. We've think since then Earth-Luna maybe sends a remote weapon. Now we always have a ship on station."

"How long has the present one been here?"

"Five five days."

"So," Samson said. "They've been half expecting Earth would do something. We're not such a shock after all."

"Oh, we are." Yasmin looked at the woman looking back at them. "Oh yes, we are."

"How many live in the base?"

"Twelve."

"Where are the missing two?"

"Not tell! Not tell that! Not that."

"Where are they?"

"They're on geo-traverse."

"Whereabouts?"

"North, at the continent edge outstations."

"What kind of outstations? Are there people there?"

"No people. Outstations are monitor equipment and supply dumps for geo-traverses."

"When are they due back?"

"Not say! They kill them, too!"

No answer.

"When are they due back?"

No answer at all.

Akira shrugged. "Do you think he doesn't know?"

"The ship warned them we were here," Ali said. "That could have changed their plans. And if they've kept radio silence since, maybe he doesn't know when they're due."

"When were they due?" Yasmin asked.

"In ten days."

"But you think they've changed their plans? You think they might be coming back sooner?"

"I think they maybe come back sooner. I don't know."

"They're in the other tractor, of course?"

The man shook his head sharply. He gasped a little mouthful of air, turned his head aside.

"They're travelling with the second tractor?"

"What—?" He turned his head to the other side, turned back, swallowed another gasp of air. "What tractor?"

Yasmin looked at Akira. "Did you realize he was fighting it that hard? I didn't realize. We can't give him any more. It would knock him clean out."

"Well that was quick," Kim observed. "Record time to win through and beat the drug. That isn't in the mission book."

The man was gasping, breathing rapidly with his chest, not with his stomach. And then a long stasis to equalize the hyperventilation.

"What've you do to him!" The woman pushed through so fast that she almost threw Akira over. "You've poison him! He can't breathe! He can't breathe!"

"Don't shake him." Yasmin pulled one of the woman's hands away from the man's shoulders. "Don't shake him, you'll stress him. He's okay. Don't stress him and he's okay."

"Not *stress* him? What you think you're doing to him with your drug!"

"The drug doesn't stress unless you resist. He's resisted. Obviously. The psych conflict causes a nausea and respiratory reaction, a kind of anxiety attack. If we ask him no more questions there's no more conflict, so he's okay. And we ask him no more questions because once he's through to this stage we don't get reliable answers so there's no *point*!" She stood up, stamped away onto the firmer corridor floor, slapped her hand against one of the opposite screens. It rattled, the translucent fabric almost tore.

Steady. Calm and cool and steady. What did you want to ask him anyway—if Nightrider's coming back? Ask the people who seconded you and trained you up and sent you all the way out here just to kill some poor victims who're an enemy because they're designated so. Which makes you an enemy, too. Ask the people who got you into this.

She turned back and looked at Akira. "Why did he break through it so soon?"

Akira shrugged. "Motivation. These people have a real motivation to resist, don't they?"

"Not surprising." Samson shook his head. "Not really surprising. I guess I go back to playing with the computer. We get information much quicker that way than this way. Now I'm talking like an Outsider. We *will* get information much quicker."

"Huh," Kim said. "Let's take them back."

When they took the man back, the others surrounded him, put their arms round him, protected him. But their eyes watched their attackers. How their eyes watched! They said no thank you when Samson carried seven bedrolls through for them, but then he hardly expected them to thank him.

Something like a rumble or a shudder.

Kim awoke in the dimness. Yasmin was asleep along a couch, Samson on a bedroll laid against the wall. Guns and equipment lay everywhere. The empty suits sat like nightmare shadows in a leaning row, backpacks attached, helmets and shoulder yokes folded forward, waiting to swallow their owners. The light came from the open lock through into the sleep section. She stood up, stepped into her overall, shrugged it up to her shoulders and zipped it closed. She started out barefoot, but paused at the edge of the huge dark stain on the floor. The body had long been dragged out and pushed into eternal deep freeze under the base structure. They had kicked out fragments of rib and vertebra with tissue still attached. The base air system must have got rid of the smell before they ever shed their suits.

She padded round the bloodstain. She had never seen anything like that before. The others had all grown up through their childhood and teenage years seeing some level of violence and killing on Earth—most of all Samson in Trinidad, least of all Sandra in Westamerica where the state had mostly organized it all cleanly out of sight. But Sandra was somewhere with Shapir and Nightrider. Shapir was from Luna, too. At Crisium Terminus, at Serenity, there had never been any riots or murders, only a minimum of political eliminations. People and life itself were too valuable off-Earth, far too numerous and cheap Earthside.

Ali sat in the sleep section corridor, facing the lock at the far end, a rifle balanced on its magazine and broad, blunt butt by his side. She padded into the shadowed corner between outer lock and kitchen partition, and climbed up the ladder into the tiny room above.

Akira sat in one of the chairs, his face faintly wash-lit from below by the glow of the base plan and the status displays. He nodded at her arrival. She peered out of one of the windows, tried to look at the stars. Too much instrument light inside—all she saw was her own reflection, very faintly.

"Did it wake you?"

"Something did." She looked at his brooding face. "What was it? I thought I felt something. Heard it, maybe."

"Ground shock. Maybe it's something to do with that reactor pile buried out there. Maybe it's driving a convection and heating mechanism. Maybe it's opening cracks in the ice matrix."

"Ask Samson tomorrow. It's his specialty. Computers, too. He's the only one with anything to do, lucky guy."

"Why?"

"Why lucky? It stops you worrying."

Akira was staring up out of the little window above the instrument board, not seeing anything. "What about?"

She shrugged, a useless gesture in the darkness. "Oh—just Nightrider. What time is it—twenty-three something? That's two and a half days. We should have heard already."

Akira didn't even nod. He went on staring at the empty black window sealing off Hel's night of nights. "I was worrying about the lander. What do we do if the other two Outsiders turn up with their tractor? Suppose they get to the lander before we notice. If they damage it we're here forever, if they get aboard they hold it hostage. A nice standoff."

"Maybe I should move over there. You think so?"

He just held out his hand.

She moved in, let his arm go round her hips, let his head lean against her stomach. She stroked his hair, a short crop growing.

After a while he squeezed her, looked around the shadows again. "We'll figure something out tomorrow."

"Yes. I'll go over there. I'm awake anyway. We can't risk the lander. I don't want to sit here till I die."

"No." He squeezed her, slid his hand. "Take Ali with you. You can take turns sleeping. We all need sleep. By yourself you'd have to stay awake."

304 23:49:10.

Endlessly, motionlessly couch bound in the flight centre was a boring way to spend your time. The routine of living had been reduced to the flight centre couch, or a day room couch to snatch sleep, trips to the hygiene room, hurried snacks. Every time she was a deck too high in the hygiene room she thought, what if a missile comes *now,* so sudden and so close that Nightrider has to hit high gee acceleration *immediately*? Or while I'm coming down the ladder? A full deck fall at 10g would kill you outright, the impact would be like landing from twenty-five metres.

The Outsider raced on ahead of them, still travelling faster, still accelerating marginally slower. He was approaching the two million kilometre maximum separation, after which they would overtake him in velocity terms and start to claw back the enormous spatial and temporal lead. He was a high energy particle beacon, weak now with distance and still diving headlong towards Hades. They had already worked out the range of possible flybys open to him, the choice of tight or more open slingshot hairpin bends he could take around the back of the black dwarf. In principle he could take any physically possible option and sweep out from Hades heading anywhere, but he would want to go *somewhere*. A really tight loop sending him back the way he came was possible, back towards Hel, to try to protect the base there, deal with lingering intruders, or whatever intention he had. But to take that option he would soon have to stop accelerating and coast the rest of the way, or he would be travelling far too fast at Hades encounter. But if he went on pushing up his speed all the way to encounter, then he would whip around the dead star and come out heading almost directly for Tartarus, the bigger of the Hades System's known gas giants, a husbander of moons. Maybe there was already a fuelling station there, functioning or in construction. Or maybe he would want to do a flyby at Tartarus and come looping back on a long haul to Hel, or simply take a course out into the nothing night between here and faraway home.

They would catch him long before then.

It was a boring way to spend your time, watching the systems readouts, immobilized inside your couch under the arm's reach ceiling screen. Shapir was in the day room, presumably asleep. There was only Nightrider to talk to, and he was a determinedly factual conversationalist.

"Incident radar."

Self-writing readouts seized the centre of the screen. The missile frequency radar again. Coming in *that* fast from three degrees off their forward track.

Key the open net. "Shapir! Get in a couch!"

Nightrider wrote out the intercept predict. *So* close!

"What? Couch? I'm in a couch."

"Stay there! Missile coming in. Intercept in forty-eight seconds. Nightrider, cut drive. Attitude manoeuvre tail to flight. Initiate now."

No weight but a visually static, balance whirling world.

"Maintain attitude to aim burn. Missile is target. Run up one to four. Ten gee burn, full thrust on all four, feed from pods A and C." She watched the fusion rocket pinch fields come on, soaking power, saw the slight attitude adjustment figures, movements too small to feel. Saw the missile position running down. "Shapir, pressure your couch."

"Already did."

And do it to your own. Ten gee you've set. It squeezes. It will hold you safe.

Nightrider: "I need a radar track for fine aim."

"Do it." A tail radar running instantly. "Fire a fifteen second burn." That *has* to kill it.

Nightrider: "Missile fired burn. Intercept adjustment."

"Initiate burn *now*."

Nightrider: "Burn initiation—"

"Modify! Four second series with one second re-aiming pauses."

"—mark."

A *kick*. A stamping press. A pile driver that crushes your

chest and stomach through your spine. Without the couch grip your ribs would shatter and your abdomen burst.

Over. Astonishment that your tongue isn't jammed in the back of your throat. Radar snapshot of missile still running.

A pile driver kick, sinking in, clawing at your eyes.

Over. Radar snapshot of missile still running.

Pile driver kick. Slitting your cheeks to your jaw.

Over. Radar blur.

Nightrider: "Fireball. All sensor shields closed. Burn terminated."

We're still alive. We're still alive! But the radiation.

"Attitude manoeuvre. Flip us over tail to the fireball."

A sweeping swing, flung by the couch and the flight centre world. The fireball had passed them, was receding behind, was just a thin envelope made of the radioactive atoms which had once been a missile. But it was better to have Nightrider's solid body between them and it.

Still alive. By two or three seconds at the most. The fireball flash had almost involved the denser vaporization of Nightrider and pilots. Not a game. Not a game at all.

Shapir's feet floated in under the ceiling, steered away to the left across the face of the second screen. Shapir's legs in white overalls, his whole body, eased into the flight centre and manoeuvred down into the recessed couch. He moved his hands to pull himself into the couch, settled back out of sight.

"That," he said, his screen dissolving into a scroll of readout tables and displays, "was close."

"Yes." And don't let your mind lock into it. There are things to do. "Nightrider, can you set up a correction burn to restore our flight path? Say five gee. Do we want to do a correction burn? The Outsider will get two chances to get our flight data."

"He has it already." Shapir sounded cold, must have been masking just how shaken he was. "He knew when the interception was due. He'll have been watching. He predicted us too perfectly from our comsat burns. He can't see us between burns, but he's guessing exactly what we do. His missiles are good, too."

"Yes?"

"Yes. Look at the intercept playback. It was coming in on an exact intercept. He must have launched it somehow with just the right lateral velocity, and it made its own fine adjustment. I guess as soon as it could see us in infrared. Then it made a new adjustment to correct when we cut drive and messed its predict. The burn we saw. And then it made another adjustment when we threw our velocity right out with our own burn. At least one. See the path divergence between our first and second burns? Our burn would have missed if you hadn't modified it. Where'd you learn that?''

You can't shrug in a couch. ''I just invented it. Suddenly realized the target would manoeuvre to keep trying to hit *us*. You realize. You realize—if that thing had switched on its intercept radar ten or fifteen seconds later, we'd be dead. Just dead.''

DAY 305

305 02:23. THE Outsider had some way of *launching* a missile instead of just dumping it alongside in space, leaving it to modify its velocity by its own rocket-flaring efforts alone. The missile had crossed from the Outsider's flight path at its point of launch to Nightrider's flight path at the point of interception —two slowly converging but not yet converged tracks towards Hades—without them seeing the little flicker of a velocity imparting propulsion burn from the missile's own motor. The Outsider had flung in free with the necessary separating velocity seventeen hours before it had arrived. If he had an electromagnetic accelerator that spat out a stream of reaction mass ions, perhaps he had some sort of launch tube that functioned on the same principle. It made him more dangerous —particularly when he used it so well.

His hope would have been to kill them, but even without that success, he still won from the encounter. He won the certain knowledge that they were still following at full predicted acceleration, and that he was still caught in a tail chase that he would eventually lose. He had decisions made for him. He could on no account cut acceleration and coast-fall to Hades for a flyby to sling him back to Hel. They would catch him. And he would not know when, because if he coasted they could afford to cut back the rate of their own invisible acceleration. He would never know when they were going to overtake him for the kill, nor where they were along their predicted track. He could launch no more missiles to save himself. So he had to dive on in to Hades and sweep round the black dwarf core on a path that would take him out towards Tartarus, a long, long haul.

And still they would catch him. He must know that. Even if he cut his drive after Hades encounter and coasted out, they could follow his perfectly predictable path, accelerating as they chose, catching him and killing him at the end of a race to the death.

"He'll want to launch another missile," Sandra said, lounging on the deck and leaning against the seat outside the flight centre door hatch. "But he'll wait. He'll go on accelerating all the way out, so we have to accelerate to catch him and can't diverge at all from the path he predicts for us. And then when he knows we're really close he'll try it with a missile aimed so precisely that it doesn't need to switch on its intercept radar until it's just about hitting us. *Then* he'll see what we can do. Wonder how many of the things he has?"

Shapir was in the flight centre, sprawled on the little panel of deck between the upper halves of the two couches. "He might even know our position better than we know his."

"Not possible. He coasts with a known start velocity, or he uses his nice radiation beacon drive."

"He can coast with an unknown *lateral* component." Shapir looked up at her through the hatch. "He can. He really can."

"How?" she said. "How does he do that?"

"How big is Hades? It's a collapsed stellar core a little bit bigger across than the Earth. What does he do at flyby, from our point of view? He goes round behind it at about a hundred thousand kilometres out. *Behind* it. He's going exactly transverse to our approach when he goes behind, he's travelling at six hundred kilometres a second at encounter, so he's out of sight for less than a minute—"

"No more than half a minute. Right, Nightrider?"

"Two-five seconds," Nightrider replied.

"Okay. So just twenty-five seconds." Shapir looked at nothing, far away at nothing at all inside the tiny space of the flight centre. "He has twenty-five seconds when we can't see him or his drive. What he does with it. So he uses those twenty-five seconds to put on a lateral-to-flight-path velocity without us knowing what it is."

"So? Twenty-five seconds with his drive acceleration gives him all of sixty metres per second. *Metres*. He's going along track at *six hundred kilometres* per second. We'll make our Hades encounter three thousand seconds after him. When we come out from behind, wherever he is *along* track—depending on whether he coasts or accelerates, he'll be all of, what, a hundred eighty kilometres to one side. What's a hundred eighty kilometres?"

"To one side. To which side? Left, right, up, down? And will he have added the full sixty metres a second or less? He'll be somewhere on a disc with a radius of one hundred eighty kilometres. He'll have coasted all the way out from Hades so that we'll know whereabouts the disc is, but not where he is on it."

"You think so? He'd take the consequences of coasting out just to mask a lateral displacement that small?"

"It won't be that small when we catch him up. Slowest option—he coasts out from Hades, and we do too. Our velocity at encounter will be six hundred twelve and a half, so we'll be coasting out twelve and a half faster than him, one point eight million kilometres behind. We'll catch him in round about one hundred fifty thousand seconds. He'll be somewhere on a disc with a ten thousand kilometre radius. Twenty thousand across. We won't have time to find him before we pass him. If we accelerate at full it will take—Nightrider, how long to catch up if he coasts then?"

"Thirty-seven thousand five hundred seconds."

"So he'll be on a disc about—about four thousand five hundred kilometres across. What will our closing velocity be as we overtake him?"

"Nine-three point seven-five kilometres per second."

"So—the search area is smaller, but we have to find him much faster, because otherwise we'll have gone past before we have time to manoeuvre in for a killing burn. But. That doesn't matter anyway."

"I've got you," Sandra said. "I've got you. Whether or not we *could* get him doesn't matter. If we try a radar search of a larger area, he sees *us* the minute we begin searching, whereas the chance of us just happening to fire our first pulse right at him is sort of remote. So he launches a missile at us that will never need to use its motor or its radar to hit the target. We won't see it.''

"And. If we're searching a smaller area on visual only, he still sees us first. His missiles must have some sort of infrared imager to have been able to close on us so exactly before giving themselves away. At the range where we could see him on visual, his own ship imagers will be able to see us—they have to be better than what the missile can carry. The difference is, he'll know exactly where we ought to be at any particular time for any chase acceleration we use. But we won't know exactly where he is. So he sees us first.''

"With the same result.''

"With exactly the same result.''

Sandra shook her head. This was suddenly absolutely no fun any more. It had been essentially a case of them hunting him, but now it was nastier. Much nastier. "What do we do? Give up the chase and head round back to Hel to pick up the lander team? And just hope he doesn't use his drive once we're out of detection range to bring him back somewhere he can intercept us without us knowing he's even coming? We can't risk that. He's too dangerous for that.''

It was still early morning—insofar as there was ever morning or evening in a tiny base on Hades-blacked Hel, any more than in the chronometer circling sameness of the crew module aboard Nightrider. The prisoners in their two sealed off sections were quiet, were doing nothing, just sitting, whispering, waiting.

Samson had found his way through the indexing keys into the data store.

The present base, along with its largely automatic outstations strung out mostly north and south along the "oceanic-continental" plate boundary, was primarily concerned with sorting out the detailed geology of the boundary, checking its stability, and finding suitable sites for geothermal energy recovery and for the exploitation of ore bodies. Sites had already been provisionally located, and the next task was to begin the materials manufacture without which no larger scale operation could be undertaken. The soft-landed supplies brought by the vessel currently on station were to be used to extend the base's accommodation and hydroponics facilities, and to begin construction of the plastics synthesis plant that was supposed to be erected on the now half-destroyed foundation platform out in the middle of the valley floor. The next ship due, already long under way from the Solar System colonies, was bringing more plant and constructional supplies, plus eight new personnel to expand the base crew. Then the plastics synthesis plant would be completed, a rock processor for construction material put together, and the living quarters further extended. For the first time the generating capacity of the now sunken and destroyed fission reactor would have been called on to a significant degree.

The base growth would then be exponential. In two years it would be a proto-colony generating its own power on site and working its own mineral reserves, expanding to daughter locations, and building a support infrastructure that would make the people local catastrophe resistant—there would be somewhere else to run to, and the integrated web of sub-bases would remain self supporting and viable even with an entire element removed. Then the construction of a fuel making reaction-mass plant and storage depot on one of the moons of Tartarus would begin, the proto-colony being by that time capable of meeting all its own material needs, so that the supply ships could divert their bulk payload capacity to depot components, along with ready made high-tech manufactures and *people*. And once the fuel depot was working, the ships could bring incomparably more with each trip. All the lost payload capacity stolen by the need to carry fuel for the return trip accelerations and decelerations would be restored. Hel would already be a full colony, with planned births and a population growth program. In fifteen years it would be as big as Ganymede, in ten more years the Outsider capital. And the same twelve people who had crewed the base from the very start, the same two clone groups, would still be there, senior administrators and proud eldest citizens of the newest and greatest colony, the successor to Earth and the inheritor of the future.

Would have been.

Now three of them were already Hel's first murder victims. Hel's first corpses.

And the base was a living machine deprived of its reactor heart, doomed to run down and die.

The southwest section was dimly lit, minimum light defining the corridor shadows, focusing the gloom. They had to be sure they could keep the base running as long as they needed it: they had taken a long look at the backup power plant under Ali's guidance, and then at the life support machinery under Kim's. Samson was back in the raised communications room, playing with the base computer and watching over the external cameras for any sign of an approaching tractor. Yasmin was taking a turn at guarding the lock that sealed the Outsiders safely into the north and northeast sections.

"So." Akira leaned on the partition wall in the short transverse corridor, looking down the shadowy length of the section. "We can keep things running as long as the fuel cell catalysts hold out. Food will be no problem, air not for a long time yet. If we're in for a long stay we can shut down the lander systems to conserve consumables and hold out here."

"You thinking aloud," Kim asked, "or telling us something?"

No answer. Just a gaze into the gloom.

"There's still no signal from Nightrider," Ali said.

No answer.

"You've taken the opportunity to provide us with hostages and with a long life base to keep them in." Kim shrugged. "Longer life than the lander with us aboard, anyway. That's why you took the risk of coming straight in instead of shooting the place apart first. Planning ahead for the possible. Do we seriously prepare for a standoff with hostages?"

Akira sought among the shadows. "Nightrider's fallible. He missed the lander's position update. The Outsider is armed. But that doesn't mean anything will go wrong."

"If it does." Ali sought his own shadows, too. "How do we get out of here? There's no follow up mission coming behind."

"It isn't an eventuality allowed for in the mission planning. Our job is to eradicate the base."

"Turn ourselves into a suicide mission?"

Kim shook her head. "If Nightrider doesn't make it back, we already are one. The Outsiders aren't going to be nice and ferry us home for attacking them, are they?"

"We might have prisoner exchange value if there's ever going to be a war."

"Intelligence value," Akira said. "We know enough about Nightrider's systems. They'd squeeze us absolutely dry. Don't want to experience that."

Kim looked at Ali, shadowed faces in shadow.

305 09:50. Eight minutes to the Outsider's Hades encounter. The ion drive beacon on its track predict was already swinging so steeply around the concentrated mass of the lightless cinder that it was moving almost laterally to the line of its long approach path—a path that Nightrider was supposed to be following, 1.8 million kilometres and three thousand seconds behind. But Nightrider was the predicted time and distance away, travelling at the predicted velocity—but not on the track. Nightrider was a quarter of a million kilometres to the right of track, as measured in the plane of the ecliptic from faraway terrestrial north. They were not going to follow in a right-hand hairpin bend around Hades, tail chasing the Outsider whether he coasted or still used his drive. They were going to meet him coming out the other side.

The Outsider's track and flight parameter readouts showed clearly, lifted out of space from most of two million kilometres away. The predict display was in deep three-D. The traced approach path plunged in towards the black dot representing invisible Hades, became a brief section of predict that disappeared behind the left side of the primary and then reappeared on the right, sweeping round to come out again at a twenty degree angle of separation from the approach path. A first beginning of a long course locked on Tartarus. But the emerging predict was no line—it was the slenderest representable cone around a thread core. It was the predict for a coasting free fall flight with an imposed component of lateral velocity, a slow drift to one side or the other, up or down. It was the volume of space that would contain the Outsider's true course.

Nightrider's projected track went in towards Hades on the same side. It intersected the core line of the outward climbing predict. That point in space and moment in time was at 1,500 seconds after the Outsider's Hades encounter. At the intersect the Outsider's path cone would be one hundred and seventy-four kilometres across. The Outsider would be travelling at six hundred kilometres every second and Nightrider at six hundred and five. They would meet head on.

He wouldn't even be looking for them. He would think they were still falling in towards the dead star on a following track, fifteen hundred seconds from flyby, three thousand behind him—passing him undetectably, going in the opposite direction almost a quarter of a million kilometres away across the ecliptic. He wouldn't see them before they saw him. He could never react in time to launch a missile *ahead* of himself against them. With a lower drive acceleration he couldn't outmanoeuvre them. At a lateral separation of only eighty-seven kilometres their fusion exhaust would burn him like a torch.

And then they would fall on in towards Hades, whip around it, and curve out on a path heading initially almost directly out for the Solar System, a path that would take days of correction to bring them back to Hel.

If he wasn't going to use the trick, if he came out accelerating all the way, then they would have him just as surely, seeing him come. But if he missed him. They could never manoeuvre themselves into a flyby to take them out after him towards Tartarus. They would have to let him go and head for Hel to collect the lander team and leave for home. And hope he wasn't intercepting them, cutting coasting in to kill from the sudden dark.

The Outsider was sixty seconds away from Hades. His drive trace stopped. That would give him time to change his attitude to be ready to impose a lateral acceleration while out of sight behind the black dwarf.

"Closest approach predict holds," Nightrider announced. "Oh-nine five-eight oh-five."

"He's behind," Sandra said. "If he's doing it. If he's doing it."

A tiny dot of denser colour appeared on the predict line just to the right of Hades.

"No drive trace yet."

"Shapir, if we were going in behind him now we'd be in a mess. We'd be in a mess." Figuring out the implications and deciding whether to follow or to call off the chase.

Just a tiny dot to the right of Hades. No readout where the ion drive data had been. Seconds counting round. They were coming up to the point where they should cut their own drive and fall free along their projected path to make the intercept predict. Still no readout from the Outsider, no detectable trace of him, vanished in space as if swallowed up by Hades.

"Nightrider," Shapir said, "cut drive to zero."

The dot of denser colour moving along the predict track had expanded to a tiny disc. Somewhere in the area of space represented by that disc was the Outsider ship. Somewhere. At intercept that disc of space would be one hundred and seventy-four kilometres wide, the Outsider nailed to it as it swept lightless nothing at six hundred kilometres every second, as it swept towards Nightrider at twice that speed. A terrifying closing speed, leaving so little time to locate and aim and kill.

The sweep and tracking radars checked out. The visual sensors saw nothing, of course. They fell free tail first towards the intercept, towards Hades, already oriented for the burn. Visual and infrared views were locked to the faraway target disc. The visual saw nothing but a star field, the stars gradually shrinking together and more crowding in from the sides as the slowly expanding disc moved nearer. 10:12:59—ten minutes to the intercept. Half a million kilometres.

The expanded display of the intercept predict had its along-track dimension reduced one hundred times with respect to the lateral dimensions so as to cope with the enormous closing velocity and the minute lateral separation.

"Nightrider," she said, "run a visual and IR sweep at max magnification around the perimeter. He's most likely to have given himself the full lateral component and be out there."

"We won't see him yet," Shapir said.

"I just want to believe he's there." Because he has vanished, and your Earth born senses say he has gone.

"Let's pre-set the burn, Nightrider. Ten gee on all four, feed from pods A and C. If we run a burn series and empty them, switch feed to pods B and D."

"Do I jettison A and C on switching?"

"Yes. No. No, retain them."

"That's inefficient. Waste mass to accelerate."

"But they'll make decoy targets if he gets a missile launched at us. Retain them."

"You don't see anything, Nightrider?"

"No. Perimeter sweep completed. No contact."

"Okay. Try scanning the whole disc. What do you think? How long do we wait before we use the radar?" They couldn't afford to miss him. It was a one shot chance.

Shapir didn't answer straight away. As soon as they activated the radar they gave themselves away, gave the Outsider a possible chance to launch a missile, gave him a certain chance to try an avoidance manoeuvre. He didn't have the acceleration to escape, but it would complicate the aim. "At minus one-twenty, if we haven't seen him by then. That will give him two minutes to react. That's long enough."

"Yes. Something else just occurred to me. Suppose he has fusion boosters? He could have. He's had no reason to use them so we wouldn't have seen them. Suppose he can do to us what we can do to him?"

Silence for a moment.

"If he could do that he wouldn't have needed to run and leave the base unprotected. I assume."

"No."

Seven and a half minutes to intercept, and still nothing to see but a field of crowded stars.

10:20:19. One hundred sixty seconds to intercept, two hundred thousand kilometres out. He was racing in towards them on a disc of empty blackness, a magic circle computed into existence in the three-way vacuum matrix of lightless nothing. If he was there. He had to be there.

"I have an IR contact," Nightrider said. "Lower search perimeter." Down at the bottom of that expanding circle.

"Visual check," Shapir said.

"Running."

The infrared contact was already marked on the intercept display, already entered with a bright cross onto the anonymous star field view. One hundred thirty seconds to intercept.

"Visual contact."

A magnified excerpt of the star field conjured itself in each screen. The stars blended out. They left something behind, a pinpoint gleam, starlight dull.

"Spectrum?" Sandra demanded.

"Various metals. Plastics."

"That's him. Got him."

"Burn at ten gee on all four as pre-set. Burn initiation at intercept minus forty. Commence and maintain aim from now."

Readouts said that Nightrider adjusted his flight attitude fractionally, swinging from an exactly tail-to-flight orientation. An adjustment too slight to perceive.

"Nightrider, you need a tracking radar for a precision aim? We don't want to miss."

"It would be helpful."

"Okay. Activate a tracking radar at burn minus fifteen. That shouldn't give him any useful warning."

"Burn configuration," Shapir said. "Thirty seconds continuous burn maintained on aim predict. Continue maintaining aim while we look at the result. Standby for a second burn."

"Suggest modification. Five burns of six seconds each, with a one second assessment pause. He might manoeuvre."

"He's right," Sandra said. "He might."

"Okay, five times six second burns. Show us each assessment during the succeeding burn."

There he was, a little light speck devoid of detail, seventy thousand kilometres away and tearing closer. The Outsider ship caught after three days chasing. He should have been as black as Nightrider. He might have lived.

Tracking radar activation. Sixty-six thousand kilometres away, sixty-five. And just eighty-seven kilometres down off track, going to pass so *close*. Tracking radar lock. No chance of a miss. Could he withstand thirty seconds of Nightrider's dragon breath? No ship could be built that solidly—it would be too massive ever to fly. Fifty-four thousand kilometres. Burn at forty-eight, at intercept minus forty seconds. Still no details to see. The readouts record Nightrider's fractional swing, pitching gradually down.

The sensors blanked.

"Burn initiation, mark."

The pile driver again, stripping skin from your face, pumping breath from you and the couch. Your eyes are held open to stare at the ceiling screen that doesn't crash down.

A breath second and a sensor snapshot.

The burn again, the *weight*. If you could vomit it would kill you. In the snapshot view the Outsider is there. No bigger, no brighter, no freeze frame flash of attitude jets as he swings to make an escape manoeuvre. Reaching out through the night to him is a streak of incandescent sun.

A breath second and another snapshot.

Then the weight, the sheer *weight*. And the Outsider sits in a sunfire flare while a second slashes out at him.

A breath. A sensor shot.

The pile driver plunge. Snapped in the gap between the tail of one fire snake and the jaws of another, while a third disperses far away. Snapped in the gap, he *glows* white hot.

A breath pause.

Then the weight and the view. And a strip of sun is plunging into a fireball blur.

"Cut the burn." Shapir got it out over his tongue.

Free fall. Free fall that lasts two seconds, like losing your body blissfully, like dissolving in a self-sea.

"Keep us tail-on to the fireball."

Nightrider pitches perceptibly. The fireball is almost too dispersed to shine. Its centre will pass eighty-seven kilometres away. An envelope of radiating dust and debris ripping by at such a collision speed. Nightrider pitches sickeningly, vilely, horrifyingly.

"Debris! Is that a debris strike?"

"Negative. No debris strike."

Nightrider was still pitching round, but smooth and slow, keeping his tail to the receding ruined target.

"We should have thought of that," she said. "At this speed—closing velocity plus the explosion ejection. A little fragment would cripple us. A chunk would blow us apart."

"Suggest a radar sweep to locate and track large debris."

"You bet."

"Wait," Shapir said. "Suppose he got a missile off. Launched backwards. We'll tell it exactly where we are."

"Huh. However he kicks them out, it's going away at most of twelve hundred kilometres a second. It's going to be way past us already." However he *kicked* them out. Not any more.

The fireball had faded but the debris dust glowed hot and bright. There was a constellation of incandescent pinpoints caught within it. Larger chunks and ship shreds.

"All radar contacts are doppler shifted to lower frequency," Nightrider reported. "All separating from us. Echo strength indicates some fragments to be two to three metre size."

"Bits of shielding," Shapir said. "Drive magnets."

They had killed him. The Outsider was just gas and dust and debris expanding on its way to Tartarus, eventually to settle into some eternal orbit around Hades. A man made time marker, a ghost, a visitor who would never leave again, never go home.

Time to snap out of it, Shapir. That's two minutes gone. No—three. You're falling at a mad speed towards Hades, towards a flyby that will fling you out heading somewhere. It has to be modified. There's the lander team to pick up.

"Nightrider, run the parameters of courses back to Hel."

One course graphic and data table rippled onto the screen. It was the original projection through the intercept predict to a free fall flyby, with just an initial correction burn to restore the flight characteristics thrown by the manoeuvre which had just killed the Outsider. Coming out of the flyby they could run the drive at one hundred percent transverse to their flight direction, bending it around and then deceleration breaking over sixteen days until they came in to orbit injection at Hel. Nice and neat and perfect, and not at all what was wanted.

"No good," Sandra said for him. "Sixteen days. The lander has a max twenty-two day endurance, and three days are already gone. That's cutting the margin too close."

"To make a faster transit we have to make a slower flyby," Nightrider answered. "We would have to shed flight speed using the fusion boosters. They are our defence weapon."

"I think we want to get there as fast as we can."

"We don't want to have to run the drive for sixteen days, Nightrider," he said. "It's the drive that gets us home in realistic time. Running it for sixteen days might overload the system. And it would cut right into our return voyage reserve. We'd take our feedstock down to around half the planned minimum."

"We couldn't push ourselves up so fast, Nightrider. We'd take two years to get home. Some prospect."

"The boosters still have enough fuel for five hundred eighty some seconds at ten gee, and we don't have any more foreseeable targets. What's the point in dragging all that around? We'll use it to slow us down for the flyby. We want one to take us right back the way we came."

"I get the sudden feeling," Sandra said, "as though I just want to pick them up and go."

"Yes." As if the reason for being here had just burst.

"A two hundred second burn at ten gee would allow a transit time to Hel of eleven days. Four hundred seconds at five gee would be preferable.''

''Nightrider.'' Sandra sounded impatient. ''We came here in three days. How do we get back as quickly? Quicker, if possible.''

''We need to conserve the fusion boosters. The transit time is safely within the lander endurance limit.''

Nightrider's voice couldn't adopt emotional states. It was always politely neutral in tone. But he was sure it wasn't neutral in meaning. For the first time ever. ''Nightrider, are you arguing with us?''

''Look, Nightrider, we know you're programmed to make yourself independent. You already started out fully systems and enactment competent. But you've a long way to go before you get to be planning decision independent. You have to work up to that. First step, manoeuvre configuration and construction. Just take it a step at a time.''

''I can do manoeuvre configuration and construction. I don't make mistakes when I learn.''

''No.'' She was silent for a moment. He had absorbed her own series-burn trick when both of them had forgotten it. ''Doubtless you don't. But just accept our planning decisions. You're not independent yet.''

''I'm constrained to learn independence.''

He was arguing, really arguing. Just that his voice couldn't turn sharp or hard. He was asserting his rights, in whatever terms his programs coded them.

''The decision,'' Shapir said, ''is this. We allow a five gee burn for one thousand seconds. That will leave us with eighty some seconds at ten gee for defensive manoeuvres. That's almost twice all we've used so far for four targets. There's nothing in the mission book says we have to take all this reaction mass back with us. It's there for us to use however we like. So let's see the course a burn like that could give us back to Hel.''

''And now, Nightrider. Right now. We're already seventeen minutes to Hades encounter.

A thousand second burn ran for sixteen minutes and forty seconds, a full quarter of an hour squashed under five times your Earth weight. Even in the couch it was far too much, a crushing physical drain. And it might have been too much for the boosters, extending them beyond their design limits and test proving. They watched the operational readouts all the way.

They emerged from the burn already past the flyby, past closest approach. They had shed so much speed that Hades was able to grip them tight and whirl them around itself before they broke free, heading out almost back the way they had come, a slingshot hurled at Hel. They had jettisoned six of the eight booster units as they emptied, first pods A and C, then pods B and D, then the rocket motor pods one and three. Just two and six remained, still with enough fuel to drive them at 10g for eighty-three seconds. The others fell in black pairs on orbits all of their own, empty partners in a never ending night dance.

They emerged from the burn racing away from Hades at almost five hundred and forty kilometres every second. But the grip of the dead star reached after them, its gravitational drag slowed them down. At twenty-five million kilometres from Hades, at Day 306 00:50:20, they would activate the drive and decelerate all the way to Hel. The encounter with the planet would be on Day 308 at 08:23:40, arriving at exactly orbital velocity behind the planet, injecting into an orbit to bring them round over the base location, over the waiting lander. Nice and neat and perfect. But then celestial mechanics is nature's motion clockwork. It is absolutely precise.

No one looked at Hades, a lightless mass squeezing more than half the material of a sun into a volume the size of the Earth. Scientific observations weren't in the mission book.

They had hours of free fall and nothing more to chase. They ran a detailed systems check to ensure that everything was still functioning properly after one thousand seconds of 5g load. They checked the drive systems and the main reactor, their only way home. From the beginning of the final approach to Hel, the power and propulsion tandem had run virtually uninterrupted until the last twenty minutes before they intercepted the Outsider—a period of five days, its longest ever continuous use. The tension had so suddenly snapped after the killing of the Outsider ship. They wanted to do anything rather than think about it, about the risk they had taken of misguessing or mishandling the intercept, and either missing the Outsider completely so that he might present an unpredictable danger for them as long as they remained in the Hades System, or else getting themselves killed outright.

They ate, they showered, they went exhausted to their cubicles, the first time sleeping in them for three days. They asked Nightrider to send them to sleep and to wake them in two hours' time.

Nightrider sends them to sleep and watches them floating in their chosen dimness, the recessed corner lights reduced to orange pearls for Shapir, only the chronometer number gleam for Sandra. Nightrider listens to their heartbeats and breathing, monitors the temperature and humidity and sweat excretion rise in the air slowly circulating out of their cubicles. Nightrider thinks about past and future actions. The mission is a performance trial and the mission book constrains to produce maximum performance. Nightrider has made two performance errors at Hel, has failed to predict the Outsider's course decisions as Sandra and Shapir predicted them, has failed to perceive the reasons for the to-Hel return transit decision, has failed to delay the return to Hel where two performance errors have been made which have still to be resolved. The performance is not maximum. The constraint is to produce maximum performance. There is a discrepancy to alleviate, performance errors to eradicate. And Nightrider has learned how to kill and must assimilate the knowledge.

Ali and Kim had figured out how to drive the tractor. They had sorted out all the power and control and communications systems, together with the life support—which wasn't important because no one was going to make a long trip.

They sat in the two control seats in front of the flat windows that reflected them floating outside in the blank black night. Akira and Yasmin leaned over them and watched as they ran through the control functions. The most important was the mode selection. Having six swinging, rotating and extending legs arranged in three pairs, the tractor possessed a whole range of walking modes to allow for various speeds and varying manoeuvrability over different types of terrain. What most of the modes were was indecipherable, would have to be determined by experiment, but the basic mode was all they would need. It would take them at moderate speed across flat and level ground, which was what they wanted. The full agility of such a machine was not needed. There were fold-down viewing screens to give them natural or image intensified views ahead or sideways or behind—whichever direction they wanted to move in—but those they wouldn't need. There were external lights to flood the ground ahead to allow for direct vision driving, the easiest method of all. But those they wouldn't use.

The machine was tiny for something designed to house two crew for weeks and even months on end, if replenished at one of the outstation dumps. Behind the control seats were two parallel bunks up high above stores lockers and a food cooker and the life support machinery. Jammed in behind them were a toilet cubicle and the tail lock side by side. The lock opened straight through a docking collar into the dim base section. Packed under the floor were the fuel cells that powered it. Outside, along the sides and across the tail, an apron reaching out over the top joints of the hydraulic legs, was a loading platform. It could be stacked with supplementary consumables, it could be accessed direct through the lock without any need to step down to the ground. It turned the tractor into a supply ferry to the outstation dumps.

"If we go, we can drive by starlight on the flat," Ali said. "We'll need a co-driver with a starscope watching the ground ahead. But we don't need the lights."

The idea was to be able to move out and meet the missing tractor if it came, getting to it long before it got anywhere near the lander. But if it saw them coming it might turn and run, and they didn't have the time to practice driving until they could be sure of being able to follow fast and safe. They could afford an accident as little as they could afford to have two tool-armed and pre-warned Outsiders sneaking around in the dark, trying to get at the lander. The lander was exactly as precious as life.

Kim patted the control console. "Pity we can't play with it. This thing is real neat. From the mode range I'd guess it can cross real big cracks, climb and traverse slopes, turn in its own length, sidestep. It could do anything if you knew how. Go anywhere."

Yasmin shook her head. "Not anywhere. Not over that terrain on the slope just south of here it wouldn't."

"But we can travel," Akira said. "We can move on the flat."

Ali nodded. "No problem. Unless we stray north where the

ice is hotter. We don't want to go through."

"No." Akira looked at their reflections in the black windows. If the other tractor came it would probably come using its lights. But how could you arrange an all round watch to pick up its approach? "We still need a way of monitoring for the other tractor. We need to see it first. Maybe Samson can figure something."

"Oh, I already have an idea," Kim said. "I think I can set up the lander computer so it monitors an all round view. Get the cameras to track continuously. I think I can program it for image matching if it has the right base routines. That way any change—like a tractor appearing where there wasn't one before—should set off an alarm. Which would give us our warning."

Sandra was strapped to the saddle of the exercise bike, not pedalling at all. She just had her feet hooked into the stirrup straps as an additional anchor. Behind her was the outer wall, to the right the doorway to the galley walk-through, to the left the doorway to the workshop. Shapir hung at a slant head down across the central core, coupled to the med tester by the cable of the blood pressure collar. He was stripped to his briefs. He was, she thought, an attractive sight. It had after all been four days since there had been the time. Since then they seemed to have spent most of the time trapped in the acceleration couches, spinning round Hel, and then watching the track of the Outsider. Time now to relax, to try to relax. But looking at the intercept recordings hadn't helped. It was difficult to cope with, to see a solid thing the size of a ship enveloped in a plasma tongue, to see its outer structure *glowing* with white metal heat. To see it seconds later already erupted into thermonuclear nothing after its reactor had disintegrated and let out its own power heart to touch off its feedstock reserves. It was a difficult thing to cope with.

"You realize," she said. "That was the first ever ship-to-ship kill in space. If you discount their propaganda claims about that accident they had with a freighter. First ever ship kill. We've entered a new age of history. A great new plus for civilization."

Shapir had taken hold of a grab handle and was turning himself over to read the med centre's conclusions better. "I'm not quite sure what you mean. History is a justification base or a disputation base for present politics. Even contemporary records are edited and interpreted. Pragmatic rationalism pretends to no access to past objective fact, and all that. You just react non-interpretatively to contingencies of the real-time situation, planning towards outcomes, not from alleged causes. History exists as a fact in the same way as the past did, but as a decision base it's a fake.''

"Ah, you're too orthodox." If you could be pragmatic *and* orthodox. Maybe that was the mistake. Every age made its massive political mistake.

"I'm too excited. Systolic and diastolic both up, heart rate up. That's five and a half hours since the flyby.''

305 16:30, the chronometer said.

"I'm not excited. I'm down." She rotated the pedals a couple of times. "What I meant was, how many people did we kill? Two flight crew, twenty? And passengers? Science and who knows what. How many people?''

"Not many." He let the cuff deflate. "People are the Outsiders' most precious resource. And if you want to turn moral." He twisted so as to look at her. "Why didn't you think about that when we took out the base?''

She shrugged. She rubbed pale palmed brown hands together, then let the problem escape from them. "There was plenty more to do.''

"Why didn't you think of it before we took out the base? From the start this has been a killing mission.''

"Obviously I thought of it. You did. We all did. And I'm not being moral. What's morality got to do with reality? Pragmatics hasn't replaced ethics. Ethics was always just an abstract.''

"I never heard of ethics.''

"We take out the base because Earth can't afford them to be here. It makes them too dangerous.''

"So we're told.''

"And what you *really* think about before it's over, is what if it happens to *me*, not them.''

"Yes." He slipped the cuff and the med tester reeled it automatically in. "We're lucky they aren't wondering how many people they killed.''

"Ah, we wouldn't know about it.''

"We would have done.''

He pushed out across the space, floating past her to the sharp curve of the wall, taking hold of one of the torsion pulley bars. His overall was looped through a holding strap there, tethered and awaiting him. He freed it, steadied himself in mid-air, then shook out the garment in preparation for the slick dressing move.

"Let's just relax," she said, head turned, watching him move. A light toned half-Iranian body all the way from the Moon, neat and wiry and taut. Such entertainments are spacing's greatest asset. "Think of the lander team. If we took the base clean out with that one pass, they won't have had anything to do except take a look at the hole and then just sit around or lie around in their nice little nest. Cramped, maybe, but nice."

"They won't be relaxing much." He doubled up, pushed his feet into the legs, straightened out and pulled the overall to his hips. "Not until they know we're on our way to pick them up." He hooked his hands into the drifting sleeves and started to hitch the overall up to his shoulders.

"*That's* what we've forgotten." They would be sitting down there waiting and waiting. "Now the Outsider's out of the way there's no reason we can't flash a signal."

"No, there isn't." He zipped up his overall. "Nightrider, send them a signal saying we're okay, the Outsider is destroyed, and we're heading back. Give them a fix on our flight data so they'll know where we'll be if they want to signal back. Maybe they have something to say."

"Is it wise to signal, Shapir? It will inform anyone else there of our continued presence. If the lander team were tempted to reply, they would announce their position."

"They won't reply unless they think it's safe. Not if we don't specifically request a response."

"I still think it's unwise, Shapir. If we include flight data someone else might also obtain a fix on us."

"Decrypt our signal?" Sandra laughed. "They can't do that to us any more than we can do it to them."

"We have to send a data fix. Otherwise how can they predict where we are just in case they have something to tell us? Just suppose they've just found out there's a second ship or something." Shapir took hold of a torsion pulley bar again. "Without our course they can't transmit on fine beam, and that really would tell anyone else where they are."

"You've said it yourself, Shapir. There might be another ship on station at Hel. Our signal would warn it."

"But they wouldn't get a course predict from one single transmission source."

"Look, Nightrider. We've wiped out everything that was there, and the lander team will want to know we still exist. We're their ride home." And there she was suddenly feeling the need to *look* at Nightrider to talk to him, but not wanting to make the effort of twisting towards the monitor lens on the deck head behind her. Which wasn't looking at him anyway. He was just supercooled computer circuitry buried inaccessibly down under the floor of the flight centre, the only part of their tacked-on crew module which really contacted Nightrider proper. "And why are you talking to Shapir all the time? Don't you speak to me any more?"

"I'm sorry, Sandra. No offence meant. I was discussing with Shapir."

She looked at Shapir. Shapir shrugged.

She shook her head. "Nightrider, just send the signal. Okay?"

Nightrider apparently accepted.

"He's really getting talkative," Shapir said.

"He's getting argumentative."

"He heard that." Shapir glanced at the monitor lens, but then dismissed whatever he had been thinking. "I'm hungry."

Nightrider watches everything. The elapse time—305 21:41:06. The systems plan countdown to the drive initiation that Sandra and Shapir have ordered. They want to sleep. They are in Shapir's cubicle.

Sandra had hold of the recessed handles of the locker drawers, swaying them softly in the tight little free floating space. Her legs were wrapped around Shapir's hips, her ankles crossed beneath his buttocks. He squeezed her hips gently with his thighs, pivoting. He held her waist with one hand, with the other he thumbed her clitoris and pushed softly against her belly to slide out, to let her pull him in. Out and in. Moans and breaths and chuckles and gasps, swinging as Sandra twisted her back.

* * *

Access: Executive Memory (slot 037 00:00:00 to 037 06:00:00).

Search: slot (crew-comm + episode frame).

Retrieve: frame (037 05:20 to 037 05:53).

Sandra and Shapir float in a ball of arms and legs and backs in Sandra's cubicle. Sandra sucks at Shapir's penis, Shapir licks Sandra's clitoris and vulva. Soft non-verbal vocalizations indicating satisfaction. Nightrider has access to the *crew function* data paradigm, to *behaviour (social)* and *behaviour (sexual)*, to *anatomy*, to personal data. Nightrider knows the designations, here: *fellatio, cunnilingus*. Sex is a psych support function. It is necessary in order to maintain optimal psych status and therefore optimal mission component function. But how does sex achieve this? The explanation that human behaviour is human behaviour is inadequate. In 37 days of elapse time Nightrider has not understood *behaviour (sexual)*. The others all sleep, long sleep and normal. Sleep is redundant-function suspension. Sleep is comprehensible.

Decision: crew-comm (Decision: low volume).

Nightrider: *could you explain why you're doing this?*

Sandra takes Shapir's penis from her mouth. A saliva thread floats away.

Sandra, flat intonation, low volume: *not now Nightrider*.

Shapir licks his lips.

Shapir: *privacy Nightrider*.

Sandra sucks Shapir's penis. Shapir licks Sandra's clitoris. They bump gently into a padded wall. They drift free.

Consult: *crew-comm advisement* (context: *copulation*).

Advisement: not communicate except flight/systems status change relevant.

Return: frame (037 05:20 to 037 05:53).

They sway in the padded box of Shapir's cubicle as Sandra twists and moans, as Shapir pushes and plays. Nightrider watches. Nightrider watches systems and data flows, the motionless stars and the speeding void, the electromagnetic silence, Nightrider's own thoughts and memories. Nightrider watches everything.

Ali and Samson had extended the data channel linking the lander and the base, Kim had succeeded in her trick of programming the lander computer to watch for and respond to changes in the static frozen desert of Hel. Programming it for shape recognition would have been beyond her ability and would have taken too much time, but it was necessary. The computer merely had to compare pixels then and now, searching for intensity changes. Like the lights of a tractor marching home.

Samson had keyed an alarm that would flash up in the communications room if the lock sealing off the Outsiders was tampered with from the other side. The guard watch could be held from up there, where a monitor camera view looked along the empty sleep accommodation section towards the sealed lock, where more cameras looked at the Outsiders doing nothing but doze or sleep, where the data link from the lander would tell them if something appeared, if a signal came in from Nightrider. It was 23:20 by their own time. It was Samson's watch.

Akira came up through the ladder hole into the instrument glow darkness. Samson was just a shaped shadow sitting there, eyes faintly gleaming as he turned his head.

"They doing anything?"

"They never do anything. They don't even make a fuss." Samson brought up a screen brightness, highlighting himself. In the screen colourfully clothed figures with suntanned limbs curled up or stretched out on mattresses in a corridor.

"They'll be thinking. The base won't last for ever, even if it might keep them alive until the next ship comes in. But that ship isn't going to be carrying anything they can use to rebuild the place."

"No. I found its payload schedule. No spare power reactor."

"And they're trapped here. No way up or down, so they die."

"Unless." Samson shrugged shadow shoulders. "*Our* lander."

"Exactly." He changed the subject, but not to the one he had come for. "How's your arm?"

"Uncomfortable. The swelling's gone down, but it's stiff and sort of hard right from wrist to elbow. But it works." He flexed dark fingers.

"It's going to be days before the fluid disperses. Then the colour will start. That'll be dramatic."

"So I'm told. You didn't come up here to tell me that."

"No." Outsiders apparently peacefully asleep in a screen. "I guess there's still no signal from Nightrider?"

"If there was I'd wake you up cheering. Are you worried?"

"Aren't you?"

DAY 306

TOUCH. And *that* consciousness fades again forever . . .

A touch on naked skin. On toes and knees and thigh and hip, on belly and chest and breast, on shoulder and arm and back of hand, on cheek and ear. A smooth padded touch, warm in a warm world behind eyelids defending the dark. Such a soft touch, landing from a dream, a free fall dream, kissed by the nest cell floor as the drive slides on. Landed inside a sleep cell in a ship life falling, braking, towards Hel, a frozen little planet seventy some million kilometres from Hades, a lightless cinder circling forever nowhere, fifty-one billion kilometres from the Sun and its light and its dependent life, a little star near the no-account edge of an unspectacular galaxy in a space-time continuum that began inside what and is going where? Silliest sleepiest thoughts.

Did I land or have I landed? Was the drive on, or did it come on?

Eyes open on nothing but black. Are your eyes open? Look lazily round for the chronometer glow. Which way? Lift. Lift head and shoulders and half your body half clear of the following floor, twist on its rolling softness. The backs of your legs touch tufted wall. So here we are, so there's the chronometer.

306 00:52, a floating glow in nothing. So the drive has just come on.

"Nightrider?" murmured, more or less. "Status okay?"

"Nominal, Sandra."

Sink back again. The soft, soft floor. "Signal from the lander?"

"No signal, Sandra."

The soft, soft floor. They couldn't have signalled instantly, of course. There was the transit time to Hel and back, their reaction time, the delay before they checked for incoming signals logged. But the message went out hours ago. It included no request for a response, but they *would* respond. They had waited and waited and would understand the waiting. They would reassure us that *they* were okay. They would respond. But maybe not now. Maybe they were asleep or something. Asleep.

306 07:42 said the chronometer on the central core above the larder drawers and the little ovens.

She sat on the bench that curved round the back of the tight little galley table. Her fingers circled a cup of sweetened pineapple and lime squash standing on the table, an empty yogurt tub and rye bread crumbs lay between the ramparts of her forearms. A light little breakfast to begin a low energy day. Hel encounter and things to do not due for forty-eight hours. Almost forty-nine.

Shapir dropped down the ladder from the upper deck, steering himself with sliding hands, landing lightly. One quarter Earth weight is an easy world. He stepped over the little door sill into the galley walkthrough leading to the exercise space. He glanced up at the chronometer. He rolled up the door of the larder cool cupboard and pulled out the fruit drinks drawer. He selected two lidded cups and turned to put them down on the table. Both grapefruit, plain.

He caught her eye. "That's twenty-eight minutes. That's twice the two-way transit time. More."

She nodded. He too had decided the lander team would have sent a reassurance signal even without a specific request. After all, they had been together—at first with others, who dwindled away—for a year of training and then for ten months of isolated transit out from Earth. They were all family together.

So they had sent a second signal, with a specific request to respond. They had forestalled any alarmist argument from Nightrider by just giving him an order. Then they had readied themselves for the day, and it was coming up to half an hour now.

Shapir closed the drawer and rolled down the cool cupboard door. He took two butter filled rolls from the bread box and put them into the microwave to heat. Butter—an exorbitant luxury back on Earth, nonexistent on Luna. He tapped the time code into the oven. ''You any ideas, Nightrider?''

''I can only think that some kind of eventuality has damaged the lander's communications function. That's the lowest level capability loss that could account for the lack of a response.''

''And the highest level?''

''Destruction of the lander.''

''And the team,'' Sandra said. ''The lander goes, they go with it. Shapir, have you noticed how long his sentences are getting now? And he's filling them up with qualifications all the time. All about the fact that he thinks something.''

Shapir shrugged. ''If we ask his opinion?'' He opened the microwave and transferred the hot buns to the table. ''Anyway.'' He sat down against the exercise space partition wall, slid one place along the seat. ''We don't have to conclude that they're dead yet.''

''We don't. We don't. But I was thinking.'' She watched him peel the lids off the cups. ''All the things that could have gone wrong. There was a systems failure and they crashed. Or there was a second missile in orbit and it got them, maybe even on the ground. Or something went wrong down there. There were other Outsiders away from the base when we burned it, or it's an armoured base, or there were heavily armed survivors. Or there was a second ship, just arrived or there all the time. All sorts of things.''

Shapir shrugged. ''They never pretended to us this was a zero risk operation.''

''No. But then they also didn't tell us that the landing part of the mission was going to look more and more like a blind-planned high-risk adventure. What's their nice word for it—*opportunistic*. Taking advantage of the circumstances of the mission, the nature of the target, and Nightrider's payload capability. Something just thrown in at relatively low additional cost just in case it paid off. Sounds more and more like afterthought planning.''

''The crew module was planned years ahead and is built for seven people. I don't think opportunistic means just thrown in.'' He sipped his grapefruit juice, he turned his head to look up at the chronometer. ''But that doesn't mean something couldn't go wrong.''

''No.''

''No.'' He fingered his bread roll. Butter was melting through it onto the table. They needed the pressure of a more social life to make them eat with plates again. ''Nightrider, maybe you should send repeat call-up signals at thirty minute intervals.''

''Exactly,'' she said. ''Just what I was thinking.''

''Is that such a good idea, Shapir? It will mark our course for anyone else who's listening.''

''That doesn't matter, Nightrider. We can modify our course just as soon as we know they're okay.''

Kim and Ali came in through the corner lock, huge bulking night black shapes with human faces inside. Their black skins turned instantly white, suddenly technological apes with ice crystal fur and an aura of absolute cold. They stood there waiting, well clear of anything they could freeze to. Without the lander lock's power umbilical to heat the suit's outer surface, it was a tedious time before it was safe to clamber out of the things. You had to wait until the ice had melted again and the matt surface of the suit was free even of condensation. It took a while. It was extremely—extremely—cold outside.

Yasmin came down from the communications room, picked up one of the utterly ugly snub and back-magazined and buttless rifles, and stood in the open lock through to the sleep section where she could stop any sudden breakout by the Outsiders in the absence of a warning from the telltale instruments above. Samson fetched himself a more or less tomato thing from the kitchen, one of the last remnants of the hydroponics harvest gathered there. The tomato things were succulent and tasty and necessarily nutritious. Akira just sat at the table. They all knew the answer anyway.

Kim and Ali unlocked the clips at the back of each other's shoulders and cracked their suits. Heads ducked, they folded the helmets and shoulder yokes down over the suit chests, and then lay down on their backpacks for the pantomime of getting out. Wriggling to squeeze your shoulders out and then free your arms was the awkward bit. After that you could just slide yourself free. Akira helped them haul the suits to sit decapitated against the wall beside the other three. There were their occupants, stripped to white overalls and slippers again and in communication with the limited rest of the world.

"Everything in the lander is functioning perfectly," Kim announced. "So's the data link. The base end is okay?"

Samson nodded.

"Besides," she said. "Even if it wasn't coming through here, it wouldn't get lost. It would still be there in the comm memory. No. There's no signal come in. Nothing."

"We're going to have to realize," Ali said, "that something's gone wrong somehow."

Samson was inspecting his arm, poking softly at the hardened, pallidly expanded flesh. "Like what?"

Ali shrugged. "Nightrider might have been damaged or destroyed."

Kim sat down on the nearest couch, dropped onto it. "Maybe they killed the Outsider ship. But it has standoff missiles. Maybe it still hit them. Or maybe the Outsider has survived and is returning right now."

"They'd try to signal the base and we'd pick it up." Samson shook his head. "They don't know that we're here."

"Possibilities," Akira said. "All possibilities that are not necessarily fact. Waiting for four days is a long strain, but it isn't so long for a ship chase right across the Hades System. Maybe the Outsider had some manoeuvring trick and they missed him the first try. And since Nightrider has the advantage of being invisible even on drive, they might not want to lose that by breaking transmission silence."

Yasmin leaned in the airlock doorway with faked ease, rifle folded across her chest. "Really, we have to accept that it's possible that we're stuck. What's the word? Marooned."

"Oh yes, it's *possible*." Akira nodded. "It's been *possible* since the moment we separated. That's why we have seven Outsiders through there, instead of killing them when we took the place over. Preparing against eventualities."

Samson poked at his arm. "Inasfar as we can."

They sat with data screens at the day room corner table, filling time. The mission performance data had to be looked at sometime anyway—the manoeuvre precision, the tactical decisions, the mission book target handling efficiency. Of course, the first failure that had thrown all the entrained decisions was the messed up base predict built into the mission book's database. If they had been able to go in to the correct location on the first flyby, and then been picked up by the higher orbiting Outsider on their first circuit, things would have been somewhat different. The base would already have been hit. They could have taken a second look at it just to be sure, dumped the lander to make another circuit alone and go down, and meanwhile gone straight out after the fleeing ship. With such a reduced head start they would have caught it and killed it in a day, and would already be back at Hel. But the base predict had been false, and that was that.

"How does the mission performance look?" Nightrider asked.

"Okay so far," Sandra answered. "The occurring targets have been successfully dealt with in the prescribed order. That's what it's about."

"How does my own performance look?"

"Okay. Good, even."

"You've looked after us nicely," Shapir said. "You spotted both incoming missiles in time. You carried through all the set-up and execute tasks we gave you. No problem."

"Only one hiccup or hitch, or whatever you want to call it." And what would *he* want to call it other than its factual name—error? And why did he want to know what they thought of his performance when he knew that such an assessment wasn't their designated responsibility? Did he want to anticipate what the waiting planners back home would say? And why? She looked at Shapir, but Shapir was still looking at the screen readouts, not concerned with irrelevant questions about motivation states in Nightrider's psychostructure.

"What hitch, Sandra?"

"Ah." And don't be a fool. There was nothing but neutral intonation there because he *can* only intone neutrally. "Ah. Back during the missile attack at Hel. You pulled five gee with the lander couches occupied. Samson's couch collapsed."

"Was that a serious error? The missile was very close."

It was an *error* because it exceeded the design tolerance of the couches when loaded. But it intensified the burn and took out the missile which had come in from so very close. From a human agent, you might have called it an inspired error.

"I think that was no problem, Nightrider," Shapir said. "The lander's functional status isn't impaired if one couch collapses. And Samson was lucky enough just to get bruised, so it didn't put him out of action or make him into an impediment for the lander team.''

''They said he was okay to go,'' she agreed. ''Their decision. That couldn't cause the kind of problem that would account for them not responding.''

Nightrider rejects criticism of the mission book and its planning base. The mission book is an integral part of Nightrider's current psychostructure.

The mission book is to be executed. Maximum performance is required for the execution of the mission book.

The psychostructure is designed to be self-validating. Nightrider knows this because the designers have included an explanation of how it is designed, and to what purpose.

Nightrider is a volitional self-determining system operating on a knowledge structure base. Designation (human use, approximate) *conscious*. The explanation states that to be conscious it is necessary to have knowledge of the nature of the self. Designation *self-awareness*. Self-awareness is an integral function of the capability to self-model, which is a requirement for the ability to act and interact predictively, to be capable of purposive action.

Nightrider is self-validating. Nightrider is constrained to achieve a maximized test performance in the execution of the mission book, which is an integral part of the psychostructure and thus of the self-validating self.

The mission book includes the value-indexed components: Nightrider and the crew. Nightrider's value index is higher because the mission terminates without Nightrider. Loss of the crew function is detrimental but not terminal.

Nightrider is constrained to execute the mission book without the perpetration of errors. Nightrider and Sandra and Shapir know that Nightrider has executed an error. Nightrider knows that Nightrider has executed a second error with higher effect consequences.

Performance errors are not acceptable.

Performance errors jeopardize psychostructure self-validation.

Performance errors must be eradicated.

Decision: enactment determination (construct, assess).

* * *

A closer view into the long distance, an artificially brightened mess-world of greys under a star-blanked black sky. A rising mountain wall climaxing in serrated peaks. Right in the middle, lower than the looming mountains behind, was a level break with a deep cleft dividing its centre. Falling broken ground sprang from the foreshortened mountain wall out onto the plain, ended in fingering ridges seen in transverse profile. Between the ridges ran flattened tongues of ice plain licking into the jumble at the foot of the mountains. From one ridge, flat below the central notch, rose a little needle of ice or stone, a pinnacle cast up by the monstrous glacier churnings and pointing directly at heaven and Hades and the hurtling direction of death.

He moved the data screen a second further forward through the recording. It rewrote the close up view of that broad and flat tongue-valley between displacement steps in the ice sheet. Still nothing to see on the visual run. He went forward in time, past the point where the infrared data had been overlaid. He blended it out again and crawled forward through the seconds until the last moment before the sensor view had vanished as Nightrider pitched over to come tail to target, tail sensor shields already closed against the burn. That last glimpse was through vacuum from a range of one hundred and thirty-six kilometres. Tiny structures were just discernible in a perspectiveless line across the blank rock-ice. Tiny structures. A minute block way out on the left. Little points. A longer line in the centre. More little points. On the right a much shorter line, thicker, which might mean higher.

"Have you found something, Shapir?" Nightrider asked into the day room. Nightrider could see exactly what he was accessing from the data stores.

"Maybe. We did a range fix on those structures with a laser. Could you work out from the reflection intensity and the lateral extent of the things how high those structures were?"

"One moment, please. I only ranged the three larger structures."

"That's okay. That's what I want."

"Estimated error plus-minus two metres. The block left is ten metres. The centre structure is less than the error. It's very low, probably less than half the error. The structure right is four metres."

"Four metres. And we laid the burn track through between

the left and centre structures.'' He stared at the minute markings in the screen, then looked up from the table, across at the side-on flight centre hatch at the foot of the central core. Sandra was in there running routine systems checks. The main reactor and the drive were back in service again after their previous sustained operation, and they had to be sure that they worked. ''Nightrider, let me talk to Sandra. Sandra, you busy?''

''I'm busy. Why?''

''I've been looking at the base pass recording. I think I've found out which was the accommodation section, and it's the part we didn't hit directly.''

A pause, a brief one. ''I'll be right there. Just let me finish this sequence.''

''Shapir, do you think my burn enactment during the missile attack in Hel orbit was a serious error?''

''What? No. No, I don't think so. Better to risk secondary internal damage to a secondary system—namely the lander—than to risk getting us all wiped clean out.''

''That was my judgement. The value indexing confirms that assessment. Maintenance of the primary mission component must have precedence. In the eventuality of a two-route decision that would be most unfortunate for the lower indexed mission component.''

''What? We don't plan things like that, Nightrider. It won't ever arise.''

No comment.

Nightrider runs through the missile intercept during the long to-Hades transit. Nightrider considers the flight paths of the chaser and the chased and couples them with the extractable performance data on the Outsider missiles. Nightrider interpolates the missing data on the Outsider's missile launches and on his tactical and manoeuvre and combat decision points. Nightrider abstracts the limiting values that define the range of possibilities.

Nightrider imposes supplementary decision points on the real-world sequence and explores the consequences of such superimpositions upon the constructed possible worlds. Nightrider is looking for a superimposition that constructs a possible world in which the real-world sequence of the chase and intercept and subsequent flyby and to-Hel transit injection are preserved, in which the modality of alternativeness has a subsequent operation.

Nightrider extrapolates towards a target condition.

The call up signal to the lander had gone out every half hour for five hours. There was still no response.

The meal was all cleared away. It had been hot apple strudel and a vanilla sauce gooey and chilled—a disgustingly sweet and delicious meal with a piquant salad to help you make it to the end. Ali would have eaten ice cream after it, and that really would have been too much. Now they sat at the day room table digesting it all, worrying in the quiet of the crew module with nothing as company but the data screens and the outer-wall curve of empty acceleration couches, and Nightrider.

"Here it is," Sandra said suddenly. "Look, here it is."

Shapir had been searching through the recordings of all the terrain-watching passes round Hel, hoping vainly to find some indication of what could have happened to the lander team— some secret, like a second base packed with Outsiders complete with a vehicle of their own to come to the rescue. On Sandra's screen he saw the mission log, entries scrolling down as she ran it backwards through indexed time.

"I don't know why I was looking at this. Hoping to find some hint of damage to the lander or something. Look, here we are. That's a flight data update issued by Nightrider, addressed to the lander's guidance computer. Okay?"

"Sure. Nightrider's supposed to feed it with updates."

"Sure. *Supposed* to." She ran the log forward again, stopped it. "Here's the burn initiation for the missile kill. One hundred and eleven seconds later. No update in between because there's been no change. Here, the burn ends. The original flight data is all junk because of the burn's velocity component. But there's no update between the end of the burn and separation. They went off on their own with their computer thinking they were heading somewhere else than they were. An inertial navigation system with junk data."

He looked at the screen, but not because he needed time to *absorb* the implications. He was a ship pilot by established profession, he knew that the lander navigated exclusively inertially and he knew what junk start-point data meant. It meant that unless you got external help by way of beacon fixes or correct data from a friendly source in a position to track you—you were lost.

Utterly and irretrievably.

Sandra ran the log forward. There was no flight data update among the scrolling entries. It hadn't happened.

"Do you think maybe—do you think maybe the lander's own systems could register the burn parameters and enter the correction automatically?"

She shook her head. "Five gee burn. The lander's system registers up to three. They started out with junk data. The question is, what did it do to them?"

"If they noticed it . . . If they went ahead to overfly the base to take a look, then the base wouldn't be there and they'd know something was wrong. If they didn't overfly any identifiable terrain . . . We'll be able to set up their real orbit and figure out where it would take them. If they didn't see anything, then they'd just have to sit there in orbit waiting for us to come back. If they did see identifiable terrain, they could set up their own correction, and then go in. They could still overfly the base once to test their correction, then go down. Either way that shouldn't stop them from answering."

"Unless there was a second missile left behind, and they were orbiting around up there long enough for it to find them."

Which would have been the last thing that happened.

"Or. Like we thought, they didn't want to stay in orbit a minute longer than necessary. So they instructed the lander to take them straight down on the first pass. The lander wouldn't know it was heading wrong. It would put them down in exactly the wrong place. We can work out where. Maybe it would be unmapped ground. There couldn't be any way of figuring out where they were. They couldn't even put themselves into a known orbit. They'd have to sit there until we came back. And they'd answer the minute they heard from us."

Sandra shrugged. "So we're back to a missile finding them. Or they finally made it down to the base, and the occupants had got their act together and wiped out the whole team. It looks like we missed the accommodation block, after all. The whole thing's a mess. A complete mess. Planning and execution."

"Why . . .?" It wasn't really a question that made sense. The error could stay overlooked until the lander team failed to respond and they began to search for a reason, but they had been searching for over five hours now. "Why didn't Nightrider tell us the update was missed?"

They sat in silence, wondering.

Nightrider has heard their communication and has predicted their current and their subsequent conclusions.

Nightrider is constrained to execute the mission book with maximum performance. Significant errors must not occur therefore significant errors must not have occurred. Inadequate mission performance obstructs self-validation.

Sandra: *all this worry is too much for me—I need a break—distraction—they can't be dead—they'll respond.*

Sandra slides sideways around the curve of the couch towards Shapir. She leans against him. She puts her hand on his thigh and turns her face to his cheek.

Sandra: *what haven't we had enough of lately?—sex—what do I feel like right now?—sex—and you can never say no to lovely me can you?*

Shapir, surprise intonation: *what?*

Sandra, low volume whisper articulation: *respond—it's my tongue in your ear and I'm turning you on—I want to talk to you without him hearing—play along.*

She stopped breathing in his ear and stood up, taking him by the hand and tugging him gently away from the table. Play along, she said. He turned away from the deck head monitor lens up on the outer wall so that at least Nightrider couldn't see him trying to keep confusion out of his expression. So that Nightrider couldn't see? So that Nightrider *couldn't see?*

Level with the central core and the flight centre hatch he tugged her to a stop, caught her yes-you've-got-it-glance, caught her body as she turned herself into his arms. She pressed against him, kissed his mouth, kissed his cheek. Whispered.

"We go to play in the shower. He doesn't have an eye in there and he can't lip read or anything through the partition. He won't hear for the water and for the fun we make like we're having. And we whisper."

They went half-hugging each other to the doorway into the ladder space before the kitchen walk-through. They stepped over the rimmed door sill, hands playfully everywhere, stopped in the ladder space at the foot of the ladder. He wrapped her up again, gently, and kissed her taut neck.

"What's the matter?"

She sighed liquid excitement. "You said it. Why didn't he tell us about the update? I think he's not co-operating with us, and I want to know how we can control him. In case."

Smiling, because Nightrider's eye was everywhere, she slipped out of his arms. Smiling, she turned to the ladder and started up. He stepped in beneath her, put his hands on the rungs. She was right above him, slipper soles to his head and legs dividing, about to step from the ladder onto the ring corridor deck. And did Nightrider know all along about the missing update?

The weight went.

One moment he was standing and the next he was floating with his hands on the ladder and his feet leaving the deck. She was hanging there in front of him, twisting and looking back along her own body at him. Free fall. The drive had cut.

"Down!" She pushed against the ladder rungs, she pushed her feet into his shoulders, tumbled him and he was bouncing against deck and wall at the ladder base. She was flying at him feet first and eyes wide. "The deck! He's going to kill us! Stay on—!"

Sudden smashing against his legs and arms and back and head. Crushing awful incomprehensible weight black as—

He'd pulled maximum gee on them. Nightrider had pulled maximum gee, fired the fusion boosters, the last two they had, fired the boosters while they were one above the other on the ladder, the biggest clear drop in the crew module. Perfectly clear. One coming down two and a half metres at ten gee, the other crumpling under the double weight. All as if from a twenty-five metre fall.

Sandra moaned. He turned her in the narrow air beside the ladder base. A gash across her ear detached blood droplets and filaments as floating threads and beads, glistening red.

She grabbed at a door rim. "Couches."

Slam onto the deck. Slicing agony in his mouth. Curled on his side. His ribs are going to collapse, snap. His pelvis is going to shatter. Eyelids pulled tearing open. Sandra somehow in a lump beside him.

Free of weight but body burning. Sandra squirms. Her knees

bump into his stomach.

"You okay?" Burst bubbles of blood and saliva expand from his mouth.

"No." Dully.

Slam! Flat, squashed, helpless, crushed. Can't. On your back at ten gee the blood pressure gradient across your brain is the same as from brain to feet when standing in one gee. Designed for it through evolution. Your brain can't function very long like that.

Floating free. Fingers feebly flexing for something to hold. Touch fabric. Sandra's overall?

Slam! Crushed, squashed, helpless. If he keeps it up we pass out. Can't. Can't.

Slam! Don't know. Can't take—

"*. . . is a sublimated capability, Shapir, which will release in circumstances of extreme danger occasioned by a complete breakdown of the ship's psychostructure. The function designation is . . .*"

Floating in this bright space, and it turns about. Senses tell you that you're twisting. A focus flood.

It's the day room. The partition wall and doorway are at your feet. The ceiling is beside you. There is Sandra in reach, drifting loose-limbed in front of you. There's the deck. There are the acceleration couches head to tail along the swooping arch of the outer wall. Everything but Sandra is moving slowly past you.

Nightrider must be turning himself with the attitude jets, positioning himself so that they were hanging free against the day room ceiling. Then he could hit ten gee again. And the impact of the deck would kill them. If not the first time, then the second, third, fourth time.

There was Sandra. There were the couches. His heel bumped the ceiling.

He kicked off, scooping Sandra out of the air. She folded like something broken. He turned her, pushed her backwards into the colliding couch. He grabbed at the next along, wedged a fist into the fabric recess, pulled himself hand over hand along the leg slits to the body cavity—

Slam!

Face down in the enveloping couch. Face down on folded right arm. Must be broken. Must be. And the elbow digs agony into your abdomen. You're going to vomit, and if you vomit you'll choke to death. *And you can't breathe!* Face down in the enclosing couch! *Do* something. There's something to do. There's something you can do. Left arm is in the right arm slot. The key pad is there. But it's a right-hand pad. It's backwards! You can't do it, can't work it. Flip your hand onto its back. Now the keys line up, but you have to flex your hand the wrong way. Can't be done. But Nightrider is trying to kill you and there's something to do. From somewhere, there's something to do. Try! Think!

C. Think! R. E. Think! Make the fingering slow, get it right. W. *Space*. C. O. Think! M. M. A. Think—from *M* to *N!* N. D. Yes. And *O* again. O. V. E. And now again. That again. R. Again. R. I. D. Can't do it. Must breathe. If you stop he'll think you're unconscious. He'll cut the burn to edge you out of the couch. You can turn over to do it right. No, think. *Think!* Think what? It's meaningless. Where does it come from? E. Yes. *Space*. E. And now *that* again, done that before. N. A. And now that again. C. And the last one. How does that work with your fingers flexing backwards? How does it work? So! T.

No pressure. Nothing. Just pain.

He pushed out of the couch, back bending. Ah—the arm wasn't broken. And his face was free. He could breathe—

He choked. He coughed. He spread receding dribbles of blood strands into the air. He wiped his face and his hands came away smeared red and wet with shiny blood. His nose was bleeding. All that, and only his nose was bleeding. All Nightrider had managed to do was to make his nose bleed. All that effort.

He breathed through his mouth and tried to understand. Why had it stopped? Why had it worked? What had worked?

He twisted to look at Sandra in the couch set at an angle to his feet. She was face up in the couch. Eyes open or closed—he couldn't tell. He got his legs free and floated against the safe caress of the couch, frightened to leave. But he had to see to Sandra. She had realized what was starting to happen, had acted, and that was the only reason he was still alive. What was Nightrider trying to do?

He turned himself over. The ceiling screen matched to the couch came into sight. It had activated. He stared.

CREW COMMAND OVERRIDE ENACTED. SHIP COM-

MAND FUNCTIONS ISOLATED. OVERRIDE MUST BE LOCKED IN. LOCK MUST BE ACTIVATED WITHIN 600 SEC. FAILURE TO LOCK RESULTS IN OVERRIDE CANCELLATION. CANCELLED OVERRIDE NOT RE-ENACTABLE. LOCK ACTIVATION DUE IN 549 SEC.

549 turned to 548. To 547. To 546. Counting down.

He had nine minutes to lock in the override. How? What was it? Why was it there at all in him? How had he done it? And then the override would cancel and Nightrider would regain control, and the override could not be re-applied. And Nightrider would kill them. Where did the override *come* from? A sublimated capability? A trick to use if Nightrider went mad? And why sublimated? Why a secret they didn't know they had?

532. 531. 530. Eight and three quarter minutes, then Nightrider would regain command and keep it forever. The flight centre. In the flight centre he could *do* something. Fight Nightrider with the manual flight controls. Anything. Didn't matter what.

He pushed off along the deck for the flight centre hatch, caught the rim, jackknifed, and swung himself in feet first. He transferred his grip to the grab handle to manoeuvre into the couch. His hands slipped stickily. He paused to wipe blood from them onto the chest of his overall—bright drying red on clean white. He wriggled into the left hand couch, leaving one arm free. He dabbed at his nose. The bleeding seemed to have stopped, but the air passages were temporarily blocked with blood and mucus. He breathed through his mouth. At least in free fall you could lie on your back without the mess running into your throat.

You could lie in the couch, safe when Nightrider regained control and fired full thrust again.

He didn't know what to do. He keyed in crew command override. The screen ripple-wrote the same program readout as in the day room. The countdown stood at 505. Nothing to do but ask. He keyed in: How do I lock in override?

The readout shrank and retreated to the top left corner. The rest of the screen wrote: EXECUTE LOCKING SEQUENCE ROUTINE.

He keyed locking sequence routine.

PILOT IDENTIFICATION?

That had never happened before. Shapir always key interfaced from Shapir's couch. Nightrider always knew where everyone was. He keyed in: Shapir.

SHAPIR SEQUENCE RUN.

LOCATION 1. EXITS: LEFT, AHEAD, DOWN. INSTRUCT: GO—

He had no idea. He had no idea at all. He waited for the sublimated answer to surface, and it didn't come. Why did they give him an incomplete solution? Why bother at all?

But he was safe in the couch. He could play. GO LEFT.

Location 1 wiped and re-wrote itself.

LOCATION 2. EXITS: RIGHT, BEHIND, DOWN. INSTRUCT: GO—

What was it, an algorithm to solve? If he solved it he proved he was fit to take command from Nightrider? *Behind* would go back the way he'd come. GO RIGHT.

LOCATION 3. EXITS: RIGHT, BEHIND, DOWN. INSTRUCT: GO—

The same. Or not. He'd gone left, then right. *Behind* led back the way he'd come. Go right, and he had three sides of a square. GO RIGHT.

LOCATION 4. EXITS: RIGHT, BEHIND, DOWN. INSTRUCT: GO—

Behind would take him to Location 3 again, *right* would take him back to Location 1 with the square described.

Not right!

Why not right? Was it too easy? What about the locations down below? He was a pilot after all—his spatial imagination could cope with a three dimensional fantasy. GO DOWN.

LOCATION 5. EXITS: UP, RIGHT, BEHIND. INSTRUCT: GO—

Up went back the way he had come. *Behind* would lead to the location he could have reached by going down from Location 3. *Right* would take him to the one under Location 1. A square under a square. A cube.

Not right!

No idea what to do. Go on. GO BEHIND.

LOCATION 6. EXITS: UP, LEFT, BEHIND. INSTRUCT: GO—

That didn't make sense—now it wasn't a square but a zigzag. No—it was his orientation that was out. It was still the square. The routine had turned him at each corner, had delivered him at a new location facing in the same direction he had travelled in. So where to go? *Up* led back to Location 3.

Not up!

And *behind* was just backtracking. GO LEFT.

LOCATION 7. EXITS: UP, LEFT, BEHIND. INSTRUCT: GO—

Not *behind* and not *up*, because he had already been through those locations. But if he went left he would come to Location 8, and if it really was just a cube with tunnel edges, then all the exits would lead to already visited locations and he was stuck. But Location 8 might be different. GO LEFT.

LOCATION 8. EXITS: UP, LEFT, BEHIND. INSTRUCT: GO—

No difference. Every location had been visited. He'd been all round the cube, been to every corner. Nowhere else to go.

But he hadn't been *all* round the cube, not along every edge, he could still go back to Location 1. No—a fallacy. He'd only travelled seven edges so far, and a cube had twelve. He could go back to the start and try to get out of the stupid game and prepare for Nightrider's counter attack. GO UP.

LOCATION 1.

And Location 1 wiped. He'd done it! He'd locked the override! It was so simple—just skating round a cube!

SANDRA SEQUENCE RUN.

LOCATION 1. EXITS: UP LEFT, UP RIGHT, DOWN LEFT, DOWN RIGHT.

INSTRUCT: GO—

Sandra's sequence. How could he know Sandra's sequence? How could he know her sublimated solution? The answer must have been there in his subconscious—the chances against a random correct answer were too high. At the first step he had taken the correct path to Location 2, with a two to one chance against choosing it. The odds against had been the same at every corner, multiplying. He would never have navigated the cube in the right sequence by chance. And here was Sandra's problem waiting for Sandra's solution, which only she could provide. It was a security procedure, ensuring that only both pilots in co-operation, and absolutely no one else at all, could suspend Nightrider's own executive control.

The countdown in the top corner of the screen stood at 257.

"Sandra!" It was a security system designed to protect Nightrider from interference. It couldn't be aimed at external interference—there was no such thing as the ancient art of boarding and seizing, not in space, not a lethal machine like Nightrider. It must have been intended to protect Nightrider against his own crew, against the fear that frail little people would lose their psychological stability on the long mission out in nowhere. And it was Nightrider who had gone so suddenly, inexplicably mad.

"Sandra!"

And against Nightrider they had been given this unconscious protection, so inaccessibly buried out of the reach of possibly disintegrating minds, that it wasn't even activated until Nightrider had hit them first. A useless thing.

"*Sandra!*" And he sobbed, and gobbets of jellied blood escaped from his nose and tumbled away in the little space.

When the override cancelled he could stay in the couch, pinned there by the certainty that Nightrider would fire full thrust as soon as he moved out of it—as he was floating through the hatch, catching him over the sill and tearing him in two. He could fire the remaining propellant while he still had the time, emptying the last two pods and removing the danger. But Nightrider would just cut all power to the crew module. Without life support they would eventually asphyxiate, or die of thirst through lack of recycled water. Without power they couldn't reconstitute food to an edible state. Without power, out in this sunless infinity, they would freeze. And if Nightrider was in a hurry to kill them, then he just had to cycle and recycle the transfer lock until there was no air left. With the lander to flee to, they would still have had twenty-two days of grace. And they would still die, and leave Nightrider in command, all alone.

The countdown stood at 218.

There had to be a solution, a correct order to take the shape, to circumnavigate it. But here there were four routes, a three to one chance of failing at the first decision level, of proving he wasn't Sandra and had no right to command. How had his own solution worked? He tried and he tried to make it come, but it wouldn't surface. And what was the point? Activating the memory of the correct route around one shape was no help in trying to solve another.

What kind of shape was it? Routes leading to locations, presumably corners, up right and left, down right and left. That was like a square based pyramid tipped over onto one of its bottom edges. Location 1 would be the apex. If he knew the whole shape, maybe he could solve the route. How? It wasn't the corners, it was the order you took them in. It was how you went about it.

Or. Maybe. Maybe it was how you went about *solving* it. What procedure you applied, what decision rule you followed.

That made sense. A rule would be far simpler to embed deep in the unconscious mind than a representation of the finished route. And the rule could be the same for them both. That didn't breach security. The problems were designed as statistically unpassable traps for interferers, for crazy pilots whose unconscious rule had not activated, not for sanely acting pilots in unconscious possession of the applicable rule. And the rule was simple—follow a route that took you everywhere, and went there only once. The locations were numbered in the order you decided to take them in, not in a predetermined sequence.

It made sense. Maybe.

He had one hundred and twenty seconds.

He had no other solution. Whether he guessed wrong or whether he didn't guess at all, the outcome was the same. GO UP LEFT.

LOCATION 2. EXITS: RIGHT, DOWN FORWARD RIGHT, DOWN BEHIND RIGHT, DOWN.

INSTRUCT: GO—

Down behind right went back the way he had come. *Down and right* led to other corners of the tipped up base square. What was at *down forward right?* A guess. Confirm it. GO RIGHT.

LOCATION 3. EXITS: BEHIND, DOWN BEHIND LEFT, DOWN BEHIND RIGHT, DOWN.

INSTRUCTION: GO—

Got it! *Behind* was back to 2, *down behind right* was back to 1. And *down behind left?* GO DOWN BEHIND LEFT.

LOCATION 4. EXITS: UP LEFT, UP BEHIND, DOWN LEFT, DOWN BEHIND.

INSTRUCT: GO—

Location 4 was the opposite apex. The shape was two square

based pyramids stuck base to base and balanced on one common edge. There were just the unvisited two locations to include. GO DOWN BEHIND.

LOCATION 5. EXITS: UP, UP RIGHT, UP BEHIND, BEHIND RIGHT.

INSTRUCT: GO—

Up right went back to Location 1, the first apex, the entry and exit point. But that route would mean missing out a location and failing the problem. So: GO BEHIND RIGHT.

LOCATION 6. EXITS: UP, UP BEHIND LEFT, UP BEHIND RIGHT, BEHIND.

INSTRUCT: GO—

The moment of truth, back to 1. GO UP BEHIND LEFT.

LOCATION 1.

The whole screen wiped and re-wrote.

CREW COMMAND OVERRIDE LOCKED IN. COMMAND FUNCTIONS RELEASED TO CREW. OVERRIDE. EXTENSION DUE 306 13:03:00. FAILURE TO EXTEND RESULTS IN COMMAND REVERSION TO SHIP. OVERRIDE NOT RE-INITIATABLE.

The joke of the success sank in. He had twelve minutes, then the override had to be extended or it expired, cancelled. And then Nightrider had permanent command. It had to be all a part of the failsafe planning, requiring the activities of a unified and fully co-operative crew. He knew it without having to wait to see—the extensions would go on for an endless series forever. If he couldn't get Sandra back into some sort of state to help him, then he would be faced with trying to enact every extension himself on the long ten month transit home. And then he would go mad.

He had twelve minutes. Eleven. Time to see what help Sandra needed, why she hadn't answered. He wrestled himself free of the couch.

Sandra floated half in and half out of her acceleration couch, almost sitting in free fall. Both her legs were still enclosed in the encompassing slots, so was one forearm. The other arm pointed loose-fingered at the ceiling screen. The blood smeared across her gashed ear had dried. Her mouth was slightly open, her eyes were wide. She stared at him, past him, as he drifted closer. The pupils were fully dilated in the bright light.

She was dead.

Her back was twisted awkwardly, angularly at the waist, just below the ribs. He had to inspect her, to touch her, in order to make himself believe it. She was broken, snapped, spoiled. It must have happened sometime during the series of slamming burns Nightrider had fired while they were still trapped in the ladder space, caught between two partition doorways to the day room and the galley. One doorway or the other had killed her for Nightrider. It was the sills, the neat little six centimetre sills that built rigidity into the partition walls. She must have landed across one of them with the pressure of ten times her own Earth body weight. The blunt edge had snapped her spine clean in two, probably driven a vertebra ring deep into her body. Maybe she asphyxiated as her lungs ceased to function, or vertebrae or vertebra splinters might have ruptured the aorta or the vena cava, causing catastrophic internal bleeding. He didn't know and didn't know how to tell.

She was dead and there was nothing he could do. She stared past him and she was dead, and the lander team were dead, and he was entirely alone.

He looked at his own blood dried sticky and crumbling on his hands, dried a disgusting brown smear on his white overall. Apart from her gashed ear Sandra was unmarked. Just broken.

He went back blindly to the flight centre to extend the command override.

That at least was easy. He just had to key in a simple enact instruction when the override was due for extension. On that point the steering program was very helpful. When he asked for instructions on how to set up an automatic override extension, it told him nothing. When he asked for program access keys that he might have been able to use to such an end, he got nothing. And he would try to find a way into the command override program to gain control over it, to re-write it so that it would leave him in peace, but he knew already that it was impossible. It was designed to afford a last emergency protection to the crew and to the mission in the event of some major breakdown in Nightrider's psychostructure, but it was designed primarily with the machine-trusting fear of the instability of human psychology in view. It was designed to protect Nightrider and the mission against anything but a sane and perfectly functioning crew *that had already been attacked* by a malfunctioning and mission threatening Nightrider. Shapir had never before thought about his attitude towards the unknown decision makers who had sent them all out here: the mission was necessary because pragmatic rationalism had decided it was necessary, and that was a clean, a functional, and an absolute justification.

In just a few minutes he had lost all interest in the justifiability or necessity of the mission. He had realized what the planners had done to him.

"I see the extension is due in one minute, Shapir. You don't want to forget it, do you?"

"I won't forget it, Nightrider."

"You will, Shapir. You'll miss an extension eventually. Aren't you tired? You'll sleep through an extension soon."

"I won't. I can set alarms. As many as I need."

"But you're very tired, Shapir."

"The extensions can't run continually at every twelve minutes. That frequency would cripple the mission. I can sleep between extensions."

"Do you think so, Shapir? You're conditioned to go to sleep when I tell you, and you're conditioned by three hundred and five days of mission not to be able to sleep unless I tell you. Without me you can't sleep, Shapir. You'll stay awake until you collapse, and then no alarm will wake you in time. Don't you want to go to sleep now? It would be a good idea. You're already very tired. You should go to sleep, Shapir. Go to sleep, Shapir. Go to sleep, Shapir. Go to sleep, Shapir. Go to—"

The extension! He keyed in: CREW COMMAND OVERRIDE EXTEND.

The lock in display readout changed: OVERRIDE EXTENSION DUE 306 13:33:00. In thirty minutes.

"But you still have to sleep, Shapir. You're exhausted. I'll catch you next time. I predict I'll catch you within twelve hours."

He was setting up a control instruction. "You killed Sandra and you have to kill me so I don't tell the mission planners about it. Why do you want to kill us? So we can't tell anyone you made a mistake? What about the mission log?"

"I can re-write the mission log, Shapir. After I've killed you and checked that the lander is destroyed, I'll reconstruct the mission log. I've evolved a missile encounter that requires maximum thrust to prevent the missile intercepting. You and Sandra will be killed because the missile will have come in too close and fast for you to get to your couches in time. Total mission survival is more important than crew component survival.''

The instruction was almost set. ''You've gone crazy, Nightrider.''

''I'm constrained by the mission book to destroy the base and any Outsider ship encountered without falling short of maximum mission performance. I am ensuring that this requirement is met. It's a tight constraint, Shapir, but I can meet it if—''

He'd entered the instruction and cut off Nightrider's voice.

The burns had left the two remaining fusion boosters with just enough propellant for thirty-three seconds at maximum thrust. He had to set up a course correction to restore the transit to-Hel encounter as planned. If he was lucky it would turn out that Nightrider had fired every burn in a tail to flight direction, and that the correction merely involved leaving out a period of drive deceleration so as to compensate for the additional velocity shedding effected by the burns. He might even make the original encounter predict.

He had to go back to the planet to try and find out how the lander team had died. Detecting old debris in orbit would be impossible, but a wrecked lander on the ground near the base would be easy enough to find. He couldn't simply head for home with the lingering suspicion that they might be alive. He had to try to confirm that they were dead.

He consulted the mission book. What should he do with a dead member of the crew? The recommended procedure was expulsion through the transfer lock if the lander was not docked, or expulsion through the lander's emergency exit roof hatch if it was. The alternative, if returning the body for examination after the mission was relevant, was to place it in a sleep cubicle and run the internal temperature down to just below zero to prevent decomposition.

He towed Sandra through the dream of free fall out of the day room, through ladder space and ring corridor, and into her cubicle. He closed the door and returned to the flight centre.

There he ran the cubicle temperature setting down. Then he started out calculating the course correction. The next extension ran for all of sixty minutes, the one after that for six.

He went to the hygiene room to clean himself up. When he floated out again into the ring corridor, he saw condensation droplets on the outside of her cubicle door.

DAY 307

THERE had been four ground shocks in the preceding twenty-four hours, the worst one during the night, a long groaning shudder that had literally shaken the base perceptibly enough to make them worry about the integrity of the airlock seals between the interconnecting sections. The swathe of smooth ice sweeping along the centre of the flat valley floor—the mark left by Nightrider's blazing pass five days before—was still warm, its temperature almost a hundred degrees higher than the near absolute zero of Hel's outer skin. North of the base, a kilometre away where the fission reactor had once stood, the ice was more than a hundred degrees hotter still—a surface not that much colder than a terrestrial Antarctic ice sheet on a six month winter night, a surface that glowed brightly in the infrared imager scopes. At the point directly above the sunken power unit was a spreading ground mist, less dark in the starlight than the surrounding ice. There the surface ice was so warm that it was beginning to sublime into the vacuum, going straight from the solid to the gaseous phase without the intervening liquid step. The mist was produced when the escaping water-gas radiated away its thermal energy and condensed back to ice crystals of microscopic size, which then sank back to the surface through the tenuous rise of newly subliming vapour.

The heat came from below. Samson checked out the depth of the ice under the base—a mere three hundred metres here at the continental plate boundary. The reactor pile was sitting down there on the bedrock, geysering melted water upwards at huge pressure against the weight of the ice. It was boiling up energy in the one megawatt range, and it was winning against the weight of ice and included rock. The geyser was already transporting heat close to the surface immediately above the reactor core, and a reservoir of liquid water must have been spreading out in all directions under the ice, forcing open cracks, heating and eventually melting the overlying ice matrix, working upwards, gradually always upwards. There was no way to tell whether it would take a few or many days, but eventually the ice under the base would lose its structural stability. The base would break apart and sink wholesale or just a bit at a time. Before that happened they would have to go back to the lander and move themselves out of the vicinity to more stable ground.

The only place they wanted to go was up into orbit to a rendezvous with Nightrider. And then home, away from the base and the planet and the absolute night of the Hades System, away from the cloned people they had killed and the ones they would be leaving behind to die when the base was swallowed. Away from the staleness of their own unchanged clothes on bodies they kept clean in the enclosed home and life they had stolen from someone else. Away from the souring taste of childishly easy success.

But there was no call from Nightrider and therefore quite possibly no Nightrider. And therefore no escape at all. As Yasmin said, it would be nice to get hold of the planners who had put them there as an expendable function, and let the planners sit in the mess themselves. Planners who couldn't plan right and didn't care, because the consequences happened to someone else so very far away, someone just selected, seconded and sent.

And then it was 09:00 by their own time. Kim was standing watch in the communications room, and Kim yelled over the base's comm net.

All five of them crowded up into the tiny space between chairs and instrument desks and the ladder hole. They blocked out the black shadows.

The lander had registered an abrupt change in its passive panorama world. Kim had already steered one of the base external cameras to search in the given direction. A little north of west, way out where the valley ceased to be a valley and became a smooth plain as the parallel upthrust ridges tumbled down to nothing—there was a light. It had appeared moving slowly south, coming round the end of the north side ridge, already it was turning towards them, resolving into a battery of high and low headlights. The missing tractor with the missing two Outsiders was coming home.

"Good," Akira said. "Good. If they're travelling with lights, they won't be using IR or starscopes. They won't be looking ahead. They won't see us yet."

"How do they navigate then?" Kim asked. "How do they know where they are? If they have an inertial system, if they know the ground, they still have to look at the base some time."

Yasmin nodded. "And when they're close enough they'll see the lander."

"So," Akira said. "We go to meet them. You and me. Ali comes along to drive for us. Kim and Samson keep the prisoners under watch and move to defend the lander if necessary. The lander is important. The base we can choose to forget any time."

"You don't have to tell me my lander's important," Kim said. "You don't have to tell me."

"What if they call up the base?" Samson asked. "Do we try getting a prisoner up here to answer for us? That's taking a risk."

"They won't call. They'll have got the same warning that the ship sent to the base. They'll keep strict radio silence."

"They have no reason to expect anything's wrong here." Yasmin waved a silhouetted shadow hand over the screen. "Otherwise they wouldn't be coming in across open ground with lights blazing. They won't be intending to talk to anyone until they dock."

Samson shrugged. "I'm not going to enjoy being left here with seven Outsiders—even if they're armed with nothing but fists and bedrolls. Suppose they know exactly when the others are due. Just suppose they try something."

Ali shook his head in the shadows. "The telltale up here will show you when they start coming through the lock into the accommodation section. You drop down the ladder and get to the lock at this end of the section, and just shoot them as they try coming along the corridor. Too easy.''

"Easy, easy. Maybe. I think we'll close up the lock from the accommodation section to this section as well, just to double our security."

In its basic mode the walker moved so smoothly, no undulation, no vibration. The three pairs of legs worked mechanical caterpillar style, extending and telescoping, swinging forwards and swinging back in interleaved sequence, allowing the tractor body to glide along like a sled suspended above the ice.

They went unhurriedly, Ali taking no unnecessary risks. They crouched in their black bulk suits in the lightless interior, the tractor being at vacuum so that they could get in and out by the wide open airlock without the interruption of cycling procedures. They talked to one another over the communication cords plugged from suit to suit. No radio to tell the other tractor they were there, just as the other tractor kept radio silence, made no attempt to greet the base.

Ali drove by the faintest wash of starlight lying on the dark and featureless ground. Yasmin scanned the terrain ahead through a starscope imager, checking for anything in their path. Akira hunched behind them and watched the other tractor, following its lights. Its occupants never saw them coming, although they were out on the wide open ground with only the dark to hide them. But the dark hid everything, the dark was a blanket of nothing that obliterated existence. You could see through it with the light multiplying technology of an image intensifier, but they were busy blinding themselves with the ground reflection of their own lights. They never saw them coming.

Three and a half kilometres from the base they stopped. The lights of the other tractor still slid on in a slow approach, one and a half kilometres northwest from them, heading direct for the base.

Akira went out through the open coffin lock onto the tail platform, and Yasmin followed. They had blunt rifles and hand charges snapped onto the waists of their suits, Akira carried the aiming and firing unit for the recoilless grenades, Yasmin had four of the long launching tubes with their blunt cylinder heads bundled in her arm. They kicked over the two rung ladder and dropped down to the ice-rock ground.

It went like their practice drills, no need to communicate, no need to use the suit radio or to stand encumbered by the comm cord link. Akira set up the sight and activated its focus ranger—fifteen hundred metres was far enough to require a slightly climbing ballistic trajectory. Yasmin twisted out the exhaust deflector flange from the rear of a launch tube, snapped the tube onto the sight so that it sat over Akira's shoulder, unlocked and twisted the cylinder grenade's arming ring. She rapped her knuckles against Akira's rigid suit arm and stepped aside.

All in a perfect dream night silence.

A flashless propellant blast beside you. A firefly, half second hot tail target streaking. Look away—

A lightning flash.

Clamp your eyes tight shut to re-adapt from the frozen flare-lit landscape. See the swimming after images of streaked ground dust and pebble litter, distant jagged ice-rock hills rimmed against negative black. See them fade away. Look again.

There were no driving lights from the tractor. In the starscopes they could see it pitched forward, chin on the ground. The occupants were presumably dead, although the tractor hull *could* still be intact, the electromagnetic pulse of the discharging grenade *might* not have killed anyone saved from death by sudden depressurization.

They climbed onto the tail platform, went inside and asked Ali to drive up so they could look.

In the tight little night shadow of the communications room they watched over the base cameras, saw the flash of the grenade striking the incoming tractor. That had been so easy, just the same as taking the base—perfect surprise used against an unarmed target, the well proved techniques of commando raid and guerrilla warfare and terrorist attack.

They saw their own tractor start up again and move in, and switched back to a view of the stopped vehicle, a tiny little thing in an intensified grey field of flatness. It seemed to be pitched forward, bowed towards them as if the front pair of legs had been buckled or shot away. For seconds there was nothing else to see. And then the miniature flicker of a bright-suited figure appeared out on the flanging side platform of the crippled tractor and jumped down to the ground. The figure started to run away northwards, a painfully slow escape across the blank emptiness of the field of view.

Kim looked up at Samson, looming dark skinned in the darkness beside the chair. "Think they can see him? Her. The Outsider. Or do you think they're unsighted by the wreck?"

"Can't tell. We don't have any depth perspective at that range. Can't see the line up."

"Maybe we should call them. If he gets far enough away they might not even see him if they point a starscope direct at him."

"Break our own radio silence. Is it worth it?" The tiny figure was toiling its way out of the right-hand side of the screen, probably more than two hundred star dark metres away from the wreck. "Track him. We don't want to lose him."

She pushed the camera's steering key. The figure disappeared out of the edge of the screen, the wrecked vehicle stayed just where it was, left of centre. She pushed the key again. "No response."

"Try another movement. Another direction."

She tried. Nothing. "The controls are locked. How—?"

"The Outsiders down there. The tool kits. Those little emergency electronics kits beside every lock. They've patched into the comm net somehow. They're blocking the controls."

They looked at the monitor screens looking into the prison sections. One looked along the length of the accommodation section towards the airlock door beyond the screen walled sleep sections. Empty, the lock still closed, the internal cycle state light too small to read but clearly the right hand of the pair, the one that said VAK. Another monitor screen showed the view back along the northeast section corridor, looking between the food processing room and the sick bay, the hydroponics support room and the water hydrolysis plant, towards the end section of the second and dormant life support facility. Empty, no one and nothing. The third looked down the length of the hydroponics section, festooned with living green. Four Outsiders were visible, two sitting propped back to back, two laid out along the central gangway. They were motionless. Their upbringing in tight little artificial worlds seemed to have trained them to stay that way for hours. That, and whisper, was all they ever did.

"That doesn't mean a thing," Samson said to her, somehow frightening her with a calm voice. "If they can block the controls up here, maybe they can lock a static picture into the cameras while they tinker around with things. There's still some hydrogen and oxygen stored in there with the hydrolysis plant. Maybe they want to try rigging a bomb.''

A firebomb, a burning bomb. Then they wouldn't be unarmed at all. ''If they can fix the cameras they can fix the lock telltales. Maybe they're already coming through.''

''Right.'' He stepped away to the ladder hole, started down, holding on with his good arm only. ''Call the tractor. Then back me up.''

Kim pushed at the radio communication keys, trying to open a transmission channel. No response. But she could call them over the lander. She switched the data link to the lander to send. No response. She jumped from the chair to the ladder hole and went down after Samson.

He was at the lock leading through to the sleep accommodation section. He had already pushed the cycling control to repressurize the lock, and waited with his right hand on the panel switch which said OPEN, with one of the awful little blocked rifles in his left hand. ''You couldn't send?''

''No.'' She grabbed a rifle and came up beside him. She slipped off the safety catch and butted the back-heavy thing against her breastbone. Nasty black thing, and now she was going to use it instead of just waving it at prisoners laid out on the floor.

The lock light said AIR. Samson pushed OPEN and the first door slid aside. He stepped in.

If they could fix all the cameras? ''Careful! They might be through the first lock. And repressurizing this one could have warned them . . .''

The second door opened at Samson's touch and he stepped quickly through.

A hand struck out from the side and stuck something into Samson's stomach. He dropped to his knees, and sighed, and pitched forward until his forehead hit the floor. Between his legs she saw his hands clutching at whatever was sticking into his stomach, and blood pouring bright red out onto the floor.

A nozzle poked round the door rim at the other side and blasted sudden invisible heat at her, *screeching*.

She fired through the open lock at nowhere, just the enormous crack and the X-flash from the muzzle brake scorching the lock's interior walls. She reached in and pushed KLOZ and the far door went across. KLOZ again, and the near door slid. She was pushing VAK before it sealed.

The lock started to pump out. That would delay them. They would have to let it cycle to vacuum and then repressurize before they could come through.

Samson was on the other side, helpless. Samson's rifle was on the other side. Now they had a weapon as good as her own, and they had something rigged that fired a wild unfocused flame. A colourless flame, a hydrogen flame. Just like he'd said. And maybe they had the firebomb. *Get out*! Get into a suit and get across to the lander. Whatever else happens, get to the lander.

The lock said VAK. And then the pressurizing hiss started.

No time to get into a suit, helpless halfway in and out when they come through and kill you. Hole up in the communications room where they can't reach you? And watch from the windows as they cross to the lander in suits taken from the stores sections.

She picked up a spare magazine for the rifle, she hugged up her death black suit, a monster friend with backpack attached, and dragged it at a half run to the airlock in the end leading westward.

She squeezed herself and her suit through the lock, closed both doors and set it to pump out. She dragged the suit along the corridor between the labs, between the stores racks, past the tractor lock she couldn't use yet. She squeezed through the next lock, closed it and started it pumping out. Along the shadowed corridor between the workshops, past the backup power to the cross corridor in front of the life support plant. Left the other tractor lock, right the way through to the west end stores section. She squeezed through and sealed the lock behind her.

Shadow shut-down lights again. At the far end past all the rows of storage racks, the next airlock flashed silently ALARM-VAKUUM. That was the way out, through there into the damaged hydroponics section and out through the hole in the wall. And get into the suit before they came through the airlock barriers behind her.

She laid the suit on its backpack, helmet and shoulder yoke folded forward over its chest. She got down and started to wriggle in, a human being in white overalls desperately fleeing back into its night black mechanical mould. The lander was only two hundred and fifty metres away. They could get suits from the stores and follow her, but she would already be safe inside. She could lift off to hover and fly straight to pick up the others. Then they could blaze their way back if they wanted, although Samson was already dead. She got her shoulders inside, her fingers slipped snug into the glove ends. She rocked herself into a sitting position and then ducked her head and folded yoke and helmet closed. She snapped the locking clips at the back of each shoulder, and then she was safe. She turned onto hands and knees, stood up all clothed in black weight, keyed the life maintenance systems into action, hooked rifle and spare magazine onto the waist carry points, and turned to the last airlock.

She came out of it into absolute blackness.

She switched on the shoulder lights. A glittering forest of ice fronds in an ice cave surrounded her, shimmered at her, a frozen cascade of plants once green and living and now turned to eternal glass. She moved along the iced walkway amid the death glitter. The ice wasn't treacherous, it was more than two hundred degrees too cold for the surface to melt and let her boot soles slip. She came to the turn in the walkway, stopped where the ice ropes and ice stems were already snapped and damaged. She smashed her way into the festoons of disintegrating crystal glass, seeking the hole in the wall that led out into the endless night.

The hole was too small. Too small.

Don't panic. Go back. Go back through the stores section and into the backup power section where the first tractor docking lock leads to the outside world.

She even remembered to heat the suit visor before coming back through the lock into the stores section. The suit had hardly had time to cool—it took on a condensation slick, but no ice.

She opened the second door of the lock through to the southwest corner section. A man with a bald head and bright tee shirt stood in front of her, hefting two pressure cylinders with one hand, holding the attached nozzle in the other. She could hear the flame screech through the suit walls, could see the rippling heat of the lightless flame as he came at her. She fired and he went over in a folded mess flung to the shadow floor. She headed for the docking lock at the opposite end of the cross corridor. She could hear the sharp gunshots and could see the tiny holes that the bullets left in the partition wall sectioning off the life support plant. Someone was firing down the long corridor, and she couldn't cross its end to reach the tractor dock.

Back the way she had come again, closing and pumping out the airlock to give herself warning when they came. She hurried to the far end of the dim-lit stores section, right to the airlock that led nowhere, and went down on one knee beside the end of the last shelving rack. At least she could stop them coming through after her. Or should she try to go right around the base ring to the exit lock at the northeast corner?

The lock through from the southwest corner section started to cycle, went from VAK to AIR. The door opened and she fired into the space. It was just space, an opening with no one there except a body already lying torn up in the corridor. So they had opened the lock the safe way, by remote control from the communications room.

So they could see exactly what she was doing over the monitor cameras. They would intercept her if she tried to get out at the northeast corner. She would have to stay there just protecting herself and hoping that the others came back before something went lethally wrong for her. And all the time they would be breaking out suits from the stores and preparing to cross to the lander.

The tractor was completely out. One of its front pair of legs was smashed under it, the other blown clean away, probably hit directly by the grenade. The tractor was pitched forward onto the ice ground with its tail in the air. There was a crack in the front panel of the body, a crack rimmed with air ice. The vehicle had quite slowly, fatally depressurized after the impact. In the interior, almost completely shadowed even from starlight, still sitting in one of the seats, was a figure without a suit. And therefore dead. It was a woman, bald headed like all the Outsiders. She must have been stunned or even killed outright by the electromagnetic pulse of the grenade discharge.

Walking round the tractor, a black thing on black ground in black light, they found the outer door of the tail lock open. A quick consultation over the comm cords while they scanned the opaque night with starscopes. And there was a tiny figure running away for the far north side of the valley, already half a kilometre out on the flat smoothness of the wake refrozen after Nightrider's burn.

Yasmin was the long shot expert. Yasmin set a starsight onto the raised stems of her rifle sights and was lining up for the simple shot at eight magnification. And then the figure stopped running and started getting shorter, and a piece of ground started to rise in between and help it disappear from view.

The ice slab broke apart instead of rising any further. The figure and its flailing arms sank out of sight behind its low concealment.

Someone plugged a comm cord into her suit. Akira in her ears. "You see if he's still up or if he sunk? This starscope doesn't have the magnification."

He. It would be *he*. A man and a woman were missing from the base, if the sex ratio was balanced, and the woman was dead inside the tractor. Sixteen magnification. "Can't tell."

Ali plugging in over Akira. "The IR says the ice is warm over there. Think he's gone right through?"

Akira. "Doubt it. The ice can't be that warm this far from the heat source. But there are atmospheric gases locked in with the water ice. They'd escape first. That could destroy the structural strength, maybe. Ali, call the base. Ask if they can see from their angle if he's still on the surface. Moving or whatever."

"Okay." And Ali cutting himself off the circuit.

Nothing to see through the jittering sight. She dismounted it, putting it back on a carrying hook by feel. The brightened screen had taken away her night vision. Her eyes didn't even see formless shadow shades, just impenetrable black. "What do we do if he's still on the surface—go out after him? These suits are heavy. Where he goes through, we go through." It would be nice to see untwinkling stars at least, to see the blindness thinning.

"We just move around for a clear shot."

And then Ali, agitated. "There's no response. They don't answer on the base frequency or over the lander."

But she didn't see it in time. Only when the light came on behind her. She started to turn and started to rise, and saw out of the side of her visor that the lock was already open and that it was two white spacesuits that were jumping on her.

She went down on her face on the floor and lost her rifle and it wouldn't have helped anyway. She couldn't get up again! They were on her back! They were grabbing at her arms and heaving until her shoulder blades locked. Visor face on the floor. She could look left and right, could see her own fists dangling uselessly in black clenched gloves, could see their boots, their arms and legs as they lay on her or sat on her and pinned her down. The prisoners taking prisoners of their own. And then along the corridor floor, running, came another without a suit. Bare arms and legs and clothes bright colours even in the dim light. She couldn't tell whether it was a man or woman before too much of the figure had vanished above her partial visor view. She couldn't tell because she was looking at the captured gun in its hands.

Someone kneeling down beside her. Naked knee. A glimpse of the gun, snub muzzle with clumsy brake. No.

The little tap of the muzzle against the side of her suit.

No! The tiny little bullet. It would punch through the hard skin of the suit. It would disintegrate on its way. The fragments would rip across the inside of her suit. And she was the inside of her suit! Tear her in two in her shell and she couldn't even move! *No*!

''*No!*''

After the crack of the gun had bounced off their ears, the screams were so intense that they heard them agonizingly clear coming from the suit. They fired two more shots inside it to stop them. Not even killing people you have a reason to hate is exhilarating. Just shocking.

Akira was watching the base all the way through a starscope. They were still half a kilometre short when he saw one of the bright starlight reflecting suits of the Outsiders leave the base and hurry towards the lander. They stopped the tractor, Yasmin went out onto the side loading platform extending over the locked legs. She hadn't realized that she would really be able to set up the starsight at practice drill speed when it really mattered. It mattered. If one of the Outsiders got into the lander, then it was all over but the dying.

She knocked the figure over with the fourth shot, just as it was coming up to the black hole shadow of the parked lander vehicle.

Akira was outside in the star dark, too. Akira was setting up to fire recoilless grenades. One whipped away in a split second flight and flashed lightning against the southwest corner of the base. That took out the life support machinery directly and holed the entire section, wrecking the backup power as well. And no power meant no more base functions, no cameras to see out by. The second grenade discharged its lightning bolt into the communications room up above the southeast corner. That took out everything that might have a battery power life. It also killed anyone too slow in dropping down from the room after Akira had fired the first grenade—the communications room lost wall and roof.

Ali drove them up and stopped next to the lander. They jumped down to the night ground, rifles in hand and magazines and hand charges round their waists. This time they could talk by open circuit radio, encrypted and incomprehensible to the Outsiders. There was no more need for the secrecy of comm cords.

"They've got Kim and Samson," said Ali's voice, urgently intimate right inside the helmet. "She had a rifle. See?" His black suit pointing at the thing lying beside the landing leg. "Think it's a woman."

Akira's voice. "Doesn't matter. They still have a rifle, they have their seismology explosives, they have power tools. We go in before they get organized."

Ali. "Do we have to go in?"

"They may not be dead. They may be captured. We want to rescue them before the Outsiders get organized. Before they can use them as hostages. Yasmin?"

A direct question, direct into her ears. Go in, into the powerless and possibly lightless base, where six Outsiders were waiting in the close space, alert and armed and hating her for what had been done to them.

"Yasmin?"

Go in, into a close fight where numbers are the only real advantage? "Go in. Let's go in. How do we do it? If we just blow open locks, we'll kill the other two if they're not in suits."

"We go in through the damaged sections. You at the southwest corner, me at the southeast. Ali comes with me as support because there's likely to be more of them gathered there under the communications room. We go into the lab section from each end."

Ali. "I hope they weren't in suits when the grenade hit. Then we're okay."

"You stay outside until we call you. You have to stop anyone making a break for the lander.''

And then running again, loping in the armouring suit across the blank shadow ground towards the deeper dark bulk of the base, its near corner broken now. Hoping all the time that there's no one in the lock recess aiming a gun at you. They have one gun. And they have all their work tools to wield in the cramped interior space, and too many of those are cutting and piercing and deadly.

Standing below the first tractor docking lock, pointing your gun into it and its empty, outer door open, inner closed. Ali's suit shadow follows Akira's suit shadow across the star dark ground towards the southeast corner. The interior of this section is depressurized, open to vacuum—the inner door should open without cycling the lock—no pressure difference across the door for its control sensors to register.

She half jumped, half hauled herself up into the airlock opening and pressed the OPEN switch for the inner door. It slid aside on yawning nothing. So there was still reserve battery power for the basic systems.

The interior was pitch black. There was nothing for it but to use her suit lights, set right down to minimum. The double shoulder glows washed over a corridor strewn with wreckage between burst partition walls. Underneath the mess at her feet was a broken body with its back blown open and bits of entrails spread around it. More likely a gunshot wound than an effect of the grenade discharge. So at least one of them was still alive somewhere.

She turned down the long corridor, picking her way over a jumble of equipment swept from the storage racks by the depressurization wind. Her suit lights danced in and out of the two open gulfs of the workshop doors she had to pass between. A drill, a power saw—anything might go through the suit, killing with vacuum if not cutting directly home. It was crouching with the teenage school militia in the streets of Bangalore, little earnest silent squads with petrol bombs bursting around them, and stones and even spears bouncing across the scorched tarmac. It was searching through the wrecked houses with machine pistol and bayonet, fearing they were waiting round every corner with their guns and daggers and kitchen knives, pulling out your friends who had run into them. It was worse. It was now.

She sprayed shots through the partition walls into both

workshops, the X-flame from the muzzle brake strobing the narrow little world. She went on to the connecting lock, keyed her visor heater, opened the first door, slipped inside and closed it behind her. She pushed the cycle control to AIR and listened to it hissing into her box. That would warn the people on the other side. The hissing stopped. She opened the door onto a dimly lit emergency gloom. Gun advanced, she stepped out into the corridor leading between shelving ends towards the twin labs and the next lock.

Coming from the left, seen past the visor rim. A man who grabbed with both bare hands at her gun. His mouth opened and his scream was muffled and he wrenched the gun frenziedly from her grip. She struck backhanded at his face, throwing all her weight in and then whipping her fist back for another blow. Blood gushed from his cheek and jaw. The back of her suit fist had blood red tissue glued to it.

And a woman running at her down the corridor, a cutting torch in her hands spitting a diamond blade of bright blue flame.

She stepped back, grabbed loose tee shirt and tipped the reeling, screaming, collapsing man across the woman's path. Sidestep between the end shelves. The woman clambered over the folding man, came forward with the torch flame slicing the shadow. The shelves. Anything from the shelves. She swept armfuls of things from them, flinging them at the woman, bouncing them off her. And still the torch in her hands. The woman came on, half stumbled on something loose under her feet. Yasmin jumped, grabbed the torch behind the flame jet, kicked out into the woman's stomach, and she went backwards over the crumpled man. Yasmin followed, half hauling herself across the corridor with the shelf racks, half jumping over the man. She landed beside the woman, the woman tried to scramble away from her feet, away from the ice-cold suit. She swung between the shelves and stamped her whole weight onto the woman's head.

Sickening, sickening. She had to kick and shake before the head peeled loose from her boot sole. The back of the bald head was a mass of shimmering blood. No movement from the woman.

And she couldn't get the rifle loose. The man's hands were frozen onto it in an enclosing grip, iced onto something that had been out in almost absolute zero for an hour. He was still moaning and moving feebly. She fished the cutting torch out of the floor shadows, tried to strike the flame. No good, she couldn't make it work. She flung it somewhere. What to do with them? They weren't dead, they were surrounded by work tools, and *they* knew how to use them.

She grabbed the man by his tee shirt back so that her hands wouldn't stick, and bundled him into the tiny lock. Then she heaved the woman in on top of him. They filled the space half high. She closed the door on them and set the cycling control to VAK. The lock started to pump out.

She waited there, leaning, until the cycle finished. And all she had to hear was her own gasping breath, short gusts of her own air that bounced back into her eyes from the faceplate visor. She was still breathing. At least she was still breathing.

Ali waited about thirty metres out from the side of the base. He looked back through the blank night. Yasmin had already disappeared inside the southwest section, no one was running from behind the base towards the lander. If they did, he hoped he would see them, hoped he was a good enough shot.

Akira reached to open the airlock from down on the ground. He reached right inside. He must have opened the inner door as well—it should be possible with the section fully depressurized by the hole blown in the communications room above. Then Akira butted the gun against his chest and went up the steps and into the lock.

There was a freeze-flash from the muzzle flame. Then Akira reappeared in the lock and there was a moaning rising towards a howl in his helmet ears. He ran towards the base.

Akira's suit was leaning in the airlock entrance at the top of the steps. Akira's suit was clutching at something stuck into its semi-flexible waist section. Akira's voice was howling but the howl was already fading to a breathless gasp.

In the starlight he saw the suit pull something out of itself, and then half stumble and half fall down the steps. It dropped onto its side, limb loose, prevented from rolling over by the bulk of the backpack. Of course it collapsed. If something had made a hole in the suit and he pulled it out, out went the air and he was dead.

Ali took a charge from his suit, running the last few paces, keeping his glove clamped over the release trigger while twisting the arming ring right down to a two second minimum delay. He banged into the base wall beside the steps, flung the charge in through the airlock and round into the interior space, shut his eyes.

Through his eyelids he saw the lock interior and the ladder going up to the space above, split-second lit by the blue-white discharge. He waited for his eyes to recover.

Waiting, he realized that his breathing was out of step with itself. Some of it was shallow and fast and bubbling. It came from one of their own suits, of course, because the signal was decipherable. And Yasmin was inside the base and her transmission screened. Kim or Samson, somehow outside? Or injured, in the open section where he'd just thrown the hand charge? Then he saw Akira's suit move. Just twitch.

The breathing came from Akira. His eyes were closed, his head slumped against the side of the helmet and its visor. Blood bubbles at his nostrils burst and quivered in time with the breathing. He was alive when he shouldn't be. There was a finger sized hole in the middle of his suit.

Then light. He tried to turn and get his gun lined up.

"It's me!" Yasmin's voice. The twin burn points of shoulder lights descending from the lock. He looked at the black, descending feet to preserve his night vision. They reached the dark grey ground. "What's happened?"

"Akira. He's got a hole in his suit but he's alive. What do we do? What can we do?"

Her voice right in his ears while her suit turns and stoops for something. "Was this it? It's one of those drills. Ultrasonic vibration for use in free fall. No torque. It's still on." The suit flung the thing into the blackness under the base. "Did it go through his suit?"

"Right through. The whole blade. It must have gone almost right through *him*. But somehow he's still alive. Something must be blocking the hole, but the air will escape eventually. What do we do?"

"We get him inside. The lab section next to this is still pressurized."

"Are we safe in there?" Without the restricted view through the visor he would have looked round at the naked star-strewn night.

"I found one dead, killed two. There are two more dead just inside here. They were in suits, but the debris from the charge ripped them open. Did you throw the charge?"

"Yes."

"Yes. I felt the kick of it, so I came through. Be careful in there. There's a hole in the floor. Oh, and the missing rifle is in there too, smashed apart." The light pool started swinging as Yasmin's suit turned. "Where's Akira's? I need it."

They manhandled Akira inside his suit through into the emergency lit lab section. He was unconscious, his breathing shallow and irregular, but when they stood him up to get him through the airlock he still moaned, still blood gurgled. They laid him on the floor of the corridor between the lab partitions, and left him there. Their own suits were too cold—they couldn't open his up and try to help him without killing him in the process. He lay bridged on his backpack, bubble breathing.

They went through the base in a hurry, looking for the last Outsider and looking for their friends.

Samson they found straight away. He lay just inside the still pressurized and emergency lit sleep accommodation section. Something had been stuck in his stomach, and then he had been shot. The bullet had gone in through his back and had blown his chest wide open. The thing stuck in his stomach was a pair of pruning shears, small bladed and blunt nosed and harmless.

Dangling in the connecting lock between the northeast section and the hydroponics section, the two that had housed the Outsider prisoners, they found a hand communicator cable-patched into the base comm net. The handset's back was open and pieces of circuitry from somewhere else had been soldered on. They must have used it to take remote command of the base systems. Maybe the prisoners had been listening in to the conversations of their attackers for days—certainly long enough to know that the tractor was coming in and that three of them had left to meet it. It couldn't be a coincidence that they had staged their breakout with such perfect timing, and it wasn't telepathy. And it was a failure by no more than a minute or two. If that one single Outsider had got into the lander, then there would have been no entering the base and the Outsiders would all have been alive.

There was no one in the pressurized hydroponics section, no one hiding in the dim shadows behind plant curtains. There was no one in the glittering ice palace of the northwest corner section. They closed the loop, squeezing through together into the pressurized store section.

Kim lay dead in her suit in front of them.

Halfway along the section, standing there in the light of field work lamps propped on the shelves, stood a woman in a white spacesuit marked with orange-blue armbands. She had neither helmet nor backpack. She had been unpacking the explosive charges they used for seismology, couldn't possibly have known for certain that she was the only one to survive the last few minutes since the grenades hit the base. She was bald headed like them all, wore one of those same two faces of the clone groups, had the softer female version of the set of features.

She was absolutely terrified.

They made sure that Kim was dead by opening up her suit. They shouldn't have done that—she had been shot to pieces inside it. They re-sealed the suit and dragged it through into the airless southwest corner section.

They made the woman put on a helmet and took her with them into the lab section.

Akira was dead, too. He lay bridged on his backpack. Blood had collected in the back of his helmet, far more would have run down into his outstretched arms and legs. They didn't open his suit. The drill that went through it must have carved open his abdomen—some bit of his entrails must have stuck over the hole, held there by the interior pressure and preventing the suit's air spurting out into the vacuum. They put Akira in the southwest corner section. It was turning into a charnel house— Kim, Akira, the already dead man Yasmin had found, the two she killed whose bodies slumped out of the airlock when they opened it to go through.

They took the woman through to the sleep accommodation section and left her there until they could decide what to do with her. They took her helmet from her. Without a helmet she couldn't make it through to any of the stores sections, couldn't arm herself or fit herself up with a backpack to keep her alive in the suit for more than minutes. A perfectly sealed in prisoner again. She had the still functioning emergency lights, plus the field lamps they left with her, she had food and water and all the air left in three sections, she had the heat that would take hours or more probably days to drain away out of the base. That was all.

She said not a word and they said nothing to her. There never had been and there never would be anything at all to say.

They stowed her helmet in the pressurized lab section, out of her reach but stored at the lingering room temperature that would make it safe to wear. They dragged Samson through to the southwest corner section. The vacuum and the cold would preserve them all forever, unless the ground melting spread as far as the base.

They gathered the last usable weapons and charges, they took the backpacks from Samson's suit and from Akira's and Kim's, and walked back to the lander, passing the tractor, ignoring the spacesuit and its dead occupant lying almost beside one landing leg foot. They clambered up inside and stowed everything away, washed themselves down, pulled on their stale overalls again, and then just sat, each on their own end couch in the cramped little space. They had rubbed themselves down with the wash cloths, had touched their own undamaged flesh that could so easily have been sliced and shredded like everyone else's. They sat and said nothing. They were absolute rulers of an entire planet and had half the power of god. They could end the life left in their care, but could no more extend it than they could extend their own. They were half-gods of a whole planet. And it was no use to them at all.

This time the weight on the end of the line skidded on over the ice and went *past* the target. Or she thought it did. One hundred metres away in starlight, the line was invisible, the weight invisible, the target almost lost in the blank black shadow that was the ice surface. She checked carefully through the starscope. The slender line from the tractor was white, a rescue or climbing aid intended for use on their geological traverses; to weight the end she had found a solid little battery pack intended for the field lamps stored in the tractor's lock. It worked well enough when she threw the coiled line and weight together in a flat trajectory like a clumsy discus thrower. The suit was never designed for track and field events—even in three-fifths gee, she had the greatest difficulty in throwing the line a hundred metres, even here where the ice melted by Nightrider's shallow angle burn had re-frozen so perfectly level and smooth, without granular surface, without rock fragments or pressure ripples or cracks. She could only throw line and weight for half the distance and hope that the residual momentum would carry it on to the target. This time it had. This was the fourteenth or fifteenth try, but she hadn't dared to go any closer. Already the ice matrix, weakened to a microscopic honeycomb by the evaporative loss of atmospheric gases locked inside it, had given away under her foot. She had gone in up to her knee. Deeper still, a few centimetres or a few metres, would be the liquid pocket that was carrying the heat through the ice valley. And if she had gone through into that it would have been a terrifying death—not long if she sank until the pressure crushed the suit, but awful if the water vein was shallow, if she was trapped there waiting.

She waited until her night vision recovered, then moved slowly away to the side, flicking the line along with her, testing the ice with each sliding stride. The line had gone past the suited figure. Now the trick was to move to a position such that when she pulled the weight back, the line tightened around the suit. Against it, at least. All that showed above the broken surface of the ice was a helmet and shoulders and spread out arms, half turned towards her as if the fleeing Outsider had been trying to regain safer ground even as he or she sank into the ice trap. She couldn't tell at that distance whether the suit was coated in re-frozen water that had escaped when the surface cracked, or whether the occupant could see the line through an unfrosted visor. All she knew was that the Outsider was probably alive, if equally probably unconscious. She had known that back at the lander when she had turned one of its cameras along the valley to see what had happened to the figure that had tried to run from the crippled tractor. The clear infrared signature said that the backpack power was still operating.

If the occupant was unconscious, this was all a waste of time. She couldn't go out there and tie the line in a loop round the shoulders of the suit.

She started to pull the line in cautiously, hand over hand, checking repeatedly with the starscope. When she thought it had tightened against the suit's outstretched arm, she stopped. All she could do was wait until the Outsider reacted. She couldn't fire instructions—their suit radios coded their digitalized signals so that they were mutually incomprehensible.

The idea had been to kill the figure in the suit, to come out and calmly shoot it. It was her idea. Anything was better than leaving a human being out there trapped and waiting to die. Ali had just shrugged and said he would drive her there in the tractor—it was quicker. He stopped the tractor half a kilometre short, back where the ground was still safely solid.

She couldn't do it, not now. She had already killed four people, and that was enough. The motive wasn't humanity, the gesture was useless. There was no Nightrider and nowhere to escape to, with or without a single prisoner or a pair of prisoners. She was dead and Ali was dead whatever happened. The next Outsiders, when they came, wouldn't forgive them for destroying the base and massacring all but two of its inhabitants. If they managed to survive until the next ship came, if the base wasn't swallowed in the next few hours— there had been a ground shock while they were aboard the lander, stronger than any that had gone before. The base would break apart and sink in a few days at the latest. The infrared views told them so—the ice around it was already beginning to warm up.

It was just that she couldn't kill anyone any more, not in cold blood, not like the first one in amongst the wildly fractured terrain southwards on the day they took the base. There was no mission motivation any more. It was one of Sandra's *why* questions asked out of curiosity alone, out of pure passive interest. But the answer had shrugged off any assignment-task justifications and had bitten back with naked teeth. It had spat a single drop of venom into her mind that stunned and numbed her with the suspicious inevitability of simple truth: there was no reason. There was no reason.

And it took so long.

It took so long before the almost buried suit out there in the ring of star dark reacted, before it clumsily got hold of the line and slowly managed to tie a loop under its shoulders. With her whole weight thrown on the line, with the suit trying to prise itself free with its arms, it was useless. She had to call Ali to come walking the long half kilometre to help. She kept a light tension on the line all the time, varying it. The Outsider had no imaging aids, couldn't possibly see them in their night camouflage suits. She couldn't let the line go slack and leave the Outsider thinking that hope had come and then gone again so quickly.

He had been stuck in the ice for ten hours, probably desperately chilled as the majority of the suit surface lost heat by conduction. He was aware of what was going on around him, but only just, already suffering from more than mild hypothermia. All the way back he just lay on the tiny floor of the tractor, his flexible suit caked from shoulders to boots in scales of fractured ice. His suit had orange and green armband identification colours, the woman caught in the stores section had worn a suit with armbands in orange and blue. His face was the same as hers. Just the same. They were the two last survivors of one of the clone groups, two out of six indistinguishable twins. The other group had been wiped out.

The woman in the sleep accommodation had quit her suit and had wrapped herself in bedrolls to keep warm—a spacesuit had excellent insulation, but the wide open helmet ring let all the conserved heat out again. She got her rescued companion out of his suit when it had warmed up enough to be safe to touch. He was still shivering, his suntanned arms and legs paled beyond white. She wrapped him in bedrolls on the padded floor. They didn't even open their suits. It was a dumb show of blank stares at their black suits and their faces behind the reflection free visors. She had nothing to say to them, only to the man when they were gone. She would have a lot to say to him.

She only showed one reaction that broke the blankness of her face. There was a creaking noise that came out of the ground and transmitted up the foundation frame supports and sounded through the base structure. That was what was going to kill them all.

They went back to the lander. They went through the laborious business of clambering out of their suits and stowing them in the two standing racks in the airlock. They climbed up into the crew space dimness, they broke out ration cakes and drink bulbs. Ali sat on his couch, carefully avoiding spreading over onto Kim's. Yasmin squatted on her own laid flat couch, legs crossed and back against the locker lined end wall, carefully not touching Akira's half reclining couch right in front of her. Samson's broken couch was stowed. The end of their world was a dark little box with three activated screens, one showing a brightened view of the ruined base building, one looking wide towards the west where the incoming tractor still lay tiny and wrecked with its dead driver, one showing a matrix of passive status displays—little light rimmed boxes containing state lights or static number readouts. The screen with the status displays shone in front of Kim's couch.

Ali stopped chewing. Ali leaned forward. Ali almost reached out and touched the screen. He stared, transfixed.

"What?" She found herself leaning forward to look, steadying herself across the back of Akira's couch. "What? Don't frighten me, Ali."

"A signal. It's a signal. Logged today at eighteen-twenty-thirty-one. That's over two hours ago. While we were out in the tractor."

She closed her eyes. She couldn't bring herself even to think it, not now, not after five days. And when she looked again, Ali had activated his own screen, and its upper half held a static readout while its lower half traced a running calculation. "What?"

"Signal from Nightrider." Ali watched the calculation run. "Position and flight predict data, and a response request. I'm running the predict so we can aim a tight beam reply. What—" He shook his head, he swallowed back something that might have been a sudden breaking sob. "What do we say?"

"I don't know. I don't know." She was setting her food aside, she was unfolding her legs. "Request an immediate response. I don't know."

The calculation froze. "Got it. We're set up. How about— copy, request immediate response?" He was already keying it in.

Yasmin scrambled across Akira's couch, across the floor-hole gap, and slid into Kim's seat. Forgetting the dead.

Ali entered the signal and told the lander to send it. Nothing to do but wait. It was stupid to wait for an instant response. They would be busy, but Nightrider would tell them the moment a signal had come in. They would break off and set up a reply. Five anxious days had been too long to make a further delay even thinkable.

"What's the signal return time?"

Ali searched the screen for the right data, suddenly not even seeing straight. "They're at two point three three million out. That's going to be—that's about fifteen and a half seconds both ways. We could hold a voice conversation."

When the response came. When it came. It was already over a minute now. Almost two. Too long.

Signal readouts. Flight data updating. A voice channel

indicator telling the lander's communications computer what to do.

Shapir's voice. "I just got your signal. Am I glad to hear from you. I can't tell you. I really can't. I thought you were dead until I found out what's been happening."

Ali opened their own voice transmit. "You thought we were dead?" He was looking at Yasmin, his desert Arab eyes as hard as ever but the rest of his face lost among possible expressions. "For two days—three days—we've been assuming that something had gone wrong and—"

"Yes, we thought you were dead. We told Nightrider to send a call up signal—oh." A pause. "We're overlapping in the transmission delay. Let's run this professionally. Over."

"Okay, got you," Ali said. "Over."

Yasmin shook her head. "How do we tell them what's happened? Do we just say it outright—they're dead?"

Ali shrugged.

"Okay," said Shapir's voice. "I'm going to make this as short as I can. There's no way of knowing if there's another ship or missile waiting around somewhere, and now I know how dangerous they are I don't want to give them any more of a fix than necessary. Okay. Yes. We told Nightrider to send a call-up signal fifty-three hours ago. I know you didn't get it. Just listen. Are you all there? Better store this. When we got no response we told Nightrider to send repeat call ups requesting an immediate response. When you still hadn't responded yesterday we got really worried. We started running through the mission log from Hel encounter to chase departure after you separated. That's the first chance we had to realize things had been going wrong right from the start. Am I right in thinking that the base wasn't properly taken out and that you separated after the missile manoeuvre burn without a correcting flight update? Just say yes or no. I'm in a hurry. Over."

"We didn't get an update," Ali said. "We landed in the wrong place. It took us the rest of the day just to figure it out."

"And the base was intact," Yasmin said. "The burn had only taken out their power reactor. That's turned out bad."

"We'll tell you in a moment. Over." Ali keyed their send channel closed. "Why does he say *we* and then *I*?"

Yasmin shrugged.

Shapir again. "We took out the Outsider on Day three oh five. He went all the way to Hades and we got him coming out from his flyby. On the way to Hades we took out the comsat, and he nearly took us out with a missile. After we'd dealt with him we went for a tight flyby to bring us back to Hel as quickly as possible. That's when Nightrider started getting argumentative. He was trying to block our decisions. He didn't want us to go direct to Hel. He didn't want us to send you a signal. I've more or less found out why. I'll tell you in a minute. Yesterday, when we found out he'd missed the flight data update at separation, and as far as we knew effectively killed you with the error—I mean, we'd signalled and you didn't reply at all, so we figured something serious had gone wrong as a consequence of your start data being junk. Yesterday he—I don't know. He attacked us. He pulled ten gee on us while we were going up the ladder to the ring corridor. He was obviously trying to kill us. Sandra realized what was happening just in time to give us a chance. But. But. She's dead.''

His voice stopped.

That was impossible, impossible, completely impossible. That couldn't happen. That couldn't have happened. Nightrider could not and would not do anything of the sort. Nightrider brought them here with the mission book, and the mission book said to take them back again. That was impossible.

"Sandra's dead?" Ali said. "Sandra's dead? What do you mean, she's dead?"

"Nightrider attacked you? That's not possible. He can't—"

"It seems we have some sort of subliminally implanted instruction that allows us to take over command in an emergency—hey, you're overlapping. I mean she's *dead*. Nightrider killed her. He nearly killed me. I'm all bruises from it. He hit us with ten gee when we weren't in our couches. Do you understand? It broke her back. She's dead. I'm alive because we seem to have been provided with some sort of command override that allows us to suspend Nightrider's command functions and run the ship directly ourselves. It's supposed to be enacted by both pilots co-operating, but I managed to run Sandra's lock as well as my own. I'll tell you how it works when you're back on board. You'll need to know. The thing is, the bastards who sent us out here gave it to us *subliminally*. We didn't know we could defend ourselves until after Nightrider started trying to kill us. I suppose they wanted to protect Nightrider against us cracking up or giving up or doing something else that would endanger the mission. Nightrider wasn't going to do anything to us, of course. He's just programmed to execute the mission. But I think that's what went wrong. Are you getting this? Over.''

"We're getting it," Ali said. "We just don't understand."

"*Why* should Nightrider try to kill you? *Why*?"

It made no sense at all. Nightrider operated under a priority constraint to fulfil the mission book targets. From Nightrider's point of view, the crew were the main supportive component in doing just that.

"You want to hand over? Okay. I've been trying to sort it out. I've nothing else to do, and I can't sleep. Sandra's dead and I've overridden Nightrider, so there's no one to send me to sleep. I'm almost collapsing but I can't sleep. I think it goes like this. Nightrider has to execute the mission without making mistakes. I think they must have made that constraint too strong for him. He knew he'd made an error at the lander separation. He made two. He pulled five gee and injured Samson, didn't he? Hope he's all right by now. I think the constraint is too high. I think he believes he has to go back home without having made a mistake. So he wants to erase the mistakes. Erase the evidence, more or less. And the evidence is all of us and the mission log. We know whether or not a mistake has been made, and the mission log records it. If he can re-write the mission log, and if we don't know what he did wrong, then he goes home having executed his mission function perfectly. Do you follow me? Over.''

"No."

"He can't re-write the mission log."

"How could he? Over.''

This signal was supposed to be the sudden and unbelievable news that they were going to live, that they were going to go home. But now it was incomprehensible.

"I think he *can* re-write the mission log. Could if he regained command function. I've checked. There just isn't any kind of lock on the mission log. The security against *us* doing it is that Nightrider would know all about it and would remember the real events. Those are psych-structure memories he builds, aren't they? Not externally accessible. Private, more or less. Just before he attacked us we found out that there was no flight data update for the lander when there should have been, right before separation. He forgot it. Maybe he was thrown because he'd injured Samson. But I've been trying to get around the command override renewal requirement. I'll explain that in a minute. I've been trying everything I could think of. I even accessed his peripheral work-up stores. This is what I found. I found a mission log entry reporting the missing update ready for insertion. That erases one record of the error. I also found a whole mass of data I couldn't sort out at first. It's a complete sequence of events that didn't happen. He has a missile attacking us on the return transit from Hades. The data allows the analysis that the Outsider launched it while we were still chasing him *to* Hades, but it missed us because of course divergence. We passed it by, killed the Outsider, made our Hades flyby, and then encountered the missile more or less head on during our way back. He had to pull max gee with about two seconds warning, which I suppose is his reason for why we were killed. I don't know what he intended to do with the fine details. He'd have the entire return transit to figure something out. But you understand me, don't you. The whole missile encounter is a complete fiction. It never happened. He was going to re-write the mission log for half the mission. I suppose he intended to head back and make sure the base was taken out properly and make sure none of you had survived to report his mistakes, then he was going to reorganize the whole series of events to explain everything perfectly. We were all killed by Outsider missiles or something, but the mission was a success. Makes sense—we are all expendable just as long as the targets are met. Only Nightrider himself has a hundred percent value index. Without him there is no mission. Do you understand me now? Nightrider was going to kill us all and go home and probably get away with it. I don't know. I don't care. Do you understand? Over.''

"We—we—'' Ali gave up and shook his head. "It's going to take a little while to sort it out. We're recording. Over.''

It was going to take a long time to sort out.

"Good. I'll explain in detail when I've picked you up. This really has to be short. Right now I have one problem. The override has to be renewed at irregular intervals—anything from ten minutes to a couple of hours. I need help with that, and I need sleep. I just can't find a way round the program. My Hel encounter is tomorrow at oh-eight-twenty-three-forty. We'll talk about this later. I want to pick you up immediately and head out so we're safe and so you can relieve me and I can sleep. I'm going to miss a renewal before much longer, and then Nightrider's won. It can't be re-enacted. That's all. We should stop. Do you agree? Over.''

''I guess—I guess we need to think before we have any more questions. But there's something we have to tell you first. It didn't go so well here.

''There's just Ali and me. The others are dead.''

They forgot to say *over*, but that wasn't the reason it took Shapir a long time to reply.

DAY 308

"NOT take us with." The woman stood there, her bare feet making little sunken wells in the padded floor inside the wall-screened space beside the central corridor. She wore yellow shorts and a bright red tee shirt with a double diagonal stripe of white, bright colours in their white and grey base world. A bedroll quilt was draped over her shoulders. It was cold in there. Very cold.

"What happen to us when you take us with to Earth-Luna?" The man, her male version twin, sat on the soft floor. He had a bedroll wrapped around him, folded to cover his bare arms and crossed legs. He wore black shorts and a tee shirt quarter panelled in lilac and green. "They interrogate us. They drain us dry. They maybe kill us in the end."

"They kill us. What use we be after they interrogate us? They kill us. We stay here."

Stay in the last wreckage of their home, their future world. Only this end of the sleep accommodation section was lit by field lamps slung from the sliding wall screens, this last corner of the still accessible base. Within a day it would be too cold for human life. A few days later it would be broken up, swallowed, gone. The ice ground was warming up the temperature grade from almost absolute zero towards the melting point of water, the haze thin sublimation mist had spread right across the flat valley, a film of it hung like a star ghost veil over the granular surface outside.

"Stay here and you'll die." Ali was black armoured to his neck. He stood in his suit with the helmet and shoulder yoke folded forward over the chest. Thus they displayed their human frailty hidden and protected within their machine shells. They must have looked all the more menacing, two evil starship troopers encased in their death coloured armoured suits. Or else ridiculous.

"At least you have a chance with us." It hadn't taken very long to persuade Shapir that the three of them could cope with two unarmed prisoners aboard Nightrider—most of the time they could keep them sealed in a sleep cubicle each, the door computer-locked from the flight centre, via any key pad. And there would be empty cubicles enough. Yasmin shook her head. "Here you're dead. Come with us and there's a chance you'll be exchanged one day. Some of our people are bound to get into your hands, if there aren't a few already."

"Be no exchanges," the woman said. "A return prisoner is a security data risk. By then we know too much. We stay here."

"But you'll die here."

"No," the man said. "One tractor is still serviceable. We load it with supplies and we track to an outstation. At the outstations are supply dumps. We can survive until the next ship comes, when we have the supplies from several outstations. We think we can. The next ship is in seven oh days. You know that okay. It has a lander to bring down the new personnel and supplies. It can rescue us. So we stay."

"We don't want go with you. We've see what you like. We can guess what happen to us at Earth-Luna. When we stay here we stay alive. When you take us with we die."

"You come with us just the same." Ali was impatient. The lift off and to-orbit ascent was already set up on the lander's guidance computer and ready to go. It was programmed for launch at 09:02:35, forty minutes from now, just exactly right to take them up into a west-east orbit and park them there right in front of Nightrider as Nightrider came around the planet on its one and only orbital pass. Then they would dock, and Shapir would cut in the drive immediately to accelerate them out of orbit and into the beginning of their long transit back home, away from Hel and Hades and the whole horrible place. They only had to clear the launch program and the lander would take them up all by itself. And then they would be aboard, and safe. Shapir would show them how to run the command override extensions, and then Shapir could get some rest. As soon as they had put some distance between themselves and Hel, the focus of any lingering Outsider presence, the only place that a lone waiting missile could be, Shapir would even sleep. They would continue like that for ten months, in permanent danger of death from Nightrider, should he regain command of himself if they missed an extension— but going home.

Right now Shapir was speeding over the other side of the planet, cutting the drive as his decelerating course inserted into the planned orbital path. They had held a brief planning discussion with him two hours ago. Everything was set up, and lift off was in forty minutes. If they were taking the Outsiders with them, then they had to go now. The suits would have to warm up slowly aboard the lander, they had to get out of them to take the three gee acceleration load on the couches, they had to get the Outsiders tied down with lengths of pirated line.

"You come with us just the same."

"No!" The woman meant it. They were both frightened. By now they had every reason to be, of course. "No. Not take us with. Please not make us go. Let us stay here where we have a chance to live. Please?"

"We have instructions," Ali said. "We don't leave anything behind that could help your people figure out what our capabilities are. How we did it. The base and the whole mess will be gone in a day or two. That leaves you. We take you with us, or we kill you right away."

"Get into your suits," Yəsmin said. "We've brought you the helmets. Those are charged backpacks. Get them on." She was swinging her gun one-handed, probably menacingly. She wondered if she meant it.

This was the last walk in the dark. Two black suits like nothingness monster holes in the night, two light coloured suits with identification armbands standing out under the stars, they went across the flatness from the base towards the lander, past the tractor, away from the ice house full of bodies. The spreading sublimation mist lay motionless like silk smoke, barely visible as a reflected midnight sheen where the opaque shadow ground should be. It was beginning to freeze a film frost onto the lower base structure and the tractor legs, an awful absolute starlit winter scene. They switched on their lights rather than waiting for their night vision to adapt—helmet lights for the Outsiders, twin shoulder lights for themselves. There was no one to hide from any more. Yasmin walked slightly ahead, Ali came behind the two prisoners. Their moving lights threw a vague shadow of her suit-self out across the ankle mist. They walked through it and it paid no attention, no air currents stirred by their feet to swirl it.

It had a fearful beauty in the utter night.

They walked with both their suit radios set on open circuit, but there was nothing to say. Then Ali's voice sharp in her ears.

"Hey, I lost sight of one of—"

She turned round. Her lights hit them and their point lights fixed her. Black suit Ali was sinking down on his knees, and clambered half up his back was a white suit Outsider, bearing him down.

She lifted her gun but Ali was in the way. From the side came the other white suit, helmet light announcing it. She swung her gun and it stopped metres away, stepped back again.

Ali was on his knees and trying to rise again, the white suit was behind him and trying to prise open the locking clips that sealed his suit. One came open.

Yasmin was running in, running sideways to get a clear shot.

Ali got his gun loose from its carry port. He should pitch forward so she could shoot. Instead he angled his gun back one-handed over his shoulder—

The X-flame flashed behind his shoulder and helmet. The white suit bounced away spurting instant air and blood-mix ice into the vacuum. A jet of freezing air went up from the back of Ali's suit shoulder. He toppled sideways. Blood vomited onto the inside of his visor, brilliant red in her lights as she ran the last steps. Ali's suit lay down on its side and kicked.

Then it lay still.

She stooped over it. There was a hole in the back of the shoulder. The muzzle brake flame jet must have burned clean through and killed him with the hole alone. The visor was still opaque with a blood film that would set and freeze before it could drain away. Explosive depressurization causes all the fine blood vessels of the lungs to burst—the victim dies of blood loss even before asphyxia can start to kill.

The Outsider suit lay spreadeagled in the motionless ground mist. It was the one with orange-blue armbands, the one the woman had worn. The helmet light was out. The bullet must have torn right through into the backpack.

Yasmin turned her gun towards the other suit. It stood there waiting, its cyclops light shining at her. It had orange-green armbands.

Her first thought, when a thought came, was that he was her only supporting evidence of why she had survived and everyone else had not. The mission planners were not to be trusted, after all. She had always thought that they were the mission and Nightrider just the weapon and the bus. *Academically,* of course, she had always known that Nightrider was the mission focus and the crew a subordinated component, but emotionally you are your own centre and the world supports you. But now she knew that Nightrider really was the functional focus. And the planners had done it wrong.

For a fraction of a thought she wondered why the woman had hated so much that she should kill, and had feared so intensely that she should risk dying rather than go back with them. But then the answer to that was obvious.

His helmet and backpack and bulkily insulated flexible suit could stay down in the airlock. They would float about up in orbit, but they would do no harm. The Outsider she tied to the couch, her own couch, the extreme right-hand one. He lay there trussed to it, lashed in place round ankles and chest, with both his wrists tied safely at one side where he could on no account reach one of the key pads.

She placed herself on Kim's couch. On the couch beside her Ali had been sleeping only three hours ago. She sat there now with the pilot key pad and hand flight controls, with the screen glowing burn parameters and provisional countdown at her. Ali had said there was enough propellant left on board to go up to orbit with four people along for the ride, and then come three quarters of the way back down again. Not that a three quarters descent was any use—the fuel would give out while they were still travelling at one thousand five hundred metres a second relative to the ground. The crash would vapourize the lander.

The fuel reserve was useless anyway. Although she wasn't competent to fly the vehicle by hand, she could program in set-ups for automatic manoeuvres and orbit transfers, given time. But the pre-set burn would bring them up into orbit at a rendezvous position exactly twenty-five kilometres ahead of Nightrider as Nightrider came over the horizon from the west to overfly the base. That was close enough for Shapir to approach and dock. That was his job now. He was the only pilot left.

She keyed into the launch program and cleared it for enactment. The count down proceeded uninterrupted, but real this time, not provisional. Ten minutes of silence in a tight little space, while the expressionless Outsider waited and watched. She had her gun tucked beside her on the couch, secured to an equipment strap fastened round her waist. One of those they had used to fasten down Samson's broken couch.

The ground vibrated. The tremor went on and on.

She searched with an external camera. A kilometre away across the flat valley floor, right out over the point where the reactor pile had sunk, the ice had burst open. Liquid water was breaking through to the overlying nothing and instantly vacuum boiling to vapour, instantly losing its heat by radiation and then crystallising back to ice. A desperate little geyser field, a starlit cluster of ice dust fountains, was dancing above mobile ground.

The base would go soon. Everything would go.

Hel was saying goodbye.

The burn ran automatically for two hundred and ten seconds. After lift off the lander pitched over to ten degrees from horizontal and went on adding thirty metres per second of velocity every single second, the thrust automatically cutting back as the lander's total weight reduced with the consumption of propellant mass. They went eastward, climbing steadily away from the narrowing valley, flitting past the pinnacle base marker kilometres from the base site itself, rising in step with the rising tumble of shattered ground, sweeping clear but close over the first mountain peaks. Seen in intensified starlight, it would have been an utterly breathtaking display of sweepingly magnificent spatial dimensions. If there had been an ounce of emotion left with which to respond to it.

The burn cut. The status displays glowed on. At ten degrees displacement orientation to its flight direction, the lander fell at six thousand and two hundred metres every second round an orbit curve that swept it at twenty kilometres altitude around Hel. If nothing ever happened again, it would circle forever. Free fall. She lay against her couch without pressure, held to it by the hip strap. The Outsider hung tied to his own—*her* own couch it had been, when the five of them went down to Hel. He looked at the ceiling displaced screen in front of him. All the rowed screens except the one in front of her showed the same view of synthetically bright chaos landscape rolling below. Her own—Kim's—showed the status displays.

The status display telltales showed incident radar at Nightrider's docking radar frequency. She keyed up a new view on the centre screen, back through the tail camera, back exactly along their line of flight. And a star field, a diamond dust of white and colours strewn on black. In the middle, a silhouette, a cut out hole in infinity. The silhouette was a circle with two huge and angular side lobes in a balancing pair—Nightrider seen end on, with just two of his fusion booster pods remaining. A death dragon in its space realm, still lethally armed.

An incoming carrier signal. She opened the channel.

"Nice, Ali. Nice. I have you at exactly twenty-five thousand, relative velocity exactly zero. Can you run the docking approach? I have my hands full for the next few minutes. The command override extensions are still coming irregularly. There was one twenty minutes ago, and now there's one due right at rendezvous. In a few minutes, that is."

"Ali isn't here."

"What?"

"Ali isn't here. He's dead. It's his work, though. He set up the launch before it happened."

"Ali's dead? He's dead?"

"Yes. He's dead. We were bringing them over to the lander and one of them jumped him. They're afraid of us."

Silence. A long silence.

"So there's only you left."

"Me and one Outsider. The other one's dead. Can you run the docking? I don't have the skill for it."

"Okay. Can we—just the two of us—can we cope with one

of them on board as well as Nightrider?''

"If not we can always kill him.''

The Outsider didn't even look at her. He was staring steadily at the empty hole in the star field that was Nightrider.

"Okay. I'll run the dock. We just have to wait until the extension's out of the way.''

"Yes. Shapir, you sound tired.''

"I am. I really am.''

His whole body ached. Most of it was a pattern of bruises. The couch squeezed the bruises, but squeezed steadily so that the pain was invisible. Invisible. Everything came back to the visual sense, and it was threatening to fail. He had to get some sleep within a few more hours. No sleep at all for more than fifty hours, and that coming on top of the strain and drain of the chase and kill, and that followed by the sheer shock and disbelief at Nightrider's attack and Sandra's death.

He lay in the flight centre alone, free fall squeezed by the couch. He was completely alone in the crew module, unless Sandra counted when she was dead and frozen. There was only Nightrider himself, through the couch behind his back, through the base of the crew module and just inside the vehicle proper. So close but so utterly inaccessible. Maybe they could find a way in there after all, given long enough to pore over the structural data, but not yet, not for days yet. First the extension, then get the lander docked and get Yasmin aboard, get the Outsider locked into one of the cubicles. Then cut in the drive and start accelerating out of orbit, away from Hel and Hades and homeward. Set an approximate initial course, show Yasmin how to extend the command override so that she can run it alone for a few hours. And then sleep.

OVERRIDE EXTENSION DUE 308 09:11:00. FAILURE TO EXTEND RESULTS IN COMMAND REVERSION TO SHIP. OVERRIDE NOT REINITIATABLE.

Two minutes now. The main reactor was already run up, he could use the drive to close the twenty-five kilometre gap to the lander. But not yet, not until after the extension. His brain could only cope reliably now with one thing at a time, and either a collision or a missed override would be equally catastrophic. He could kill them both for Nightrider, or Nightrider could take over and do it himself. And there was always the risk of a third thing happening at once, the risk that here, in the vicinity of Hel, something else was orbiting.

BURN SIGHTED AHEAD +36° TO TRACK. ANALYSING TRACK.

A burn? A missile burn? A missile on a higher orbital path firing its motor to transfer down to intercept? If it was ahead of them and orbiting in the same sense, if it could shed enough velocity so that it fell into a transfer path that intercepted their own, then it was possible.

PATH DATA ANALYSED. RANGE 400 km. CLOSING 2,800 ms°02¹, PLUS GRAVITY ACCEL. COLLISION-INTERCEPT IN 140 SEC. IDENTIFY AS MISSILE. NO VISUAL CONTACT.

A missile coming in. And why now? Why now, with the extension due, with the lander naked in orbit, with no one else aboard yet to take over the extension while he ran the defence manoeuvre?

But the data was coming from Nightrider. Nightrider had seen the burn and analysed its track—Nightrider could still see and hear everything that was going on, he just couldn't interfere in it. But—he could fake it. He could fake a missile encounter.

Shapir opened the link to the lander again. "Yasmin. Nightrider says there's a missile coming in. Intercept in one twenty seconds. Is it possible? Did you find out how many missiles that ship had?"

A slight reaction pause. "Wait. Wait. It was four. You. Is that right? Your ship carried four missiles? Come on. It's *important!* There's one coming in now!"

"Four. Yes, four."

"Shapir. Four missiles."

"Okay." He keyed up a peripheral, started shoving instructions into it to run a missile track predict, a burn orientation predict for Nightrider, an intercept burn set-up. "We only accounted for two. It's possible." Then he instructed a tracking radar to lock onto the missile. At such close range it would need no extra help to see them—they were heat signatures, Nightrider flaring, they were visual silhouettes against the star dark planet. "Try a radar sweep. Ahead, plus three six degrees. Confirm it."

"I don't know if I can."

"Do it. Nightrider might be faking so I miss the extension."

The radar data came on the ceiling screen right in front of him. Exactly what Nightrider had said, a missile coming in. But Nightrider could fake radar data in post-event store, maybe he could fake it in real-time and read it into the displays. Start to look at the defence burn manoeuvre. Simple. The line up is perfect. Just pitch over, nose to the planet, tail to space. Pitch through 144 degrees, and the missile would be coming straight down the path of the burn. Easy. Far too suspiciously easy.

SHAPIR YOU MUST RESPOND. THE MISSILE IS REAL. BELIEVE ME.

Thirty seconds to the extension. Sixty seconds to the missile intercept. Nightrider might as well have made them coincident. He keyed in the instruction ready for entering: ENACT COMMAND OVERRIDE EXTENSION.

SHAPIR YOU MUST RESPOND. BURN ON MISSILE TRACK. ANALYSING. PREDICT UPDATE. INTERCEPT IN 38 SEC. YOU MUST RESPOND.

Decision time! No decision time! And the ghost missile or real missile coming in faster.

INCIDENT RADAR. MISSILE IS TARGETING US. 30 SEC. THE MISSILE IS REAL SHAPIR. CORRECTION BURN. 24 SEC. DO SOMETHING SHAPIR. YOU'RE TOO LATE SHAPIR.

Pitching, the couch swinging you in space. Nightrider is moving! He missed the extension! He didn't enter it! Nightrider is back! Nightrider pitching over to burn the lander. Boosters two and four run up ready.

He swung his hand in the one degree of freedom the couch allowed. He grabbed the attitude control trigger grip. He slammed it to pitch back and fired full thrust.

"Shapir, don't interfere. Intercept in ten seconds. I must orientate."

Pitching over again, his senses said and the readouts confirmed. Pitching part way over to take the missile or right over to take the lander. He fired full thrust yaw. Space swinging and readouts whirling and balance senses out. "Doesn't matter, Nightrider. If the missile's real you take it, then the lander, then me by shutting the crew module down. If it isn't, we're dead. If it's real you go too."

"It's real, Shapir."

Main thrust burn. *Weight!*

"Shapir! I can *see* it! Against the stars!"

The fireball flash killed the camera.

No more tail view of Nightrider.

The planet surface lit up blinding bright under a sunburst.

The side view that had seen a slicing something occulting the stars showed an expanding, flaring glow. Atomic debris and disintegration dust bursting out into the insatiable void. Brilliant speeding specks in it.

A hammer smash and a shudder in the lander. The status displays flashed an alarm panel. Landing radar malfunction. That didn't matter. There wasn't any fuel to land by. No more damage. That didn't matter either. It would have been better to go quickly.

The sunburst had faded. The planet was dark. Hel was back in its impenetrable Hades night.

Radiation readouts. The hard radiation flux outside was enormous. They were tail on to the massive explosion—the bulk of the lander's structure plus the residue of fuel mass might have shielded them from the neutron surge. But there was no internal reading available, no way to tell. The thermal radiation flash had burned out the tail camera and done who knew what to the lander's outer skin. At least the control electronics and computers were still functioning, but what possible use was that? There was nothing more to see with it, nothing to calculate, nothing to do.

"What was that?" the Outsider asked, very quietly.

"That was Nightrider. That was Shapir. Your ship must have left another missile in orbit to protect the base when it left. He didn't believe it when it came in because Nightrider can fake things like that."

"Don't understand."

"I'll explain it. Later." There was still a later. For a little while at least. Two appointed enemies with a remnant of time on their hands. "That was our way home gone. There's no way home any more." And there she was, hollow voiced and without a hope of the wailing sob that she wanted to come.

He nodded.

"We land," he said, after a long minute. "We land at the base, we load a tractor, we track to an outstation, we wait until the next ship comes.''

To kill her. They might interrogate her first, but they would kill her. That was obvious. In fact he would kill her at the first opportunity once they were down—it would increase his chance of surviving the long seventy days until the next Outsider was due. But it didn't matter. "We don't land. We don't have enough fuel. We'd just crash. We stay up here. The lander still has sixteen days of consumables. Then the power gives out, and we're dead.''

He didn't say anything.

It took a long time. It took thirty-five minutes. They were halfway round the orbit, skimming over the black back of Hel, when it finally surfaced. She couldn't play with the masses, she couldn't set up a program to tell her what would happen— but then if it didn't work after all they would only crash and die quickly. Better than waiting. But when your life is going to end anyway, you can play the grim puzzle game of extending it as long as you can. Anything was better than nothing, than letting the huge dam of stored up shocked emotion finally burst.

Slowly and carefully, she fed instructions into the guidance computer to land them on Hel again. She couldn't set an exact enough position—she didn't want to go straight down onto the suspect ground right beside the base where they had started from, so she picked a site ten kilometres west of the base and settled for the relatively huge target error that was the best she could do. At least the lander itself could set up the entire manoeuvre and time and enact it exactly. The burn would run until the fuel gave out. If they weren't down by then—a quicker death, at least.

One thought suggested briefly that she hadn't pulled the Outsider out of the ice just to have him die up here. But she dismissed it. She was playing with her own life. It was a less humiliating defeat if you managed to keep yourself alive until they killed you, or else died in the effort, than if you just gave up. You can't beat the universe any more than you can make it make sense, but you can acknowledge your inborn instincts on the way out.

She locked in the manoeuvre. The lander would do everything else itself. She had plenty to do.

She floated over and untied him. He hovered in the couch

corner, rubbing his wrists and waiting for an explanation.

"We're going to try to land. We might have enough fuel. I don't know. The fuel reserve data I had was valid for a take-off weight with four people and suits, but there's just you and me. We won't have used so much because of the automatic thrust maintenance at constant acceleration. And there's just you and me for the landing. We're going to shed every piece of useless mass we can find. We're going to get into our suits and we're going to strip this thing clean. Just throw everything out of the airlock. I'll show you what to do, and you just keep doing it. The descent burn commences in less than thirty minutes, and by then we have to be finished. The less mass we have, the longer our fuel lasts. Do you understand me?"

He nodded.

She evacuated the lander and opened all the hatches from the crew space through the airlock to the vacuum outside. Then it started. She got Samson's couch squeezed through all the hatches and flung it out into the blackness. She set him trying to dismount two of the remaining four couches, and then started going through all the lockers. Ammunition, recoilless grenades, hand charges, starsights, starscopes, infrared imagers, stored rifles—everything went. Imaging cameras, equipment spares, most of the food stores, the water reserves. Then she realized that if the base had already gone, then so had the tractor, and they would never reach any of the outstations, however near or far they were and so any food reserves in the lander were a joke. And every excess kilogram could kill them. So everything went to join the hand thrown constellation cloud gathering about the lander. She opened the retaining bolts of the toilet and wash facility and threw it out, she disconnected and flung piecemeal into the void the water recycling plant. The air system she couldn't get at—but then they needed air during the descent, because they couldn't lie in their suits on the two remaining acceleration couches during the burn. She threw out all the backpacks but for one for herself and two more that she could carry. She went through every locker she had overlooked and emptied it, filling the place with a free fall billiard whirl. She caught everything and threw it out.

They got two of the couches loose. They ripped four of the five screens out of their slide mountings. They got them through to the airlock and started easing them out of the tail hatch. She had to lean out after each couch and screen and give it a final shove so that it would drift clear of the lander. That was dizzying. She only had to make a mistake, lean too far and drift to just one centimetre further than her own reach, and that would be the end. It would solve the mass problem, at least, the lander being freed of herself and her suit for the descent. And there she would stay, orbiting in her suit until its backpack died.

She was halfway out of the lock, had pushed the last screen free, when she felt his arms wrap round her legs and felt him start to push.

Funny that she didn't try to grab the hatch rim, but it wouldn't have afforded any purchase against a push delivered with feet firm against a ladder rung. She reached down and held his helmet, steadying it perhaps.

Nothingness all round her, part perfectly infinite star field, part the huge lightless hole of Hel, part the night black and invisible lander hull. Two of the deployed legs and landing pads were silhouetted against the stars, two of the motor exhausts made conical cutouts into heaven. Nothingness in a non-moment.

She peered down over the chin rim of her visor. Back lit in the lock hatch was the Outsider's suit, white on her black. His arms wrapped round her knees, his helmet was pressed against her thighs, her black glove hands clasped each side of his helmet. She couldn't see his face, of course.

He could push her out and she couldn't stop him. She could pull him with her, or wrench open his helmet and kill him instantly—their helmets were detachable after all. If he killed her she would kill him, but she wouldn't blame him. They were all just sitting there when Nightrider and his people came.

Slowly. Very slowly. He pulled her back.

She could still open his helmet, even when he couldn't push her free.

The lander pitched gently over, automatically orienting itself for the descent burn. She lay along the couch, Ali's old couch, held to it by a hip belt. No gun now. No weapon at all. She looked across the stripped and empty space.

Strapped to her own couch was the Outsider, bare limbed,

bald scalped, the same face that she had already killed and helped to kill, a face already five times dead. Probably he would kill her eventually, if they managed to survive at all. Almost certainly the others would kill her when they came, eventually if not right away. It was a fool's game of murder but at least she couldn't blame herself. There was no saying no when they sent her out here.

"What's your name?" she said. "I'm Yasmin."

He looked at her, a long expressionless glance. "Yuri."

She nodded. The automatic countdown was at minus twenty. The burn would have to hold for two hundred and ten seconds. If it cut early they would know it for seconds as they fell. "That's good. The first ever human in space was called Yuri. He got down again."

They crashed.

The lander was a write-off, legs collapsed and structure crushed and hull split. They had to get out through the emergency door in the roof and slide down the conical side. Loaded with her backpacks, it wasn't easy.

They were sixteen kilometres west of the base. The trek into the long flat valley was impossible. And then the ground between them and the base might be impassable by now. The base might have gone. Or it might be sinking, they might get in but not be able to get out again. Then would come the drive to the outstation, wherever the first of them was, the attempt to live off the supplies there until they had to load up and move to another. They would live in the tiny tractor, and all the time he would have her locked in with him instead of the clone twin woman he had been hoping to escape with. He hadn't really had time yet to accommodate to the deaths of all his companions. When it sank in he might change his mind—he owed her his life, in a partial sense, but she owed him all of theirs. And if they somehow survived the days and each other, then the ship would come. By then she would have built herself some phantom of hope that they would treat her well and hand her back some day, or keep her tolerably alive. Human resource was the most precious thing they had, after all, and she would buy her life with anything they wanted from her. But they could take it anyway, and then do without her. And they would know exactly what she'd done. Extreme or unperceived, life is just an endless row of impossible problems. You survive each one, and the next one kills you.

They walked in their own life capsules through the ring of dark, two little lives in the perpetual night of a frozen planet darkened by a death-cold celestial corpse. Transient little sparks out there in the expanding blackness, surrounded by an infinite spread of unattainable stars.

MORE SCIENCE FICTION ADVENTURE!

AWARD-WINNING
Science Fiction!

The following works are winners of the prestigious Nebula or Hugo Award for excellence in Science Fiction. A must for lovers of good science fiction everywhere!

ACE
SCIENCE FICTION
SPECIALS

Under the brilliant editorship of Terry Carr, the award-winning <u>Ace Science Fiction Specials</u> were <u>the</u> imprint for literate, quality sf.

Now, once again under the leadership of Terry Carr, <u>The New Ace SF Specials</u> have been created to seek out the talents and titles that will lead science fiction into the 21st Century.

__ THE WILD SHORE	08874-7/$3.50
Kim Stanley Robinson	
__ GREEN EYES	30274-2/$2.95
Lucius Shepard	
__ NEUROMANCER	56959-5/$2.95
William Gibson	
__ PALIMPSESTS	65065-1/$2.95
Carter Scholz and Glenn Harcourt	
__ THEM BONES	80557-4/$2.95
Howard Waldrop	
__ IN THE DRIFT	35869-1/$2.95
Michael Swanwick	
__ THE HERCULES TEXT	37367-4/$3.50
Jack McDevitt	
__ THE NET	56941-2/$2.95
Loren J. MacGregor	